D0105659

THE NORTON BOOK OF
THE SEA

VOLUME II FICTION

by the same author

Submariner

THE NORTON BOOK OF THE SEA

VOLUME II   FICTION

Edited by CAPTAIN JOHN O. COOTE

Introduction by HAMMOND INNES

Foreword by DAME NAOMI JAMES

with an Appreciation by
ERIC P. SWENSON

W · W · NORTON & COMPANY · NEW YORK · LONDON

Copyright © 1991 by Captain J. O. Coote
First American Edition 1993
First published in England under the title, *The Faber Book of Tales of the Sea*

All rights reserved

Printed in the United States of America
Manufacturing by The Haddon Craftsmen, Inc.

ISBN 0-393-03502-6

W. W. Norton & Company, Inc.
500 Fifth Avenue, New York, NY 10110
W. W. Norton & Company Ltd.
10 Coptic Street, London WC1A 1PU

1 2 3 4 5 6 7 8 9 0

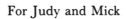

For Judy and Mick

Contents

CONTENTS

Foreword

Anyone with a passing interest in the sea likes to read about it, either in the hope of learning from the experience of others or of gaining the thrill of adventure without stirring from the sofa. Until now, I have been more or less in the first category. By reading of the exploits of other seafarers, from early explorers of the New World to the Englishman who recently sailed the Atlantic in a bottle, I have sought primarily to understand why people go to sea.

When asked to write the foreword for this anthology, my first reaction was: why do people bother with fiction when there are so many accounts of the real thing to read? What have writers like Shakespeare and Evelyn Waugh known personally about the sea? Wasn't Shakespeare's experience of tempest and shipwreck gained second-hand, on shore? Truth can, of course, be stranger than fiction; and a straightforward account of real sea adventure can be every bit as riveting as a novel by, say, Joseph Conrad. This has been my view. Until now I have never bothered to look further. Reading John Coote's anthology has, however, caused me to think again about sea fiction.

In it I find to my delight a blend of two powerful forces: the majestic, frightening, alluring magic of the sea, and the story-teller's skill in depicting this reality in moving prose. The elegant phrasing and artistry of the written language, found perhaps more often in the imagination of the master story-teller than the undemonstrative sailor, are here in abundance. Evelyn Waugh, for example, conveys in a few well-chosen words the ghastly reality of sea-sickness in a way few real sufferers can:

> Standing on the deck, Father Rothschild lent his elbows on the rail, rested his chin in his hands and surveyed the passengers coming up the gangway, each face eloquent of polite misgiving.

When the ferry is well out in the teeth of the gale (at which point I would be among the first over the lee rail), Waugh continues:

> 'The ship creaked in every plate, doors slammed, trunks fell about, the wind howled; the screw, now out of the water, now in, raced and churned, shaking down hat-boxes like ripe apples; and above all the roar and clatter there rose from the second-class ladies' saloon the despairing voices of Mrs Ape's angels, in frequently broken unison, singing, singing, wildly, desperately, as though

their hearts would break in the effort and their minds lose their reason, Mrs Ape's famous hymn, *There ain't no flies on the Lamb of God.*'

Humour, that important ingredient which puts even mal de mer at a safe distance, is successfully included in this anthology, along with such diversions as pirates in drag, beautiful women and the Bermuda Triangle.

The grim themes of mutiny, hangings at sea and war are dealt with in chilling detail; the many moods of the sea are equally convincingly drawn. Great drama, which the reader will expect, is not lacking. I particularly enjoyed *The Secret Sharer* by Conrad, for his graphic cameo of the Mate:

> At noon I gave no orders for a change of course, and the mate's whiskers became much concerned and seemed to be offering themselves unduly to my notice.

And for his spare use of words to evoke the chill prospect of the land too near at hand:

> When I opened my eyes the second view started my heart with a thump. The black southern hill of Koh-ring seemed to hang right over the ship like a towering fragment of the everlasting night. On that enormous mass of blackness there was not a gleam to be seen, not a sound to be heard. It was gliding irresistibly towards us and yet seemed already within reach of the hand. I saw the vague figures of the watch grouped in the waist, gazing in awed silence.

John Coote makes the point that many of the writings he has collected for his anthology are based on first-hand experience. One extract I *know* could not have been written by a land-lubber: Clare Francis, a contemporary of mine, makes the most of her extensive navigational experience in her writing; and Fenimore-Cooper's story of a square-rigged ship in a heavy gale has all the excitement and suspense of an eye-witness account:

> In less than a minute [the crew] were scattered along the yards, prepared to obey the signal of their officer. The mate cast a look about him: perceiving that the time was comparatively favourable, he struck a blow upon the large rope that confined one of the lower angles of the distended and bursting sail to the yard. The effect was much the same as would be produced by knocking away the key-stone of an ill-cemented arch. The canvas broke from its fastenings with a loud explosion, and, for an instant, it was seen sailing in the air ahead of the ship, as if it were sustained on wings. The vessel rose on a sluggish wave – the lingering remains of the former breeze – and settled heavily over the rolling surge, borne down alike by its own weight and renewed violence of the gusts. At this critical instance, while the seamen aloft were still gazing in the direction in which the little cloud of canvas had disappeared, a lanyard on the lower rigging parted, with a crack which reached the ears of Wilder . . .

You must read on to discover for yourself what befalls the crew high up in the rigging.

Whatever your taste, you will find it here. There is no mistaking the scope of John Coote's knowledge of sea fiction and his love of things nautical. He has succeeded admirably in the difficult task of weaving his diverse material into a cohesive whole. And the book's appeal is heightened by his illuminating notes about each author's life.

John Coote's aim is to arouse our interest in stories of the sea and encourage us to read on. He has succeeded with me.

Naomi James
Paris, July 1991

John Oldham Coote—An Appreciation

Captain J. O. Coote, R.N. (ret.) died suddenly on June 11, 1993. He leaves a painful gap in the many worlds he illuminated by his energy, intellect, wit, and friendship.

At the onset of World War II, he turned from the study of law to the Royal Navy, becoming the youngest submarine commander in the service. After the war he was lured into journalism where he rose to the position of deputy chairman of Beaverbrook Newspapers, which included the London *Daily Express*. When that empire was sold to entrepreneurs whom he found incompatible, he moved on to Boeing Aircraft as its advance man in Europe. Throughout, he indulged his love for opera, theater, sports (he was an unstoppable tennis player), music, his wife, his daughters, and his dogs.

His passion for the sea and sailing vessels was constant. He sailed and studied the oceans of the world as a naval officer and later as a celebrated offshore racer and cruiser. He was a consummate navigator in the age of the sextant who truly loved the sea, whether he was under, on, or inundated by it.

A swift and omnivorous reader, Johnnie Coote knew the literature of the sea from the Old Testament to the daily shipping news. And always he wrote brilliantly. His letters, his reviews, his articles, and his books informed and delighted all who read them. His friends were legion, devoted, and transoceanic. He is deeply missed.

Eric Swenson
September 1993

Introduction

Putting together an anthology has its similarities to arranging a dinner party for a very special occasion. Not only must the guests be chosen for what they can bring to the table, but the seating-plan, the menu and the wine list require the same care as putting on a concert that will suit an audience of wide musical tastes. What is more it must be remembered that some of the guests may have sat at the same table recently; repetition is to be avoided, no matter how great a success the earlier occasion may have been.

The fact that there are a limited number of places at the feast is often overlooked by reviewers who tear into any anthology, intent on exposing its omissions, which they unquestioningly attribute to the host's moronic cultural inadequacies. In compiling this anthology of fiction, therefore, I had to be mindful of my previous effort – *The Norton Book of the Sea*, first published in May 1989 – which happened to include some fiction. Although a number of authors appear with works of equal merit in both volumes, extracts from only two books do: from *U-boat*, one of the three greatest novels about the Second World War at sea, and *Sod's Law of the Sea*, an imperishable loo-side giggle.

My imaginary dinner party is not constrained by any time scale, a device followed by among others Nicholas Monsarrat in his unfinished book *Master Mariner*, but they all speak English. Early on, one of my guests, a much respected living writer of eighteenth-century sea stories, declined to sit at the same table as two of his contemporaries, both of them well-established writers about the same period and enjoying at least equal popular success. Much as I admire his work and feel that the anthology is impoverished by its absence, I had to deny him the right of veto which he demanded over my other guests.

In compiling any anthology of fiction, it can be assumed that most of it derives from actual experience, even though by definition it should spring from the imagination. In considering this, perhaps I hang a question-mark over Byron's dictum that truth is stranger than fiction, even though he tacked on the qualifying observation that 'novels would gain by the exchange'. Many fictional sea heroes have attained their stature and given much pleasure to readers through being the eclectic of the qualities of more than one sea-captain, just as Ian Fleming is known to have drawn on three real-life intelligence operatives in portraying his immortal Commander James Bond. Horatio Hornblower, Jack Aubrey, Richard Bolitho, Lord

Ramage, and the less well-remembered Captains Owen Kettle, Peter Blood and Harry Spink have no place in factual history, but each has made his mark in countless action-packed stories about the sea, still enjoyed by children of all ages.

My whole literary trawling process has been governed by subjective judgement, always in the hope that I might arouse readers' interests in fiction about the sea that I have enjoyed. A few new authors make their debut in the same volume as Conrad and Masefield. One is Sam Llewellyn, the Dick Francis of the hi-tech ocean-racing scene, which badly needed its own narrator.

Another factor should be borne in mind: the selection process is sometimes blurred because it is difficult to determine how relevant the sea is to the story being unfolded. For example, should a steamy love story set on a cruise-liner in the Caribbean qualify for our attention, or could it just as easily have been written against the background of a holiday camp in Morecambe Bay without losing its central point – which turns on who was in Cabin 221 at midnight on New Year's Eve?

There are narratives by single-handed sailors, from Slocum onwards, whose tales lose nothing in the telling, but cannot be called to question since they lack eye-witnesses. I have been tempted to include some highly coloured narratives of recent sea voyages, but have to be wary of exposure to action for libel if I suggest that their logs could be categorized as 'faction', even if not quite fiction. In earlier times the bible posed agonizing problems and sharp division amongst the faithful when drawing the line between the literal and the allegorical. However, a contemporary French newspaper report of the Battle of Trafalgar certainly earns its place among memorable fiction-writing about the sea.

Modern fiction about the sea dates from the sixteenth century, but was clearly influenced by earlier Greek romances, notably a long work called *On the Sphere* attributed to Achilles Tatius in the second century, which in turn followed the plot constructions of Virgil's *Aeneid*, written between 26 and 19 BC. As with modern soap operas, whodunnits, and movie screenplays during the American Hays Office era of moral censorship, plots developed along familiar lines. It was expected that any sea-captain who captured a ship would bed down the most beautiful woman he found on board. After a classic shipwreck and a miraculous survival, usually with the heroine riding ashore on a spar conveniently broken away from the wreck's rigging, there often followed a successful escape in disguise, leading eventually to a happy reunion, with all the true lovers back in their right places. This plot formula had a long run. In 1580 Sir Philip Sidney's *Arcadia* varied only in that we got two shipwrecks, one of them culminating with the lurid twist of survivors on the poop of the stricken ship cutting their throats rather than face death by drowning.

Then as now, no yarn about the sea was complete without a catastrophic shipwreck during a gale. The development of the storm itself is familiar to those who cruise the Mediterranean under sail today. Even with radio forecasts and access to synoptic charts, violent gales still erupt over calm seas with little warning. The seas are short and steep, usually it seems from right ahead. There is total overcast, with a low cloud-base. The sky darkens quickly, illuminated only by a terrifying electric storm, with forked lightning and ear-splitting thunderclaps. Passengers and crew are already in a state of panic when their ship suffers structural damage and is finally smashed on the rocks.

It is interesting to note that early prose fiction about the sea rarely concerned itself with the sort of hazards which nowadays most often account for the Lutine bell being struck at Lloyd's. Early fiction-writers seldom depicted disasters due to fog, fire at sea, collisions or piracy, let alone barratry. Nor is there much to be found about the prolonged calms which drove sailors mad when they first ventured west of the Straits of Gibraltar and were rationed to drops of brackish water as the bewildering early symptoms of scurvy broke out. Probably this was because, although the Mediterranean is 2,300 miles from one end to the other, there is no point much further than 150 miles from the nearest land, so a few sharp reminders to the slaves on the oars would soon raise a landfall.

The sixteenth-century prose-writers about ships and those who sailed them were preceded by the Anglo-Saxon epic poem *Beowulf*, and then by the two greatest names in English literature. In the fourteenth century Chaucer gave us the first definitive profile of a contemporary sailor. The Shipman was a tough, leathery West Countryman, fast on the draw with his knife, totally unscrupulous and given to making his victims walk the plank. The persistent jibe that sailors are no good on horseback certainly owes it to him. In the first scene in *The Tempest*, and again in the storm in *Pericles*, Shakespeare demonstrated his technical mastery of the subject to the extent that a case could be made for identifying him having once been a sailor, among many other professional attainments which can be read into his writings. From that point on, the sailor is increasingly depicted as the central character in works of fiction and drama, but it was not until the golden age of sail in the mid-nineteenth century that ships shared centre-stage with their crews in the eyes of writers. No one could be lyrical about the unwieldy, fetid old tubs in which Elizabethans and even Nelson's contemporaries were obliged to sail.

References to ships in the feminine – an almost exclusively British habit not adopted even by the French, let alone the Arabs – seem to have sprung from the last century when ships first had graceful lines and, above all, were very fast, showing a pretty turn of foot to their pursuers. Such courtesy cannot be accorded to a modern container-ship or super-tanker, more appropriately referred to as 'it'.

If you enjoy this book, much of the credit rests with Sally Kellett, who patiently persevered with the thankless task of tracking down and negotiating fees with those holding the republication right of any author's works whose copyright had not lapsed. Please accept my apologies if any have been overlooked; it has not been for any lack of effort on her part. I am also indebted to Frank Pike, my discreet, constructive editor at Faber and Faber, and to my old dilettante shipmate Eric Swensen, whose enthusiasm caused both anthologies to be published in the USA under the distinguished imprint of W. W. Norton.

John O. Coote, Iping, West Sussex, 1991

When we risk no contradictions,
It prompts the tongue to deal in fiction

John Gay (1720)

Tell that to the Marines – the sailors
won't believe it.

Sir Walter Scott (1824)

The sea is at its best at London, near midnight, when you are within the arms of a
capacious chair before a glowing fire, select-
ing phases of the voyages you will never
make.

H. M. Tomlinson (1912)

THE SEA

Its Mysteries

White Waves in the Indian Ocean

Most sailors are by nature superstitious, ready to accept irrational beliefs, such as that no ship should ever set sail on a Friday. Worse misfortune awaits a ship which happens to have been launched on that day. Cape Horners firmly believe that they would never drown if they were born with a caul over their heads, and members of that exclusive club often carried a tobacco pouch made from the dried membrane which had covered their heads at birth. Killing an albatross led to certain retribution, for those majestic birds of the Southern Ocean each embodied the soul of a dead sailor. Sea-serpents, mermaids, the Flying Dutchman, the maelstrom and even the Bermuda Triangle were readily accepted as facts. Long before the age when figureheads were fashioned as topless beauties tucked under the bowsprit, sailors had mystical insignia on their bows, seen to this day on Chinese junks as eyes with which to help the ship find its way across the oceans and to out-stare any evil spirit which cross their track. It would be unthinkable to go to sea without these precautions in their proper place.

Small wonder that sailors have their own explanation for exceptional natural phenomena encountered at sea, from St Elmo's Fire to the Aurora Borealis. These mystical beliefs find their way into novels by many leading writers about the sea, so it is not surprising to find them woven into the plots of sea stories by such master storytellers as Hammond Innes. One of his novels features a rusty old tramp steamer, the *Strode Venturer*, in an exciting tale about exploiting magnesium ore and political clout from Addu Atoll, near the Maldives, which had been thrown to the surface by a volcanic eruption.

Voyaging through inadequately charted waters of the Indian Ocean, the ship suddenly hits breakers at a point where for miles around the soundings show a depth of thousands of fathoms. The navigators of native craft based on the atoll know the reason, but Captain Reece, newly promoted to his first command by unscrupulous executives in Leadenhall Street who stand to gain by the voyage's failure, evidently does not.

It was shortly after eleven when I turned in. I couldn't sleep for a while. The air in the cabin was stifling and there was a queer singing in my ears. My head ached, too. I put it down to the atmosphere, which seems to press down on me. The sweat on my naked body tingled. I must have dropped off into a deep sleep, for I woke suddenly with a start to the certainty that something was wrong. I couldn't place it at first, but then I became conscious of the silence and realized that the engines were stopped.

I jumped out of bed, pulled on my shorts and padded down the alleyway and up the ladder to the wheelhouse. Peter was just ahead of me. 'What is it?' I heard him ask anxiously. 'What's happened?' And then Reece's voice: 'Breakers ahead. The lookout spotted them.'

'Breakers? How can there be breakers?'

The ship was steady as a rock, the sea flat calm.

They were out on the starboard bridge wing, their figures two black silhouettes against the peculiar luminosity. 'There man. There. Do you see them? Straight over the bows.' Reece's voice was pitched high on a note of tension as he turned and called to the helmsman, 'Slow astern.' The engine-room telegraph rang and the bridge wing juddered as the shaft turned and the screw threshed the water. There was no other sound; no sound of breakers and yet there they were, straight over the bows, a long line of white water that made my eyeballs blink with the strain of watching the waves bursting against – what? Against coral reefs? Against some laval heap that had suddenly reared itself up?

'Full astern. Starboard helm. Hard over, man.' The ring of the telegraph, the wheel turning, and then the bows began to swing. 'Christ!' It was Lennie Porter breathing down my neck. 'She's being sucked in.' The ship was broadside now to the white-fanged line of the breakers and they were much nearer, a leaping, plunging cataract of surf.

It was Blake who said quietly – 'The white water.'

'What's that? What did you say?' Reece was shouting, though there wasn't another sound in the wheelhouse.

'Christ.' Lennie said again and there was a pain in my head and behind my eyeballs as the white line of the breakers engulfed us.

They caught us broadside, great waves of broken water, great combers bursting on all sides, their tops high as the mast and all shot with blinding streaks of light. And not a sound. No hiss of surf, no growl of combers spilling, no crash of breakers thundering aboard, and the ship steady as a rock.

'He is saying' – Peter's voice was startlingly clean considering that the sea all round us appeared to be violently agitated and boiling like cauldron – 'that this is the white water.'

'What are you saying? What is it, man?' Reece's face looked ghastly white in the frightful luminosity. Everybody in the wheelhouse had a deathly pallor and his voice, sunk to a whisper, was still clearly audible, for the only sound was the hum of the engines and the click-click-click of the echo-sounder.

'An optical illusion,' Peter said. 'I've never seen it, but I've heard about it.'

'I saw it once,' Blake said. 'Off the Konkan coast. Let me see – it was wartime – '44 I think. We ploughed straight into a line of breakers. The old man knew what he was about. He knew there weren't any reefs ahead of him, and as we ploughed into it there was a sort of white mist across the bows and then it was gone and all we saw after that was streaks of light and a lot of phosphorescence.'

4

He asked permission then to turn back on to course and Reece gave it to him in a strained voice. 'You'll find it in the Pilot,' Blake said as he gave the necessary orders. 'There's quite a bit about it in the West Coast of India volume under "Luminosity of the Sea," including an eye-witness report by the master of a merchant ship.'

We were back on course and coming up to our usual eight knots and still the night was stabbed with lines of light and the sea boiled, the waves all moving with the light so that the effect was hypnotic and painful to the eyes. And then suddenly it was gone, the night clear, no humidity and the stars bright overhead.

Nobody said anything. We just stood there, too dazed, too mesmerized by what we had seen to speak. Lennie Porter was the first to find his voice. 'What was it? What the hell was it?'

But nobody could explain it. We looked it up in the Pilot. The master of the *Ariosto* had seen very much what we had seen, but off the coast of Kutch in India more than fifty years ago. In his case the phenomenon had lasted twenty minutes with the appearance of very high seas. He had described them as so agitated that they appeared 'Like a boiling pot, giving one a most curious feeling – the ship being perfectly still and expecting her to lurch and roll every instant.' And his report added, 'It turned me dizzy watching the moving flashes of light, so that I had to close my eyes from time to time.' On leaving it the line of light had presented the same appearance as on entering, as of breakers on a low beach, and after steaming through a bright, clear cloudless night for a further twenty minutes, the whole thing had been repeated, but if anything slightly worse. The Pilot recorded two other instances, both reported by naval vessels – in 1928 and 1933. But it offered no explanation, merely observing that the phenomenon could occur in the open sea as well as near land and either in calm or stormy water and that it might be caused by 'the presence of confervæ or other organic matter in the water.'

Peter had heard about the 'white water' from Don Mansoor during his voyage from Mukalla to Addu Atoll. 'He told me that he had seen it twice and each time his crew had been very frightened, thinking it was Ran-a-Maari.' Ran-a-Maari, he explained, was apparently some sort of a jinn or devil, and he added, 'The first man the Adduans recognize is Adam, the second Noah and the third Solomon, whom they call Suleiman. According to legend, Suleiman made a copper ball and confined Ran-a-Maari inside it, but it wasn't big enough to encase the jinn's legs.' He smiled, the lines at the corners of his eyes deepening. 'Suleiman threw the copper ball with Ran-a-Maari inside into the sea and it's their belief that the white water is the threshing of the jinn's legs as he struggles to release himself.'

A pleasant enough story to chuckle over beside a winter fire back in England. But out there in the Indian Ocean, in seas that were virtually uncharted, the superstitions of a primitive people seemed less absurd. Whatever the cause of the white water, our sighting of it had an unsettling effect on the ship's company. At least half the crew had been up on deck and had seen it with their own eyes, and for those who had remained in their bunks or been on duty in the engine-

5

room it was even more frightening since they had it second-hand from their companions and it was much exaggerated in the telling. And it wasn't only the lascar crew that felt uneasy; the Europeans were affected, too, for it emphasized the uncertainty of the venture, the fact that we were steaming into a little-known area and only one man knew where we were or where we were going or what to expect when we got there. Uncertainty of that sort can play the devil with a group of men cooped up in a ship and in the morning everybody was very quiet, not sullen exactly, but shut in with their thoughts, and the feeling of tension mounted as the sun rose and the heat increased.

from 'The Strode Venturer' by Hammond Innes (1965)

The Flying Dutchman Off Station

The 'Flying Dutchman' is one of the most enduring legends of the sea, possibly originating in Viking sagas, but more certainly as the story of an eighteenth-century Dutch sea-captain homeward bound from the Indies and caught by a fearful storm off the Cape of Good Hope. He swore an oath that he would defy this manifestation of God's wrath by beating his way into the anchorage of Table Bay, but he was condemned to go on sailing for eternity, bringing disaster to all sailors who crossed his path. Wagner's variation in his opera *Der Fliegende Holländer* permits the offending captain to touch port once every seven years in search of a woman whose pure love will exorcise the curse laid upon him.

The first great American naval historian, J. Fenimore Cooper, had already established himself as a novelist of the front rank before he wrote his definitive *History of the Navy of the United States* in 1839. His own experiences afloat were not exactly heroic. Expelled from Yale for using gunpowder to blow the lock off a dormitory door, he promptly shipped before the mast in a merchantman. In 1808 he enlisted in the US Navy and served as a Midshipman for three years on the Great Lakes before he married and sought to make a living by writing. In his 1827 Novel *The Red Rover* he drew on the legend of the Flying Dutchman, but shifted the scene to the treacherous waters off Cape Hatteras in North Carolina. The brig *Royal Caroline*, out of Bristol, is caught in typical Gulf Stream weather off the Cape when her young Commander, Wilder, makes a fleeting sighting of another ship. This is confirmed by a lookout aloft.

'Sail Ho!' shouted a voice from a-top. The cry sounded, in the ears of our adventurer, like the croaking of a sinister spirit.

'Where away?' he sternly demanded.

'Here on our lee-quarter, sir' returned the seaman, at the top of his voice. 'I

6

make her out a ship close-hauled; but, for an hour past, she has looked more like a mist than a vessel.'

'He is right,' muttered Wilder; 'and yet 'tis a strange thing that a ship should be just there.'

He soon summoned the officer of the watch to his councils, and they consulted together apart, for many minutes.

'Is it not extraordinary that she should be just there?' demanded Wilder, after each, in turn, had made closer examination of the faint object, by the aid of an excellent night-glass.

'She would certainly be better off here,' returned the literal seaman, who had an eye only for the nautical situation of the stranger; 'we should be none the worse for being a dozen leagues more to the eastward, ourselves. If the wind holds here at east-by-south-half-south, we shall have need of all that offing. I got jammed once between Hatteras and the Gulf—'

'Do you not perceive that she is where no vessel could or ought to be unless she had run exactly the same course with ourselves?' interrupted Wilder. 'Nothing, from any harbour south of New York, could have such northing, as the wind has held; while nothing from the colony of York would stand on this track, if bound east; or would be there, if going southward.'

The plain-going ideas of the honest mate were open to a reasoning which the reader may find a little obscure; for his mind contained a sort of chart of the ocean, to which he could refer at any time, with a proper discrimination between the various winds and all the different points of the compass. When properly directed, he was not slow to see the probable justice of his young commander's inferences; and then wonder, in its turn, began to take possession of his more obtuse faculties.

'It is downright unnatural, truly, that the fellow should be just there!' he replied, shaking his head, but meaning no more than that it was entirely out of the order of nautical propriety; 'I see the reason of what you say, Captain Wilder; and I don't know how to explain it. It is a ship to a moral certainty!'

'Of that there is no doubt. But a ship most strangely placed!'

'I doubled the Good Hope in the year '46,' continued the other, 'and we saw a vessel lying, as it might be, here on our weather-bow – which is just opposite to this fellow, since he is on our lee-quarter – but there I saw a ship standing for an hour across our fore-foot, and yet though we set the azimuth, not a degree did he budge, starboard or larboard, during all that time, which, as it was heavy weather, was, to say at least, something out of the common order.'

'It was remarkable!' returned Wilder, with an air so vacant, and to prove that he rather communed with himself than attended to his companion.

'There are mariners who say that the Flying Dutchman cruises off that Cape, and that he often gets on the weather-side of a stranger, and bears down upon him like a ship about to lay him aboard. Many is the King's cruiser, as they say, that has turned her hands up from a sweet sleep, when the look-outs have seen a double-decker come down in the night, with ports up, and batteries lighted; but then this can't be any such craft as the Dutchman, since she is, at the most, no more that a large sloop of war, if a cruiser at all.'

'No,' said Wilder, 'this can never be the Dutchman.'

'Yon vessel shows no lights; and for that matter, she has such a misty look, that one might well question its being a ship at all. Then, again, the Dutchman is always seen to windward, and the strange sail we have here lies broad on our lee-quarter!'

'It is no Dutchman,' said Wilder, drawing a long breath, like a man awaking from a trance. 'Main-topmast cross-trees, there!'

The man stationed aloft answered the hail in the customary manner, the short conversation that succeeded being necessarily maintained in shouts rather than in speeches.

'How long have you seen the stranger?' was the first demand of Wilder.

'I have just come aloft, sir; but the man I relieved tells me more than an hour.'

'And has the man you relieved come down? Or who is that I see sitting on the lee side of the mast-head?'

''Tis Bob Brace, sir; who says he cannot sleep, and so he stays upon the yard to keep me company.'

'Send the man down. I would speak with him.'

Brace confirms that the stranger has held her relative station ever since he first made her out. The Commander then orders *Royal Caroline* to alter to the other tack, but still she cannot shake off her shadower, much to the Mate's amazement.

'That fellow has truly tacked!' said Earing, after a long meditative pause, and with a voice in which awe was beginning to get the ascendency of doubt. 'Long as I have followed the sea, have I never before seen a vessel tack against such a head-beating sea. He must have been all shaking in the wind, when we gave him the last look, or we should have lost sight of him.'

'A lively and quick working vessel might do it,' said Wilder; 'especially if strong-handed.'

'Aye, the hand of Beelzebub is always strong; and a light job would he make of even a more difficult manoeuvre!'

'Mr Earing,' interrupted Wilder, 'we will pack upon the *Caroline* and try our sailing with this stranger. Get the main tack aboard, and set the top-gallant sail.'

*

The *Royal Caroline* seemed, like her crew, sensible of the necessity of increasing her speed. As she felt the pressure of the broad sheets of canvas that had just been distended, the ship bowed lower, appearing to recline on the bed of water which rose under he lee nearly to the scuppers.

Wilder tries every manoeuvre to shake off the other ship. but the *Royal*

Caroline is out-sailed at every point. The Mate's protest that the brig is dangerously overpressed is ignored.

'Is it your deliberate opinion, Captain Wilder,' he said, 'that the *Royal Caroline* can, by any human means, be made to drop yonder vessel?'

'I fear not,' returned the young man, drawing a breath so long, that all his secret concern seemed struggling in his breast for utterance.

'And, sir, with proper submission to your better education and authority in this ship, I *know* not. I have often seen these matches tried in my time; and well do I know that nothing is gained by straining a vessel with a hope of getting to windward of one of those flyers.'

'Take the glass, Earing, and tell me under what canvas the stranger is going, and what you think his distance may be,' said Wilder, without appearing to advert at all to what the other had just observed.

The honest and really well-meaning mate deposited his hat on the quarter-deck, and did as desired. When his look had been long, grave and deeply absorbed, he closed the glass with the palm of his broad hand and replied in the manner of one whose opinion was sufficiently matured, –

'If yonder sail had been built and fitted like other craft,' he said, 'I should not be backward in pronouncing her a full-rigged ship, under the three single-reefed topsails, courses, spanker and jib.'

'And yet, Earing, with all this press of canvas, by the compass we have not left her a foot.'

*

'Earing, I think there is too much southing in this breeze; and there is more brewing in yonder streak of dusty clouds on our beam. Let the ship fall off a couple of points or more, and take the strain off the spars by a pull upon the weather braces.'

The mate heard the order with an astonishment he did not care to conceal. There needed no explanation to teach one of his experience that the effect would be to go over the same track they had just passed; and that it was, in substance, abandoning the objects of the voyage.

'I hope there is no offence for an elderly seaman, like myself, Captain Wilder, in venturing an opinion on the weather,' he said. 'When the pocket of the owner is interested, my judgement approves of going about, for I have no taste for land that the wind blows on, instead of off. But by easing the ship with a reef or two, she would always be jogging seaward; and all we gain would be clear gain, because it is so much off the Hatteras. Besides, who can say that tomorrow, or the next day we sha'n't have a pull out of America, here at northwest?'

'A couple of points fall off, and a pull upon your weather-braces' said Wilder, in a way to show that he was in earnest.

The *Royal Caroline* is briefly caught wallowing without a steerage-way in the still eye of the storm, but it becomes apparent to all that she is about to be caught unprepared by winds of even greater severity from a new quarter.

The *Caroline* received the blast like a stout and buoyant ship as she was, yielding to its impulse until her side lay nearly incumbent on the element; and then, as if the fearful fabric were conscious of its jeopardy, it seemed to lift its reclining masts again, struggling to work its way through the water.

'Keep the helm-a-weather! Jam it a-weather, for your life,' shouted Wilder, amid the roar of the gust.

The veteran seaman at the wheel obeyed the order with steadiness, but in vain did he keep his eyes on the margin of his head sail, to watch the manner in which the ship would obey its power. Twice more, in as many moments, the giddy masts fell towards the horizon, waving as often gracefully upward, and then they yielded to the mighty pressure of the wind, until the whole machine lay prostrate on the water.

'Be cool!' said Wilder, seizing the bewildered Earing by the arm, as the latter rushed madly up the steep of the deck; 'bring hither an axe.' Quick as the thought which gave the order, the mate complied, jumping into the mizzen-channels of the ship, to execute with his own hands the mandate that he knew must follow.

'Shall I cut' he demanded, with uplifted arms, and in a voice that atoned for his momentary confusion, by its steadiness and force.

'Hold! Does the ship mind her helm at all?'

'Not an inch, sir,'

'Then cut!'

A single blow sufficed. Extended to the utmost powers of endurance, by the vast weight it upheld, the lanyard struck by Earing no sooner parted than each of its fellows snapped in succession, leaving the mast dependent on its wood for the support of all the ponderous and complicated hamper it upheld. The cracking of the spar came next; and the whole fell like a tree that had been snapped at its foundation.

'Does she fall off?' called Wilder, to the seaman at the wheel. 'She yielded a little, sir; but this new squall is bringing her up again.' 'Shall I cut?' shouted Earing from the main-rigging, whither he had leaped, like tiger who bounded on his prey.

'Cut!'

A louder and more imposing crash succeeded this order, though not before several heavy blows had been struck into the massive mast itself. As before, the sea received the tumbling maze of spars, rigging and sails; the vessel surging, at the same instant, from its recumbent position, and rolling far and heavily to windward.

'She rights! she rights!' exclaimed twenty voices which had been mute in a suspense that involved life and death.

'Keep her dead away!' added the calm but authoritative voice of the young commander. 'Stand by to furl the fore-top-sail – let it hang a moment to drag the ship clear of the wreck – cut, cut – cheerily men – hatchets and knives – cut *with* all, and cut *off* all!'

As the men now worked with the vigour of hope, the ropes that still confined the fallen spars to the vessel were quickly severed; and the *Caroline*, by this time dead before the gale, appeared barely to touch the foam that covered the sea. The wind came over the waste in gusts that rumbled like distant thunder, and with a power that seemed to threaten to lift the ship from its proper element. As a prudent and sagacious seaman had let fly the halyards of the solitary sail that remained, at the moment the squall approached, the loosened but lowered top-sail was now distended in a manner that threatened to drag after it the only mast which still stood. Wilder saw the necessity of getting rid of the sail, and he saw also the utter impossibility of securing it. Calling Earing to his side, he pointed out the danger, and gave the necessary order.

'The spar cannot stand such shocks much longer,' he concluded; 'should it go over the bows, some fatal blow might be given to the ship at the rate she is moving. A man or two must be sent to cut the sail from the yards.'

'The stick is bending like a willow whip,' returned the mate, 'and the lower mast itself is .prung. There would be great danger in trusting a hand in that top, while these wild squalls are breathing around us.'

'You may be right,' returned Wilder, with a sudden conviction of the truth of what the other had said. 'Stay you then here; if anything befall me, try to get the vessel into port as far north as the Capes of Virginia, at least; on no account attempt Hatteras, in the present condition of—'

'What would you do, Captain Wilder?' interrupted the mate, laying his hand on the shoulder of his commander, who had already thrown his sea-cap on the deck, and was preparing to divest himself of some of his outer garments.

'I go aloft to ease the mast of that top-sail, without which we lose the spar and possibly the ship.'

'I see that plain enough, sir; but, shall it be said that another did the duty of Edward Earing? It is your business to carry the vessel into the Capes of Virginia, and mine to cut the top-sail adrift. If harm comes to me, why, put it in the log, with a word or two about the manner in which I played my part. That is the most proper epitaph for a sailor.'

Wilder made no resistance. He assumed his watchful and reflecting attitude, with the simplicity of one who had been too long trained to the discharge of certain obligations himself, to manifest surprise that another should acknowledge their imperative character. In the mean time, Earing proceeded steadily to perform what he had just promised. Passing into the waist of the ship, he provided himself with a suitable hatchet, and then, without speaking a syllable he sprang into the fore-rigging, every strand and rope-yarn of which was tightened by the strain nearly to snapping. The understanding eyes of his observers comprehended his intention; and with precisely the same pride of station as had urged him to the dangerous undertaking, four or five of the oldest mariners jumped upon the ratlines, to mount into an air that apparently teemed with a hundred hurricanes.

'Lie down out of that fore-rigging,' shouted Wilder, through a deck trumpet; 'lie down; all, but the mate, lie down!' His words were borne past the inattentive ears of the excited and mortified followers of Earing. but for once they failed of their effect. Each man was too earnestly bent on his purpose to listen to the sounds of recall. In less than a minute, the whole were scattered along the yards, prepared to obey the signal of their officer. The mate cast a look about him; perceiving that the time was comparatively favourable, he struck a blow upon the large rope that confined one of the lower angles of the distended and bursting sail to the yard. The effect was much the same as would be produced by knocking away the key-stone of an ill-cemented arch. The canvas broke from its fastenings with a loud explosion and, for an instant, it was seen sailing in the air ahead of the ship, as if it were sustained on wings. The vessel rose on a sluggish wave – the lingering remains of the former breeze – and settled heavily over the rolling surge, borne down alike by its own weight and renewed violence of the gusts. At this critical instant, while the seamen aloft were still gazing in the direction in which the little cloud of canvas had disappeared, a lanyard of the lower rigging parted, with a crack that reached the ears of Wilder.

'Lie down!' he shouted wildly through his trumpet; 'down by the backstays; down for your lives; every man of you, down!'

A solitary individual profited by the warning, gliding to the deck with the velocity of the wind. But rope parted after rope, and the fatal snapping of the wood followed. For a moment, the towering maze tottered, seeming to wave towards every quarter of the heavens; and then, yielding to the movements of the hull, the whole fell, with a heavy crash, into the sea. Cord, lanyard, and stay snapped like thread, as each received in succession the strain of the ship, leaving the naked and despoiled hull of the *Caroline* to drive before the tempest, as if nothing had occurred to impede its progress.

A mute and eloquent pause succeeded the disaster. It seemed as if the elements themselves were appeased by their work, and something like a momentary lull in the awful rushing of the winds might have been fancied. Wilder sprang to the side of the vessel, and distinctly beheld the victims, who still clung to their frail support. He even saw Earing waving his hands, in adieu, with a seaman's heart, like a man who not only felt how desperate was his situation, but who knew how to meet it with resignation. Then the wreck of spars, with all who clung to it, was swallowed up in the body of the frightful preternatural-looking mist which extended on every side of them, from the ocean to the clouds.

'Stand by, to clear away a boat!' shouted Wilder, without pausing to think of the impossibility of one's swimming, or of effecting the least good, in so violent a tornado.

But the amazed and confounded seamen who remained needed no instruction in this matter. Not a man moved, nor was the smallest symptom of obedience given. The mariners looked wildly around them, each endeavouring to trace in the dusky countenance of some shipmate his opinion of the extent of the evil; but not a mouth opened among them all.

'It is too late – it is too late!' murmured Wilder; 'human skill and human efforts could not save them!'

'Sail, ho!' Knighthead shouted in a voice that was teeming with superstitious awe.

'Let him come on,' returned his young commander, bitterly; 'the mischief is ready done to his hands!'

'Should this be a true ship, it is our duty to the owners and the passengers to speak her, if a man can make his voice heard in this tempest,' the second mate continued, pointing, through the haze, at the dim object that was certainly' at hand.

'Speak her! – passengers!' muttered Wilder, involuntarily repeating his words. 'No; anything is better than speaking her. Do you see the vessel that is driving down upon us so far?' he sternly demanded of the watchful seaman who still clung to the wheel of the *Caroline.*

'Aye, aye, sir.'

'Give her a berth – sheer away hard to port – perhaps he may pass us in the gloom, now we are no higher than our decks. Give the ship a broad sheer, I say, sir.'

The usual laconic answer was given; and, for a few moments the Bristol trader was seen diverging a little from the line in which the other approached; but a second glance assured Wilder that the attempt was useless. The strange ship (every man on board felt certain that it was the same that had so long been seen hanging in the north-western horizon) came on through the mist, with a swiftness that nearly equalled the velocity of the tempestuous winds themselves. Not a thread of canvas was seen on board her. Each line of spars, even to the tapering and delicate top-gallant masts, was in its place, preserving the beauty and symmetry of the whole fabric; but nowhere was there the smallest fragment of a sail opened to the gale. Under her bows rolled a volume of foam that was even discernible amid the universal agitation of the ocean; and, as she came within sound, the sullen roar of the water might have been likened to the noise of a cascade. At first, the spectators on the decks of the *Caroline* believed they were not seen, and some of the men called madly for lights, in order that the disasters of the night might not terminate in an encounter.

'Too many see us there already!' said Wilder.

'No, no,' muttered Knighthead; 'no fear but we are seen; and by such eyes, too, as never yet looked out of mortal head!'

The seamen paused. In another instant, the long-seen and mysterious ship was within a hundred feet of them. The very power of that wind, which was wont usually to raise the billows, now pressed the element, with the weight of mountains, into its bed. The sea was everywhere a sheet of froth, but the water did not rise above the level of the surface. The instant a wave lifted itself from the security of the vast depths, the fluid was borne away before the tornado in glittering spray. Along this frothy but comparatively motionless surface, then, the stranger came booming with the steadiness and grandeur with which a cloud is seen sailing in the hurricane. No sign of life was discovered about her.

'She is going out of sight in the mist!' exclaimed Wilder, when he drew his breath, after the fearful suspense of the last few moments.

'Aye, in the mist or clouds,' responded Knighthead, who now kept obstinately at his elbow, watching, with the most jealous distrust, the smallest movement of his unknown commander.

'In the heavens, or in the sea, I care not, provided he be gone.'

All the doubts of Knighthead as to the character of the young stranger were now removed. He walked forward among the silent and thoughtful crew, with the air of a man whose opinion was settled. Wilder, however, paid no attention to the movements of his subordinate, but continued pacing the deck for hours; now casting his eye at the heavens, and now sending frequent and anxious glances around the limited horizon, while the *Royal Caroline* still continued drifting before the wind, a shorn and naked wreck.

from *The Red Rover* by J. Fenimore Cooper (1827)

Early Evidence of the Bermuda Triangle

In Nelson's day sailors were continually encountering mystifying or frightening natural phenomena. Michael Scott's hero Tom Cringle, a Midshipman in the sloop *Torch* on passage from Nassau to Bermuda, suddenly believes himself in danger of being shipwrecked in waters which, according to the charts, are over 2,000 fathoms deep.

The next day I had the forenoon watch; the weather had lulled unexpectedly, nor was there much sea, and the deck was all alive, to take advantage of the fine *blink*, when the man at the mast-head sung out – 'Breakers right a-head, sir.'

'Breakers!' said Mr Splinter, in great astonishment. 'Breakers! – why the man must be mad – I say, Jenkins – '

'Breakers close under the bows,' sung out the boatswain from forward.

'The devil,' quoth Splinter, and he ran along the gangway, and ascended the forecastle, while I kept close to his heels. We looked out a-head, and there we certainly did see a splashing, and boiling, and white foaming of the ocean, that unquestionably looked very like breakers. Gradually, this splashing and foaming appearance took a circular whisking shape, as if the clear green sea, for a space of a hundred yards in diameter, had been stirred about by a gigantic invisible *spurtle*, until every thing hissed again; and the curious part of it was, that the agitation of the water seemed to keep a-head of us, as if the breeze which impelled us had also floated it onwards. At length the whirling circle of white foam ascended higher and higher, and then gradually contracted itself into a spinning black tube, which wavered about, for all the world like a gigantic *loch-leech*, held by the tail between the finger and thumb, while it was poking its vast snout about in the clouds in search of a spot to fasten on.

'Is the boat gun on the forecastle loaded?' said Captain Deadeye.

'It is, sir.'

'Then luff a bit – that will do – fire.'

The gun was discharged, and down rushed the black wavering pillar in a

14

wateiy *avalanche*, and in a minute after the dark heaving billows rolled over the spot whereout it arose, as if no such thing had ever been.

This said troubling of the waters was neither more nor less than a waterspout, which again is neither more nor less than a whirlwind at sea, which gradually whisks the water round and round, and up and up, as you see straws so raised, until it reaches a certain height, when it invariably breaks. Before this, I had thought that a waterspout was created by some next to supernatural exertion of the power of the Deity, in order to suck up water into the clouds, that they, like the wine-skins in Spain, might be filled with rain.

The morning after, the weather was clear and beautiful, although the wind blew half a gale.

from *Tom Cringle's Log* by Michael Scott (1833)

Seismic Waves

Freak waves, over 100 feet high in the open ocean, have been authenticated, usually explained by a clash of wind, current and shoal water. Even in relatively calm conditions, volcanic activity or earthquakes can manifest themselves in tidal waves up to 50 feet high, sweeping across low-lying coastal areas and receding to leave craft perched on rooftops. In October 1737 such a wave in the Bay of Bengal destroyed 20,000 boats and drowned 300,000 people.

In the black depths of the oceans, however, these huge waves are eclipsed by unimaginable seismic rollers triggered off by an earthquake on the seabed. According to Rachel Carson in her classic on the subject, *The Sea Around Us* (1951), they can reach a height of 300 feet, causing unexplained surface disturbances even in calm conditions when they slam into a continental shelf or a wall of denser water, such as the Gulf Stream. Rachel Carson affirmed, however, that these monsters never reach the surface of the sea at anything like their full height.

Nevertheless, in his novel *The Poseidon Adventure*, Paul Gallico does not discount that possibility. His story concerns an 81,000 ton passenger-liner which has seen better days and, in her old age, is reduced to being a cruise-liner, her unscrupulous owners operating her on a shoestring under a Greek Captain. When she is abruptly capsized she remains afloat for a while, buoyed up by air trapped in some of her major compartments below. Eventually the upside-down hull is spotted from the air and an international rescue operation put in train, led by a US Navy frigate. A handful of survivors is finally located and freed from one of the propeller-shaft tunnels by a team from the frigate, using a blow-torch to cut through from the outside. A few more are rescued from further forward in the same way – in the nick of time before bulkheads collapse and the ship rumbles her way to the ocean bed 8,000 feet below.

Gallico is at pains to win the reader's acceptance that the world's largest passenger-liner could be rolled over by a single wave. He strings together a series of consequential circumstances, each increasing the odds on such a catastrophe: towards the end of her thirty day cruise the *Poseidon*'s cargo has all been discharged and her fuel tanks left dangerously low to save the cost of bunkers in Venezuela; in order to get more speed her reduced displacement has not been compensated by taking in water ballast; her stabilizer-fins are damaged or malfunctioning and cannot cope with the long low swell caused by lesser seismic waves, so that she rolls ominously in a calm sea. The final act which dooms the liner is the Captain's reaction on seeing a straight line paint across his track on the radar display. Knowing that the nearest land is 400 miles away, he puts the wheel hard over and meets the killer wave almost broadside on. Like the officer of the watch on *Titanic*'s bridge fifty years earlier, he might have done better to reduce the way on his ship and meet the obstruction head on.

On the bridge the Captain, thanking his stars that he had got off so lightly, nevertheless was still apprehensive. He had discarded as unnecessary as well as dangerous the idea of taking on water ballast under way, even in a calm ocean through which his ship was sailing normally again. Should there be a hurricane warning, there would still be ample time to do so to enable his ship to ride out a storm. But from all reports, high-pressure zones were holding. Once again he made the decision not to ballast. If he pushed his engines to their capacity, he would be able to make up some of the lost time and bring her in no more than a day late already provided for. Yet no skipper is ever truly comfortable when his vessel is going all out. He operated therefore with the sixth sense of the veteran seaman: weather good, forecast holding, sea track clear, nerve ends uncomfortable.

With nightfall the sky had become overcast and the surface of the flattened sea had an oily quality which was distasteful to the Master as though a leaden-coloured skin had formed over it. When his ship entered the zone of total darkness he sent a second man up into the crow's nest and posted two young officers permanently at the radar screen whose revolving arm lit up not a single blip on a fifty-mile range.

The executive, who was second-in-command and a more stolid person, could not imagine what was bugging the Skipper or keeping him striding nervously. Thrice he had asked whether the second lookout had been posted. Each time he passed the radar screen he glanced into it. He was like a man driving a car who, checking his rear vision mirror before making a turn, does not quite believe it when he sees there is no one behind him.

From time to time he went out on to the port bridge wing which projected out over the water and looked down upon the oily sea reflecting the speeding string of lights of his ship keeping pace with him on its surface. The news of the minor quake had made him conscious of what lay below. His charts showed that the submerged mountain peaks of the Mid-Atlantic Ridge, extending in a gigantic letter 'S' ten thousand miles from Iceland to the edge of the Antarctic, at that point were a mile and a half beneath his keel.

The charts, however, were not specific seismic maps and hence indicated neither the three volcanoes believed to be active pointing in line towards the top of South America, nor reflected the huge fault known to exist in the Ridge in that area.

At exactly eight minutes past nine, this fault already weakened by the preliminary tremor, now without warning shifted violently and slipped a hundred or so feet, sucking down with it some billions of tons of water.

If the *Poseidon* had not been shuddering so from the power she was generating, the bridge might have felt the sudden jolt of earthquake shock echoing upwards, though its force was downwards. Indeed, the Captain and his executive did glance at one another sharply for an instant, because of something they thought they felt in the soles of their feet. But when the *Poseidon* continued to surge forward, they relaxed and by then it was too late.

For a moment they experienced that sickening feeling at the pit of the stomach when an elevator lift drops too quickly, as the ship, sucked into the trough of the sea's sudden depression, lurched downward and began to heel. At the same time there was some babbling from the telephone to the crow's-nest and the Third Officer at the radar screen gave an unbelieving shout of 'Sir!' as, eyes popping from his head, he pointed to the blips which showed them about to run into a solid obstacle that had not been there a minute before.

The Captain tried to run in from the end of the bridge wing, but it was already going uphill. He heard the clang of the engine-room telegraph as the executive reached the levers and the order, 'Right full rudder! All engines full astern!' the almost automatic reaction to an obstacle dead ahead.

And so when the SS *Poseidon* met the gigantic, upcurling seismic wave created by the rock slip, she was more than three-quarters broadside, heeling farther from the turn. Top heavy and out of trim, she did not even hang for an instant at the point of no return, but was rolled over, bottom up, as swiftly and easily as an eight-hundred ton trawler in a North Atlantic storm.

from *The Poseidon Adventure* by Paul Gallico (1969)

A Lone Fisherman in Awe of
the Gulf Stream

Considering the amount of time he spent afloat indulging in his favourite sport of game-fishing, it is sad that Ernest Hemingway left us only one book in which he deployed his great economical skills as a wordsmith to describe the sea. Who else would have observed the 'great island of Sargasso weed that heaved and swung in the light sea as though the ocean was making love with someone under a yellow blanket', as he did in *The Old Man and the Sea*?

His description of the lone fisherman losing his fight with a marlin first appeared in 1936 as just one paragraph in an article in *Esquire* magazine:

> Another time an old man fishing along in a skiff out of Cabañas hooked a great marlin that, on the heavy sash-cord hand line, pulled the skiff far out to sea. Two days later the old man was picked up by fishermen sixty miles to the eastward, the head and forward part of the marlin lashed alongside. What was left of the fish, less than half, weighed eight hundred pounds. The old man had stayed with him a day, a night, a day and another night while the fish swam deep and pulled the boat. When he had come up the old man had pulled the boat up on him and harpooned him. Lashed alongside the sharks had hit him and the old man had fought them out alone in the Gulf Stream in a skiff, clubbing them, stabbing at them, lunging at them with an oar until he was exhausted and the sharks had eaten all that they could hold. He was crying in the boat when the fishermen picked him up, half crazy from his loss, and the sharks were still circling the boat.

Apart from its ending, this formed the synopsis of a slender book which would hardly have needed condensing for *Reader's Digest*, yet which won Hemingway the 1954 Nobel Prize for Literature.

He published nothing further until he committed suicide seven years later, aged sixty-two. His last years were spent in the depressive grip of a serious illness, possibly foreshadowed by the no-win struggle of the hero of his masterpiece, an ageing Cuban fisherman whose strength ebbs away as the big sailfish he has spent a lifetime looking for takes his deep bait and heads seawards. He has no option but to hang on to his unseen enemy until one or the other gives up through despair or exhaustion. Two days later he has the dead fish, all 18 feet and 1,500 pounds of it, lashed alongside his flimsy skiff. He then sets sail through a benign trade-wind breeze towards his village on a beach far beyond the horizon – but by the time he staggers ashore, totally exhausted, there is no flesh left on his prize; it has all been ripped off by successive waves of hungry sharks.

The action begins with the fleet of local fishing boats setting out before dawn. The old man is soon in harmony with his surroundings.

'Good luck,' the old man said. He fitted the rope lashings of the oars onto the thole pins and, leaning forward against the thrust of the blades in the water, he began to row out of the harbour in the dark. There were other boats from the other beaches going out to sea and the old man heard the dip and push of their oars even though he could not see them now the moon was below the hills.

Sometimes someone would speak in a boat. But most of the boats were silent except for the dip of the oars. They spread apart after they were out of the mouth of the harbour and each one headed for the part of the ocean where he hoped to find fish. The old man knew he was going far out and he left the smell of the land behind and rowed out into the clean early morning smell of the ocean. He saw the phosphorescence of the Gulf weed in the water as he rowed over the part of the ocean that the fishermen called the great well because there was a sudden deep of seven hundred fathoms where all sorts of fish congregated because of the swirl the current made against the steep walls of the floor of the ocean. Here there were concentrations of shrimp and bait fish and sometimes schools of squid in the deepest holes and these rose close to the surface at night where all the wandering fish fed on them.

In the dark the old man could feel the morning coming and as he rowed he heard the trembling sound as flying fish left the water and the hissing that their stiff set wings made as they soared away in the darkness. He was very fond of flying fish as they were his principal friends on the ocean. He was sorry for the birds, especially the small delicate dark terns that were always flying and looking and almost never finding, and he thought, 'The birds have a harder life than we do except for the robber birds and the heavy strong ones. Why did they make birds so delicate and fine as those sea swallows when the ocean can be so cruel? She is kind and very beautiful. But she can be so cruel and it comes so suddenly and such birds that fly, dipping and hunting, with their small sad voices are made too delicately for the sea.'

He always thought of the sea as *la mar* which is what people call her in Spanish when they love her. Sometimes those who love her say bad things of her but they are always said as though she were a woman. Some of the younger fishermen, those who used buoys as floats for their lines and had motor-boats, bought when the shark livers had brought much money, spoke of her as *el mar* which is masculine. They spoke of her as a contestant or a place or even an enemy. But the old man always thought of her as feminine and as something that gave or withheld great favours, and if she did wild or wicked things it was because she could not help them. The moon affects her as it does a woman, he thought.

He was rowing steadily and it was no effort for him since he kept well within his speed and the surface of the ocean was flat except for the occasional swirls of the current. He was letting the current do a third of the work and as it started to be light he saw he was already further out than he had hoped to be at this hour.

Reaching the edge of the land-shelf, where soundings abruptly drop to nearly 1,000 fathoms, the behaviour of a man-o'-war bird and glistening flying-fish skimming across the surface signal that he is near a school of dolphins, which his big fish might be tracking. Soon he sees many other familiar pointers near the surface of the translucent sea.

The clouds over the land now rose like mountains and the coast was only a long green line with the grey-blue hills behind it. The water was a dark blue now, so dark that it was almost purple. As he looked down into it he saw the red sifting of the plankton in the dark water and the strange light the sun made now. He watched his lines to see them go straight down out of sight into the water and he was happy to see so much plankton because it meant fish. The strange light the sun made in the water, now that the sun was higher, meant good weather and so did the shape of the clouds over the land. But the bird was almost out of sight now and nothing showed on the surface of the water but some patches of yellow, sun-bleached Sargasso weed and the purple, formalized, iridescent, gelatinous bladder of a Portuguese man-of-war floating close beside the boat. It turned on its side and then righted itself. It floated cheerfully as a bubble with its long deadly purple filaments trailing a yard behind it in the water.

'*Agua mala*,' the man said. 'You whore.'

From where he swung lightly against his oars he looked down into the water and saw the tiny fish that were coloured like the trailing filaments and swam between them and under the small shade the bubble made as it drifted. They were immune to its poison. But men were not and when some of the filaments would catch on a line and rest there slimy and purple while the old man was working a fish, he would have welts and sores on his arms and hands of the sort that poison ivy or poison oak can give. But these poisonings from the *agua mala* came quickly and struck like a whiplash.

The iridescent bubbles were beautiful. But they were the falsest thing in the sea and the old man loved to see the big sea turtles eating them. The turtles saw them, approached them from the front, then shut their eyes so they were completely carapaced and ate them filaments and all. The old man loved to see the turtles eat them and he loved to walk on them on the beach after a storm and hear them pop when he stepped on them with the horny soles of his feet.

He loved green turtles and hawks-bills with their elegance and speed and their great value and he had a friendly contempt for the huge, stupid logger-heads, yellow in their armour-plating, strange in their love-making, and happily eating the Portuguese men-of-war with their eyes shut.

He had no mysticism about turtles although he had gone in turtle boats for many years. He was sorry for them all, even the great trunk-backs that were as long as the skiff and weighed a ton. Most people are heartless about turtles because a turtle's heart will beat for hours after he has been cut up and butchered. But the old man thought, I have such a heart too and my feet and hands are like theirs. He ate the white eggs to give himself strength. He ate them all through May to be strong in September and October for the truly big fish.

He also drank a cup of shark liver oil each day from the big drum in the shack where many of the fishermen kept their gear. It was there for all fishermen who wanted it. Most fishermen hated the taste. But it was no worse than getting up at the hours that they rose and it was very good against all colds and grippes and it was good for the eyes.

Finally he hooks the big one he has been waiting for all his life and is towed far out to sea by his implacable quarry in a fight to the death lasting over two days. The old man suffers agonies from cramp and rope-burn as he constantly plays the snaking manilla to keep its tension just right for each new tactic adopted by the big fish in its unending death-struggle. But he is sure he has one thing going for him – he does not expect the weather to swing the odds abruptly against him.

He looked across the sea and knew how alone he was now. But he could see the prisms in the deep dark water and the line stretching ahead and the strange undulation of the calm. The clouds were building up now for the trade wind and he looked ahead and saw a flight of wild ducks etching themselves against the sky over the water, then blurring, then etching again and he knew no man was ever alone on the sea.

He thought of how some men feared being out of sight of land in a small boat and knew they were right in the months of sudden bad weather. But now they were in hurricane months and, when there are no hurricanes, the weather of hurricane months is the best of all the year.

It there is a hurricane you always see the signs of it in the sky for days ahead, if you are at sea. They do not see it ashore because they do not know what to look for, he thought. The land must make a difference too, in the shape of the clouds. But we have no hurricane coming now.

He looked at the sky and saw the white cumulus built like friendly piles of ice cream and high above were the thin feathers of the cirrus against the high September sky.

'Light *brisa*,' he said. 'Better weather for me than for you, fish.'

from *The Old Man and the Sea* by Ernest Hemingway (1952)

CAPTAINS AND CREWS

Hornblower

Pressing 'Volunteers' Illegally

In C. S. Forester's *A Ship of the Line*, Captain Horatio Hornblower, in command of the 74-gun HMS *Sutherland*, is part of the escort for an outward-bound convoy of East Indiamen as far as the Tagus. Off Ushant, in waters familiar to him since he served under Pellew in the blockade of Brest, two French privateers in luggers fall upon the convoy with every prospect of making their captains rich for life by capturing a fat East Indiaman. Through brilliant seamanship, Hornblower out-manoeuvres the faster luggers, dismasting one of them and frightening the other away.

After the incident bad weather prevents the ships in the convoy from visiting one another for more than a week, until just before *Sutherland* is due to detatch herself. Then a boat from *Lord Mornington*, the Commodore of the convoy's ship, comes alongside.

The boat ran alongside, and Hornblower walked forward to receive his own guests – Captain Osborn of the *Lord Mornington*, in his formal frock coat, and someone else, tall and bony, resplendent in civilian full dress with ribbon and star.

'Good afternoon, Captain,' said Osborn. 'I wish to present you to Lord Eastlake, Governor-designate of Bombay.'

Hornblower bowed; so did Lord Eastlake.

'I have come,' said Lord Eastlake, clearing his throat, 'to beg of you, Captain Hornblower, to receive on behalf of your ship's company this purse of four hundred guineas. It has been subscribed by the passengers of the East India convoy in recognition of the skill and courage displayed by the *Sutherland* in the action with the two French privateers off Ushant.'

'In the name of my ship's company I thank your Lordship,' said Hornblower.

It was a very handsome gesture, and as he took the purse he felt like Judas, knowing what designs he was cherishing against the East India convoy.

'And I,' said Osborn, 'am the bearer of a most cordial invitation to you and your first lieutenant to join us at dinner in the *Lord Mornington* .'

At that Hornblower shook his head with apparent regret.

'We part company in two hours,' he said. 'I was about to hang out a signal to that effect. I am deeply hurt by the necessity of having to refuse.'

'We shall be sorry on board the *Lord Mornington*,' said Lord Eastlake. 'Ten days of bad weather have deprived us of the pleasure of the company of any of the officers of the navy. Cannot you be persuaded to alter your decision?'

'This has been the quickest passage I have made to these latitudes,' said

25

Osborn. 'I begin to regret it now that it appears to have prevented our seeing anything of you.'

'I am on the King's service, my Lord, and under the most explicit orders from the Admiral.'

That was an excuse against which the Governor-designate of Bombay could not argue.

'I understand,' said Lord Eastlake. 'At least can I have the pleasure of making the acquaintance of your officers?'

Once more that was a handsome gesture; Hornblower called them up and presented them one by one; horny-handed Bush, and Gerard handsome and elegant, Captain Morris of the marines and his two gawky subalterns, the other lieutenants and the master, down to the junior midshipman, all of them delighted and embarrassed at this encounter with a lord.

At last Lord Eastlake turned to go.

'Good-bye, Captain,' he said, proffering his hand. 'A prosperous voyage in the Mediterranean to you.'

'Thank you, my lord. And a good passage to Bombay to you. And a successful and historic term of office.'

Hornblower stood weighing the purse – an embroidered canvas bag at which someone had laboured hard recently – in his hand. He felt the weight of the gold, and under his fingers he felt the crackle of the bank notes. He would have liked to have treated it as prize money, and take his share under prize money rules, but he knew he could not accept that sort of reward from civilians. Still, his crew must show full appreciation.

'Mr Bush,' he said, as the boat shoved off. 'Man the yards. Have the men give three cheers.'

Lord Eastlake and Captain Osborn acknowledged the compliment as they pulled away; Hornblower watched the boat creep back to the *Lord Mornington*. Four hundred guineas. It was a lot of money, but he was not going to be bought off with four hundred guineas. In that very moment he came to his decision after twenty-four hours of vacillation. He would display to the East India convoy the independence of Captain Hornblower.

'Mr Rayner,' he said. 'Clear away the launch and the long-boat. Have the helm put up and run down to leeward of the convoy. I want those boats in the water by the time we reach them. Mr Bush. Mr Gerard. Your attention please.'

Amid the bustle and hurry of wearing the ship, and tailing on at the stay tackles, Hornblower gave his orders briefly. For once in his life Bush ventured to demur when he realized what Hornblower had in mind.

'They're John Company's ships, sir,' he said.

'I had myself fancied that such was the case,' said Hornblower with elaborate irony. He knew perfectly well the risk he was running in taking men from ships of the East India Company – he would be both offending the most powerful corporation in England and contravening the Admiralty orders. But he needed the men, needed them desperately, and the ships from whom he was taking them would sight no land until they reached St Helena. It would be three or four months before any protest could reach England, and six months before any censure could reach him in the Mediterranean. A crime six months old might not be prosecuted with extreme severity, and perhaps in six months' time he would be dead.

'Give the boats' crews pistols and cutlasses,' he said, 'just to show that I'll stand no nonsense. I want twenty men from each of those ships.'

'Twenty!' said Bush, gaping with admiration. This was flouting the law on the grand scale.

'Twenty from each. And mark you, I'll have only white men. No Lascars. And able seamen every one of them, men who can hand, reef, and steer. And find out who their quarter gunners are and bring them. You can use some trained gunners, Gerard?'

'By God I can, sir.'

'Very good.'

Hornblower turned away. He had reached his decision unaided, and he did not want to discuss it further. The *Sutherland* had run down to the convoy. First the launch and then the cutter dropped into the water and pulled over to the clustered ships while the *Sutherland* dropped farther down to leeward to wait their return, hove to with main topsail to the mast. Through his glass Hornblower saw the flash of steel as Gerard with his boarding party ran up on to the deck of the *Lord Mornington* – he was displaying his armed force early so as to overawe any thought of resistance. Hornblower was in a fever of anxiety which he had to struggle hard to conceal. He shut his glass with a snap and began to pace the deck.

'Boat pulling towards us from *Lord Mornington*, , sir,' said Rayner, who was as excited as his captain, and far more obviously.

'Very good,' said Hornblower with careful unconcern.

That was a comfort. If Osborn had given Gerard a point blank refusal, had called his men to arms and defied him, it might give rise to a nasty situation. A court of law might call it murder if someone got killed in a scuffle while illegal demands were being enforced. But he had counted on Osborn being taken completely by surprise when the boarding party ran on to his deck. He would be able to offer no real resistance. Now Hornblower's calculations were proving correct; Osborn was sending a protest, and he was prepared to deal with any number of protests – especially as the rest of the convoy would wait on their Commodore's example and could be relieved of their men while the protesting was going on.

It was Osborn himself who came in through the entry port, scarlet with rage and offended dignity.

'Captain Hornblower!' he said, as he set foot on the deck. 'This is an outrage! I must protest against it, sir. At this very moment your lieutenant is parading my crew with a view to impressment.'

'He is acting by my orders, sir,' said Hornblower.

'I could hardly believe it when he told me so. Are you aware, sir, that what you propose to do is contrary to the law? It is a flagrant violation of Admiralty regulations. A perfect outrage, sir. The ships of the Honourable East India Company are exempt from impressment, and I, as Commodore, must protest to the last breath of my body against any contravention of the law.'

'I shall be glad to receive your protest when you make it, sir.'

'But—but—' spluttered Osborn. 'I have delivered it. I have *made* my protest, sir.'

'Oh, I understand,' said Hornblower. 'I thought these were only remarks preliminary to a protest.'

'Nothing of the sort,' raved Osborn, his portly form almost dancing on the deck. 'I have protested, sir, and I shall continue to protest. I shall call the attention of the highest in the land to this outrage. I shall come from the ends of the earth, gladly, sir, to bear witness at your court martial. I shall not rest – I shall leave no stone unturned – I shall exert all my influence to have this crime punished as it deserves. I'll have you cast in damages, sir, as well as broke.'

'But, Captain Osborn—' began Hornblower, changing his tune just in time to delay the dramatic departure which Osborn was about to make. From the tail of his eye Hornblower had seen the Sutherland's boats pulling towards two more victims, having presumably stripped the first two of all possible recruits. As Hornblower began to hint at a possible change of mind on his part, Osborn rapidly lost his ill temper.

'If you restore the men, sir, I will gladly retract all I have said,' said Osborn. 'Nothing more will be heard of the incident, I assure you.'

'But will you not allow me to ask for volunteers from among your crews, Captain?' pleaded Hornblower. 'There may be a few men who would like to join the King's service.'

'Well – yes, I will even agree to that. As you say, sir, you may find a few restless spirits.'

That was the height of magnanimity on Osborn's part, although he was safe in assuming that there would be few men in his fleet foolish enough to exchange the comparative comfort of the East India Company's service for the rigours of life in the Royal Navy.

'Your seamanship in that affair with the privateers, sir, was so admirable that I find it hard to refuse you anything,' said Osborn, pacifically. The *Sutherland's* boats were alongside the last of the convoy now.

'That is very good of you, sir,' said Hornblower, bowing. 'Allow me, then, to escort you into your gig. I will recall my boats. Since they will have taken volunteers first, we can rely on it that they will have all the willing ones on board, and I shall return the unwilling ones. Thank you, Captain Osborn. Thank you.'

He saw Captain Osborn over the side and walked back to the quarterdeck. Rayner was eyeing him with amazement on account of his sudden volte-face, which gave him pleasure, for Rayner would be still more amazed soon. The cutter and launch, both of them as full of men as they could be, were running down now to rejoin, passing Osborn's gig as it was making its slow course to windward. Through his glass Hornblower could see Osborn wave his arm as he sat in his gig; presumably he was shouting something to the boats as they went by. Bush and Gerard very properly paid him no attention. In two minutes they were alongside, and the men came pouring on deck, a hundred and twenty men laden with their small possessions, escorted by thirty of the *Sutherland*'s hands. They were made welcome by the rest of the crew all with broad grins. It was a peculiarity of the British pressed sailor that he was always glad to see other men pressed – in the same way, thought Hornblower, as the fox who lost his brush wanted all the other foxes to lose theirs.

Bush and Gerard had certainly secured a fine body of men; Hornblower looked them over as they stood in apathy, or bewilderment, or sullen rage, upon the *Sutherland*'s main deck. At no warning they had been snatched from the comfort of an Indiaman, with regular pay, ample food, and easy discipline, into the hardships of the King's service, where the pay was problematic, the food bad, and where their backs were liable to be flogged to the bones at a simple order from their new captain. Even a sailor before the mast could look forward with pleasure to his visit to India, with all its possibilities; but these men were destined instead now to two years of monotony only varied by danger, where disease and the cannon balls of the enemy lay in wait for them.

'I'll have those boats hoisted in, Mr Rayner,' said Hornblower.

Rayner's eyelids flickered for a second – he had heard Hornblower's promise to Captain Osborn, and he knew that more than a hundred of the new arrivals would refuse to volunteer. The boats would only have to be hoisted out again to take them back. But if Hornblower's wooden expression indicated anything at all, it was that he meant what he said.

'Aye aye, sir,' said Rayner.

Bush was approaching now, paper in hand, having agreed his figures regarding the recruits with Gerard.

'A hundred and twenty, total, sir, as you ordered,' said Bush. 'One cooper's mate – he was a volunteer, one hundred and nine able seamen – two of 'em volunteered; six quarter gunners; four landsmen, all volunteers.'

'Excellent, Mr Bush, Read 'em in. Mr Rayner, square away as soon as those boats are inboard. Mr Vincent! Signal to the convoy. "All-men-have-volunteered. Thank you. Good-bye." You'll have to spell out "volunteered" but it's worth it.'

Hornblower's high spirits had lured him into saying an unnecessary sentence. But when he took himself to task for it he could readily excuse himself. He had a hundred and twenty new hands, nearly all of them able seamen – the *Sutherland* had nearly her full complement now. More than that, he had guarded himself against the wrath to come. When the inevitable chiding letter arrived from the Admiralty he would be able to write back and say that he had taken the men with the East India Company's Commodore's permission; with any good fortune he could keep the ball rolling for another six months. That would give him a year altogether in which to convince the new hands that they had volunteered – by that time some of them at least might be sufficiently enamoured of their new life to swear to that; enough of them to befog the issue, and to afford to an Admiralty, prepared of necessity to look with indulgence on breaches of the pressing regulations, a loophole of excuse not to prosecute him too hard.

'*Lord Mornington* replying, sir,' said Vincent. ' "Do not understand the signal. Await boat"!'

'Signal "Good-bye" again,' said Hornblower.

Down on the maindeck Bush had hardly finished reading through the Articles of War to the new hands – the necessary formality to make them servants of the King, submissive to the hangman and the cat.

from *A Ship of the Line* by C. S. Forester (1938)

Hornblower Elevated to the Peerage, His Lineage Assured

A different account of this incident appeared in *The Life and Times of Horatio Hornblower*, a definitive biography of the great sailor first published in 1970.

Leighton's squadron was under orders for the Mediterranean and comprised the *Pluto*, *Caligula*, and *Sutherland*, the first of 98 and the others of 74 guns. The first duty of this force was to escort an outward-bound East India convoy out of the Channel and as far south as latitude 35°. Leighton entrusted this task to Hornblower and sent the *Caligula* with two storeships to Port Mahon, he himself escorting some transports to Lisbon before proceeding to Palamos Point, where the other two ships would rejoin his flag. As from then Leighton was to operate on the Spanish coast as commander of the Inshore Squadron, his role to harass the French forces in Spain. The squadron sailed from Plymouth on May 16th and the Sutherland soon parted from the flagship, keeping her convoy in fairly strict formation, made Ushant and set a course for Finisterre. Hornblower's main anxiety centred upon his shortage of men. He had enough to work the ship and enough to man the guns but not enough to do both. And, as luck would have it, he was in action before he had a chance to find more men or even train those he had. The six East Indiamen were attacked by two French privateer luggers and it took all Hornblower's seamanship to beat them off, leaving one of them dismasted. After thus earning the gratitude of the Company's officers and of Lord Eastlake, bound for the governorship of Bombay, Hornblower went on to press twenty seamen from each of the Company's ships. This high-handed proceeding was contrary to Admiralty instructions but he answered the protests of the Company's senior captain by an assurance that all who did not volunteer would be returned. He ended the incident by signalling that all *had* volunteered which, in a sense, was true. He parted company from the Indiamen as ordered, feeling confident that months would pass before the Admiralty would receive a protest from East India House. He also recalled that Nelson had once impressed men from an East Indiaman in London River itself, firing a broadside to suppress the resistance that had been offered. His own offence was nothing by comparison and far more remote from public notice. He had an even chance of escaping reprimand and there is no record, in fact, of any reproof ever reaching him. In the meanwhile, he had a ship properly manned and ready, or soon to be ready, for battle.

What C. S. Forester would have said, had he lived a few years longer to read this book, is a matter for conjecture. That it should have been written by Professor C. Northcote Parkinson, who postulated his own Law years before Sod's or Murphy's, is a fair warning that all is not what it seems. No doubt his interest in naval history sprang from the short time he spent as a master on the staff of the Royal Naval College, Dartmouth, before he was swept into the Army for the Second World War. He invested Hornblower with an ancestry, as the great-grandson of the corn-merchant Jeremiah Hornblower (1692–1754).

It is more difficult to see how C. S. Forester himself first got his appetite for eighteenth-century fighting ships and their crews. Born in Cairo in 1899 he was educated at Dulwich College, following in the footsteps of P. G. Wodehouse and A. E. W. Mason. No doubt another Old Boy, Ernest Shackleton, was a boyhood hero. He became keen on sailing while failing his medical studies at Guy's Hospital. He wrote *Brown on Resolution*, a fictional exploit set in the First World War, before his first Hornblower novel appeared in 1937 while he was covering the Spanish Civil War for *The Times*. He joined the RNVR for the Second World War but was invalided out and thereafter lived in Berkeley, California, until his death in 1965.

Having embarked on the twelve Hornblower novels, clearly modelling his protagonist on Nelson, Forester could not afford to have him written out of the script at Trafalgar. Instead he has Hornblower commanding the Sea Fencibles in Kent when matters come to a head after Admiral Sir Robert Calder's indecisive action has allowed Villeneuve to escape to Cadiz with his fleet largely intact. Forester then has his hero summoned to the Admiralty and sent to land near San Sebastian, carrying a set of forged orders from Bonaparte in Paris to Villeneuve. Somehow the Imperial messenger is induced to play his part in the deception plan, and Villeneuve sails into the waiting British fleet in the nick of time for its newly joined Vice-Admiral to lay down his life in the course of destroying them. But Forester's storyline left the way open for Hornblower's career to run its full course, now embellished and rounded off by all the minutiae which diligent research endows on a conscientious biographer – even a bogus one like Parkinson. We find Hornblower, by now married to Lady Barbara Wellesley, the widow of his one-time Flag Officer, Rear-Admiral Sir Richard Leighton, in retirement at Smallbridge Manor, his country seat near Maidstone in Kent. He was already a Baron when he married for a second time, but Professor Northcote Parkinson offers his own account of how he finally becomes a Viscount.

It was on a wet evening in 1848, that the unexpected visitor arrived. The Hornblowers had dined in comfort and Horatio was enjoying his glass of port while his wife had gone to read in the drawing-room, where coffee would presently be brought to them both. We may picture the contrast between the warmth of the dining room and the discomfort of the weather outside, for the rain was beating on the window panes and the wind was loud in the treetops. It was as rough an evening as anyone would want to avoid, being windy, cold and wet. The doorbell rang, the footman answered it and Hornblower's former coxswain and present butler presently reported that there was a lunatic at the door. Asked what form the lunatic took, the invaluable Brown replied that the visitor had given his name as Napoleon Bonaparte. What then was the object of the call? Mr Bonaparte wished to borrow a carriage and horses so as to catch the packet boat from Dover to Calais. Thoroughly mystified, Hornblower told Brown to show the visitor in. The man who now entered the room was aged about forty, dressed in civilian clothes under a rain-soaked cape and splattered with mud from his boots to his knees. He had no resemblance to the late Emperor, wearing in fact a heavy moustache and a tuft of beard. Although clearly a foreigner, he was fluent in English and quickly explained the disaster that had befallen him. He had been travelling by rail from London to Dover with a view to reaching Paris as quickly as possible. As a result of the recent downpour the railway embankment had given way at one point, burying the rails under hundreds of tons of earth. It might take days to clear the line – and there was not even an hour to spare! What the strange visitor wanted was a carriage to take him to Maidstone, beyond the point where the line was blocked. From there he could catch another train to Dover, and so board the steam packet for Calais which would connect again with the train for Paris. The whole future of France depended, he said, upon his arrival in time for the election.

At this point both Hornblower and Brown were convinced that they had to do with a lunatic, but each for a different reason. Hornblower had not been following the events in France with more than a passing interest. He saw it as a country in which society had been torn up by its roots, never to recover. Napoleon had been dead for a quarter of a century and more, and was without a living heir. That a lunatic should call himself Bonaparte was not improbable and that he should see himself as the saviour of France was a more or less logical corollary to his central delusion. It was merely a question of how to get rid of him! Brown was more immediately interested in the visitor's account of where he was travelling and why.

It seems that the Frenchman has been misled by a station announcement at Paddock Wood causing him to change to a local train to Maidstone. Its progress in either direction was soon blocked by landslides, so he has trudged across the wild countryside to nearby Smallbridge Manor. He is about to be shown the door when Lady Hornblower intervenes. Impressed by his old-fashioned Gallic courtesy, she orders the coach for him.

Brown and the coachman decided between them that the coach should take the Frenchman back to Paddock Wood, where there would be another train in about an hour. This plan was carried out without reference to Lord Hornblower, who believed to his dying day that his strange visitor had been taken to Maidstone. The later train should not, by rights, have connected with the steam packet but on this night the vessel was delayed and the foreigner reached his own country without loss of time.

The odd sequel to this strange incident was the discovery that the traveller *was* in fact Napoleon's nephew. He was a candidate for the office of President and was duly elected to that office in December. He became Emperor as Napoleon III in 1852. In the meanwhile he was genuinely grateful to the old Admiral who had helped him on his way. Almost his first act as President was to confer on Hornblower the insignia of a Chevalier of the Legion of Honour, with a sapphire as a present for Barbara. He did more than that, however, asking Queen Victoria to confer some further honour on a man he described as his particular friend. Wanting at that moment to conciliate the new French government, Lord John Russell agreed (rather reluctantly) to make Hornblower a Viscount. There was some opposition to this, however, and the new honour was not announced until 1850. He then became Viscount Hornblower of Smallbridge, his son assuming the courtesy title of Lord Maidstone of Boxley. This last honour, the result of a fortunate accident, was not due to the Wellesley influence. He had owed much to that in the past, his peerage included, but the family was no longer so influential. Richard Wellesley, who had long since retired from politics, had died in 1842 and the Duke was last in the cabinet in 1841–46. He was an old man now and Viscount Hornblower, as we must now call him, went over to Walmer to pay him a brief visit in 1851. He and Barbara chose to go by rail and were scolded by the Duke for taking such a risk. It was not the same thing, he admitted, as Barbara travelling by herself – *that*, he trusted, was out of the question – but it was a risk they should never run if it were avoidable. He told them the story of how poor Mr Huskisson was killed by a railway locomotive twenty years before. He had never liked the railway since and always tried to discourage ladies from travelling in so dangerous a fashion. He asked after Richard, remembering his duty as Commander-in-Chief. The trouble was, he said, that none of these young men had been in action. He went on to ask Hornblower whether he had ever fought a duel and was told that he had. The Duke disapproved of duelling, especially in the army, but had to admit that his own example told against him. He had fought Lord Winchelsea back in 1829, and could still remember that morning at Battersea . . . The two old men had a long talk but the Duke was somewhat deaf, compelling the other to shout. The visit came to an end and Lord and Lady Hornblower set off again (by rail) for Smallbridge via Paddock Wood.

This scholarly deadpan spoof ends with a succession of convincing appendices, not the least being one giving the Hornblower family tree right up to the present day.

> Richard, Lord Maidstone, the second Viscount, was succeeded by Horatio, who held minor office under the Marquess of Salisbury in 1885 and died in 1909. Richard, fourth Viscount, joined the Navy in 1878 and, remaining in service, rose to the rank of Rear-Admiral. He commanded the battleship *Collingwood* at the Battle of Jutland and retired in 1921. Horatio, fifth Viscount, served in the Grenadier Guards, won the MC as a subaltern in 1918 and commanded a battalion of his regiment before he retired in 1937. Called back to the service in 1939–45, he was wounded at Dunkirk and confined to staffwork, as Brigadier, for the rest of the war. With fortune much reduced by taxation, he was compelled to sell Boxley House in 1953, retaining only his town residence in Wilton Street, Knightsbridge. When he died in 1968 he was succeeded in the title by Richard, the sixth Viscount, born in 1921, who served in the Royal Navy during World War II, being a sub-lieutenant in the *Achilles* at the battle of the River Plate and a Lieutenant-Commander on D-Day of the landings in Normandy. He left Britain in 1952 (following his divorce) and has since lived in South Africa.

> from *The Life and Times of Horatio Hornblower*
> by C. Northcote Parkinson (1970)

Royal Navy Cadets Under Training

John Winton's brief career as a regular naval officer started when he was eighteen and reported to the Royal Naval College at Dartmouth in May 1950 for two terms' basic training, after which he went to sea in the cadet training-cruiser HMS *Devonshire*, a sedate three-stacker with generous accommodation, designed for service on the China Station before air conditioning was specified for the repertoire of the Navy's ship designers. I can vouch for the authenticity of many of the events and personalities. When he later set down his experiences in the hilarious bestseller *We Joined the Navy*, my role as his Divisional Officer is recognizable, though fortunately cloaked by an alias (as is the author himself).

The officer in overall charge, The Bodger, is a destroyer captain of the old school – a member of that raffish camaraderie of practical seamen and wonderful ship-handlers who squeezed the last drop out of life ashore and afloat. In the middle of the cadets' first term in Dartmouth, they embark in a wartime frigate for an extended weekend cruise to the Channel Islands. The Captain, Poggles, is an old term-mate of The Bodger's, so it is sure to be a lively cruise. In those days the Coxswain, who always took the wheel when the Captain needed the assurance of his presence in the wheel-house immediately under the compass platform, had a clear view ahead through an open port.

In the afternoon The Bodger produced a timetable and organized tours of the ship. Ratings of various branches called at the cadets' messdeck to conduct the tours. None of them was quite as silent as Petty Officer Moody and the Chief Stoker but on the other hand none of them was talkative. The Beattys could only get them to answer questions with the greatest difficulty. As far as normal human contact was concerned the ship's company of *Rowbottom* were as unco-operative as the men that sailed with the Ancient Mariner. It was as though the entire ship's company had successfully graduated by correspondence course from a Trappist monastery.

While the tours were going on, *Rowbottom* was steadily nearing the island of Guernsey. She anchored there in the calm of a beautiful summer evening. Six Beattys were present on the bridge when Poggles anchored his ship.

'Cox'n,' said Poggles, down the voicepipe.

'Sir?' said Petty Officer Moody.

'See that Bass Bitter advertisement dead ahead?'

'Sir.'

'Steady on that.'

'Steady on Bass Bitter, sir. Aye aye, sir.'

'Slow ahead both engines.'

'Slow ahead together.'

'Slow ahead together, sir. Both engines answered slow ahead, sir.'

'Very good.'

Poggles leaned on the parapet and sniffed the evening air.

'Good night for a run ashore, I think, Bodger. We might take a glass or three of the local vino, what do you think?'

'*Splendid* idea!' replied The Bodger.

'Yes, I think so. A few tots won't do us any harm.'

'Alka-Seltzer bearing one-four-zero, sir,' said *Rowbottom*'s Navigating Officer.

'*Alka*-Seltzer?' said Poggles. 'What's Alka-Seltzer got to do with it?'

'Sorry, sir. Hennessy. Three star, two-five-two, sir.'

'*That's* better. Steady on Guinness, Cox'n.'

'Steady on Guinness, sir. Aye aye, sir.'

'Just coming up to transit between Martini and Sandeman's Port, sir.'

'Very good. Let me know when we reach Johnny Walker.'

'Aye aye, sir.'

'Stop together. I seem to remember a little popsy the last time we were in here . . . what in hell was her name now? Said she loved naval officers and would go miles to get one.'

'Johnny Walker, sir!'

'Very good. Half astern together.'

Poggles languidly let go a small green flag. Down on the cable deck the blacksmith swung his hammer. The Blake slip parted, the cable thundered up out of the locker, thumped over the scotsman and down through the hawsepipe. A gesticulating signalman began to make signs with flags.

'Stop together.'

'Stop together, sir. Both engines answered stop sir.'

'Very good.'

The cable stopped rattling. The signalman held one flag out at rest. The Cable Officer looked out over the guardrail at the water and held up his thumb. Poggles stretched wearily. *Rowbottom* had anchored.

'That was neatly done, if I may say so, Poggles,' said The Bodger.

Poggles shrugged his shoulders modestly.

'Aw shucks,' he said.

The Beattys, too, were impressed. The captain had found his way to an exact spot on the chart, guided unerringly not by radar, echo-sounders, light-houses, buoys or leading marks, but by brewers' signs. It had been a magnificent performance.

The training-cruiser gave most of the Cadets their first taste of an unin-hibited run ashore in a foreign port. As often as not, Gibraltar was the setting for them to retrace the unsteady steps of the generations of young officers who had got into trouble before them. The frontier at La Linea was wide open. So was the action behind countless swing-doors or bead curtains. In Winton's account it is the thankless task of the Principal Medical Officer (PMO) to warn the cadets of some of the pitfalls literally lying in wait for them.

On the evening before *Barsetshire* reached Gibraltar, her first foreign port of the cruise, the PMO gave a lecture and film show to the junior cadets. The PMO's lecture and film show was famous in the training cruiser. Some of the officers on the staff attended it every cruise; they looked forward to it, as concert-goers look forward to the Promenade Concerts every year.

The PMO was six feet tall, with iron grey hair and blue eyes. He was an Irishman from County Cork, a gentle and unsuspicious man by nature. Twenty years in the Navy, listening to sailors describe their complaints, had made him cynical, but had not erased the last traces of his native brogue. The PMO still spoke with a slight lisp and occasionally introduced an aspirate into his dental consonants.

'Tomorrow we'll be getting to Gibraltar,' said the PMO to the junior cadets, 'and I have no doubt at all that some of you'll be putting your private parts where I wouldn't be putting my walking-stick. So let me be saying from the start that I'm not meaning to give you any *advice*. Nobody takes the least bit of notice of advice, and nor they should. You'll not be the first to go ashore in Gib and you'll not be the last. I'm telling ye now some of the things I've noticed in the past and which might be of use to you to know. Whether you take any notice of them at all is up to you entirely.'

The PMO opened a sheaf of notes and spread them out on a table.

'There's a very awkward and unpleasant disease which people catch in the Mediterranean. It's a form of dysentery and it's known as the Malta Dog. Some people catch it because they're not used to the water, or because they've eaten something which doesn't agree with them. You can catch it from shellfish or from meat that's a bit too old. So when you go ashore to have a meal, watch out for things like prawns or lobsters or greens that have not been washed. If you do get it, come along to the Sick Bay and we'll give you some cement. Everybody has their own remedies. I always take a glass of equal parts of port and brandy.

'It'll be a bit hotter from now on than most of ye're used to. Whenever you're in a hot climate you have to take extra care to keep yourself clean. You'll have to wash yourself more often or you'll get rashes and toe rot.

'I'll not be telling ye never to sleep with strange women. That's a thing that every man has to decide for himself and the sooner the better. But if you do decide to have a little bit of excitement, don't be thinkin' ye're giving the poor frustrated girl the one night of delirious joy in her drab and dreary existence. Not at all. Ye're a part of the rent, or just a little bit on the groceries bill, or something to keep the butcher happy for a while. There'll be two types. Either she'll tell you the price straight away or she'll stay quiet and look at ye. If it's the first, then you're clear where you stand. It's the second you have to be careful of. She'll be wondering how much you're good for and she"ll likely over-estimate a little and you'll have to beat her down and there's no more degrading sight than a naval officer haggling with a woman over the price of a little bit of copulation.'

The Bodger sat in the front row, restraining his laughter. As a newcomer to the ship, he had never before heard the PMO's lecture and he now realized that he had been missing the performance of a natural showman. The PMO's droll delivery and perfect timing might have made him famous on the stage.

'Now I'll come to the bit ye'll all be wanting to hear,' said the PMO solemnly. 'The chances of catchin' something. I'll be frank with you. There's no real safeguard against venereal disease except total abstinence, just as there's no real safeguard against getting drunk except not drinkin'. But it would be a poor world without women and drink, would it not? The next best thing to abstinence is continence. If you can't contain yourself, then at least control yourself. And take care. My Chief Nightingale up at the Sick Bay will be delighted to fix you up. I can't be tellin' ye that too often.'

The PMO put away his notes in his pocket.

'All I've been tellin' ye,' he went on, 'goes all to hell if you've been drinkin' too much. If you're drunk, you'll behave like an animal and an animal has never heard of birth control. It's easily done. Several of you go ashore together. On the way you have a drop to drink until one of you has a drop too much. He's the one we'll call Paddy. When you all decide to go, Paddy wants to stay where he is, where it's warm and he can see the women. He won't be wantin' to be pushed into the cold where there's no beer and no women. So he stays where he is and the rest of you go on without him. From that minute, Paddy is half-way to the Sick Bay. Now that'll be enough from me. I've got some films to show you which'll let ye see what happens to Paddy after you've left him. They'll not need any comment from me so I'll leave ye to them. I tried to get you the ones they show to the Wrens but they're booked up for years ahead so you'll just have to make do with these.'

The PMO left the messdeck. After everyone else had sat down again The Bodger remained standing.

'Before we see the PMO's blue films,' he said, 'I want to emphasize what the PMO said on the subject of liquor. Most of the local drinks in the Mediterranean are an acquired taste. Stuff like Spanish brandy, absinthe, ouzo and arrack are drunk by the local inhabitants by the quart. But if you start drinking them you'll get drunk very quickly. Some of the worst stuff will not only make you drunk, it may send you blind. In the old days they used to sell a white stick with every crate of it. Things are not so bad now as they used to be, but even now quite a lot of the local hooch will do you a power of no good. Stick to sherry or beer. Sherry is very cheap in Gibraltar and Spain and you can get some first class stuff for very little compared with what you would have to pay for it in England. That's all I have to say on that. Now for the PMO's ciné bleu.'

*

In the first few hundred yards from the landing stage the cadets met more American patrols than Gibraltarians, but once up the steps and into Main Street they found themselves swallowed up in the beginnings of an evening which Gibraltar had come to know very well.

The bars were all similar. They had swing doors, a band with a female trumpeter on a dais, and they were full of sailors. The bars sounded the same, with the jarring notes of a trumpet, drums and castanets, shouts and songs and the accumulated sound of voices talking, bottles clinking and shuffling feet. In the street, bullfight posters were pasted on the blank spaces of the wall by the lottery stand. The shops offered highly coloured rugs, cigarette lighters, cameras, clocks, shirts, watches, bales of cloth, handbags, bullfight photographs, toy monkeys and perfume. There were very few cars and those made their way slowly between the crowds who walked in the centre of the narrow street. American and British sailors jostled small, swarthy men in pastel-shaded suits. The women watched from their tiny balconies with latticed and fretted windows on the first floor.

As the sun went down in rose and scarlet and finally indigo far out in the Atlantic beyond the Pillars of Hercules, the noise in Main Street swelled. The music from the bars grew louder and the swing doors belched out a stream of sailors who tumbled into the street, picked themselves up and tottered to the bar next door. The tinkling of broken glass attracted a patrol from the other side of the street and they went into the bar to quell the first fight. Their entrance was the cue for redoubled shouts from inside and higher and more frenzied notes on the trumpet while castanets carried on their steady ticking without a break in their rhythm. The Gibraltar evening was warming up according to its traditional schedule.

The cadets ate prawn cocktails, swordfish steaks and pineapple fruit salad and afterwards drank beer quietly in bars where girls of fourteen or fifteen in flaring skirts danced the paso doble with dark youths in tight-fitting trousers and short black jackets.

*

They changed their money into pesetas at the end of Main Street and took a taxi to the border. They walked across into Spain, where the frontier guards took no more notice of them than if they had been Spanish flies, although they looked concerned when George Dewberry lurched towards a bullfight poster.

George Dewberry led the way by instinct into the first bar.

The walls were tiled with scenes from the bullfight. The bar itself was of hard black wood polished with a wet cloth and barrels of sherry were stacked to the roof behind it. The bartender kept each customer's score chalked on the bar and no money passed until the customer was ready to leave. Each drinker was besieged by a clamouring crowd of shoe-shine boys, men selling fountain pens and postcards, and small girls holding baskets of peanuts and flowers.

The bar was crowded with officers from *Barsetshire*, among them The Bodger, who had his arm around the bartender's wife, and was loudly calling for Fundador for both of them.

Raymond Ball looked around him.

'Might as well be back in *Barsetshire*,' he said disgustedly. 'Come on, Paul. Let's try somewhere else. This place is too sordid for words.'

They collected George Dewberry, who, in one crowded minute, had had his right shoe polished and had bought three bags of peanuts, a carnation and a postcard of two women wrestling with a donkey, and went outside.

Deeper in the town they came upon a street which reeked of lechery. The air smelt sickly, over-ripe with the smell of offal and garbage. The very houses huddled lewdly together and women in the doorways winked invitingly at the cadets and leapt out into the streets to snatch at them.

'Golly!' said Paul. 'This is like something out of Hogarth in one of his juicier moods. Let's get out of the light before we all get raped.'

*

Raymond Ball was separated from the main party in the next bar. He was much taken with a girl who, until he noticed her, had been sitting by herself and taking no part in the entertainment.

'I say, Mike, lend me thirty pesetas, will you?'

'Surely,' said Michael.

'Thanks.'

Raymond Ball went over to the girl, who looked up enquiringly.

'Hello, my dear,' he said, in his most engaging manner, which made Michael think of the Walrus talking to the Oysters. 'How about a little bit of je ne sais quoi?'

'Eighty-five pesetas,' said the girl briskly.

'Whatever you say, my dear.'

'Well, I'll be goddamned,' said Paul. 'Would you like to take a walk? Let's go and find our own exibeesh, Mike.'

'Good idea,' said Michael.

from *We Joined The Navy* by John Winton (1959)

John Winton followed his enormous initial success as a novelist with a succession of equally light-hearted accounts of life as a submariner and other aspects of the naval service. Later he established himself as a naval historian of the front rank with his biographies of Raleigh and Jellicoe, followed by *Convoy*, a major definitive study of the Defence of Sea Trade over the last century.

Midshipmen

Initiation

Frank Mildmay, the hero of Captain Marryat's novel of that name, runs away from school at the beginning of the nineteenth century and announces to his father that he intends to join the Navy. With an elder son at Oxford waiting to inherit the estate, his father readily falls in with this plan. So, decked out in a dazzling new uniform and with a brass-bound sea-chest strapped on top of the stage-coach, young Frank sets out for Plymouth to join his first ship.

On arrival he finds the ship in dockyard hands with her Captain living ashore at an inn, whence he is bidden to dine. Their companions at table are the First Lieutenant and Murphy, a senior midshipman of indeterminate age and the scourge of the gunroom. Frank's first lesson in the customs of the Service seems innocent enough.

A captain seldom waits for a midshipman, and we took good care he should not wait for us. The dinner was in all respects one 'on service'. The captain said a great deal, the lieutenants very little, and the midshipmen nothing at all; but the performance of the knife and fork and wine-glass (as far as it could be got at) were exactly in the inverse ratio. The company consisted of my own captain, and two others, our first lieutenant, Murphy, and myself.

As soon as the cloth was removed, the captain filled me out a glass of wine, desired I would drink it, and then go and see how the wind was. I took my first admonitory hint in its literal sense and meaning; but having a very imperfect idea about the points of a compass, I own I felt a little puzzled how I should obtain the necessary information. Fortunately for me, there was a weathercock on the old church steeple; it had four letters, which I certainly did know were meant to represent the cardinal points. One of these seemed to respond so exactly with the dial above it, that I made up my mind that the wind must be west, and instantly returned to give my captain the desired information, not a little proud with my success in having obtained it so soon. But what was my surprise to find that I was not thanked for my trouble; the company even smiled and winked at each other; the first lieutenant nodded his head, and said, 'Rather green yet.' The captain, however, settled the point according to the manners and customs in such cases used at sea. 'Here, youngster,' said he, 'here is another glass for you: drink that, and then Murphy will show you what I mean.' Murphy was my chaperon; he swallowed his wine – rather a *gorge déployée* – put down his glass very energetically, and, bowing, left the room.

When we had got fairly into the hall, we had the following duet: – 'What the h— brought you back again, you d—d young greenhorn? Could you not take a hint and be off, as the captain intended? So I must lose my wine for such a d—d young whelp as you. I'll pay you off for this, my tight fellow, before we have been many weeks together.'

I listened to this elegant harangue with some impatience and much more indignation. 'I came back,' said I, 'to tell the captain how the wind was.'

'You be d—d,' replied Murphy; 'do you think the captain did not know how the wind was? and if he had wanted to know, don't you think he would have sent a sailor like me instead of such a d—d lubberly whelp as you?'

Once on board Frank is shown the gunroom (or midshipmen's berth, as it was commonly called) abreast the mainmast at waterline level. His future residence was a square hole they called a berth:

... it was ten feet long by six, and about five feet four inches high; a small aperture, about nine inches square, admitted a very scanty portion of that which we most needed, namely fresh air and daylight. A deal table occupied a very considerable extent of this small apartment, and on it stood a brass candlestick, with a dip candle, and a wick like a full-blown carnation. The table-cloth was spread, and the stains of port wine and gravy too visibly indicated, like the midshipman's dirty shirt, the near approach of Sunday. The black servant was preparing dinner, and I was shown the seat I was to occupy. 'Good Heaven!' thought I, as I squeezed myself between the ship's side and the mess-table, 'and is this to be my future residence? – better go back to school; there, at least, there is fresh air and clean linen.'

*

I had now more leisure to contemplate my new residence and new associates, who, having returned from the duty of the dockyard, were all assembled in the berth, seated around the table on the lockers, which paid 'the double debt' of seats and receptacles; but in order to obtain a sitting, it was requisite either to climb over the backs of the company, or submit to 'high pressure' from the last comer. Such close contact, even with our best friends, is never desirable; but in warm weather, in a close, confined air, with a manifest scarcity of clean linen, it became particularly inconvenient. The population here very far exceeded the limits usually allotted to human beings in any situation of life, except in a slave ship. The midshipmen, of whom there were eight full-grown, and four youngsters, were without either jackets or waistcoats; some of them had their shirt-sleeves rolled up, either to prevent the reception or to conceal the absorption of dirt in the region of the wrist-bands. The repast on the table consisted of a can or large black-jack of small beer, and a japan bread-basket full of sea-biscuit. To compensate for this simple fare, and at the same time to cool the close atmosphere of the berth, the table was covered with a large green cloth with a yellow border, and many yellow spots withal, where the colour had been discharged by slops of vinegar, hot tea, etc. etc.; a sack of potatoes stood in one corner, and the shelves all round, and close over our heads, were stuffed with plates, glasses, quadrants, knives and forks, loaves of sugar, dirty stockings and shirts, and still fouler table-cloths, small-tooth-combs, and ditto large, clothes brushes and shoe brushes, cocked hats, dirks, German flutes, mahogany writing-desks, a plate of salt butter, and some two or three pairs of naval half-boots. A single candle served to make darkness visible, and the stench had nearly over-powered me.

The initiation of a newly joined midshipman in Nelson's day varied only in degree to that accorded those arriving from Dartmouth between the world wars. Frank soon realizes that Murphy has singled him out as a prime target. During his first uneasy night in a hammock he has it abruptly cut down at his head. He quickly retaliates by cutting Murphy down, having first placed an ammunition locker under his head so that Murphy is knocked out cold and seriously injured on hitting it.

It is time to take stock of the midshipmen's mess and the jungle laws which shape the characters of its young inmates.

Their only pursuits when on shore were intoxication and worse debauchery, to be gloried in and boasted of when they returned on board. My captain said that everything found its level in a man-of-war. True; but in a midshipman's berth it was the level of a savage, where corporal strength was the *sine qua non*, and decided whether you were to act the part of a tyrant or a slave. The discipline of public schools, bad and demoralizing as it is, was light compared to the tyranny of a midshipman's berth in 1803.

A mistaken notion has long prevailed that boys derive advantages from suffering under the tyranny of their oppressors at school; and we constantly hear the praises of public schools and midshipmen's berths on this very account, namely, 'that boys are taught to find their level'. I do not mean to deny that the higher orders improve by collision with their inferiors, and that a young aristocrat is often brought to his senses by receiving a sound thrashing from the son of a tradesman. But he that is brought up a slave will be a tyrant when he has power; the worst of our passions are nourished to inflict the same evil on others which we boast of having suffered ourselves. The courage and daring spirit of a noble-minded boy are rather broken down by ill-usage, which he has not the power to resist, or, surmounting all this, he proudly imbibes a dogged spirit of sullen resistance and implacable revenge which becomes the bane of his future life.

The latter was my fate; and let not my readers be surprised or shocked if, in the course of these adventures, I should display some of the fruits of that fatal seed so early and so profusely sown in my bosom. If, on my first coming into the ship, I shrank back with horror at the sound of blasphemy and obscenity – if I shut my eyes to the promiscuous intercourse of the sexes, it was not so long. By insensible degrees I became familiarized with vice, and callous to its approach. In a few months I had become nearly as corrupt as others. I might have indeed have resisted longer; but though the fortress of virtue could have held out against open violence, it could not withstand the undermining of ridicule. My young companions, who, as I have observed, had only preceded me six months in the service, were already grown old in depravity; they laughed at my squeamishness, called me milksop and boarding-school miss, and soon made me as bad as themselves. We had not quite attained the age of perpetration, but we were fully prepared to meet it when it came.

Peace lasts only as long as Frank's tormentor is laid up with an injury.

Murphy had also recovered from his fall, and returned to his duty; his malice towards me increased, and I had no peace or comfort in his presence. One day he threw a biscuit at my head, calling me at the same time a name which reflected on the legitimacy of my birth, in language the most coarse and vulgar. In a moment all the admonitions which I had received, and all my sufferings for impetuosity of temper, were forgotten; the blood boiled in my veins and trickled from my wounded forehead. Dizzy, and almost sightless with rage, I seized a brass candlestick, the bottom of which (to keep it steady at sea) was loaded with lead, and threw it at him with all my might; had it taken effect as I intended, that offence would have been his last. It missed his head, and struck the black servant on the shoulder; the poor man went howling to the surgeon, in whose care he remained for many days.

Murphy started up to take instant vengeance, but was held by the other seniors of the mess, who unanimously declared that such an offence as mine should be punished in a more solemn manner. A mock trial (without adverting to the provocation I had received) found me guilty of insubordination 'to the oldsters', and setting a bad example to the youngsters. I was sentenced to be *cobbed* with a worsted stocking filled with wet sand. I was held down on my face on the mess-table by four stout midshipmen; the surgeon's assistant held my wrist, to ascertain if my pulse indicated exhaustion; while Murphy, at his own particular request, became the executioner. Had it been any other but him, I should have given vent to my agonizing pain by screams, but like a sullen Ebo, I was resolved to endure even to death, rather than gratify him by any expression of pain. After a most severe punishment, a cold sweat and faintness alarmed the surgeon's assistant. I was then released, but ordered to mess on my chest for a fortnight by myself.

from *Frank Mildmay* by Captain Frederick Marryat (1829)

Frank is then sent to Coventry, but not before he publicly acknowledges having cut Murphy's hammock down and promised to knock his block off unless he desists from further tyranny. Luckily Murphy quickly shows himself a coward and withdraws into the shadows, leaving our hero free to organize the junior midshipmen's defences against further gross physical aggression.

It is also fortunate that the frigate now joins *Victory* off Cadiz, where few of her company or others in the fleet do not respond wholeheartedly to Nelson's signal to do their duty in the face of the enemy, as England expects.

Discipline

Flogging Round the Fleet

Douglas Reeman, who also writes under the pen-name of Alexander Kent, is not only the most prolific living fiction-writer about the sea, concentrating mainly on Nelson's day, but in his accuracy and grasp of technical and factual detail matches the most meticulous and informed naval historians. As Alexander Kent, he has created a series of action-packed stories around the central character of one Richard Bolitho, a native of Falmouth whose promotion through the ranks of the Royal Navy owes nothing to influence or birth. In reality the Bolitho family are part of Cornish legend, mostly as landowners, bankers, masters of foxhounds and distinguished soldiers. Indeed old copies of the Navy List do not show any members of the family having held commissions afloat between Nelson's day and the Crimean War, although during my lifetime there was an outrageous but lovable eccentric retired naval Captain of that name whose memorial at the Royal Yacht Squadron in Cowes is a three-bottle ship's port decanter which has to be consumed at a sitting.

The fictional Richard Bolitho of 1795 bears little resemblance to him. He is the hero of *The Flag Captain*, serving in that appointment in the three-decked ship-of-the-line *Euryalus*, a former French flagship which he has taken against all odds as a prize in a bloody encounter. While at anchor in his home port of Falmouth, awaiting the arrival of the hard-nosed aristocratic Vice-Admiral Sir Lucius Broughton to form a new squadron, Taylor, an old shipmate from days gone by, struggles to Bolitho's home with sinister news. He is now serving as Master's Mate (navigator's assistant) in the frigate *Auriga*, which has been detached from the fleet during the Spithead Mutiny and is now in nearby Veryan Bay, with her sadistic Captain and officers held at bayonet-point by the mutineers. They are minded to hand her over to the French and take their chances on the run in Europe. Taylor has persuaded them instead to throw themselves at the mercy of Captain Bolitho, who then brings the *Auriga* to anchor off Falmouth under the guns of his own ship, which the new Admiral has already joined. He picks on the loyal Taylor as scapegoat for the mutiny in *Auriga* and orders him to be flogged round the fleet – without the formality of a court-martial, which was required by King's Regulations before such a severe punishment. Bolitho questions this decision, but the Admiral is quick to point out that Taylor will otherwise be hung at the yard-arm – a matter of indifference to the wretched Taylor, who dies under punishment and is later buried on a sandbank at low water. The grim ritual of flogging round the fleet has never been more movingly described.

Bolitho held up his arms to allow the big coxswain to buckle the sword around his waist and then let them fall to his sides. Through the thick glass windows he could see the distant town swinging gently as wind and tide took the *Euryalus* under control. He was again aware of the silence which had fallen over the whole ship since Keverne had come down to repeat that the lower decks were cleared and that it was close on eight bells.

He picked up his hat and glanced briefly around the cabin. It should have been a good day for quitting the land. A fair breeze had sprung up from the south-west overnight and the air was clean and crisp.

He felt Broughton watching and deliberately turned away. But it *did* matter, and he *did* care, and he knew he could not change. Not for Broughton, or to further his own chances of promotion in the Service he loved and now needed more than ever before.

He heard Keverne clear his throat and then something like a sigh from the watching seamen on the gangways.

Around the bows of *Zeus*, the nearest seventy-four, came in a procession of longboats, one from each ship in the squadron, the oars rising and falling with the 'Rogue's March' of the drum. He could see *Euryalus*'s boat second in line, dark green like those now lashed in their tier and crowded with silent men. Each one in the procession carried marines, the lethal glitter of their bayonets and gleam of scarlet bringing colour to the grim spectacle as the boats turned slightly and headed for the flagship.

Broughton said softly, 'This should not take too long, I think.'

'Way 'nough!'

The *Auriga*'s longboat glided alongside and hooked on to the main chains, while the others swayed above their reflections to witness punishment.

Bolitho took the Articles of War from Keverne and walked quickly to the entry port. Spargo, the surgeon, was already down in the boat accompanied by the boatswain's mates, and he glanced up as Bolitho's shadow fell across the rigid oarsmen.

He said, 'Fit for punishment, sir.'

Bolitho made himself look at the figure in the forepart of the frigate's longboat. Bent almost double, his arms lashed out on a capstan bar as if crucified, it was hard to believe it was Taylor. The man who had come to ask for help. For forgiveness and . . . He removed his hat, opened the book and began to read the Articles, the sentence and punishment.

Below the boat, Taylor stirred slightly, and Bolitho paused to look once again.

The thwarts and planking of the boat were covered with blood. Not the blood of battle, but black. Like the remnants of torn skin which hung from his mangled back. Black and ripped, so that the exposed bones shone in the sunlight like polished marble.

The boatswain's mate glanced up and asked thickly, 'Two dozen, zur?'

'Do your duty.'

Bolitho replaced his hat and kept his eyes on the nearest two-decker as the man drew back his arm and then brought the lash down with terrible force.

A step sounded beside him and Broughton said quietly, 'He seems to be taking it well enough.' No concern or real interest. Just a casual comment.

Just as suddenly it was over, and as the boat cast off again to continue its way to the next ship Bolitho saw Taylor trying to turn his head to look up at him. But he did not have the strength.

Bolitho turned away, sickened by the sight of the contorted face, the broken lips, the thing which had once been John Taylor.

He said harshly, 'Dismiss the hands, Mr Keverne.' He glanced involuntarily back again at the re-formed procession. Two more ships to go. He would never live through it. A younger man possibly, but not Taylor.

He heard Broughton's voice again, very near. 'If he had not been one of your old ship's company – er, the *Sparrow* was it?' – he sighed – 'you would have not have felt so involved, so vulnerable.'

He sighed and walked from the cabin, past the table and its untouched breakfast, through the door with the rigid sentry and towards the bright rectangle of sunlight and the open quarterdeck beyond.

Keverne was waiting, his dark features inscrutable as he touched his hat and said formally, 'Two minutes, sir.'

Bolitho studied the lieutenant gravely. If Keverne was brooding about his sudden removal from possible command he did not show it. If he was thinking about his captain's feelings he concealed that too.

Bolitho nodded and walked slowly to the weather side of the deck where the ship's lieutenants were already mustered. Slightly to leeward the senior warrant officers and midshipmen stood in neat lines, their bodies swaying easily to the ship's motion.

A glance aft told him that Giffard's marines were fallen in across the poop, their tunics very bright in the fresh sunlight, the white cross-belts and polished boots making their usual impeccable array.

He turned and walked to the quarterdeck rail, letting his eyes move over the great press of seamen who were crowded along the gangways, in the tiered boats and clinging to the shrouds, as if eager to watch the coming drama. But he could tell from the silence, the air of grim expectancy, that hardened to discipline and swift punishment though they were, there was no acceptance there.

Eight bells chimed from the forecastle and he saw the officers stiffen as Broughton, accompanied by Lieutenant Calvert, walked briskly on to the quarterdeck.

Bolitho touched his hat but said nothing.

Across the anchorage the air shivered as a solitary gun boomed out, and then came the doleful sound of drumming. He saw the surgeon below the break in the poop whispering to Tebbutt, the boatswain, and his two mates, one of whom carried the familiar red baize bag. The latter dropped his eyes as he realized his captain was looking at him.

Broughton's fingers were tapping the hilt of his beautiful sword, seemingly in time with the distant drum. He appeared relaxed, and as fresh as ever.

Bolitho tensed as one of the young midshipmen wiped his mouth with the back of his hand, a quick nervous gesture which brought back a sudden memory like the feel of an old wound.

He had been only fourteen himself when he had witnessed his first flogging through the fleet. He had seen most of it in a mist of tears and nausea, and the nightmare had never completely left him. In a service where flogging was commonplace and an accepted punishment, and in many cases more than justified, this final spectacle was still the worst, where onlookers felt degraded almost as much as the victim.

Broughton remarked, 'We will be weighing this afternoon, Bolitho. Our destination is Gibraltar, where I will receive further orders and news of developments.' He looked up at his flag at the fore and added, 'A fine day for it.'

Bolitho looked away, trying to shut the persistent drumming from his ears.

'All the ships are fully provisioned, sir.' He stopped. Broughton knew that as well as he did. It was just something to say. Why should this one event mar everything? He should have realized by now that the days when he had been a young frigate captain were gone for good. Then, faces and people were real individuals. When one suffered it was felt throughout the cramped confines of the ship. Now he had to realize that men were no longer individuals. They were necessities, like the artillery and the rigging, the fresh water supply and the very planking upon which he now stood.

When Bolitho did not reply he added curtly, 'An example has to be made. They'll not forget it, I think.'

Bolitho straightened his back and faced him, his voice steady as he replied, 'Neither will I, sir.'

For just a few more seconds their eyes held, and then the shutter seemed to fall as Broughton said, 'I am going below. Make the signal for all captains as soon as possible.' Then he was gone.

Bolitho took a grip of his thoughts, his anger and disgust.

'Mr Keverne, you will instruct the midshipmen of the watch to bend the signal for all captains to repair on board.'

Keverne watched him curiously, 'When shall it be hoisted, sir?'

A voice called, 'Signal from *Valorous*, sir. Prisoner has died under punishment.'

Bolitho kept his eyes on Keverne. 'You may hoist it now.' Then he turned on his heel and strode aft to his cabin.

from *The Flag Captain* by Alexander Kent (1971)

Hanging by Verdict of Court-martial

Punishment by death lingered on as a possible sentence in the Royal Navy's Articles of War until relatively recently. A wide range of offences were prescribed as 'punishable by death or such other punishment as may hereinafter be described'. In fact, the last man to be hung from the yard-arm was a Royal Marine on the China Station in 1860 for the trifling offence of attempting to murder his captain and navigator. Over a quarter of a century after Frederick Marryat ran away to sea in 1805 the threat still carried weight and the drill for its execution needed little rehearsal. Indeed, it was the practice for the local Commander-in-Chief to advertise his trump card in enforcing discipline by a widespread poster campaign after each judicial hanging within his Command. As a Midshipman in his early teens, Marryat served in the frigate *Imperieuse* under the redoubtable Thomas Cochrane. Cochrane commanded in turn the navies of Chile, Brazil and Greece during a long period of disgrace from the Royal Navy after he had publicly charged his superior, Admiral Lord Gambier, with not pressing home the advantage he created for him at the Battle of Basque Roads in 1809.

Marryat's first novel, written in 1829 before he retired to become a full-time author, was not considered at the time to be autobiographical, partly owing to the depravity of some of its characterization, but it is significant that its hero, Frank Mildmay, bears the author's initials. In 1909, in his masterly *The British Tar in Fact and Fiction*, Commander C. N. Robinson judged *Frank Mildmay* to have been 'visibly autobiographical', flawed by being used as a vehicle for Marryat's revenge on various officers who made his life miserable as a young man. In his later books a more generous view emerges of such men as Admiral Cochrane.

Frank Mildmay has also been faulted for painting too lurid a picture of its hero's love life, but within the social mores and judgements of the day it seems credible enough. There is the torrid affair with Eugenia, one of a company of strolling players whom Frank joins while on the books of the guardship at Portsmouth. She contrives a neat ending to the tale by losing his bastard son in a trout-stream and then bequeathing to Frank a considerable legacy before being carried off with a brain haemorrhage as our hero chases her across France.

In the meantime he whiles away his leisure hours in Nassau in the arms of Carlotta, a voluptuous Creole whom he cheerfully abandons when the next passing HM ship offers him a passage home. There Emily, the unsullied English rose, the girl-next-door (give or take a few landed estates) of impeccable background, is waiting at the altar with a broad-minded octogenarian bishop ready to tie the knot. In a revealing moment of self-analysis Frank recognizes his virtuous intended as being 'what the Dutchman's best anchor was to him – he kept it at home for fear of losing it'.

Fact or fiction, it makes a fast-moving adventure story based on every conceivable incident Marryat's impressionable young mind had stored away. One chapter concerns the fate of two mutineers after a long, morale-slapping blockade of an enemy port without any action, in conditions of unimaginable squalor and privation. This account of the ultimate penalty, written 150 years before Alexander Kent, has the authentic ring of eye-witness reportage.

While I was on board of this ship two poor men were executed for mutiny. The scene was far more solemn to me than anything I had ever beheld. Indeed, it was the first thing of the kind I had been present at. When we hear of executions on shore, we are always prepared to read of some foul, atrocious crime, some unprovoked and unmitigated offence against the laws of civilised society, which a just and a merciful government cannot allow to pass unpunished. With us at sea there are many shades of difference; but that which the law of our service considers a serious offence is often no more than an ebullition of local and temporary feeling, which in some cases might be curbed, and in others totally suppressed, by timely firmness and conciliation.

The ships had been a long time at sea, the enemy did not appear – and there was no chance either of bringing him to action, or of returning into port. Indeed, nothing can be more dull and monotonous than a blockading cruise 'in the team', as we might call it, that is, the ships of the line stationed to watch an enemy. The frigates have, in this respect, every advantage; they are always employed on shore, often in action, and the more men they have killed, the happier are the survivors. Some melancholy ferment on board the flagship I was in caused an open mutiny. Of course it was very soon quelled, and the ringleaders having been tried by a court-martial, two of them were condemned to be hanged at the yardarm of their own ship, and were ordered for execution on the following day but one.

Our courts-martial are always arrayed in the most pompous manner, and are certainly calculated to stike the mind with awe – even of a captain himself. A gun is fired at eight o'clock in the morning from the ship where it is to be held, and a union flag is displayed at the mizzen-peak.. If the weather be fine, the ship is arranged with the greatest nicety; her decks are as white as snow – her hammocks are stowed with care – her ropes are taut – her yards square – her guns run out – and a guard of marines, under the order of a lieutenant, prepared to receive every member of the court with the honour due to his rank. Before nine o'clock thay are all assembled; the officers in their undress uniform, unless an admiral is to be tried. The great cabin is prepared, with a long table covered with a green cloth. Pens, ink, paper, prayer-books, and the articles of war, are laid round to every member.

'Open the court,' says the president.

The court is opened, and officers and men indiscriminately stand round. The prisoners are now brought in under the charge of the provost-marshal, a master-at-arms, with his sword drawn and placed at the foot of the table, on the left hand of the judge-advocate. The court is sworn to do its duty impartially, and if there is any doubt, to let it go in favour of the prisoner. Having done this, the members sit down, covered, if they please.

The judge-advocate is then sworn, and the order for the court-martial read. The prisoner is put on his trial: if he says anything to commit himself, the court stops him, and kindly observes, 'We do not want your evidence against yourself; we want only to know what others can prove against you.' The unfortunate man is offered any assistance he may require; and when the defence is over, the court is cleared, the doors are shut, and the minutes, which have been taken down by the judge-advocate, are carefully read over, the credibility of the witnesses weighed, and the president puts the question to the youngest member first, 'Proved, or not proved?'

All having given their answer, if seven are in favour of proved, and six against, proved is recorded. The next question – if for mutiny or desertion, or other capital crime – 'Flogging or death?' The votes are given in the same way: if the majority be for death, the judge-advocate writes the sentence, and it is signed by all the members, according to seniority, beginning with the president, and ending with the judge-advocate.

The court is now opened again, the prisoner brought in, and an awful and deep silence prevails. The members of the court all put their hats on, and are seated; every one else, except the provost-marshal, is uncovered. As soon as the judge-advocate has read the sentence, the prisoners are delivered to the custody of the provost-marshall, by a warrant from the president, and he has charge of them until the time for the execution of the sentence.

About three o'clock in the afternoon, I received a message from one of the prisoners, saying he wished much to speak to me. I followed the master-at-arms down to the screened cabin, in the gun-room, were the men were confined with their legs in irons. These irons consist of one long bar and a set of shackles. The shackles fit the small part of the leg, just above the ankle: and, having an eye on each of them, they receive the leg. The end of the bar is then passed through, and secured with a padlock. I found the poor fellows sitting on a shot-box. Their little meal lay before them untouched; one of them cried bitterly; the other, a man of the name of Strange, possessed a great deal of equanimity, although evidently deeply affected. This man had been pretty well educated in youth, but having taken a wild and indolent turn, had got into mischief, and to save himself from a severe chastisement, had run away from his friends, and entered on board a man-of-war. In this situation he had found time, in the intervals of duty, to read and to think; he became, in time, sullen, and separated himself from the occasional merriment of his mess-mates; and it is not improbable that this moody temper had given rise to the mutinous acts for which he was to suffer.

This man now apologized for the liberty he had taken, and said he would not detain me long.

'You see, sir,' said he, 'that my poor friend is quite overcome with the horror of his situation; nor do I wonder at it. He is very different from the hardened malefactors that are executed on shore; we are neither of us afraid to die: but such a death as this, Mr Mildmay – to be hung up like dogs, an example to the fleet, and a shame and reproach to our friends – this wrings our hearts! It is this consideration and to save the feelings of my poor mother, that I have sent for you. I saw you jump overboard to save a poor fellow from drowning; so I thought you would not mind doing a good turn for another unfortunate sailor. I have made my will, and appointed you my executor; and with this power of attourney you will receive all my pay and prize money, which I will thank you to give to my dear mother, whose address you will find written here. My motive for this is, that she may never learn the history of my death. You can tell her that I died for my country's good, which is very true, for I acknowledge the justice of my sentence, and own that a severe example is wanting. It is eleven years since I was in England; I have served faithfully the whole of that time; nor did I ever misbehave except in this one instance. I think if our good king knew my sad story he would be merciful: but God's will be done! Yet, if I had a wish, it would be that the enemy's fleet would come out, and that I might die, as I have lived, defending my country. But, Mr Mildmay, I have one very important question to ask you – do you believe that there is such a thing as a future state?'

'Most surely,' said I; 'though we all live as though we believed there was no such thing: but why do you doubt it?'

'Because,' said the poor fellow, 'when I was an officer's servant, I was one day tending the table in the wardroom, and I heard the commander of a sloop of war, who was dining there with his son, say that it was all nonsense – that there was no future state, and the Bible was a heap of lies. I have never been happy since.'

I told him that I was extremely sorry that any officer should have used such expressions at all, particularly before him; that I was incapable of restoring his mind to its proper state; but that I should recommend his immediately sending for the chaplain, who, I had no doubt, would give him all the comfort he could desire. He thanked me for this advice, and profited by it, as he assured me in his last moments.

'And now, sir,' said he, 'let me give *you* a piece of advice. When you are a captain, as I am very sure you will be, do not worry your men into mutiny by making what is called a smart ship. Cleanliness and good order are what seamen like; but niggling, polishing, scraping iron bars and ring-bolts, and the like of that, a sailor dislikes more than a flogging at the gangway. If, in reefing topsails, you happen to be a minute later than another ship, never mind it, so long as your sails are well reefed, and fit to stand blowing weather. Many a sail is split by bad reefing, and many a good sailor has lost his life by that foolish hurry which has done incredible harm in the navy. What can be more cruel or unjust than to flog the last man off the yard? seeing that he is necessarily the most active and cannot get in without the imminent danger of breaking his neck; and, moreover, that one man *must* be last. Depend upon it, sir, "that nothing is well done which is done in a hurry." But I have kept you too long. God bless you, sir; remember my poor mother, and be sure you meet me on the forecastle to-morrow morning.'

The fatal morning came. It was eight o'clock. The gun fired – the signal for punishment flew at our mast-head. The poor men gave a deep groan, exclaiming, 'Lord have mercy upon us! – our earthly career and troubles are nearly over!' The master-at-arms came in, unlocked the padlock at the end of the bars, and, slipping off the shackles, desired the marine sentinels to conduct the prisoners to the quarter-deck.

Here was a scene of solemnity which I hardly dare attempt to describe. The day was clear and beautiful; the top-gallant yards were crossed on board of all the ships; the colours were flying; the crews were all dressed in white trousers and blue jackets, and hung in clusters, like bees, on the side of the rigging facing our ship; a guard of marines, under arms, was paced along each gangway, but on board of our ship they were on the quarter-deck. Two boats from each ship lay off upon their oars alongside of us, with a lieutenant's and a corporal's guard in each, with fixed bayonets. The hands were all turned up by the boatswain and his mates with a shrill whistle and calling down each hatchway, 'All hands attend punishment!'

You now heard the quick trampling of feet up the ladders, but not a word was spoken. The prisoners stood on the middle of the quarter-deck, while the captain read the sentence of the court-martial and the order from the commander-in-chief for the execution. The appropriate prayers and psalms having been read by the chaplain, with much feeling and devotion, the poor men were asked if they were ready; they both replied in the affirmative, but each requested to have a glass of wine, which was instantly brought. They drank it off, bowing most respectfully to the captain and officers.

The admiral did not appear, it not being etiquette; but the prisoners desired to be kindly and gratefully remembered to him: they then begged to shake hands with the captain and all the officers, which having done, they asked permission to address the ship's company. The captain ordered them all to come aft on the top and quarter-deck. The most profound silence reigned, and there was not an eye but had a tear in it.

William Strange, the man who had sent for me, then said, in a clear and audible tone of voice, 'Brother sailors, attend to the last words of a dying man. We are brought here at the instigation of some of you who are now standing in safety among the crowd; you have made fools of us, and we are become the victims to the just vengeance of the laws. Had you succeeded in the just design you contemplated, what would have been the consequences? Ruin, eternal ruin, to yourselves and your families; a disgrace to your country, and scorn of those foreigners to whom you proposed delivering up the ship. Thank God you did not succeed. Let our fate be a warning to you; and endeavour to show by your future acts your deep contrition for the past. Now, sir,' turning to the captain, 'we are ready.'

This beautiful speech from the mouth of a common sailor must as much astonish the reader as it then did the captain and officers of the ship. But Strange, as I have shown, was no common man; he had had the advantage of education, and, like many of the ringleaders at the mutiny of the Nore, was led into the error of refusing to *obey*, from the conscious feeling that he was born to *command*.

The arms of the prisoners were then pinioned, and the chaplain led the way, reading the funeral service; the master-at-arms, with two marine sentinels, conducted them along the starboard gangway to the forecastle; here a stage was erected on either side, over the cathead, with steps to ascend to it; a tail block was attached to the boom iron, at the outer extremity of each fore-yardarm, and through this a rope was rove, one end of which came down to the stage. The other was led along the yard into the catharpings, and thence down upon the main-deck. A gun was primed and ready to fire, on the fore part of the ship, directly beneath the scaffold.

I attended poor Strange to the very last moment; he begged me to see that the halter, which was a piece of line like a clothes line, was properly made fast round his neck, for he had known men suffer dreadfully from the want of this precaution. A white cap was placed on the head of each man, and when both mounted the platform, the cap was drawn over their eyes. They shook hands with me, with their messmates, and with the chaplain, assuring him that they died happy, and confident in the hopes of redemption. They then stood still while the yard-ropes were fixed to the halter by a toggle in the running noose of the latter; the other ends of the yard-ropes were held by some twenty or thirty men on each side of the main-deck, where two lieutenants of the ship attended.

All being ready, the captain waved a white handkerchief, the gun fired, and in an instant the poor fellows were seen swinging at either yardarm. They had on blue jackets and white trousers, and were remarkably fine-looking young men. They did not appear to suffer any pain, and at the expiration of an hour, the bodies were lowered down, placed in coffins, and sent on shore for interment.

On my arrival in England, nine months after, I acquitted myself of my promise, and paid to the mother of William Strange upwards of fifty pounds, for pay and prize-money. I told the poor woman that her son had died a Christian, and had fallen for the good of his country; and having said this, I took hasty leave for fear she should ask questions.

from *Frank Mildmay* by Captain Frederick Marryat (1829)

The Handsome Sailor Swings For It

Herman Melville's literary fame rests mainly on his imperishable classic about harpooning whales in open long-boats in the Southern Ocean. *Moby*

Dick was published in 1851 when its author was thirty-two and had long since swallowed the anchor, married and become a full-time customs officer in New York City.

The story of the whaling-ship *Pequod* and Captain Ahab, with his relentless obsession with tracking down and killing the great white whale Moby Dick in revenge for a leg lost during an earlier encounter, is so well known – perhaps especially as a feature film – that it tends to be an anthologist's automatic choice as an example of Melville's writing about the sea. I would have liked instead to have chosen extracts from his *White Jacket*, written after a year's service in a US Navy frigate, as the best portrayal of uniformed life at sea in the 1840's, but it is so transparently autobiographical that it cannot qualify as fiction.

I have in the end picked the last story Melville wrote, published in 1891 after his death. Later *Billy Budd* became better known as an opera by Benjamin Britten, first performed in 1951. It concerns a twenty-one year-old fore-topman, the archetypical Handsome Sailor, the hero of drama and song about the Navy during the closing years of the eighteenth century. Billy is the most highly regarded sailor in a homeward-bound East Indiaman when she is boarded and he alone is pressed into service in the 74-gun HMS *Indomitable* on passage to join the Mediterranean Fleet. She is commanded by Captain Vere, nicknamed Starry Vere for his habit of gazing at the night sky from the weather rail of the quarter-deck, wrapped in impenetrable transcendental meditation.

It is the year of the mutinies amongst HM ships at Spithead and the Nore. Sailors who were present have been dispersed as widely as possible; their arrival in ships which have not been affected is viewed with as much apprehension as is that of pressed men, who are assumed to be the sweepings of waterfront jails, or to be on the run from some desperate felony.

But on board the seventy-four in which Billy now swung his hammock very little in the manner of the men and nothing obvious in the demeanour of the officers would have suggested to an ordinary observer that the Great Mutiny was a recent event. In their general bearing and conduct the commissioned officers of a warship naturally take their tone from the commander, that is if he have that ascendency of character that ought to be his.

Captain the Honourable Edward Fairfax Vere, to give his full title, was a bachelor of forty or thereabouts, a sailor of distinction, even in a time prolific of renowned seamen. Though allied to the higher nobility, his advancement had not been altogether owing to influences connected with that circumstance. He had seen much service, been in various engagements, always acquitting himself as an officer mindful of the welfare of his men, but never tolerating an infraction of discipline; thoroughly versed in the science of his profession, and intrepid to the verge of temerity, though never injudiciously so. For his gallantry in the West Indian waters as flag-lieutenant under Rodney in that admiral's crowning victory over De Grasse, he was made a post-captain.

Ashore in the garb of a civilian, scarce anyone would have taken him for a sailor, more especially that he never garnished unprofessional talk with nautical terms, and grave in his bearing, evinced little appreciation of mere humour. It was not out of keeping with these traits that on a passage when nothing demanded his paramount action, he was the most undemonstrative of men. Any landsman observing this gentleman, not conspicuous by his stature and wearing no pronounced insignia, emerging from his retreat to the open deck, and noting the silent deference of the officers retiring to leeward, might have taken him for the King's guest, a civilian aboard the King's ship, some highly honourable discreet envoy on his way to an important post. But, in fact, this unobtrusiveness of demeanour may have proceeded from a certain unaffected modesty of manhood sometimes accompanying a resolute nature, a modesty evinced at all times not calling for pronounced action, and which shown in any rank of life suggests a virtue aristocratic in kind.

As with some others engaged in various departments of the world's more heroic activities, Captain Vere, though practical enough upon occasion, would at times betray a certain dreaminess of mood. Standing alone on the weather-side of the greater deck, one hand holding by the rigging, he would absently gaze off at the black sea. At the presentation to him then of some minor matter interrupting the current of his thoughts, he would show more or less irascibility; but instantly he would control it.

*

The lieutenants and other commissioned gentlemen forming Captain Vere's staff it is not necessary here to particularize, nor needs it to make mention of any of the warrant-officers. But among the petty officers was one who, having much to do with the story, may as well be forthwith introduced. This portrait I essay, but shall never hit it.

This was John Claggart, the master-at-arms. But that sea-title may to landsmen seem somewhat equivocal. Originally, doubtless, that petty officer's function was the instruction of the men in the use of arms, sword, or cutlass. But very long ago, owing to the advance in gunnery making hand-to-hand encounters less frequent, and giving to nitre and sulphur the pre-eminence over steel, that function ceased; the master-at-arms of a great warship becoming a sort of chief of police charged among other matters with the duty of preserving order on the populous lower gun-decks.

Claggart was a man of about five-and-thirty, somewhat spare and tall, yet of no ill figure upon the whole. His hand was too small and shapely to have been accustomed to hard toil. The face was a notable one; the features, all except the chin, cleanly cut as those on a Greek medallion; yet the chin, beardless as Tecumseh's, had something of the strange protuberant heaviness in its make that recalled the prints of the Rev. Dr Titus Oates, the historical deponent with the clerical drawl in the time of Charles II, and the fraud of the alleged Popish

Plot. It served Claggart in his office that his eye could cast a tutoring glance. His brow was of the sort phrenologically associated with more than average intellect; silken jet curls partly clustering over it, making a foil to the pallor below, a pallor tinged with a faint shade of amber akin to the hue of time-tinted marbles of old.

This complexion singularly contrasting with the red or deeply bronzed visages of the sailors, and in part the result of his official seclusion from the sunlight, though it was not exactly displeasing, nevertheless seemed to hint of something defective or abnormal in the constitution and blood. But his general aspect and manner were so suggestive of an education and career incongruous with his naval function, that when not actively engaged in it he looked like a man of high quality, social and moral, who for reasons of his own was keeping incognito. Nothing was known of his former life. It might be that he was an Englishman; and yet there lurked a bit of accent in his speech suggesting that possibly he was not such by birth, but through naturalization in early childhood. Among certain grizzled sea-gossips of the gun-decks and forecastle went a rumour perdue that the master-at-arms was a chevalier who had volunteered into the King's Navy by way of compounding for some mysterious swindle whereof he had been arraigned at the King's Bench. The fact that nobody could substantiate this report was, of course, nothing against its secret currency.

*

Life in the foretop well agreed with Billy Budd. There, when not actually engaged on the yards yet higher aloft, the topmen, who as such had been picked out for youth and activity, constituted an aerial club, lounging at ease against the smaller stun'-sails rolled up into cushions, spinning yarns like the lazy gods, and frequently amused with what was going on in the busy world of the decks below. No wonder then that a young fellow of Billy's disposition was well content in such society. Giving no cause of offence to anybody, he was always alert at a call. So in the merchant service it had been with him. But now such puntiliousness in duty was shown that his top mates would sometimes good-naturedly laugh at him for it. This heightened alacrity had its cause, namely: the impression made upon him by the first formal gangway-punishment he had ever witnessed, which befell the day following his impressment. It had been incurred by a little fellow, young, a novice, an after-guardsman absent from his assigned post when the ship was being put about, a dereliction resulting in a rather serious hitch to that manœuvre, one demanding instantaneous promptitude in letting go and making fast. When Billy saw the culprit's naked back under the scourge gridironed with red welts, and worse; when he marked the dire expression in the liberated man's face, as with his woollen shirt flung over him by the executioner he rushed forward from the spot to bury himself in the crowd, Billy was horrified. He resolved that never through remissness would he make himself liable to such a visitation, or do or omit aught that might merit even verbal reproof. What then was his surprise and concern when ultimately he found himself getting into petty trouble occasionally about such matters as the stowage of his bag, or something amiss in his hammock, matters under the police oversight of the ship's corporals of the lower decks, and which brought down on him a vague threat from one of them.

So heedful in all things as he was, how could this be? He could not understand it, and it more than vexed him. When he spoke to his young topmates about it, they were either lightly incredulous, or found something comical in his unconcealed anxiety. 'Is it your bag, Billy?' said one; 'well, sew yourself up in it, Billy boy, and then you'll be sure to know if anybody meddles with it.'

It is at this time that Billy is tipped off by a veteran of Nelson's fleet that Jemmy Legs – as Master-at-Arms Claggart was known on the lower deck – has it in for him. His immediate anxiety is lessened when a sudden lurch of the ship causes him to spill the contents of his soup-pan over the newly scrubbed deck just as the Master-at-Arms is passing through the mess-deck. Instead of a whack from his ratan, the incident draws only a heavily sarcastic comment: 'Handsomely done, my lad! And handsome is as handsome does it, too!'

A more sinister turn of events comes when Billy is awoken by two strangers from another part of ship, identifying themselves also as pressed men and inviting him to join them in some unspecified mutinous act. They are *agents provocateurs* and they provide Claggart with enough evidence to force the Captain to confront Billy in the privacy of the after cabin.

Now when the foretopman found himself closeted, as it were, in the cabin with the captain and Claggart, he was surprised enough. But it was a surprise unaccompanied by apprehension or distrust. To an immature nature, essentially honest and humane, forewarning intimations of subtler danger from one's kind came tardily, if at all. The only thing that took shape in the young sailor's mind was this: 'Yes, the captain, I have always thought, looks kindly upon me. I wonder if he's going to make me his coxswain. I should like that. And maybe now he's going to ask the master-at-arms about me.'

'Shut the door there, sentry,' said the commander. 'Stand without and let nobody come in. Now, master-at-arms, tell this man to his face what you told of him to me'; and stood prepared to scrutinize the mutually confronting visages.

With the measured step and calm collected air of an asylum physician approaching in the public hall some patient beginning to show indications of a coming paroxysm, Claggart deliberately advanced within short range of Billy, and mesmerically looking him in the eye, briefly recapitulated the accusation.

Not at first did Billy take it in. When he did the rose-tan of his cheek looked struck as by white leprosy. He stood like one impaled and gagged. Meanwhile the accuser's eyes, removing not as yet from the blue, dilated ones, underwent a phenomenal change, their wonted rich violet colour blurring into a muddy purple. Those lights of human intelligence losing human expression, gelidly protruding like the alien eyes of certain uncatalogued creatures of the deep.

The first mesmeric glance was one of surprised fascination; the last was the hungry lurch of the torpedo-fish.

'Speak, man!' said Captain Vere to the transfixed one, struck by his aspect even more than by Claggart's. 'Speak! defend yourself.' Which appeal caused but a strange, dumb gesturing and gurgling in Billy; amazement at such an accusation so suddenly sprung on inexperienced nonage; this, and it may be horror at the accuser, serving to bring out his lurking defect, and in this instance for the time intensifying it into a convulsed tongue-tie; while the intent head and entire form, straining forward in an agony of eagerness to obey the injunction to speak and defend himself, gave an expression to the face like that of a condemned vestal priestess in the moment of being buried alive, and in the first struggle against suffocation.

Though at the time Captain Vere was quite ignorant of Billy's liability to vocal impediment, he now immediately divined it, since vividly Billy's aspect recalled to him that of a bright young schoolmate of his whom he had seen struck by much the same startling impotence in the act of eagerly rising in the class to be foremost in repsonse to a testing question put to it by the master. Going close up to the young sailor, and laying a soothing hand on his shoulder, he said, 'There is no hurry, my boy. Take your time, take your time.' Contrary to the effect intended, these words, so fatherly in tone, doubtless touching Billy's heart to the quick, prompted yet more violent efforts at utterance – efforts soon ending for the time in confirming the paralysis, and bringing to the face an expression which was as a crucifixion to behold. The next instant, quick as the flame from a discharged cannon at night, his right arm shot out, and Claggart dropped to the deck. Whether intentionally, or but owing to the young athlete's superior height, the blow had taken effect full upon the forehead, so shapely and intellectual-looking a feature in the master-at-arms; so that the body fell over lengthwise, like a heavy plank tilted from erectness. A gasp or two, and he lay motionless.

'Fated boy.' breathed Captain Vere, in tone so low as to be almost a whisper, 'what have you done! But here, help me.'

The twain raised the felled one from the loins up into a sitting position. The spare form flexibly acquiesced, but inertly. It was like handling a dead snake. They lowered it back. Regaining erectness, Captain Vere with one hand covering his face stood to all appearance as impassive as the object at his feet. Was he absorbed in taking in all the bearings of the event, and what was best not only now at once to be done, but also in the sequel? Slowly he uncovered his face; and the effect was as if the moon emerging from eclipse should reappear with quite another aspect than that which had gone into hiding. The father in him, manifested towards Billy thus far in the scene, was replaced by the military disciplinarian. In his official tone he bade the foretopman retire to a state-room aft (pointing it out), and there remain till thence summoned. This order Billy in silence mechanically obeyed.

*

Accordingly a drum-head court was summarily convened, he electing the individuals composing it – the first lieutenant, the captain of marines, and the sailing-master.

In associating an officer of marines with the sea-lieutenant in a case having to do with a sailor, the commander perhaps deviated from general custom. He was prompted thereto by the circumstance that he took that soldier to be a judicious person, thoughtful and not altogether incapable of grappling with a difficult case unprecedented in his prior experience. Yet even as to him he was not without some latent misgiving, for withal he was an extremely good-natured man, an enjoyer of his dinner, a sound sleeper, and inclined to obesity. The sort of man who, though he would always maintain his manhood in battle, might not prove altogether reliable in a moral dilemma involving aught of the tragic. As to the first lieutenant and the sailing-master, Captain Vere could not but be aware that though honest natures, of approved gallantry upon occasion, their intelligence was mostly confined to the matter of active seamanship, and the fighting demands of their profession. The court was held in the same cabin where the unfortunate affair had taken place. This cabin, the commander's, embraced the entire area under the poop-deck. Aft, and on either side, was a small state-room – the one room temporarily a jail, and the other a dead-house – and a yet smaller compartment leaving a space between, expanding forward into a goodly oblong of length coinciding with the ship's beam. A skylight of moderate dimensions was overhead, and at each end of the oblong space were two sashed port-hole windows easily convertible back into embrasures for short carronades.

All being quickly in readiness, Billy Budd was arraigned, Captain Vere necessarily appearing as the sole witness in the case, and as such temporarily sinking his rank, though singularly maintaining it in a matter apparently trivial, namely, that he testified from the ship's weather-side, with that object having caused the court to sit on the lee-side. Concisely he narrated all that had led up to the catastrophe, omitting nothing in Caggart's accusation, and deposing as to the manner in which the prisoner had received it. At this testimony the three officers glanced with no little surprise at Billy Budd, the last man they would have suspected, either of mutinous design alleged by Claggart, or of the undeniable deed he himself had done. The first lieutenant taking judicial primary, and turning toward the prisoner, said, 'Captain Vere has spoken. Is it or is it not as Captain Vere says?' In response came syllables not so much impeded in the utterance as might have been anticipated. They were these: –

'Captain Vere tells the truth. It is just as Captain Vere says, but it is not as the master-at-arms said. I have eaten the King's bread, and I am true to the King.'

'I believe you, my man,' said the witness, his voice indicating a suppressed emotion not otherwise betrayed.

'God will bless you for that, your honour!' not without stammering, said Billy, and all but broke down. But immediately was recalled to self-control by another question, to which with the same emotional difficulty of utterance he said, 'No, there was no malice between us. I never bore malice against the master-at-arms. I am sorry that he is dead. I did not mean to kill him. Could I have used my tongue I would not have struck him. But he foully lied to my face, and in the presence of my captain, and I had to say something, and I could only say it with a blow. God help me!'

Captain Vere has no choice but to carry out the death penalty at first light the next morning.

At sea in the old time, the execution by halter of a military sailor was generally from the fore-yard. In the present instance, for special reasons, the main-yard was assigned. Under an arm of that yard the prisoner was presently brought up, the chaplain attending him. It was noted at the time, and remarked upon afterwards, that in this final scene the good man evinced little or nothing of the perfunctory. Brief speech indeed he had with the condemned one, but the genuine Gospel was less on his tongue than in his aspect and manner toward him. The final preparations personal to the latter being speedily brought to an end by two boatswain's-mates, the consummation impended. Billy stood facing aft. At the penultimate moment, his words, his only ones, words wholly unobstructed in the utterance, were these – 'God bless Captain Vere!' Syllables so unanticipated coming from one with the ignominious hemp about his neck – a conventional felon's benediction directed aft toward the quarters of honour; syllables, too, delivered in the clear melody of a singing-bird on the point of launching from the twig, had a phenomenal effect, not unenhanced by the rare personal beauty of the young sailor, spiritualized now through late experiences so poignantly profound.

Without volition, as it were, as if indeed the ship's populace were the vehicles of some vocal current-electric, with one voice, from alow and aloft, came a resonant echo – 'God bless Captain Vere!' And yet at that instant Billy alone must have been in their hearts, even as he was in their eyes.

At the pronounced words and the spontaneous echo that voluminously rebounded them, Captain Vere, either through stoic self-control or a sort of momentary paralysis induced by emotional shock, stood erectly rigid as a musket in the ship-armourer's rack.

The hull, deliberately recovering from the periodic roll to leeward, was just regaining an even keel, when the last signal, the preconcerted dumb one, was given. At the same moment it chanced that the vapoury fleece hanging low in the east, was shot through with a soft glory as of the fleece of the Lamb of God seen in mystical vision, and simultaneously therewith, watched by the wedged mass of upturned faces, Billy ascended; and ascending, took the full rose of the dawn.

In the pinioned figure, arrived at the yard-end, to the wonder of all, no motion was apparent save that created by the slow roll of the hull, in moderate weather so majestic in a great ship heavy-cannoned.

from *Billy Budd* by Herman Melville (1891)

Later Captain Vere dies of wounds received in action. His last words are: 'Billy Budd, Billy Budd.'

The Handsome Sailor becomes a legend in the Fleet. For years to come parings from the yard-arm on which he was strung up are held by sailors with the same veneration as pieces of the Cross, even when it comes to end its days as a boom in a dockyard.

Shanghaied

The Press-gang Interrupts a Wake

Michael Cott's stories about Midshipman Tom Cringle were originally published anonymously in *Blackwood's* magazine in 1833, ten years after the author had returned to his native Glasgow from being an estate manager in Jamaica – the setting for most of his yarns. I suspect many modern writers of fiction about life in the Royal Navy during the early years of the nineteenth century have drawn heavily on his work for authenticity of background.

Tom, like many other lads after Trafalgar, has set his heart on following in Nelson's footsteps. After pulling every string he knows, he contrives to interest Vice Admiral Sir Barnaby Blueblazes, KB, who has him appointed to the frigate *Breeze*. Then follows a spell of dull blockade duty in the ship-of-the-line *Kraaken* before he gets away on independent service in the 18-gun sloop *Torch*. After various skirmishes afloat and ashore in the Baltic approaches, she sails for Cork, where Tom has many relations. *Torch* is ordered to join an outward-bound convoy, but, as usual, they are seriously under-manned. The Second Lieutenant, Mr Trenail, therefore sends Tom, disguised as a sailor, to reconnoitre the various crimp-shops in search of ten men known to have jumped ship. First he calls at a disreputable grog-shop on the Quay.

I heard a step within, and a very pretty face now appeared at the wicket.

'Who are you saking here, an' please ye?'

'No one in particular, my dear; but if you don't let me in, I shall be lodged in jail before five minutes be over.'

'I can't help that, young man,' said she; 'but where are ye from, darling?'

'Hush – I am run from the Guava, now lying at the Cove.'

'Oh,' said my beauty, 'come in;' and she opened the door, but still kept it on the chain in such a way, that although by bobbing, I creeped and slid in beneath it, yet a common-sized man could not possibly have squeezed himself through. The instant I entered, the door was once more banged to, and the next moment I was ushered into the kitchen, a room about fourteen feet square, with a well-sanded floor, a huge dresser on one side, and over against it a respectable show of pewter dishes in racks against the wall. There was a long stripe of a deal table in the middle of the room – but no tablecloth – at the bottom of which sat a large, bloated, brandy, or rather whisky-faced savage, dressed in a shabby great-coat of the hodden gray worn by the Irish peasantry, dirty swandown vest, and greasy corduroy breeches, worsted stockings, and well-patched shoes; he was smoking a long pipe. Around the table sat about a dozen seamen, from whose wet jackets and trowsers the heat of the blazing fire, that roared up the chimney, sent up a smoky steam that cast a halo round a lamp which depended from the roof, and hung down within two feet of the table, stinking abominably of coarse whale oil. They were, generally speaking, hardy, weather-beaten men, and the greater proportion half, or more than half drunk. When I entered, I walked up to the landlord.

'Yo ho, my young un! whence and whither bound, my hearty?'

'The first don't signify much to you,' said I, 'seeing I have wherewithal in my locker to pay my shot; and as to the second, of that hereafter; so, old boy, let's have some grog, and then say if you can ship me with one of them colliers that are lying alongside the quay?'

'My eye, what a lot of brass that small chap has!' grumbled mine host. 'Why, my lad, we shall see to-morrow morning; but you gammons you so about the rhino, that we must prove you a bit; so, Kate, my dear.' – to the pretty girl who had let me in – 'score a pint of rum against— Why, what is your name?'

'What's that to you?' rejoined I, 'let's have a drink, and don't doubt but the shiners shall be forthcoming.'

'Hurrah!' shouted the party, most of them now very tipsy. So the rum was produced forthwith, and as I lighted a pipe and filled a glass of swizzle, I struck in, 'Messmates, I hope you have all shipped?'

'No, we han't,' said some of them.

'Nor shall we be in any hurry, boy,' said others.

'Do as you please, but I shall, as soon as I can, I know; and I recommend all of you making yourselves scarce to-night, and keeping a bright look-out.'

'Why, boy, why?'

'Simply because I have just escaped a press-gang, by bracing sharp up at the corner of the street, and shoving into this dark alley here.'

This called forth another volley of oaths and unsavoury exclamations, and all was bustle and confusion, and packing up of bundles, and settling of reckonings.

'Where,' said one of the seamen, – 'where do you go to, my lad?'

'Why, if I can't get shipped to-night, I shall trundle down to Cove immediately, so as to cross at Passage before daylight, and take my chance of shipping with some of the outward-bound that are to sail, if the wind holds, the day after to-morrow. There is to be no pressing when the blue Peter flies at the fore – and that was hoisted this afternoon, I know, and the foretopsail will be loose to-morrow.'

'D--n my wig, but the small chap is right,' roared one.

'I've a bloody great mind to go down with him,' stuttered another, after several unavailing attempts to weigh from the bench, where he had brought himself to anchor.

'Hurrah!' yelled a third, as he hugged me, and nearly suffocated me with his maudlin caresses, 'I trundles wid you too, my darling, by the piper!'

'Have with you, boy – have with you,' shouted half-a-dozen other voices, while each stuck his oaken twig through the handkerchief that held his bundle, and shouldered it, clapping his straw or tarpaulin hat, with a slap on the crown, on one side of his head, and staggering and swaying about under the influence of the poteen, and slapping his thigh, as he bent double, laughing like to split himself, till the water ran over his cheeks from his drunken half-shut eyes, while jets of tobacco-juice were squirting in all directions.

I paid the reckoning, urging the party to proceed all the while, and indicating Pat Doolan's at the Cove as a good rendezvous; and promising to overtake them before they reached Passage, I parted company at the corner of the street, and rejoined the lieutenant.

Next morning we spent in looking about the town – Cork is a fine town – contains seventy thousand inhabitants *more* or *less* – safe in that – and three hundred thousand pigs, driven by herdsmen, with coarse gray great-coats. The pigs are not so handsome as those in England, where the legs are short, and tails curly; here the legs are long, the flanks sharp and thin, and tails long and straight.

All classes speak with a deuced brogue, and worship graven images; arrived at Cove to a late dinner – and here follows a great deal of nonsense of the same kind.

By the time it was half-past ten o'clock, I was preparing to turn in, when the master at arms called down to me, –

'Mr Cringle, you are wanted in the gunroom.'

I put on my jacket again and immediately proceeded thither, and on my way I noticed a group of seamen, standing on the starboard gangway, dressed in pea-jackets, under which, by the light of a lantern, carried by one of them, I could see they were all armed with pistol and cutlass. They appeared in great glee, and as they made way for me, I could hear one fellow whisper, 'There goes the little beagle.' When I entered the gunroom, the first lieutenant, master, and purser, were sitting smoking and enjoying themselves over a glass of cold grog – the gunner taking the watch on deck – the doctor was piping any thing but mellifluously on the double flageolet, while the Spanish priest, and aide-de-camp to the general, were playing at chess, and wrangling in bad French. I could hear Mr Treenail rumbling and stumbling in his stateroom, as he accoutred himself in a jacket similar to those of the armed boat's crew whom I had passed, and presently he stepped into the gunroom, armed also with cutlass and pistol.

'Mr Cringle, get ready to go in the boat with me, and bring your arms with you.'

I now knew whereabouts I was, and that my Cork friends were the quarry at which we aimed. I did as I was ordered, and we immediately pulled on shore, where, leaving two strong fellows in charge of the boat, with instructions to fire their pistols and shove off a couple of boat-lengths should any suspicious circumstance indicating an attack take place, we separated, like a pulk of Cossacks coming to the charge, but without the *hourah*, with orders to meet before Pat Doolan's door, as speedily as our legs could carry us. We had landed about a cable's length to the right of the high precipitous bank – up which we stole in straggling parties – on which that abominable congregation of the most filthy huts ever pig grunted in is situated, called the Holy Ground. Pat Doolan's domicile was in a little dirty lane, about the middle of the village. Presently ten strapping fellows, including the lieutenant, were before the door, each man with his stretcher in his hand. It was a very tempestuous, although moonlight night, occasionally clear, with the moonbeams at one moment sparkling brightly in the small ripples on the filthy puddles before the door, and on the gem-like water-drops that hung from the eaves of the thatched roof, and lighting up the dark statue-like figures of the men, and casting their long shadows strongly against the mud wall of the house; at another, a black cloud, as it flew across her disk, cast everything into shade while the only noise we heard was the hoarse dashing of the distant surf, rising and falling on the fitful gusts of the breeze. We tried the door. It was fast.

'Surround the house, men,' said the lieutenant in a whisper. He rapped loudly. 'Pat Doolan, my man, open the door, will ye?' No answer. 'If you don't, we shall make free to break it open, Patrick, dear.'

All this while the light of a fire, or of candles, streamed through the joins of the door. The threat at length appeared to have the desired effect. A poor decrepid old man undid the bolt and let us in. '*Ohon a ree! Ohon a ree!* What make you all this boder for – come you to help us to wake poor ould Kate there, and bring you the whisky wid you?'

'Old man, where is Pat Doolan?' said the lieutenant.

'Gone to borrow whisky, to wake ould Kate, there; – the howling will begin whenever Mother Doncannon and Misthress Conolly come over from Middleton, and I look for dem every minute.'

There was no vestige of any living thing in the miserable hovel, except the old fellow. On two low trestles, in the middle of the floor, lay a coffin with the lid on, on the top of which was stretched the dead body of an old emaciated woman in her grave-clothes, the quality of which was much finer than one could have expected to have seen in the midst of the surrounding squalidness. The face of the corpse was uncovered, the hands were crossed on the breast, and there was a plate of salt on the stomach.

An iron cresset, charged with coarse rancid oil, hung from the roof, the dull smoky red light flickering on the dead corpse, as the breeze streamed in through the door and numberless chinks in the walls, making the cold, rigid, sharp features appear to move, and glimmer, and gibber as it were, from the changing shades. Close to the head, there was a small door opening into an apartment of some kind, but the coffin was placed so near it, that one could not pass between the body and the door.

'My good man,' said Treenail, to the solitary mourner, 'I must beg leave to remove the body a bit, and have the goodness to open that door.'

'Door, yere honour! It's no door o' mine – and it's not opening that same, that old Phil Carrol shall busy himself wid.'

'Carline,' said Mr Treenail, quick and sharp, 'remove the body.' It was done.

'Cruel heavy the old dame is, sir, for all her wasted appearance,' said one of the men.

The lieutenant now ranged the press-gang against the wall fronting the door, and stepping into the middle of the room, drew his pistol and cocked it. 'Messmates,' he sung out, as if addressing the skulkers in the other room, 'I know you are here – the house is surrounded – and unless you open that door now, by the powers, but I'll fire slap into you.' There was a bustle, and a rumbling tumbling noise within. 'My lads, we are now sure of our game,' sung out Treenail, with great animation, 'Sling that clumsy bench there.' He pointed at an oaken form about eight feet long, and nearly three inches thick. To produce a two-inch rope, and junk it into three lengths, and rig the battering-ram, was the work of an instant. 'One, two, three,' – and bang the door flew open, and there were our men stowed away, each sitting on the top of his bag, as snug as could be, although looking very much like condemned thieves. We bound eight of them, thrusting a stretcher across their backs, under their arms, and, lashing the fins to the same by good stout lanyards, we were proceeding to stump our prisoners off to the boat, when, with the innate devilry that I have inherited, I know not how, but the original sin of which has more than once nearly cost me my life, I said, without addressing my superior officer, or any one else, directly, – 'I should like now to scale my pistol through that coffin. If I miss, I can't hurt the old woman; and an eyelet hole in the coffin itself, will only be an act of civility to the worms.'

I looked towards my superior officer, who answered me with a knowing shake of the head. I advanced, while all was silent as death – the sharp click of the pistol lock now struck acutely on my own ear. I presented, when – crash – the lid of the coffin, old woman and all, was dashed off in an instant, the corpse flying up in the air, and then falling heavily on the floor, rolling over and over, while a tall handsome fellow, in his striped flannel shirt and blue trowsers, with the sweat pouring down over his face in streams, sat up in the shell.

'All right,' said Mr Treenail, 'help him out of his berth.'

He was pinioned like the rest, and forthwith we walked them all off to the beach.

from *Tom Cringle's Log* by Michael Scott (1833)

A Pressing-boat on the Thames

Roderick Random is the hero of an autobiographical novel published in 1748 by Tobias George Smollett, whose full-blooded adventure stories have inspired many who have followed him. Like the author, Roderick Random was born on the banks of the Clyde, graduated from Glasgow University and then apprenticed to a partnership of local surgeons. As many such have done since, he makes his way to London. There he qualifies as a naval surgeon's mate, but not before having tasted a dissolute life with a whore who has already slid a long way down the ladder. They part: she to start afresh in a country village, he to go to sea.

As for my own part, I saw no resource but the army or navy, between which I hesitated so long, that I found myself reduced to a starving condition. – My spirit began to accommodate itself to my beggarly fate, and I became so mean, as to go down towards Wapping, with an intention to enquire for an old school-fellow of mine, who (I understood) had got the command of a small coasting vessel, then in the river, and implore his assistance. – But my destiny prevented this abject piece of behaviour; for as I crossed Tower-wharf, a squat tawny fellow, with a hanger by his side, and a cudgel in his hand, came up to me, calling, 'Yo, ho! brother, you must come along with me.' – As I did not like his appearance, instead of answering his salutation, I quickened my pace in hopes of ridding myself of his company; which he perceiving, whistled aloud, and immediately another sailor appeared before me, who laid hold of me by the collar and began to drag me along. – Not being of a humour to relish such treatment, I disengaged myself of the assailant, and with one blow of my cudgel, laid him motionless on the ground: and perceiving myself surrounded in a trice, by ten or a dozen more, exerted myself with such dexterity and success, that some of my opponents were fain to attack me with drawn cutlasses; and after an obstinate engagement, in which I received a large wound on the head, and another on my left cheek, I was disarmed, taken prisoner, and carried on board a pressing tender; where, after being pinioned like a malefactor, I was thrust down into the hold, among a parcel of miserable wretches, the sight of whom well nigh distracted me. – As the commanding officer had not humanity enough to order my wounds to be dressed, and I could not use my own hands, I desired one of my fellow-captives who was unfettered, to take a hankerchief out of my pocket and tie it round my head to stop the bleeding. He pulled out my handkerchief ('tis true) but instead of applying it to the use for which I designed it, went to the grating of the hatchway, and with astonishing composure, sold it before my face to a bum-boatwoman then on board, for a quart of gin, with which he treated his companions, regardless of my circumstance and intreaties.

I complained bitterly of this robbery, to the midshipman on deck, telling him at the same time, that unless my hurts were dressed, I should bleed to death. But compassion was a weakness of which no man could justly accuse this person, who squirting a mouthful of dissolved tobacco upon me, through the gratings, told me, 'I was a mutinous dog, and that I might die and be damned.' – Finding there was no other remedy, I appealed to patience, and laid up this usage in my memory, to be recalled at a fitter season. – In the mean time, loss of blood, vexation and want of food, contributed, with the noisome stench of the place, to throw me into a swoon; out of which I was recovered by a tweak of the nose, administered by the tar who stood centinel over us, who at the same time regaled me with a draught of flip, and comforted me with the hopes of being put on board of the Thunder next day, where I would be freed from handcuffs, and cured of my wounds by the doctor.

Help comes from unexpected quarters, besides the sentry who revives our hero with a measure of flip (mulled ale topped up with gin). Jack Rattlin frees him from his irons and fetches the other surgeon's mate, a Mr Thomson. He then shows our hero to his berth on board in the black depths of the hold.

However, making a virtue of necessity, I put a good face on the matter, and next day was with the other pressed men put on board of the Thunder lying at the Nore. – When we came along-side, the mate who had guarded us thither, ordered my hand-cuffs to be taken off, so that I might get on board the easier; which being perceived by some of the company who stood upon the gangboards to see us enter, one of them called to Jack Rattlin, who was busied in doing this friendly office for me; 'Hey, Jack, what Newgate galley have you boarded in the river as you came along? Have we not thieves enow among us already?' Another observing my wounds, which still remained exposed to the air, told me, my seams were uncaulked, and that I must be new payed. – A third, seeing my hair clotted together with blood, as it were, into distinct cords, took notice, that my bows were manned with red ropes, instead of my side. – A fourth asked me, if I could not keep my yards square without iron braces? and in short, a thousand witticisms of the same nature, were passed upon me, before I could get up the ship's side. – After we had been all entered upon the books, I enquired at one of my ship-mates where the surgeon was, that I might have my wounds dressed, and had actually got as far as the middle deck (for our ship carried eighty guns) in my way to the cock-pit, when I was met by the same midshipman who had used me so barbarously in the tender: He seeing me free from my chains, asked, with an insolent air, who had released me? To this I foolishly answered, with a countenance that too plainly declared the state of my thoughts; 'Whoever did it, I am persuaded did not consult you in the affair.' – I had no sooner uttered these words, than he cried, 'D--n you, you saucy son of a b--ch, I'll teach you to talk so to your officer.' – So saying, he bestowed on me several severe stripes, with a supple Jack he had in his hand; and going to the commanding officer, made such a report of me, that I was immediately put in irons by the master at arms, and a centinel placed over me. – Honest Rattlin, as soon as he heard of my condition, came to me, and administered all the consolation he could, and then went to the surgeon in my behalf, who sent one of his mates to dress my wounds. This mate was no other than my old friend Thomson, with whom I had become acquainted at the Navy-Office.

*

... my friend Thomson carried me down to the cock-pit, which is the place allotted for the habitation of the surgeon's mates: And when he had shewn me their birth (as he called it) I was filled with astonishment and horror. – We descended by divers ladders to a space as dark as a dungeon, which I understood was immersed several feet under water, being immediately above the hold: I had no sooner approached this dismal gulph, than my nose was saluted with an intolerable stench of putrified cheese, and rancid butter, that issued from an apartment at the foot of the ladder, resembling a chandler's shop, where, by the faint glimmering of a candle, I could perceive a man with a pale meagre countenance, sitting behind a kind of desk, having spectacles on his nose, and a pen in his hand. – This (I learned of Mr Thomson) was the ship's steward, who sat there to distribute provision to the several messes, and to mark what each received. – He therefore presented my name to him, and desired I might be entered in his mess; then taking a light in his hand, conducted me to the place of his residence, which was a square of about six feet, surrounded with the medicine chest, that of the first mate, his own, and a board by way of table fastened to the mizen-mast; it was also enclosed with canvas nailed round to the beams of the ship, to screen us from the cold, as well as the view of the midshipmen and quarter-masters, who lodged within the cable tiers on each side of us: In this gloomy mansion, he entertained me with some cold salt pork, which he brought from a sort of locker, fixed above the table; and calling for the boy of the mess, sent him for a can of beer, of which he made excellent flip to crown the banquet. – By this time I began to recover my spirits . . .

from *The Adventures of Roderick Random* by Tobias Smollett (1748)

Abducted for an Inheritance

In spite of the fame which *Treasure Island* brought to Robert Louis Stevenson, he was not particularly proud of being a storyteller. 'Fiction,' he said, 'is to grown men what play is to a child,' and he wrote relatively little about the sea. His knowledge of it must have stemmed in part from what he learned as a boy about the stormy waters around Scotland and the Western Isles from his father, who was a distinguished builder and civil engineer responsible for lighthouses in that area. During the last two decades of his brief life, when Stevenson wrote about eighteenth-century sailors and their way of life, it was as though he had sailed with them a century before he was born.

David Balfour, the hero of *Kidnapped*, is abruptly introduced to life afloat when his evil uncle seeks to cheat him of his family inheritance by having him shipped to the Carolinas in the brig *Covenant*. The first crew member we meet is the cabin-boy Ransome, who delivers a letter from Captain Hoseason to Uncle Ebenezer which lights the fuse of treachery by inviting them to meet on board off Queensferry in the Firth of Forth.

Uncle Ebenezer trudged in the ditch, jogging from side to side like an old ploughman coming home from work. He never said a word the whole way; and I was thrown for talk on the cabin-boy. He told me his name was Ransome, and that he had followed the sea since he was nine, but could not say how old he was, as he had lost his reckoning. He showed me tattoo marks, baring his breast in the teeth of the wind and in spite of my remonstrances, for I thought it was enough to kill him; he swore horribly whenever he remembered, but more like a silly schoolboy than a man; and boasted of many wild and bad things that he had done: stealthy thefts, false accusations, ay, and even murder; but all with such a dearth of likelihood in the details, and such a weak and crazy swagger in the delivery, as disposed me rather to pity than to believe him.

I asked him of the brig (which he declared was the finest ship that sailed) and of Captain Hoseason, in whose praises he was equally loud. Heasy-oasy (for so he still named the skipper) was a man, by his account, that minded for nothing either in heaven or earth; one that, as people said, would 'crack on all sail into the day of judgment'; rough, fierce, unscrupulous, and brutal; and all this my poor cabin-boy had taught himself to admire as something seamanlike and manly. He would only admit one flaw in his idol. 'He ain't no seaman,' he admitted. 'That's Mr Shuan that navigates the brig; he's the finest seaman in the trade, only for drink; and I tell you I believe it! Why, look 'ere'; and turning down his stocking he showed me a great, raw, red wound that made my blood run cold. 'He done that – Mr Shuan done it,' he said, with an air of pride.

'What!' I cried, 'do you take such savage usage at his hands? Why, you are no slave, to be so handled!'

'No,' said the poor moon-calf, changing his tune at once, 'and so he'll find. See 'ere'; and he showed me a great case-knife, which he told me was stolen. 'O,' says he, 'let me see him try; I dare him to; I'll do for him! O, he ain't the first!' And he confirmed it with a poor silly, ugly oath.

I have never felt such pity for anyone in this wide world as I felt for that half-witted creature; and it began to come over me that the brig *Covenant* (for all her pious name) was little better than a hell upon the seas.

'Have you no friends?' said I.

He said he had a father in some English seaport, I forget which. 'He was a fine man, too,' he said; 'but he's dead.'

'In Heaven's name,' cried I, 'can you find no reputable life on shore?'

'O, no,' says he, winking and looking very sly; 'they would put me to a trade. I know a trick worth two of that, I do!'

I asked him what trade could be so dreadful as the one he followed, where he ran the continual peril of his life, not alone from the wind and sea, but by the horrid cruelty of those who were his masters. He said it was very true; and then began to praise the life, and tell what a pleasure it was to get on shore with money in his pocket, and spend it like a man, and buy apples, and swagger, and surprise what he called stick-in-the-mud-boys.

Captain Hoseason awaits them at the inn, where he closets himself with Uncle Ebenezer. David meanwhile makes his way down to the slipway and meets other members of the *Covenant's* crew.

Away I went, therefore, leaving the two men sitting down to a bottle and a great mass of papers; and crossing the road in front of the inn, walked down upon the beach. With the wind in that quarter, only little wavelets, not much bigger than I had seen upon a lake, beat upon the shore. But the weeds were new to me – some green, some brown and long, and some with little bladders that crackled between my fingers. Even so far up the firth, the smell of the sea water was exceedingly salt and stirring; the *Covenant,* besides, was beginning to shake out her sails which hung upon the yards in clusters; and the spirit of all that I beheld put me in thoughts of far voyages and foreign places.

I looked, too, at the seamen with the skiff – big brown fellows, some in shirts, some with jackets, some with coloured handkerchiefs about their throats, one with a brace of pistols stuck into his pockets, two or three with knotty bludgeons, and all with their case-knives. I passed the time of day with one that looked less desperate than his fellows, and asked him of the sailing of the brig. He said they would get under way as soon as the ebb set, and expressed his gladness to be out of a port where there were no taverns and fiddlers; but all with such horrifying oaths, that I made haste to get away from him.

Captain Hoseason finally lures David on board for half an hour before the tide turns so that he can look round the brig and share a bowl before being put ashore.

By this time we were at the boat-side, and he was handing me in. I did not dream of hanging back; I thought (the poor fool) that I had found a good friend and helper, and I was rejoiced to see the ship. As soon as we were all set in our places, the boat was thrust off from the pier and began to move over the waters; and what with my pleasure in this new movement and my surprise at our low position, and the appearance of the shores, and the growing bigness of the brig as we drew near to it, I could hardly understand what the captain said, and must have answered him at random.

As soon as we were alongside (where I sat fairly gaping at the ship's height, the strong humming of the tide against its sides, and the pleasant cries of the seamen at their work) Hoseason, declaring that he and I must be the first aboard, ordered a tackle to be sent down from the main-yard. In this I was whipped into the air and set down again on the deck, where the captain stood ready waiting for me, and instantly slipped back his arm under mine. There I stood some while, a little dizzy with the unsteadiness of all around me, perhaps a little afraid, and yet vastly pleased with these strange sights; the captain meanwhile pointing out the strangest, and telling me their names and uses.

'But where is my uncle?' said I, suddenly.

'Ay,' said Hoseason, with a sudden grimness, 'that's the point.'

I felt I was lost. With all my strength I plucked myself clear of him, and ran to the bulwarks. Sure enough, there was the boat pulling for the town, with my uncle sitting in the stern. I gave a piercing cry – 'Help, help! Murder!' – so that both sides of the anchorage rang with it, and my uncle turned round where he was sitting, and showed me a face full of cruelty and terror.

It was the last I saw. Already strong hands had been plucking me back from the ship's side; and now a thunderbolt seemed to strike me; I saw a great flash of fire, and fell senseless.

*

I came to myself in darkness, in great pain, bound hand and foot, and deafened by many unfamiliar noises. There sounded in my ears a roaring of water as of a huge milldam, the thrashing of heavy sprays, the thundering of the sails, and the shrill cries of seamen. The whole world now heaved giddily up, and now rushed giddily downward; and so sick and hurt was I in body, and my mind so much confounded, that it took me a long while, chasing my thoughts up and down, and ever stunned again by a fresh stab of pain, to realize that I must be lying somewhere bound in the belly of that unlucky ship, and that the wind must have strengthened to a gale. With the clear perception of my plight, there fell upon me a blackness of despair, a horror of remorse at my own folly, and a passion of anger at my uncle, that once more bereft me of my senses.

When I returned again to life, the same uproar, the same confused and violent movements, shook and deafened me; and presently, to my other pains and distresses, there was added the sickness of an unused landsman on the sea. In that time of my adventurous youth, I suffered many hardships; but none that was so crushing to my mind and body, or lit by so few hopes, as these first hours aboard the brig.

*

The glimmer of the lantern, as a trap opened, shone in like the heaven's sunlight; and though it only showed me the strong, dark beams of the ship that was my prison, I could have cried aloud for gladness. The man with the green eyes was the first to descend the ladder, and I noticed that he came somewhat unsteadily. He was followed by the captain. Neither said a word; but the first set to and examined me, and dressed my wound as before, while Hoseason looked me in my face with an odd, black look.

'Now, sir, you see for yourself,' said the first; 'a high fever, no appetite, no light, no meat; you see for yourself what that means.'

'I am no conjurer, Mr Riach,' said the captain.

'Give me leave, sir,' said Riach; 'you've a good head upon your shoulders, and a good Scotch tongue to ask with; but I will leave you no manner of excuse; I want that boy taken out of this hole and put in the forecastle.'

*

Thereupon the captain ascended the ladder; and I, who had lain silent throughout this strange conversation, beheld Mr Riach turn after him and bow as low as to his knees in what was plainly a spirit of derision. Even in my then state of sickness, I perceived two things: that the mate was touched with liquor, as the captain hinted, and that (drunk or sober) he was like to prove a valuable friend.

Five minutes afterwards my bonds were cut, I was hoisted on a man's back, carried up to the forecastle, and laid in a bunk on some sea-blankets; where the first thing that I did was to lose my senses.

It was a blessed thing indeed to open my eyes again upon the daylight, and to find myself in the society of men. The forecastle was a roomy place enough, set all about with berths, in which the men of the watch below were seated smoking, or lying down asleep. The day being calm and the wind fair, the scuttle was open, and not only the good daylight, but from time to time (as the ship rolled) a dusty beam of sunlight shone in, and dazzled and delighted me. I had no sooner moved, moreover, than one of the men brought me a drink of something healing which Mr Riach had prepared, and bade me lie still and I should soon be well again. There were no bones broken, he explained: 'A clout on the head was naething. Man,' said he, 'it was me that gave it ye!'

Here I lay for the space of many days a close prisoner, and not only got my health again, but came to know my companions. They were a rough lot indeed, as sailors mostly are; being men rooted out of all the kindly parts of life, and condemned to toss together on the rough seas, with masters no less cruel. There were some among them who had sailed with the pirates and seen things it would be a shame even to speak of; some were men that had run from the king's ships, and went with a halter round their necks, of which they made no secret; and all, as the saying goes, were 'at a word and a blow' with their best friends. Yet I had not been many days shut up with them before I began to be ashamed of my first judgment, when I had drawn away from them at the Ferry pier, as though they had been unclean beasts. No class of man is altogether bad; but each has its own faults and virtues; and these shipmates of mine were no exception to the rule. Rough they were, sure enough; and bad, I suppose; but they had many virtues. They were kind when it occurred to them, simple even beyond the simplicity of a country lad like me, and had some glimmerings of honesty.

There was one man, of maybe forty, that would sit on my berth-side for hours and tell me of his wife and child. He was a fisher that had lost his boat, and thus been driven to the deep-sea voyaging. Well, it is years ago now: but I have never forgotten him. His wife (who was 'young by him,' as he often told me) waited in vain to see her man return; he would never again make the fire for her in the morning, nor yet keep the bairn when she was sick. Indeed, many of these poor fellows (as the event proved) were upon their last cruise; the deep seas and cannibal fish received them; and it is a thankless business to speak ill of the dead.

Among other good deeds that they did, they returned my money, which had been shared among them; and though it was about a third short, I was very glad to get it, and hoped great good from it in the land I was going to. The ship was bound for the Carolinas; and you must not suppose that I was going to that place merely as an exile. The trade was even then much depressed; since that, and with the rebellion of the colonies and the formation of the United States, it has, of course, come to an end; but in those days of my youth, white men were still sold into slavery on the plantations, and that was the destiny to which my wicked uncle had condemned me.

The cabin-boy Ransome (from whom I had first heard of these atrocities) came in at times from the round-house, where he berthed and served, now nursing a bruised limb in silent agony, now raving against the cruelty of Mr Shuan. It made my heart bleed; but the men had a great respect for the chief mate, who was, as they said, 'the only seaman of the whole jing-bang, and none such a bad man when he was sober.' Indeed, I found there was a strange peculiarity about our two mates: that Mr Riach was sullen, unkind, and harsh when he was sober, and Mr Shuan would not hurt a fly except when he was drinking. I asked about the captain; but I was told drink made no difference upon that man of iron.

I did my best in the small time allowed me to make something like a man, or rather I should say something like a boy, of the poor creature, Ransome. But his mind was scarce truly human. He could remember nothing of the time before he came to sea; only that his father had made clocks, and had a starling in the parlour, which could whistle 'The North Countrie'; all else had been blotted out in these years of hardship and cruelties. He had a strange notion of the dry land, picked up from sailors; stories that it was a place where lads were put to some kind of slavery called a trade, and where apprentices were continually lashed and clapped into foul prisons. In a town, he thought every second person a decoy, and every third house a place in which seamen would be drugged and murdered. To be sure, I would tell him how kindly I had myself been used upon that dry land he was so much afraid of, and how well fed and carefully taught both by my friends and my parents: and if he had been recently hurt, he would weep bitterly and swear to run away; but if he was in his usual cockbrain humour, or (still more) if he had had a glass of spirits in the roundhouse, he would deride the notion.

from *Kidnapped* by Robert Louis Stevenson (1886)

Soon afterwards David is moved aft to wait upon the officers in their own mess; the vacancy arising after Mr Shuan has killed the boy Ransome in a drunken rage for serving him brandy in a dirty pannikin.

Covenant is battling to round Cape Wrath in thick fog and high seas when she runs down an open boat, out of which one survivor manages to catch hold of the brig's bowsprit and leap aboard. He introduces himself as Alan Breck Stewart, who had hoped to rendezvous with a French ship which was to have carried him and his belt of gold to join other Jacobite supporters in France. He bribes Hoseason to put him ashore in a friendly part of the Western Isles, anywhere out of reach of the Redcoats or the bloodthirsty clan Campbell. This involves navigating without charts around the south-west coast of Mull, with the inevitable consequence that the brig is wrecked and lost on the rocks. All ends well for Alan and David, but their subsequent adventures set in the wild Highlands as they make their way to Edinburgh, do not concern us here.

Robert Louis Stevenson wrote most of his books in Bournemouth, before going to Samoa in 1888, where he died six years later aged 44. The house in Bournemouth was named *Skerryvore* after one of his father's light-houses situated so as to warn mariners of the very dangers upon which the brig *Covenant* foundered.

The Medical Care of Jack

Eighteenth-century Surgery and Yellow Fever

Having been pressed on board HMS *Thunder*, as we saw in the previous
extract (pp. 68–70), Roderick Random, the hero of Smollett's novel, is
finally able to assert his rightful position as one of the two surgeon's mates,
responsible to Mr Mackshane, a medical officer of uncertain qualifications
and little experience afloat.

We staid not long at the Downs, but took the benefit of the first easterly wind
to go round to Spithead; where having received on board provisons for six
months, we sailed from St Helens, in the grand fleet bound for the West-Indies
on the ever memorable expedition of Carthagena.

It was not without great mortification, I saw myself on the point of being
transported to such a distant and unhealthy climate, destitute of every con-
venience that could render such a voyage supportable; and under the dominion
of an arbitrary tyrant, whose command was almost intolerable: However, as
these complaints were common to a great many on board, I resolved to submit
patiently to my fate, and contrive to make myself as easy as the nature of the
case would allow. – We got out of the channel with a prosperous breeze, which
died away, leaving us becalmed about fifty leagues to the westward of the
Lizard: But this state of inaction did not last long; for next night our main-topsail was split by the wind, which in the morning encreased to a hurricane. – I
was wakened by a most horrible din, occasioned by the play of the gun carriages
upon the decks above, the creaking of cabins, the howling of the wind through
the shrouds, the confused noise of the ship's crew, the pipes of the boatswain
and his mates, the trumpets of the lieutenants, and the clanking of the chain-
pumps. – Morgan, who had never been at sea before, turned out in a great
hurry, crying, 'Got have mercy and compassion upon us! I believe we have got
upon the confines of Lucifer and the d--ned!' – while poor Thomson lay quaking
in his hammock, putting up petitions to heaven for our safety. – I got out of
bed and joined the Welchman, with whom (after having fortified ourselves with
brandy) I went above; but if my sense of hearing was startled before, how must
my sight be appalled in beholding the effects of the storm? The sea was swelled
into billows mountain-high, on the top of which our ship sometimes hung, as
if it was about to be precipitated to the abyss below! Sometimes we sunk
between two waves that rose on each side higher than our topmast head, and
threatened by dashing together, to overwhelm us in a moment! Of all our fleet,
consisting of a hundred and fifty sail, scarce twelve appeared, and these driving
under their bare poles, at the mercy of the tempest. At length the masts of one
of them gave way, and tumbled over-board with a hideous crash! Nor was the
prospect in our own ship much more agreeable; – a number of officers and

sailors run backward and forward with distraction in their looks, hollowing to one another, and unknowing what they should attend to first. Some clung to the yards, endeavouring to unbend the sails that were split into a thousand pieces flapping in the wind; others tried to furl those which were yet whole, while the masts, at every pitch, bent and quivered like twigs, as if they would have shivered into innumerable splinters! – While I considered this scene with equal terror and astonishment, one of the main-braces broke, by the shock whereof two sailors were flung from the yard's arm into the sea, where they perished, and poor Jack Rattlin thrown down upon the deck, at the expence of a broken leg. Morgan and I ran immediately to his assistance, and found a splinter of the shin-bone thrust by the violence of the fall through the skin: As this was a case of too great consequence to be treated without the authority of the doctor, I went down to his cabin, to inform him of the accident, as well as to bring up dressings, which we always kept ready prepared. – I entered his apartment without any ceremony, and by the glimmering of a lamp, perceived him on his knees, before something that very much resembled a crucifix; but this I will not insist upon, that I may not seem too much a slave to common report, which indeed assisted my conjecture on this occasion, by representing doctor Mackshane as a member of the church of Rome. – Be this as it will, he got up in a sort of confusion, occasioned (I suppose) by his being disturbed in his devotion, and in a trice, snatched the object of my suspicion from my sight. – After making an apology for my intrusion, I acquainted him with the situation of Rattlin, but could by no means prevail upon him to visit him on deck where he lay; he bid me desire the boatswain to order some of the men to carry him down to the cockpit, and in the mean time he would direct Thomson in getting ready the dressings. – When I signified to the boatswain the doctor's desire, he swore a terrible oath, that he could not spare one man from the deck, because he expected the masts would go by the board every minute. – This piece of information did not at all contribute to my peace of mind; however, as my friend Rattlin complained very much, with the assistance of Morgan, I supported him to the lower deck, whither Mr Mackshane, after much intreaty, ventured to come, attended by Thomson with a boxful of dressings, and his own servant, who carried a whole set of capital instruments. – He examined the fracture and the wound, and concluding from a livid colour extending itself upon the limb, that a mortification would ensue, resolved to amputate the leg immediately. – This was a dreadful sentence to the patient, who recruiting himself with a quid of tobacco, pronounced with a woful countenance, 'What! is there no remedy, doctor? must I be dock'd? can't you splice it?' – 'Assuredly, doctor Mackshane (said the first mate) with submission, and deference, and veneration to your superior abilities, and opportunities, and stations (look you) I do apprehend, and conjecture, and aver, that there is no occasion nor necessity to smite off this poor man's leg.' – 'God almighty bless you, dear Welchman! (cried Rattlin) may you have fair wind and weather wheresoever you're bound, and come to an anchor in the road of heaven at last.' – Mackshane, very much incensed at his mate's differing in opinion from him so openly, answered, that he was not bound to give an account of his practice to him; and in a peremptory tone, ordered him to apply the tourniquet. – At the sight of which, Jack starting up, cried, 'Avast, avast! d--n my heart, if you clap your nippers on me, till I know wherefore! – Mr Random, won't you lend a hand towards saving of my precious limb? Odd's heart, if lieutenant Bowling was here, he would not suffer Jack Rattlin's leg to be chopped off like a piece of old junk.' – This pathetic address to me, joined to my inclination to serve my honest friend, and the reasons I had to believe there was no danger in delaying the amputation, induced me to declare myself of the first mate's opinion, and affirm that the preternatural colour of the skin, was owing to an inflammation occasioned by a contusion, and common in all such cases, without any indication of an approaching gangrene. Morgan, who had a great opinion of my skill, manifestly exulted in my fellowship, and asked Thomson's sentiments of the matter, in hopes of strengthening our association with him too; but he being of a meek disposition, and either dreading the enmity of the surgeon, or speaking the dictates of his own judgment, in a modest manner, espoused the opinion of Mackshane, who by this time, having consulted with himself, determined to act in such a manner, as to screen himself from censure; and at the same time revenge himself on us, for our arrogance in contradicting him. – With this view, he demanded to know if we would undertake to cure the leg at our peril; that is, be answerable for the consequence. – To this Morgan replied, that the lives of his creatures are in the hands of Got alone; and it would be great presumption in him to undertake for an event that was in the power of his maker, no more than the doctor could promise to cure all the sick to whom he administered his assistance; but if the patient would put himself under our direction, we would do our endeavour to bring his distemper to a favourable issue, to which, at present, we saw no obstruction. – I signified my concurrence; and Rattlin was so over-joyed, that shaking us both by the hands, he swore no body else should touch him, and if he died, his blood should be upon his own head. – Mr Mackshane, flattering himself with the prospect of our miscarriage, went away, and left us to manage it as we should think proper; accordingly, having sawed off part of the splinter that stuck through the skin, we reduced the fracture, dressed the wound, applied the eighteen-tailed bandage, and put the leg in a box, *secundum artem*. – Every thing succeeded according to our wish, and we had the satisfaction, of not only preserving the poor fellow's leg, but likewise of rendering the doctor contemptible among the ship's company, who had all their eyes on us during the course of this cure, which was compleated in six weeks.

Life does not become any easier for Roderick during the long voyage to the West Indies under the tyrannical Captain Oakhum, the sadistic Midshipman Crampley (formerly in charge of the press-gang at the Tower) and the malicious surgeon Mackshane, whose hatred knows no bounds after Jack Rattlin survives without the amputation he had prescribed for him. On a trumped-up charge, he has Roderick put in irons on the poop and left there during a close-range engagement with a French man-o'-war. Roderick is made sharply aware of the danger to which this exposes him when a nearby Royal Marine officer is decapitated, his blood and brains splattering all over Roderick, followed by the entrails of a drummer boy. So unnerved by the whole affair is Roderick's friend Thomson that he throws himself over the side rather than spend another day in that unhappy ship.

After the siege of Bocca Chica in Carthagena, the squadron withdraws to face a much deadlier foe – yellow fever.

Just as we sailed from Bocca Chica on our return to Jamaica, I found myself threatened with the symptoms of this terrible distemper; and knowing very well that I stood no chance for my life, if I should be obliged to lie in the cockpit, which by this time, was grown intolerable even to people in health, by reason of the heat and unwholsome smell of decayed provision; I wrote a petition to the captain representing my case, and humbly imploring his permission to lie among the soldiers in the middle-deck, for the benefit of the air: But I might have spared myself the trouble; for this humane commander refused my request, and ordered me to continue in the place allotted for the surgeon's mates, or else be contented to lie in the hospital, which, by the bye, was three degrees more offensive and more suffocating than our own birth below. – Another in my condition, perhaps, would have submitted to his fate, and died in a pet; but I could not brook the thought of perishing so pitifully, after I had weathered so many gales of hard fortune: I therefore, without minding Oakhum's injunction, prevailed upon the soldiers (whose good-will I had acquired) to admit my hammock among them; and actually congratulated myself upon my comfortable situation, which Crampley no sooner understood, than he signified to the captain my contempt of his orders; and was invested with power to turn me down again into my proper habitation. – This barbarous piece of revenge, incensed me so much against the author, that I vowed, with bitter imprecations, to call him to a severe account, if ever it should be in my power; and the agitation of my spirits increased my fever to a violent degree. – While I lay gasping for breath in this infernal abode, I was visited by a serjeant, the bones of whose nose I had reduced and set to rights, after they had been demolished by a splinter during our last engagement: He being informed of my condition, offered me the use of his birth in the middle-deck, which was inclosed with canvas and well-aired by a port-hole that remained open within it. – I embraced this proposal with joy, and was immediately conducted to the place, where I was treated, while my illness lasted, with the utmost tenderness and care by his grateful halberdier, who had no other bed for himself than a hen-coop, during the whole passage. – Here I lay and enjoyed the breeze, notwithstanding of which, my malady gained ground, and at length my life was despaired of, though I never lost hopes of recovery, even when I had the mortification to see from my cabbin window, six or seven thrown overboard every day, who died of the same distemper.

*

The parson having felt my pulse, enquired into the nature of my complaints, hemmed a little, and began thus: 'Mr Random, God out of his infinite mercy hath been pleased to visit you with a dreadful distemper, the issue of which no man knows. – You may be permitted to recover, and live many days on the face of the earth: and, which is more probable, you may be taken away and cut off in the flower of your youth: It is incumbent on you, therefore, to prepare for the great change, by repenting sincerely of your sins; of this there cannot be a greater sign, than an ingen'ous confession, which I conjure you to make without hesitation or mental reservation; and when I am convinced of your sincerity, I will then give you such comfort as the situation of your soul will admit of. Without doubt, you have been guilty of numberless transgressions, to which youth is subject, as swearing, drunkenness, whoredom, and adultery; tell me therefore, without reserve, the particulars of each, especially of the last, that I may be acquainted with the true state of your conscience: For no physician will prescribe for his patient until he knows the circumstances of his disease.' As I was not under any apprehensions of death, I could not help smiling at the doctor's inquisitive remonstrance, which I told him savoured more of the Roman than of the Protestant church, in recommending auricular confession, a thing, in my opinion, not at all necessary to salvation, and which, for that reason, I declined.

*

I started up in a kind of frantic fit, with an intention to plunge myself into the sea, and as my friend the serjeant was not present, would certainly have cooled myself to some purpose, had I not perceived a moisture upon my thigh, as I endeavoured to get out of my hammock: The appearance of this revived my hopes, and I had reflection and resolution enough to take the advantage of this favourable symptom, by tearing the shirt from my body and the sheets from my bed, and wrapping myself in a thick blanket, in which inclosure, for about a quarter of an hour, I felt the pains of hell; but it was not long before I was recompensed for my suffering by a profuse sweat, that bursting from the whole surface of my skin, in less than two hours, relieved me from all my complaints, except that of weakness; and left me as hungry as a kite. – I enjoyed a very comfortable nap, after which I was regaling myself with the agreeable reverie of my future happiness . . .

*

. . . we were now safely arrived at Jamaica, where I had the benefit of fresh provision, and other refreshments, I recovered strength every day, and in a short time, my health and vigour were perfectly re-established. – When I got up at first, and was just able to crawl about the deck, with a staff in my hand, I met doctor Mackshane, who passed by me with a disdainful look, and did not vouchsafe to honour me with one word: After him came Crampley, who strutting up to me, with a fierce countenance, pronounced, 'Here's fine discipline on board, when such lazy sculking sons of b--ches as you, are allowed, on pretence of sickness, to lollop at your ease, while your betters are kept to hard duty!' – The sight and behaviour of this malicious scoundrel, enraged me so much, that I could scarce refrain from laying my cudgel across his pate; but when I considered my present feebleness, and the enemies I had in the ship, who wanted only a pretence to ruin me, I restrained my passion, and contented myself with telling him, I had not forgot his insolence and malice, and that I hoped we should meet one day on shore. – At this he grinned, shook his fist at me, and swore he longed for nothing more than such an opportunity.

from *The Adventures of Roderick Random* by Tobias Smollett (1748)

Burial at Sea

William Golding's classic sea trilogy started with *Rites of Passage* in 1980. This covers the first part of an outward voyage to Australia by an obsolescent and, curiously enough, unnamed ship-of-the-line carrying emigrants of different classes and reliefs for the military garrison in New South Wales. The trilogy concluded in *Fire Down Below* (1989) with a bang, the unseaworthy ship having been reduced to an unrigged hulk as the guardship in Sydney Harbour. She is secured alongside a powder-barge when she catches fire from the residual glow of extempore repairs to her foremast step, involving the contraction of red-hot iron bands and bolts.

On the long, dreary voyage Edmund Talbot keeps a detailed account for his nobleman godfather, under whose patronage he is travelling to take up an appointment as an assistant to the Colonial Governor. This chronicle covers some unusual happenings. Becalmed in the Doldrums six weeks outward bound, the ship falls in company with a frigate which is at first taken to be an enemy Frenchman, but turns out to be the frigate *Alcyone*, twenty-seven days out from Plymouth with the news that the war with France is over. The ships secure alongside one another for a programme of festivities which includes a ceremonial full-dress ball danced to the music of a mixed bunch of unrehearsed musicians drawn from each ship. Our hero promptly falls in love with the orphaned teenage ward of the wife of *Alcyone*'s patrician Captain Anderson, all three of whom were bound for Madras. Much of the remaining two volumes is taken up with Edmund's love-sick fantasies about the delectable Miss Chumley. Don't worry – all ends happily.

Another ceremony, that of Crossing the Line, leads to a sad end for the solitary parson on board, one of the few passengers whose social status earns him accommodation in the officers' quarters under the poop. His presence had taken Captain Anderson by surprise. In those days there were never enough surgeons or chaplains to go round the ships of the fleet. The former gap might be filled by an unqualified surgeon's mate capable of tying a tourniquet and dishing out laudanum in safe doses, but the equivalent of lay preachers were never accepted, partly because all sailors held to the unworthy belief that men of the cloth brought bad luck on board – a belief held by submariners to this day. (A tale is told of a padre who went out for a day's deep-diving exercise in a Malta-based submarine in high summer. The poor man suffered from an explosive attack of local dysentery. After he had cleaned up under a shower he was provided with a suit of overalls to replace the steaming fetid heap of what had recently been an immaculately starched white uniform – and the Captain ordered the whole lot to be shot out of a torpedo tube with the day's gash.) Captain Anderson's aversion to Parson Colley's presence on the passenger list drives him to paroxysms of rage every time their paths cross. His paranoia runs deeper than mere superstition, for the bluff sea-captain, who is painfully making his way up the Post List thanks to the distant interest of a titled kinsman, is himself the bastard son of a clergyman.

The Rev. Robert Colley has taken to, or rather been put into, his bunk after Father Neptune and Bacchus had got matters out of hand. The amateur diagnosis of a high-octane hangover is displaced in the log by 'low fever', a term encompassing almost any inexplicable physical deterioration. When Colley dies, Captain Anderson proves well rehearsed in the drill.

> At three o'clock we were all assembled in the waist. There was a guard, composed of Oldmeadow's soldiers, with flintlocks, or whatever their ungainly weapons are called. Oldmeadow himself was in full dress and unblooded sword, as were the ship's officers. Even our young gentlemen wore their dirks and expressions of piety. We passengers were dressed as sombrely as possible. The seamen were drawn up by watches, and were as presentable as their varied garments permit.
>
> *
>
> The ship's bell was struck, muffled. A party of sailors appeared, bearing the body on a plank and under the union flag. It was placed with its feet towards the starboard, or honourable side, by which admirals and bodies and suchlike rarities make their exits. It was a longer body then I had expected but have since been told that two of our few remaining cannon balls were attached to the feet. Captain Anderson, glittering with bullion, stood by it. I have also been told since, that he and all the other officers were much exercised as to the precise nature of the ceremonies to be observed when, as young Mr Taylor expressed it, 'piping a sky pilot over the side'.
>
> Almost all our sails were *clewed up* and we were what the *Marine Dictionary* calls, technically speaking – and when does it not? – *hove to*, which ought to mean we were stationary in the water. Yet the spirit of farce (speaking perfectly exquisite Tarpaulin) attended Colley to his end. No sooner was the plank laid on the deck than I heard Mr Summers mutter to Mr Deverel:
>
> 'Depend upon it, Deverel, without you aft the driver a handspan she will make a sternboard.'
>
> Hardly had he said this when there came a heavy and rhythmical thudding from the ship's hull under water as if *Davey Jones* were serving notice or perhaps getting hungry. Deverel shouted orders of the *warrarroohoowassst!* variety, the seamen leapt, while Captain Anderson, a prayerbook clutched like a grenade, turned on Lieutenant Summers.
>
> 'Mr *Summers!* Will you have the sternpost out of her?'

Summers said nothing but the thudding ceased. Captain Anderson's tone sank to a grumble.

'The pintles are loose as a pensioner's teeth.'

Summers nodded in reply.

'I know it, sir. But until she's rehung—'

'The sooner we're off the wind the better. God curse that drunken superintendant!'

He stared moodily down at the union flag, then up at the sails which, as if willing to debate with him, boomed back. They could have done no better than the preceding dialogue. Was it not superb?

At last the captain glanced round him and positively started, as if seeing us for the first time. I wish I could say that he *started like a guilty thing upon a fearful summons* but he did not. He started like a man in the smallest degree remiss who has absentmindedly forgotten that he has a body to get rid of. He opened the book and grunted a sour invitation to us to pray – and so on. Certainly he was anxious enough to get the thing over, for I have never heard a service read so fast. The ladies scarce had time to get out their handkerchiefs (tribute of a tear) and we gentlemen stared for a moment as usual into our beavers, but then, reminded that this unusual ceremony was too good to miss, all looked up again. I hoped that Oldmeadow's men would fire a volley but he has since told me that owing to some difference of opinion between the Admiralty and the War Office, they have neither flints nor powder. However, they presented arms in approximate unison and the officers flourished their swords. I wonder – was all this proper for a parson? I do not know, neither do they. A fife shrilled out and someone rattled on a muffled drum, a kind of overture, or postlude should I call it, or would *envoi* be a better word?

You will observe, my lord, that *Richard is himself again* – or shall we say that I have recovered from a period of fruitless and *perhaps* unwarranted regret?

And yet – at the last (when Captain Anderson's grumbling voice invited us to contemplate that time when there shall be no more sea) six men shrilled out a call on the bosun's pipe. Now, your lordship may never have heard these pipes so I must inform you that they have just as much music in them as the yowling of cats on heat! And yet and yet and *yet!* Their very harsh and shrill unmusicality, their burst of high sound leading to a long descent that died away through an uneasy and prolonged fluttering into silence, seemed to voice something beyond words, religion, philosophy. It was the simple voice of Life mourning Death.

I had scarcely time to feel a touch of complacency at the directness of my own emotions when the plank was lifted and tilted. The mortal remains of the Reverend Robert James Colley shot from under the union flag and entered the water with a single loud phut! as if he had been the most experienced of divers and had made a habit of rehearsing his own funeral, so expertly was it done. Of course the cannon balls assisted. This subsidiary use of their mass was after all in keeping with their general nature. So the remains of Colley dropping *deeper than did ever plummet sound* were to be thought of as now finding the solid base of all. (At these necessarily ritualistic moments of life, if you cannot use the prayer book, have recourse to Shakespeare! Nothing else will do.)

Now you might think that there was then a moment or two of silent tribute before the mourners left the churchyard. Not a bit of it! Captain Anderson shut his book, the pipes shrilled again, this time with a kind of temporal urgency. Captain Anderson nodded to Lieutenant Cumbershum, who touched his hat and *roared*:

'*Leeeoonnawwll!*'

Our obedient vessel started to turn as she moved forward and lumbered clumsily towards her original course. The ceremonially ordered ranks broke up, the people climbed everywhere into the rigging to spread our full suit of sails and add the stun's'ls to them again. Captain Anderson marched off, grenade, I mean prayerbook, in hand, back to his cabin, I suppose to make an entry in his journal. A young gentleman scrawled on the traverse board and all things were as they had been. I returned to my cabin to consider what statement I should write out and sign. It must be such as will cause his sister least pain. It shall be a *low fever*, as the captain wishes. I must conceal from him that I have already laid a trail of gunpowder to where your lordship may ignite it. God, what a world of conflict, of birth, death, procreation, betrothals, marriages for all I know, there is to be found in this extraordinary ship!

from *Rites of Passage* by William Golding (1980)

It later emerges that the Rev. Colley has died of shame, tormented by nightmare flashbacks to an act of gross indecency committed in the fo'csle heads during the orgy of the Crossing the Line ceremony. One of the raunchiest sailors admits having been given, for the first time in his uninhibited life, a chew by a parson. And he didn't mean tobacco . . .

Marriage on the High Seas

Another right exercised by the captain of a ship on the high seas was to conduct legitimate marriage ceremonies when occasion demanded. It seldom did in HM ships unless there were passengers on board. In William Golding's *Fire Down Below* it arises out of bizarre circumstances. Among the passengers in the afterguard is Aloysius Prettiman, heading for a new life in the Antipodes armed with a printing press, a blunderbuss and fiercely non-conformist views towards the attitudes of the establishment, including the most sacred superstitions held by sailors. He spends the early days of the voyage pacing the quarterdeck with his loaded piece, waiting for the opportunity to slay an albatross and demonstrate that no disaster ensues.

A bad fall during a storm forces him to take to his bunk with a fractured leg. There he stays, convinced that his days are numbered. He is tended for the most part by the ship's canon's daughter, the prim, middle-aged Letitia Granham. Entered in the manifest as a governess, Miss Granham harbours hidden fires of passion, as Edmund Talbot suspects when he clutches her to save her from a heavy fall and finds that she is not wearing stays. Romance blossoms in the putrid dank twilight of Mr Prettiman's hutch, and he determines to reward the lady with his modest fortune by marrying her. On the big day the whole ship is in gala mood.

... there was an outbreak of the warm remark, the *risqué*, even the downright salacious, and some drinking to go with it, as is customary on these occasions. Inevitably it was young Mr Tommy Taylor who went far beyond what was proper, even at a wedding. For looking forward to an hypothetical, an impossible honeymoon, he remarked in a voice breathless and split with his usual hyaena laughter – I call it usual, but as the months passed it seemed to me that the boy began to disappear and the 'hyaena' become customary – I have lost myself. He remarked, and in the presence of at least one lady, that Miss Granham was about to resemble an admiral's handrope. When rashly asked what the similarity was, he replied that the lady was about to be 'wormed, parcelled and served'. In sheer disgust I took it on myself to give him a clout over the head which must have made that organ ring and did, I was glad to see, leave him with his eyes crossed for as much as a minute.

The congregation which assembled in the lobby was gallant and pathetic. A procession of emigrants emerged the wrong, the way forbidden to them, up the ladder from the gundeck to the passenger lobby. They mixed, uninvited, with the passengers – Mr Brocklebank wearing a stock of pink material and divested of his coach cloak! The men wore favours, some, I thought, dating back to the 'entertainment'. The women had made efforts and were neat in costume if nothing more. Naturally enough, I changed into the appropriate costume. Bowles and Oldmeadow had never been out of it. Little Mr Pike was not to be seen. There was much chattering and laughter.

Now the most extraordinary change occurred, as if 'Heaven smiled' on the ceremony! For there came a new noise altogether. The watch on deck was dragging the canvas cover and then the planking off the skylight. The gloom of the lobby was changed so that for a time we were in the same kind of modified daylight as you would find in some ancient village church. I am sure the change caused as many tears as smiles, this reminder of distant places.

Six bells rang in the forenoon watch. The canvas chair was bundled out of Prettiman's cabin. The noise of assembly diminished suddenly. Captain Anderson appeared, glum as ever, if not indeed more so. Benét followed him, carrying under his arm a large brown-covered volume which I supposed rightly to be the ship's log. The captain wore the rather splendid uniform in which he had dined in *Alcyone*. I had a mental picture of Mr Benét (the image of a flag lieutenant) murmuring to him, *'I think, sir, it would be appropriate if you was to wear your number ones.'* Well, for sure, Benét was wearing his and meditating, it might be, a polite, poetical tribute to the bride. The groom, of course, remained helplessly in his bed. Captain Anderson went into Prettiman's hutch.

Miss Granham appeared. There was a gasp and a murmur, then silence again. Miss Granham wore white! The dress may have been hers, of course I cannot tell. But the veil which concealed her was one which Mrs Brocklebank had worn to protect her complexion. Of that I am sure, for it had provided a provoking concealment. Behind Miss Granham and from her hutch – how had they managed to cram themselves in? – came Mrs East, Mrs Pike and Mrs Brocklebank. The bride moved the few feet from her hutch to the bridegroom's with a certain stately grace, not diminished by the fact that she kept a cautious hand near the rail. As she passed, the women curtsied or bobbed, the men bowed or knuckled their foreheads. Miss Granham stepped over the threshold and entered her fiancé's cabin. Benét stood outside. I and Oldmeadow pushed our way to the door. Benét was contemplating Miss Granham's back in a kind of trance. I plucked him by the sleeve.

'We are the witnesses. Oblige us by stepping back.'

Benét obeyed at last and a murmur rose from the crowd and passed away. Miss Granham was standing by the bunk, level with Prettiman's shoulders, and all at once a simple idea occurred to me – so simple that it seemed no one had thought of it. Prettiman lay with his head to the stern!

Miss Granham put back her veil. It is, I think, unusual for the bride to face the congregation – but then, everything was unusual. Her face was pink – with embarrassment, I suppose. The colour did not look like fard.

I now have to report a series of shocks which Edmund Talbot experienced. To begin with, after she had put back her veil, the bride shook her head. This set her earrings in motion. They were garnets. I had last seen them ornamenting the ears of Zenobia Brocklebank during that graceless episode when I had had to do with her. I remembered them distinctly, their little chains flying about Zenobia's ears in the extremity of her passion! This was disconcerting; but I have to own, and it may have been the influence of the general air of lawful lubricity, that I found the fact flattering.

Miss Granham carried a bouquet. She did not know what to do with it, for she had no bridesmaids and the only publicly *plausible* recipient was Miss Brocklebank, now declining in her cabin. The bouquet was not made of cloth as were the favours which some of the congregation wore. It consisted of real flowers and greenery! I know that. For in the absence of a bridesmaid, the bride looked round her, then thrust out her arm at me and forced the bunch into my hands! All the world knows what will happen to the lucky girl who gets the bouquet, and there was an exclamation from Oldmeadow, then a howl of laughter from the congregation. At once my face was far redder than Miss Granham's. I clutched the thing and felt the softness and coolness of real leaves and flowers. They were, they must have been, from Captain Anderson's private paradise! Benét must have induced the sacrifice. *'I think, sir, the whole ship would be gratified if you was to honour the lady with a flower or two from your garden!'*

The next and last shock was delivered by the captain to everyone who heard it. He raised his prayer book, cleared his throat and began.

'Man that is born of woman—'

Good God, it was the burial service! Miss Granham, that intelligent lady, went from pink to white. I do not know what I did but the next time I looked at my bouquet it was sadly damaged. If any words followed this awful mistake I never heard them in the shrieks and giggles of hysteria which were followed by a rustle as our Irish contingent crossed themselves over and over again. Benét took a step past me and I had to haul him back. Captain Anderson fumbled with his book, which he had opened so thoughtlessly or which had opened itself at the fatal page, and now he dropped it, picked it up and fumbled again. Even his hands, accustomed to all emergencies and dangers, were trembling. The roots of our nature were exposed and we were afraid.

His voice was firm and furious.

'Dearly beloved—'

The service had been taken flat aback and was some time in returning to an even keel. Mr East, muttering what may have been an apology, pushed in past me and Anderson and placed the bride's hand in his. Benét was trying to get in and I held him back, but he hissed at me:

'I have the ring!'

So the thing was done. Did I detect a faint trace of scorn on the bride's face as she found herself literally being handed over? Perhaps I imagined it. Everyone held their peace as far as possible. No objections having been raised, this spinster and this bachelor were now both of them cleared for the business of the world and might do with each other what they would or could. Anderson neither congratulated the groom nor felicitated the bride. There was a sense, I suppose, in which such an omission was proper, seeing how little joy the two had to expect of the marriage. However, he leaned down over the writing flap and fiddled with documents. He opened the ship's log, signed papers on the opened page, then held the book open over the sick man. Prettiman made a sad job of signing his name upside down. Miss Granham, not according to custom, signed her new name, Letitia Prettiman, firmly and legibly. I signed, Oldmeadow signed. The captain presented her 'lines' to the bride rather as if he had been giving a receipt. He grunted at Prettiman, nodded round, and left with the ship's log which I had no doubt be felt had been rendered a little ridiculous by the unusual entry.

We had now to complete our business. I felicitated Mrs Prettiman in a low voice and touched Prettiman's hand. It was cold. Rivulets of perspiration coursed past his closed eyes.

from *Fire Down Below* by William Golding (1989)

Sir William Golding's trilogy ends with all the loose ends neatly tied up soon after the ship secures alongside in Sydney, leaving little room for a further instalment from the fertile imagination of the Nobel Prize winner. At least he leaves the Prettimans heading towards the setting sun, the bridegroom fully recovered and his printing press ready to spread his choleric views amongst the prosperous 'government men', as the released convicts were known.

Death in Childbirth at Sea

For most of the nineteenth century there was a strong demand in England for patriotic melodrama on the stage and in books, glorifying those heroic tars who were the supporting players in creating the legend of Horatio Nelson and his Band of Brothers. William Kingston deserves to be remembered as one of the most prolific contributors to this genre, setting a pace which only Edgar Wallace or Georges Simenon matched later in other fields. Kingston was born in Harley Street, but spent much of his early life in Portugal, where his father had a business, and in travelling all over the world. From 1850 until he died, thirty years later, he churned out an endless series of yarns for children of all ages, many of them appearing in *Union Jack*, a weekly magazine that he started.

The story of True Blue is typical of Kingston's work. Its sub-title says it all: 'A British Seaman of the Old School'. The action begins in the 74-gun ship *Terrible*, caught in a hurricane on passage to the West Indies. Most records of women at sea in the Royal Navy in those days portray them as waterfront sluts who have been smuggled aboard to carry on plying their trade. But long after Nelson's day, when women were officially banned from being at sea in HM ships, a blind eye was turned on a few legitimate wives – mostly Petty Officers' – who sailed with the fleet, provided they could stand the hardship and lend a hand. Such was Molly Freeborn.

The watch below had hitherto remained in their hammocks, and most of them, in spite of the gale slept as soundly as ever. What cared they that the ship was rolling and tumbling about? They knew that she was water-tight and strong, that she had plenty of sea-room, and that they would be roused up quickly enough if they were wanted. There was one person, however, who did not sleep soundly – that was her Captain, Josiah Penrose. He could not forget that he had the lives of some eight hundred beings committed to his charge, and he knew well that, even on board a stout ship with plenty of sea-room, an accident might occur which would require his immediate presence on deck. He was therefore sitting up in his cabin, holding on as best he could, and attempting to read – a task under all circumstances, considering that he had lost an eye, and was not a very bright scholar, more difficult of accomplishment than may be supposed. He had lost an arm, too, which made it difficult for him to hold a book; besides, his book was large, and the printing was not over clear, a fault common in those days; and the paper was a good deal stained and injured from the effects of damp and hot climates, and the gallant old sailor's eyesight was not as good as it used to be, though of this he had not yet convinced himself.

He was aroused from his studies by a signal at the door, and the entrance of one of the quartermasters.

'What is it, Pringle?' asked the Captain, looking up.

'Why, sir, Molly Freeborn is taken very bad, and the doctor says that he thought you would like to know,' was the answer. 'He doesn't think as how she'll get over it. Maybe, sir, you'd wish to see the poor woman?'

'Certainly, yes; I'll go below and see her,' answered the Captain in a kind tone. 'Poor Molly! But where is her husband – where is Freeborn? It will be a great blow to him.'

'It is his watch on deck, sir. No one liked to go and tell him. He could do no good, and the best chance, the doctor said, was to keep Molly quiet. But I suppose that they'll let him know now,' answered the quartermaster.

'Yes, do you go and find him, and take him below to his wife, and just break her state gently to him, Pringle,' said the Captain.

Captain Penrose stopped a moment to slip on his great-coat, and to jam a sou'wester tightly down over his head, before he left the cabin on his errand of kindness when a terrific clap was heard, louder than one of thunder, and the ship seemed to quiver in every timber fore and aft. The Captain sprang on deck, for the moment, in his anxiety for the safety of his ship, forgetting his intention with regard to Molly Freeborn.

Poor Molly! There she lay in the sick-bay, which had been appropriated to her own, gasping out her life amid the tumult and disturbance of that terrific storm. She was one of three women allowed in those days, under certain circumstances, to be on board ship for the purpose of acting as nurses to the sick, and of washing for the officers and men. Her husband was captain of the maintop, and as gallant and fine a seaman as ever stepped. Everybody liked and respected him.

But Molly was even a greater favourite. There was not a kinder hearted, more gentle, sensible, and judicious person in existence. She was amply supplied indeed, with all the best feminine qualities of heart and mind; but her personal appearance, at a first glance, was not in her favour. She had been probably not bad-looking when she was young, but her features were large, and bore the marks of severe buffetings with winds, and rains, and hot suns; for she had faithfully followed her husband's fortunes for many years, and through many climes. Her figure was stout, her arms were strong, and her hands large; but these very qualities enabled her to administer to the wants of the sick and wounded with greater effect, and no one could be more gentle and tender than she was when using those big hands of hers. No one had a greater variety of receipts for all sorts of ailments, and no one could more artistically cook dishes better suited to the taste of the sick.

Most of the officers, who had from time to time been ill and wounded, acknowledged and prized her talents and excellences; and the Captain declared that he considered he owed his life, under Providence, entirely to the care with which she nursed him through an attack of fever when the doctor despaired of his life. This was in another ship, and he was glad to get her and William

Freeborn on board the 'Terrible.' Her husband adored her – not in a maudlin way, but with good, hearty, honest love, admiration, and respect; and there was not a man among the crew who would not have gone through fire and water to serve her. Even the other women on board regarded her without a spark of envy, and she never had an angry word with any of them. She was as brave, too, as a man. She had been in several actions; and though she had to go below and attend to the wounded, she had stood as long as she could by her husband's side, amid showers of round-shot and bullets, as fearless of them as if they had been hailstones. Any one hearing her speak, however, without seeing her, would have supposed that she was a refined, delicate young woman: there was something so gentle and sweet in her voice, the storms of wind and showers of spray she had encountered had not been able to make it harsh; and then to hear her sing, how blythe and musical were her notes, or soothing and calming when she sat by the bedside of a sufferer and wished to lull him to sleep!

Although William and Molly had been married for many years, they had had no children. However, this state of things was not always to continue. The fact is, that when the old 'Terrible,' after being refitted, was again commissioned, Molly ought to have remained on shore; but she could not bear the thoughts of being parted from her husband, and so she did not say what she thought was going to occur, but as usual went to sea with him. She did not dread the consequences in the least. She knew that she would have plenty of nurses for the baby, at all events, and enough for herself, with a good doctor; indeed, she came to the conclusion that she should be better off afloat than on shore, for she was not a woman to do anything of so much importance without due consideration. She kept her counsel, therefore; and though her husband might have had his suspicions, he asked no questions, lest he might have to betray her secrets, and he had been so long accustomed to look up to her that he was convinced whatever she did was right.

Poor Molly had, however, not calculated that the anticipated event would take place during a hurricane; and she was also sadly mistaken as to her own strength and power of endurance. From the time the doctor came to her, he had too much reason to anticipate the worst; but she would not have her husband sent for – she would not draw him from his duty or alarm him sooner than was necessary. The faithful creature, who had never given him a moment's anxiety or pain, was anxious now to put off the infliction of it – inevitable as she feared it must be – as long as possible.

'All hands on deck!' was the order given as soon as the Captain saw what had occurred. The main-topsail had been blown from the bolt-ropes, and the tattered remnants were now lashing and slashing about in the gale, twisting into inextricable knots, and winding and wriggling round the main-topsail yard, rendering it a work of great danger to go out on it. The boatswain's whistle sounded shrilly through the storm a well-known note. 'All hands shorten sail!' was echoed along the decks. 'Rouse out there – rouse out – idlers and all on deck!' Everybody knew that there was work to be done; indeed, the clap made by the parting of the sail had awakened even the soundest sleepers. Among the first aloft, who endeavoured to clear the yard of the fragments of the sail, was William Freeborn, the captain of the main-top. With knives and hands they worked away in spite of the lashing they got, now being almost strangled, and now dragged off the yard.

The Captain resolved to heave the ship to. The wind had shifted, and if they ran on even under bare poles, they would be carried on too much out of their course. It was a delicate and difficult operation. A new main-topsail had first to be bent. It took the united strength of the crew to hoist it to the yard. At length the sail was got up and closely reefed, hauled out, strengthened in every possible way to resist the fury of the gale. It was an operation which occupied some time. The fore-topsail had to be taken in. The helm was put down, and, as she came slowly up to the wind, the after-sail being taken off also, she lay to, gallantly riding over the still rising seas. Though she did not tumble about, perhaps, quite as much as she had been doing, her movements were far from easy. She did not roll as before, as she was kept pressed down on one side; still every now and then she gave a pitch as she glided down into the trough of the sea, which made every timber and mast creak and quiver, and few on board would have been inclined to sing:

> 'Here's a sou'wester coming, Billy,
> Don't you hear it roar now!
> Oh help them! How I pity those
> Unhappy folks on shore now!'

At length William Freeborn was relieved from his post aloft, and came down on deck. Paul Pringle, his old friend and messmate, who had been hunting for him though the darkness, found him at last. Paul grieved sincerely for the news he had to communicate, and, not liking the task imposed on him, scarcely knew how to begin.

'Bill,' said he with a sigh, 'you and I, boy and man, have sailed together a good score of years, and never had a fall-out about nothing all that time, and it goes to my heart, Bill, to say anything that you won't like; but it must be done – that I sees – so it's no use to have no circumbendibus. Your missus took very bad – very bad indeed – just in the middle of the gale, and there was no one to send for you – and so, do you see—'

'My wife – Molly! – oh, what has happened, Paul?' exclaimed Freeborn, not waiting for an answer; but springing below, he rushed to the sick-bay, as the hospital is called. The faint cry of an infant reached his ears as he opened the door. Betty Snell, one of the other nurses, was so busily employed with something on her knees, that she did not see him enter. The dim light of a lantern, hanging from a beam overhead, fell on it. He saw that it was a new-born infant. He guessed what had happened, but he did not stop to caress it, for beyond was the cot occupied by his wife. There she lay, all still and silent. His heart sank within him; he gazed at her with a feeling of terror and anguish which he had never before experienced. He took her hand. It fell heavily by her side. He gasped for breath. 'Molly!' he exclaimed at length, 'speak to me, girl – what has happened?'

There was no answer. Then he knew that his honest, true-hearted wife was snatched from him in this world for ever. The big drops of salt spray, which still clung to his hair and bushy beard, dropped on the kind face of her he had loved so well, but not a tear escaped his eyes. He gladly would have wept, but he had not for so many a long year done such a thing, and he felt too stunned and bewildered to do so now. He had stood as a sailor alone could stand on so unstable a foothold, gazing on those now placid and pale unchanging features for a long time – how long he could not tell – when Paul Pringle, who had followed him to the door of the sick-bay, came up, and, gently taking him by the shoulders, said:

'Come along, Bill; there's no use mourning: we all loved her, and we all feel for you, from the Captain downwards. That's a fact. But just do you come and have a look at the younker. Betty Snell vow that he's the very image of you, all except the beard and pig-tail.'

The latter appendage in those days was worn by most sailors, and Bill Freeborn had reason to pride himself on his. The mention of it just then, however, sent a pang through his heart, for Molly had the morning before the gale dressed it for him; indeed, it had been her pride to dress and plait it, and to set it off to the best advantage, a favour she did not often condescend to bestow on anybody else.

Freeborn at first shook his head and would not move; but at last his shipmate got him to turn round, and then Betty Snell held up the poor little helpless infant to him, and the father's heart felt a touch of tenderness of a nature it had never before experienced, and he stooped down and bestowed a kiss on the brow of his new-born motherless child. He did not, however, venture to take it in his arms.

'You'll look after it, Betty, and be kind to it?' said he in a husky voice. 'I'm sure you will, for her sake who lies there?'

'Yes, yes, Bill; no fear,' answered Betty, who was a good-natured creature in her way, though it was a rough way, by the bye.

She was the wife of one of the boatswain's mates. Her companion, Nancy Bolton, who was the wife of the sergeant of marines, was much the same sort of person; indeed, it would not have been done for the style of life they had to lead, to have had too refined characters on board.

'Bless you, Freeborn – take care of the baby, of course we will!' added Nancy, looking up from some occupation about which she had been engaged. 'We'll both be mothers to him, and all the ship's company will act the part of a father to him. Never you fear that. As long as the old ship holds together, he'll not want friends; nor after it, if there's one of us alive. Set your mind at rest now.'

'Yes, that we will, old ship,' exclaimed Paul Pringle, taking Freeborn's hand and wringing it warmly. 'That's to say, if the little chap wants more looking after than you can manage. But come along now. There's no use staying here.

Bet and Nancy will look after the child better than we can, and you must turn in. Your hammock is the best place for you now.'

This was good advice, and almost mechanically poor Freeborn turned into his narrow bed, when, swung from side to side with a dead leaden feeling at his heart, in spite of the still raging storm he in time forgot his grief in sleep.

The gale at length ceased; the ship was put on her proper course for the West Indies, whither she was bound; the sea went down, the clouds cleared away, and the glorious sun came out and shone brightly over the blue ocean. All the officers and men assembled on the upper deck, and then near one of the middle ports was placed a coffin, covered with the Union Jack. There ought to have been a chaplain, but there was none, and so the Captain came forward with a Prayer-Book, and in an impressive, feeling way, though not without difficulty, read the beautiful burial service to be used at sea for a departed sister; and the two women stood near the coffin, one holding a small infant; and there stood William Freeborn, supported by Paul Pringle, for by himself he could scarcely stand; and then slowly and carefully the coffin was lowered into the waves, and as they closed over it, in the impulse of the moment, the bereaved widower would have thrown himself after it, not knowing what he was about, had not Paul Pringle held him back. Down sank the coffin rapidly, and was hid to sight by the blue ocean – the grave of many a brave sailor, and of thousands of the young, and fair, and brave, and joyous, and of the proud and rich also, but never of a more kind-hearted honest woman than was Molly Freeborn. So all on board the 'Terrible' declared, and assuredly they spoke the truth.

After fifty years covered by twenty-seven episodes in the long-running serial, our hero returns in triumph as a Boatswain to enjoy the autumn of his life with his old sweetheart from Emsworth. The moral of the story is encapsulated in the final exhortation, which might have given Baden-Powell himself a few ideas:

True Blue had a numerous family of sons, every one of whom served his country afloat, all becoming warrant-officers; while these sons again, from their intelligence and steady conduct, although they entered before the mast, obtained the same rank.

True Blue himself, who lived to enjoy a hearty and hale old age, gave the same advice to his grandchildren which he received from Paul Pringle.

'Lads,' he used to say, 'be content with your lot. Do your duty in whatever station you are placed, on the quarter-deck or fo'castle, in the tops aloft or at the guns on the main or lower deck, and leave the rest to God. Depend on it, if you obey His standing orders, if you steer your course by the chart and compass He has provided for you, and fight your ship manfully, He will give you the victory.'

from 'True Blue', in *Popular Sea Stories* by W. H. G. Kingston (*c.* 1890)

Stowaways

Homeward Bound from Siam

No collection of tales about the sea would be complete without featuring stowaways, those desperate enough to seek a free passage by hiding on board a ship before her departure on a long voyage. Most were driven by despair or poverty at home; some were fugitives from justice. This was long before the days when a plea for political asylum might persuade the courts at the destination not to ship the refugees back whence they had come.

On being discovered on board ship, a stowaway would normally be made to work his passage, then would be almost invariably turned over to the police on arrival, since neither the crew-list nor the passenger manifest could readily be fudged. Unless, of course, the master of the ship risked his ticket by becoming a sympathetic accomplice – which was about as likely as a PLO hit-man without a boarding pass being accorded guest status by the pilot of an El Al Boeing 747. In the two extracts which follow, the stowaways get the luck they deserve.

The first is by the greatest fiction-writer about the sea of his time – the Pole Teodor Józef Konrad Korzeniowski, better known as Joseph Conrad, the name he adopted when in 1894 he finally ended up in England, the haven of his choice, both his parents having met untimely deaths under the Tsar's regime. Although most of Conrad's work is thinly veiled autobiography and he knew the Gulf of Siam from having sailed there, there is no evidence that the bizarre plot of *The Secret Sharer* is anything but fiction. It can't, however, have been particularly unusual for a master of a ship to find himself harbouring a deserter who would probably face the hangman if he turned him in at the end of the voyage.

Conrad's Captain has just taken command of a barque homeward bound from Siam. A tug had hauled her out to an anchor-berth 2 miles offshore, where they await a breeze to set them off on their long voyage. Feeling that his crew has earned a night in after the hectic days of preparation for the voyage, the Captain does not set an anchor watch, but elects to take the first part of the still night on deck himself. He finds the rope Jacob's ladder hanging over the side, where it has last been used by the tugboat captain to take their mail ashore, and, as the ladder is light enough, he makes to haul it inboard himself. When it refuses to budge, the Captain looks over the side.

The side of the ship made an opaque belt of shadow on the darkling glassy shimmer of the sea. But I saw at once something elongated and pale floating very close to the ladder. Before I could form a guess a faint flash of phosphorescent light, which seemed to issue suddenly from the naked body of a man, flickered in the sleeping water with the elusive, silent play of summer lightning in a night sky. With a gasp I saw revealed to my stare a pair of feet, the long legs, a broad livid back immersed right up to the neck in a greenish cadaverous glow. One hand, awash, clutched the bottom rung of the ladder. He was complete but for the head. A headless corpse! The cigar dropped out of my gaping mouth with a tiny plop and a short hiss quite audible in the absolute stillness of all things under heaven. At that I suppose he raised up his face, a dimly pale oval in the shadow of the ship's side. But even then I could only barely make out down there the shape of his black-haired head. However, it was enough for the horrid, frost-bound sensation which had gripped me about the chest to pass off. The moment of vain exclamations was past too. I only climbed on the spare spar and leaned over the rail as far as I could, to bring my eyes nearer to that mystery floating alongside.

As he hung by the ladder, like a resting swimmer, the sea-lightning played about his limbs at every stir; and he appeared in it ghastly, silvery, fish-like. He remained as mute as a fish, too. He made no motion to get out of the water, either. It was inconceivable that he should not attempt to come on board, and strangely troubling to suspect that perhaps he did not want to. And my first words were prompted by just that troubled incertitude.

'What's the matter?' I asked in my ordinary tone, speaking down to the face upturned exactly under mine.

'Cramp,' it answered, no louder. Then, slightly anxious, 'I say, no need to call anyone.'

'I was not going to,' I said.

'Are you alone on deck?'

'Yes.'

I had somehow the impression that he was on the point of letting go the ladder to swim away beyond my ken – mysterious as he came. But, for the moment, this being appearing as if he had risen from the bottom of the sea (it was certainly the nearest land to the ship) wanted only to know the time. I told him. And he, down there, tentatively:

'I suppose your captain's turned in.'

'I am sure he isn't,' I said.

He seemed to struggle with himself, for I heard something like the low, bitter murmur of doubt. 'What's the good?' His next words came out with a hesitating effort.

'Look here, my man. Could you call him out quietly?'

I thought the time had come to declare myself.

'*I* am the Captain.'

I heard a 'By Jove!' whispered at the level of the water. The phosphorescence flashed in the swirl of the water all about his limbs, his other hand seized the ladder.

'My name's Leggatt.'

The voice was calm and resolute. A good voice. The self-possession of that man had somehow induced a corresponding state in myself. It was very quietly that I remarked:

'You must be a good swimmer.'

'Yes. I've been in the water practically since nine o'clock. The question for me now is whether I am to let go this ladder and go on swimming till I sink from exhaustion, or – to come on board here.'

I felt this was no mere formula of desperate speech, but a real alternative in the view of a strong soul. I should have gathered from this that he was young; indeed, it is only the young who are ever confronted by such clear issues. But at the time it was pure intuition on my part. A mysterious communication was established already between us two – in the face of that silent, darkened tropical sea. I was young too; young enough to make no comment. The man in the water began suddenly to climb up the ladder, and I hastened away from the rail to fetch some clothes.

Before entering the cabin I stood still, listening in the lobby at the foot of the stairs. A faint snore came through the closed door of the chief mate's room. The second mate's door was on the hook, but the darkness in there was absolutely soundless. He too was young and could sleep like a stone. Remained the steward, but he was not likely to wake up before he was called. I got a sleeping-suit out of my room and, coming back on deck, saw the naked man from the sea sitting on the main-hatch, glimmering white in the darkness, his elbows on his knees and his head in his hands. In a moment he had concealed his damp body in a sleeping-suit of the same grey-stripe pattern as the one I was wearing and followed me like my double on the poop. Together we moved right aft, barefooted, silent.

'What is it?' I asked in a deadened voice, taking the lighted lamp out of the binnacle and raising it to his face.

'An ugly business.'

He had rather regular features; a good mouth; light eyes under somewhat heavy, dark eyebrows; a smooth, square forehead; no growth on his cheeks; a small, brown moustache and well-shaped, round chin. His expression was concentrated, meditative, under the inspecting light of the lamp I held up to his face; such as a man thinking hard in solitude might wear. My sleeping-suit was just right for his size. A well-knit young fellow of twenty-five at most. He caught his lower lip with the edge of white, even teeth.

'Yes,' I said, replacing the lamp in the binnacle. The warm, heavy, tropical night closed upon his head again.

'There's a ship over there,' he murmured.

'Yes, I know. The *Sephora*. Did you know of us?'

'Hadn't the slightest idea. I am the mate of her . . .' He paused and corrected himself. 'I should say I *was*.'

'Aha! Something wrong?'

'Yes. Very wrong indeed. I've killed a man.'

'What do you mean? Just now?'

'No, on the passage. Weeks ago. Thirty-nine south. When I say a man—'

'Fit of temper,' I suggested confidently.

The shadowy, dark head, like mine, seemed to nod imperceptibly above the ghostly grey of my sleeping-suit. It was, in the night, as though I had been faced by my own reflection in the depths of a sombre and immense mirror.

'A pretty thing to have to own up for a *Conway* boy,' murmured my double distinctly.

'You're a *Conway* boy?'

'I am,' he said, as if startled. Then slowly: 'Perhaps you too . . .'

It was so; but being a couple of years older I had left before he joined. After a quick interchange of dates a silence fell; and I thought suddenly of my absurd mate with his terrific whiskers and the 'Bless my soul – you don't say so' type of intellect. My double gave me an inkling of his thoughts by saying:

'My father's a parson in Norfolk. Do you see me before a judge and jury on that charge? For myself I can't see the necessity. There are fellows that an angel from heaven . . . And I am not that. He was one of those creatures that are just simmering all the time with a silly sort of wickedness. Miserable devils that have no business to live at all. He wouldn't do his duty and wouldn't let anybody else do theirs. But what's the good of talking! You know well enough the sort of ill-conditioned snarling cur . . .'

He appealed to me as if our experiences had been as identical as our clothes. And I knew well enough the pestiferous danger of such a character where there are no means of legal repression. And I knew well enough also that my double there was no homicidal ruffian. I did not think of asking him for details, and he told me the story roughly in brusque, disconnected sentences. I needed no more. I saw it all going on as though I were myself inside that other sleeping-suit.

'It happened while we were setting a reefed foresail, at dusk. Reefed foresail! You understand the sort of weather. The only sail we had left to keep the ship running; so you may guess what it had been like for days. Anxious sort of job, that. He gave me some of his cursed insolence at the sheet. I tell you I was overdone with this terrific weather that seemed to have no end to it. Terrific, I tell you – and a deep ship. I believe the fellow himself was half crazed with funk. It was no time for gentlemanly reproof, so I turned round and felled him like an ox. He up and at me. We closed just as an awful sea made for the ship. All hands saw it coming and took to the rigging, but I had him by the throat, and went on shaking him like a rat, the men above us yelling: "Look out! Look out!" Then a crash as if the sky had fallen on my head. They say that for ten minutes hardly anything was to be seen of the ship – just the three masts and a bit of the forecastle head, and of the poop all awash driving along in a smother of foam. It was a miracle that they found us, jammed together behind the forebits. It's clear that I meant business, because I was holding him by the throat still when they picked us up. He was black in the face. It was too much for them. It seemed they rushed us aft together, gripped as we were, screaming "Murder!" like a lot of lunatics, and broke into the cuddy. And the ship running for her life, touch and go all the time, any minute her last in a sea fit to turn your hair grey only a-looking at it. I understand that the Skipper too started raving like the rest of them. The man had been deprived of sleep for more than a week, and to have this sprung on him at the height of a furious gale nearly drove him out of his mind. I wonder they didn't fling me overboard after getting the carcass of their precious shipmate out of my fingers. They had rather a job to separate us, I've been told. A sufficiently fierce story to make an old judge and a respectable jury sit up a bit. The first thing I heard when I came to myself was the maddening howling of that endless gale, and on that the voice of the old man. He was hanging on to my bunk, staring into my face out of his sou'wester.

' "Mr Leggatt, you have killed a man. You can act no longer as chief mate of this ship." '

His care to subdue his voice made it sound monotonous. He rested a hand on the end of the skylight to steady himself with, and all that time did not stir a limb, so far as I could see. 'Nice little tale for a quiet tea-party,' he concluded in the same tone.

One of my hands, too, rested on the end of the skylight; neither did I stir a limb, so far as I knew. We stood less than a foot from each other. It occurred to me that if old 'Bless my soul – you don't you say so' were to put his head up the companion and catch sight of us, he would think he was seeing double, or imagine himself come upon a scene of weird witchcraft; the strange captain having a quiet confabulation by the wheel with his own grey ghost. I became very much concerned to prevent anything of the sort. I heard the other's soothing undertone.

'My father's a parson in Norfolk,' it said. Evidently he had forgotten he had told me this important fact before. Truly a nice little tale.

'You had better slip down into my state-room now,' I said, moving off stealthily. My double followed my movements; our bare feet made no sound; I let him in, closed the door with care, and, after giving a call to the second mate, returned on deck for my relief.

'Not much sign of any wind yet,' I remarked when he approached.

'No, sir. Not much,' he assented sleepily, in his hoarse voice, with just enough deference, no more, and barely suppressing a yawn.

'Well, that's all you have to look out for. You have got your orders.'

'Yes, sir.'

I paced a turn or two on the poop and saw him take up his position face forward with his elbow in the ratlines of the mizzen-rigging before I went below. The mate's faint snoring was still going on peacefully. The cuddy lamp was burning over the table on which stood a vase with flowers, a polite attention from the ship's provision merchant – the last flowers we should see for the next three months at the very least. Two bunches of bananas hung from the beam symmetrically, one on each side of the rudder-casing. Everything was as before in the ship – except that two of her captain's sleeping-suits were simultaneously in use, one motionless in the cuddy, the other keeping very still in the captain's state-room.

It must be explained here that my cabin had the form of the capital letter L, the door being within the angle and opening into the short part of the letter. A couch was to the left, the bed-place to the right; my writing-desk and the chronometers' table faced the door. But anyone opening it, unless he stepped right inside, had no view of what I call the long (or vertical) part of the letter. It contained some lockers surmounted by a bookcase; and a few clothes, a thick jacket or two, caps, oilskin coat, and such like, hung on hooks. There was at the bottom of that part a door opening into my bathroom, which could be entered also directly from the saloon. But that way was never used.

The mysterious arrival had discovered the advantage of this particular shape. Entering my room, lighted strongly by a big bulkhead lamp swung on gimbals above my writing-desk, I did not see him anywhere till he stepped out quietly from behind the coats hung in the recessed part.

'I heard somebody moving about, and went in there at once,' he whispered.

I, too, spoke under my breath.

'Nobody is likely to come in here without knocking and getting permission.'

He nodded. His face was thin and the sunburn faded, as though he had been ill. And no wonder. He had been, I heard presently, kept under arrest in his cabin for nearly seven weeks.

Leggatt had seized his first chance to jump over the side from *Sephora*, which was when she had been anchored behind some offshore islands to await the tide before going upriver to her destination. Instead of making for the nearby islands, he struck out towards the riding-light of the barque lying to seaward. The new Captain is impressed by the man's manner and by the story of how he saved *Sephora* from being overwhelmed by huge seas in the Indian Ocean by managing to gain some measure of downwind control through setting a reefed foresail in hurricane conditions, while her master had been paralysed into inactivity through fear. He therefore hides him in his sleeping-cabin. Despite the growing suspicions of his steward, and a visit made by the master of *Sephora*, the Captain and his stowaway manage to avoid detection. At last a breeze makes up, and the barque is able to set off.

The Captain agrees to shape his course close enough to the Cambodian islands to let Leggatt slip over the side and make his escape, although this involves standing too close inshore for comfort in fluky winds with unreliable charts and uncertain cross-currents. Conrad's description of the struggle to get the unwieldy barque on to a clearing tack is frighteningly realistic – but suddenly the Captain sees in the water something that tells him all he needs to know.

At noon I gave no orders for a change of course, and the mate's whiskers became much concerned and seemed to be offering themselves unduly to my notice. At last I said:

'I am going to stand right in. Quite in – as far as I can take her.'

The stare of extreme surprise imparted an air of ferocity also to his eyes, and he looked truly terrific for a moment.

'We're not doing well in the middle of the gulf,' I continued casually. 'I am going to look for the land breezes tonight.'

'Bless my soul! Do you mean, sir, in the dark amongst the lot of them islands and reefs and shoals?'

'Well – if there are any regular land breezes at all on this coast one must get close inshore to find them, mustn't one?'

'Bless my soul!' he exclaimed again under his breath. All that afternoon he wore a dreamy, contemplative appearance which in him was a mark of perplexity. After dinner I went into my state-room as if I meant to take some rest. There we two bent our dark heads over a half-unrolled chart lying on my bed.

'There,' I said. 'It's got to be Koh-ring. I've been looking at it ever since sunrise. It has got two hills and a low point. It must be inhabited. And on the coast opposite there is what looks like the mouth of a biggish river – with some town, no doubt, not far up. It's the best chance for you that I can see.'

'Anything. Koh-ring let it be.'

He looked thoughtfully at the chart as if surveying chances and distances from a lofty height – and following with his eyes his own figure wandering on the blank land of Cochin China, and then passing off that piece of paper clean out of sight into uncharted regions. And it was as if the ship had two captains to plan her course for her. I had been so worried and restless running up and down that I had not had the patience to dress that day. I had remained in my sleeping-suit, with straw slippers and a soft floppy hat. The closeness of the heat in the gulf had been most oppressive, and the crew were used to seeing me wandering in that airy attire.

'She will clear the south point as she heads now,' I whispered into his ear. 'Goodness only knows when, though, but certainly after dark. I'll edge her in to half a mile, as far as I may be able to judge in the dark—'

'Be careful,' he murmured warningly – and I realized suddenly that all my future, the only future for which I was fit, would perhaps go irretrievably to pieces in any mishap to my first command.

I could not stop a moment longer in the room. I motioned him to get out of sight and made my way on to the poop. That unplayful cub had the watch. I walked up and down for a while thinking things out, then beckoned him over.

'Send a couple of hands to open the two quarter-deck ports,' I said mildly.

He actually had the impudence, or else so forgot himself in his wonder at such an incomprehensible order, as to repeat:

'Open the quarter-deck ports! What for, sir?'

'The only reason you need concern yourself about is because I tell you to do so. Have them open wide and fastened properly.'

He reddened and went off, but I believe made some jeering remark to the carpenter as to the sensible practice of ventilating a ship's quarter-deck. I know he popped into the mate's cabin to impart the fact to him, because the whiskers came on deck, as it were by chance, and stole glances at me from below – for signs of lunacy or drunkenness, I suppose.

A little before supper, feeling more restless than ever, I rejoined, for a moment, my second self. And to find him sitting so quietly was surprising, like something against nature, inhuman.

I developed my plan in a hurried whisper.

'I shall stand in as close as I dare and then put her round. I shall presently find means to smuggle you out of here into the sail-locker, which communicates with the lobby. But there is an opening, a sort of square for hauling the sails out, which gives straight on the quarter-deck and which is never closed in fine weather, so as to give air to the sails. When the ship's way is deadened in stays and all the hands are aft at the main-braces you shall have a clear road to slip out and get overboard through the open quarter-deck port. I've had them both fastened up. Use the rope's end to lower yourself into the water so to avoid a splash – you know. It could be heard and cause some beastly complication.'

He kept silent for a while, then whispered, ' I understand.'

'I won't be there to see you go,' I began with an effort. 'The rest . . . I only hope I have understood too.'

'You have. From first to last' – and for the first time there seemed to be a faltering, something strained in his whisper. He caught hold of my arm, but the ringing of the supper bell made me start. He didn't, though; he only released his grip.

After supper we didn't come below again till well past eight o'clock. The faint, steady breeze was loaded with dew; and the wet, darkened sails held all there was of propelling power in it. The night, clear and starry, sparkled darkly, and its opaque, lightless patches shifting slowly against the low stars were the drifting islets. On the port bow there was a big one, more distant and shadowily imposing by the great space of sky it eclipsed.

On opening the door I had a back view of my very own self looking at a chart. He had come out of the recess and was standing near the table.

'Quite dark enough,' I whispered.

He stepped back and leaned against my bed with a level, quiet glance. I sat on the couch. We had nothing to say to each other. Over our heads the officer of the watch moved here and there. Then I heard him move quickly. I knew what that meant. He was making for the companion; and presently his voice was outside my door.

'We are drawing in pretty fast, sir. Lands looks rather close.'

'Very well,' I answered. 'I am coming on deck directly.'

I waited till he was gone out of the cuddy, then rose. My double moved too. The time had come to exchange our last whispers, for neither of us was ever to hear each other's natural voice.

'Look here!' I opened a drawer and took out three sovereigns. 'Take this, anyhow. I've got six and I'd give you the lot, only I must keep a little money to buy fruit and vegetables for the crew from native boats as we go through Sunda Straits.'

He shook his head.

'Take it.' I urged him, whispering desperately. 'No one can tell what—'

He smiled and slapped meaningly the only pocket of the sleeping-jacket. It was not safe, certainly. But I produced a large old silk handkerchief of mine, and tying the three pieces of gold in a corner, pressed it on him. He was touched, I suppose, because he took it at last and tied it quickly round his waist under the jacket, on his bare skin.

Our eyes met; several seconds elapsed, till, our glances still mingled, I extended my hand and turned the lamp out. Then I passed through the cuddy, leaving the door of my room wide open.

*

I came out on deck slowly. It was now a matter of conscience to shave the land as close as possible – for now he must go overboard whenever the ship was put in stays. Must! There could be no going back for him. After a moment I walked over to leeward and my heart flew into my mouth at the nearness of the land on the bow. Under any other circumstances I would not have held on a minute longer. The second mate had followed me anxiously.

I looked on till I felt I could command my voice.

'She will weather,' I said then in a quiet tone.

'Are you going to try that, sir?' he stammered out incredulously.

I took no notice of him and raised my tone just enough to be heard by the helmsman.

'Keep her good full.'

'Good full, sir.'

The wind fanned my cheek, the sails slept, the world was silent. The strain of watching the dark loom of the land grow bigger and denser was too much for me. I had shut my eyes – because the ship must go closer. She must! The stillness was intolerable. Were we standing still?

When I opened my eyes the second view started my heart with a thump. The black southern hill of Koh-ring seemed to hang right over the ship like a towering fragment of the everlasting night. On that enormous mass of blackness there was not a gleam to be seen, not a sound to be heard. It was gliding irresistibly towards us and yet seemed already within reach of the hand. I saw the vague figures of the watch grouped in the waist, gazing in awed silence.

'Are you going on, sir?' inquired an unsteady voice at my elbow.

I ignored it. I had to go on.

'Keep her full. Don't check her way. That won't do now,' I said warningly.

'I can't see the sails very well,' the helmsman answered me, in strange, quavering tones.

Was she close enough? Already she was, I won't say in the shadow of the land, but in the very blackness of it, already swallowed up, as it were, gone too close to be recalled, gone from me altogether.

'Give the mate a call,' I said to the young man who stood at my elbow as still as death, 'and turn all hands up.'

My tone had a borrowed loudness reverberated from the height of the land. Several voices cried out together: 'We are all on deck, sir.'

Then stillness again, with the great shadow gliding closer, towering higher, without a light, without a sound. Such a hush had fallen on the ship that she might have been a bark of the dead floating in slowly under the very gate of Erebus.

'My God! Where are we?'

It was the mate moaning at my elbow. He was thunderstruck, and as it were deprived of the moral support of his whiskers. He clapped his hands and absolutely cried out, 'Lost!'

'Be quiet,' I said sternly.

He lowered his tone, but I saw the shadowy gesture of his despair. 'What are we doing here?'

'Looking for the land wind.'

He made as if to tear his hair, and addressed me recklessly.

'She will never get out. You have done it, sir. I knew it'd end in something like this. She will never weather, and you are too close now to stay. She'll drift ashore before she's round. Oh, my God!'

I caught his arm as he was raising it to batter his poor devoted head, and shook it violently.

'She's ashore already,' he wailed, trying to tear himself away.

'Is she? . . . Keep good full there!'

'Good full, sir,' cried the helmsman in a frightened, thin child-like voice.

I hadn't let go the mate's arm, and went on shaking it. 'Ready about, do you hear? You go forward' – shake – 'and stop there' – shake – 'and hold your noise' – shake – 'and see these head-sheets properly overhauled' – shake, shake – shake.

And all the time I dared not look towards the land lest my heart should fail me. I released my grip at last and he ran forward as if fleeing for dear life.

I wondered what my double there in the sail-locker thought of this commotion. He was able to hear everything – and perhaps he was able to understand why, on my conscience, it had to be thus close – no less. My first order, 'Hard alee!' re-echoed ominously under the towering shadow of Koh-ring as if I had shouted in a mountain-gorge. And then I watched the land intently. In that smooth water and light wind it was impossible to feel the ship coming-to. No! I could not feel her. And my second self was making now ready to slip out and lower himself overboard. Perhaps he was gone already . . .

The great black mass brooding over our very mastheads began to pivot away from the ship's side silently. And now I forgot the secret stranger ready to depart, and remembered only that I was a total stranger to the ship. I did not know her. Would she do it? How was she to be handled?

I swung the mainyard and waited helplessly. She was perhaps stopped, and her very fate hung in the balance, with the black mass of Koh-ring like the gate of the everlasting night towering over her taffrail. What would she do now? Had she way on her yet? I stepped to the side swiftly, and on the shadowy water I could see nothing except a faint phosphorescent flash revealing the glassy smoothness of the sleeping surface. It was impossible to tell – and I had not learned yet the feel of my ship. Was she moving? What I needed was something easily seen, a piece of paper, which I could throw overboard and watch. I had nothing on me. To run down for it I didn't dare. There was no time. All at once my strained, yearning stare distinguished a white object floating within a yard of the ship's side. White on the black water. A phosphorescent flash passed under it. What was that thing? . . . I recognized my own floppy hat. It mast have fallen off his head . . . and he didn't bother. Now I had what I wanted – the saving-mark for my eyes. But I hardly thought of my other self, now gone from the ship, to be hidden for ever from all friendly faces, to be a fugitive and a vagabond on the earth, with no brand of the curse on his sane forehead to stay a slaying hand . . . too proud to explain.

And I watched the hat – the expression of my sudden pity for his mere flesh. It had been meant to save his homeless head from the dangers of the sun. And now – behold – it was saving the ship, by serving me for a mark to help out the ignorance of my strangeness. Ha! It was drifting forward, warning me just in time that the ship had gathered sternway.

'Shift the helm,' I said in a low voice to the seaman standing still like a statue.

The man's eyes glistened wildly in the binnacle light as he jumped round to the other side and spun round the wheel.

I walked to the break of the poop. On the over-shadowed deck all hands stood by the forebraces waiting for my order. The stars ahead seemed to be gliding from right to left. And all was so still in the world that I heard the quiet remark, 'She's round,' passed in a tone of intense relief between two seamen.

'Let go and haul.'

The foreyards ran round with a great noise, amidst cheery cries. And now the frightful whiskers made themselves heard giving various orders. Already the ship was drawing ahead. And I was alone with her. Nothing, no one in the world should stand now between us, throwing a shadow on the way of silent knowledge and mute affection, the perfect communion of a seaman with his first command.

Walking to the taffrail, I was in time to make out, on the very edge of the darkness thrown by a towering black mass like the very gateway of Erebus – yes, I was in time to catch an evanescent glimpse of my white hat left behind to mark the spot where the secret sharer of my cabin and of my thoughts, as though he were my second self, had lowered himself into the water to take his punishment: a free man, a proud swimmer striking out for a new destiny.

from *The Secret Sharer* by Joseph Conrad

A Fugitive from Justice on a River-boat

Boyd Cable (pen-name of Colonel E. A. Ewart, publicity manager of P. & O. Shipping, for whom he wrote a history in 1937) published *His Duty* in 1927. Captain Boult of the paddle-wheel steamer *Boomerang* faces much the same dilemma as Conrad's hero. On a late run ashore, the ageing river boat skipper is mugged by two youths, but saved from serious injury by the timely intervention of young Able Seaman Ned Underwood, who has deserted from his ship after refusing orders and striking the mate. As soon as he hears of Ned's problem, Boult offers him a passage upriver to take him beyond the reach of the local law. The old paddler's departure into the teeth of a rising gale is hastened by the appearance on the dockside of a sergeant of police with a warrant for Ned's arrest. At the last moment, the Sergeant jumps on board the moving ship and orders her immediate return alongside. Pleading stress of weather and the vulnerability of the paddles, the Captain refuses. Out in the open sea, *Boomerang*'s wild rolling soon has the Sergeant clinging to the lee rail, not caring about anything beyond his own survival. Ned, the only sailor on board with offshore experience, takes the wheel to nurse the old ship into the rising steep seas.

'The wind's easin' a trifle,' said Ned. 'Now's the chance to shove her ahead a bit.'

As he had expected, the *Boomerang* made heavy weather of it when she was driven into the running seas, and the skipper watched with some concern the waves plunging over the bows and cascading aft.

'I don't half like it,' he said, shaking his head. 'If she – what's that?'

He broke off at the sound of a dull rumble from below and the boom of escaping steam. The paddles ceased to turn, and the boat's head immediately began to fall off. The skipper was out of the wheel-house and down the ladder in a flash, and in less than a minute he was back again.

'She's blown out the end of the cylinder or something,' he said breathlessly. 'No hope o'steam for hours! What's to do? Anchor, eh?'

'That's right,' said Ned briefly – 'and sharp, too. If we get broadside on to this sea—'

The skipper vanished, and Ned stayed, trying rather vainly to make the ship answer her helm. He heard the clank and clatter of iron through the roar of the wind, and then the harsh rumble of the chain. With a sharp jerk the steamer yielded to the pluck of the anchor chain that held her by the nose, the stern swung away from the wind, and she lay plunging, head on again to the run of the seas. With some uneasiness Ned felt the sharp, snapping jerks with which she tore at her anchor.

'These chaps,' he muttered, 'they don't know a thing about anchorin' in a seaway.' The skipper came up the ladder and into the wheelhouse, and Ned spoke quickly. 'Have you given her plenty of chain, cap'n? She feels like she was held a bit short.'

'Isn't much depth o' water here?' said the skipper. 'The anchor's holdin' all right, I think.'

'I'd give her every inch you've got aboard,' said Ned – 'an' a hawser after that. If she's anyways short she might snap that – an' by Harry! She's done it! Now for trouble. Have you a spare anchor?'

Together he and the skipper scrambled down to the lower deck, and clambered forward to the bows. There was no second anchor, and the chain had snapped off short, almost at the bows. The boat was swinging broadside to the waves again, and rolling wildly and appallingly. It was rapidly growing dark, and the angry crests, racing up out of the gloom, had a vicious and dangerous weight and drive in them.

'She won't stand much of this!' bawled Ned to the skipper. 'She'll roll over, sure as eggs. Have you any gear aboard that would make a sea-anchor?'

'What sort o' gear? What's a sea-anchor?' bellowed the skipper.

'A beam o' any sort!' Ned snapped. 'Any sort o' timber that'll float – the bigger the better. Have you anything like it?'

'There's some planks in the deck cargo aft,' said the skipper.

'Good enough,' said Ned. 'Get them for'ard here to me – and some stout line for lashing. Now, then, some o' you, a tarpaulin? Right! – fetch it here! Where's the longest and strongest hawser you've got? An' what's in them cases lashed along the rail? That'll do; get that hawser bent to the end o' your chain!'

Skipper, mate, and crew flung themselves on the work, and, under Ned's directions, a sea-anchor was roughly, but efficiently, put together. An edge of the tarpaulin lashed to the planks, the lower edge well weighted, stout lines to the corners – everything watched and tested and made doubly secure by Ned – and the sea-anchor was ready.

With some difficulty it was launched over the side, and the line paid out. Presenting the bigger surface to the wind, the steamer drove astern before it, while the huge, weighted bag of the tarpaulin dragged heavily from the bows, brought her head to the wind and into comparative safety again.

'Great notion, that, lad!' shouted the skipper. 'Looks like holding her.'

'It'll hold her head to sea,' replied Ned, 'but she's drifting like smoke, remember. Sooner your engine's under way again, the less chance o' you hittin' that shoal you spoke of.'

Suddenly the skipper leaped past him, and, with an angry oath, seized by the shoulder a man who was edging his way round amongst the crew and peering closely at each one.

'What are you doin' here?' he roared. 'Get back where I told you, or, by Christmas! I'll tie you up an' lock you in there! Can't you leave your cussed man-huntin' for a minute? You may know any blessed minute what it feels like to be hunted yourself – by the fishes. Now, then, are you goin', or will you be carried?'

'I'm going,' said the sergeant grimly. 'I fancy there is a man there I'll have a word with by and by. But no hurry – I can wait.'

He made his way aft and up to the little mess-room again, while the skipper growled and fumed.

'Better keep down there, lad,' he said to Ned. 'Come down to the engine-room. You'll be out o' the way there, an' we'll see how Jock is goin' on. I'll tell him about you and that cussed hawk. You've just about saved us all from swimmin' for it, an' there isn't a man aboard but'll help see you through, if we have to throw that beast an' sit on his head while you gets away.'

They found Jock Crauford, the engineer, working like a nigger.

'Ah've nae time t'talk the noo,' he said abruptly, when the skipper would have explained the position.

'Ay, ay, he can bide here if he'll no' get in the road. Can ye haud a spanner? Weel, see this. Gie me anither ten or fifteen meenits, skipper, an' Ah'll gie ye steam again. I canna dae mair, if she was duntin' hersel' on the shore this meenit. Bit dinna fash me the noo. Hae – you! Tak' a grup o' this!'

Inside his fifteen minutes he was piling the fuel into his furnace and watching the steam rise in the gauge. The tiny steamer came to life again, and her paddles thumped and hammered and thrust her driving through the seas once more. It was none too soon, however, for by the soundings Ned was taking at the finish with a hastily improvised lead-line, and by the shorter and steeper chop of the seas, they knew they were actually verging on the shoals when the welcome word came from the engine- room that all was right again.

The worst was over now. The wind was dropping, and in that shallow water the waves subside almost as quickly as the wind. It was well, too, since about dawn Jock Crauford came up to report that his stock of fuel was running low.

'What d'you think, lad?' said the skipper to Ned. 'Are we safe to put her broadside to it again?'

'We'll give her a good slant in anyway,' said Ned. 'I'll come up in the wheelhouse again, if you like, and tell you when I think it's safe to take the sea abeam. It's dropping fast now.'

'Just wait a minute,' said the skipper, 'and I'll go and see that sergeant's safe in the mess-room. If he's not, I'll have him there mighty quick!'

He marched off, and presently beckoned Ned up to the wheelhouse. Ned took the wheel and for an hour nursed the boat slantingly through the waves, turning her head into them to steady her when she began to develop a roll, swinging her back again at the first chance.

When the cook-steward came to announce breakfast the skipper went to have his, leaving Ned with the mate at the wheel, and saying he'd see the sergeant fed and then send him down to the lower deck aft, so that Ned could go and have his breakfast.

The skipper waited till the sergeant finished his meal, and then gave his orders about going below.

'Very well,' said the sergeant, quietly rising and putting on his cap. 'You command here, skipper. But it's rather a farce, you know, keeping me out of the way like this. Of course, I know my man is on board—'

'Have you seen him? Can you take an oath he is?' demanded the skipper.

'No,' said the sergeant; 'but I'll be able to before he leaves the boat.'

The skipper eyed him savagely.

'I suppose,' he said bitterly, 'you would run a man in just the same if you knew he had saved you and every soul on board last night? If he was the only man in the crowd with enough knowledge to do the right thing in a desperate fix and save the ship goin' ashore?'

'I would suppose,' said the sergeant evenly, 'that it was just as important to save himself as the rest on board.'

The skipper snorted angrily, and the sergeant smiled bleakly.

'You hadn't thought of it that way,' he said, and walked out on deck.

It was just at this moment that Ned, thinking it was safe enough now, and pressed by another urgent message from the engineer, put his wheel over and swung the *Boomerang* broadside to the swell and straight for the entrance to the river. The sergeant was walking back to the steps aft of the paddle-box, when the first beam sea canted the deck sharply. He went down the steep slant with a staggering run, clutched at the rail, missed it, and went reeling overboard.

The skipper saw the whole thing, and in a couple of strides was into the wheel-house.

'Go astern,' he shouted, and banged the gong down to the engine-room. 'Man overboard! The sergeant – that roll caught him!'

Before he had finished speaking, Ned had flung his coat off and was out of the wheel-house. The skipper leaped after him and caught him at the rail.

'Let another man go, lad,' he said. 'He'll recognize you, and then the game's up.'

Without answering, Ned climbed the rail and dived. He was a good swimmer, but in the nasty lop of a sea he found it hard work to make progress. But the sergeant had found it harder, and he was dead beat and sinking as Ned came up with him and seized him. It was another good fifteen minutes before the boat was able to manoeuvre alongside and haul the pair of them on board, and both Ned and the sergeant were utterly exhausted.

An hour later, as the *Boomerang* steamed into comparatively smooth waters, Ned sat on the bunk in the skipper's cabin listening to the urgings of the skipper for him to clear out.

'We'll see he don't interfere wi' you,' said Skipper Boult. 'Any decent white man would let you slide after what you've done for us an' for him. But not that cold-blooded brute. He was pretty far gone when we hauled you aboard, but he wasn't too far gone to look mighty hard at you an' make sure who you was. He'll nail you, right enough, so don't give 'im the chance.'

Ned shook his head.

'It would only get you into trouble,' he said. 'He'd arrest you for helpin' me to bolt, the minute your gang-plank was down ashore. An' he'd use the telegraph all round and get me after all. I might just as well go back wi' him an' have it over.'

Neither of them had heard a light footstep on the deck outside the door as the sergeant stood a minute at the little square of open window. The skipper was renewing his urging when a tap came to the door, and, before either could move, it opened, and the sergeant stepped in and closed it behind him.

'It's a matter of duty with me, and I just want you to listen while I read this out,' he said; and without waiting for any answer, went on to read from the water-smudged paper: 'Ned Underwood, able seaman, assaulted mate and deserted from barque *Chesapeake*. Description: Tall, heavily built, age twenty-four, complexion fair, eyes grey, slight scar back of left hand' – he checked to glance at the hand on the edge of the bunk; Ned made a slight movement to hide it, then let it lie – 'wearing blue serge suit and peaked cap.'

The skipper growled savagely as he finished.

'I've half a mind—' he exploded

The sergeant interrupted him.

'I think you'll agree that the description doesn't fit this man a bit, Captain,' he said briskly, and folded his paper while Ned and the skipper stared at him in surprise. 'I should say he was short and lightly built, and his eyes are – well, brown. We had information this Underwood was on board, but I'll have to go back and report that it was a mistake!'

For a moment there was a tense stillness in the little cabin; the sergeant turned to the door.

'I've a wife and two kids back there,' he said softly. 'I've got my duty to do – to them.'

The skipper of the *Boomerang* dived for his hand, seized it, and pump-handled vigorously.

'Sergeant,' he said, 'you're white. Dash me, an' I thought you was – I apologize! I'm dead sorry! Oh, dash me – lad, where's that bottle?'

from *His Duty* by Boyd Cable (1927)

Sundays at Sea

The routine for Sundays in an HM ship at sea or in harbour went unchanged for two centuries. Hornblower's inspection of his ship's company at Divisions, followed by compulsory church, survived until well after the end of the Second World War. The existence of non-Protestants was recognized by allowing them to attend their own devotions, if available. As the hands fell in for church, the pipe 'Fall out the Roman Catholics' embraced those of Jewish or Islamic beliefs as well. They all doubled away and made themselves scarce, some of them taking advantage of the temporary lapse in discipline to have 'a dry one', as sailors called having a smoke in the heads at a time when smoking was forbidden anywhere.

Hornblower took a last pull at his cigar when he heard the drum beating to divisions. He exhaled a lungful of smoke, his head thrown back, looking out from under the cover of the stern gallery up at the blissful blue sky, and then down at the blue water beneath, with the dazzling white foam surging from under the *Sutherland*'s counter into her wake. Overhead he heard the measured tramp of the marines as they formed up across the poop deck, and then a brief shuffle of heavy boots as they dressed their line in obedience to the captain's order. The patter of hundreds of pairs of feet acted as a subdued accompaniment as the crew formed up round the decks. When everything had fallen still again Hornblower pitched his cigar overboard, hitched his full dress coat into position, settled his cocked hat on his head, and walked with dignity, his left hand on his swordhilt, forward to the halfdeck and up the companion ladder to the quarterdeck. Bush was there, and Crystal, and the midshipman of the watch. They saluted him, and from farther aft came the snick-snack-snick of the marines presenting arms.

*

Ten days of hard work, of constant drill, of unsleeping supervision, of justice tempered by good humour, had done much to settle the hands to their duty. He had had to order five floggings three days ago, forcing himself to stand apparently unmoved while the whistle and crack of the cat o' nine tails sickened his stomach. One of those floggings might do a little good to the recipient – an old hand who had apparently forgotten what he had learned and needed a sharp reminder of it. The other four would do none to the men whose backs had been lacerated; they would never make good sailors and were mere brutes whom brutal treatment could at least make no worse. He had sacrificed them to show the wilder spirits what might happen as a result of inattention to orders – it was only by an actual demonstration that one could work on the minds of uneducated men. The dose had to be prescribed with the utmost accuracy, neither too great nor too small. He seemed, so his sweeping glance told him, to have hit it off exactly.

Once more he looked round to enjoy the beauty of it all – the orderly ship, the white sails, the blue sky; the scarlet and pipeclay of the marines, the blue and gold of the officers; and there was consummate artistry in the subtle indications that despite the inspection the real pulsating life of the ship was going on beneath it. Where four hundred and more men stood at attention awaiting his lightest word, the quartermaster at the wheel kept his mind on the binnacle and the leach of the main course, the lookouts at the masthead and the officer of the watch with his telescope were living demonstrations of the fact that the ship must still be sailed and the King's service carried on.

*

Hornblower passed on down the line, scanning each man closely. Faces well remembered, faces it was still an effort to put a name to. Faces that he had studied two years back in the far Pacific on board the *Lydia*, faces he had first seen when Gerard brought back his boat-load of bewildered captures from St Ives. Swarthy faces and pale, boys and elderly men, blue eyes, brown eyes, grey eyes. A host of tiny impressions were collecting in Hornblower's mind; they would be digested together later during his solitary walks in the stern gallery, to form the raw material for the plans he would make to further the efficiency of his crew.

*

'That man Simms ought to be rated captain of the mizzen-top. He's old enough now. What's this man's name? Dawson? No, Dawkins. He's looking sulky. One of Goddard's gang – it looks as if he's still resenting Goddard's flogging. I must remember that.'

The sun blazed down upon them, while the ship lifted and swooped over the gentle sea. From the crew he turned his attention to the ship – the breechings of the guns, the way the falls were flemished down, the cleanliness of the decks, the galley and the forecastle. At all this he need only pretend to look – the skies would fall before Bush neglected his duty. But he had to go through with it, with a show of solemnity. Men were oddly influenced – the poor fools would work better for Bush if they thought Hornblower was keeping an eye on him, and they would work better for Hornblower if they thought he inspected the ship thoroughly. This wretched business of capturing men's devotion set Hornblower smiling cynically when he was unobserved.

'A good inspection, Mr Bush,' said Hornblower, returning to the quarterdeck. 'The ship is in better order than I hoped for. I shall expect the improvement to continue. You may rig the church now.'

It was a Godfearing Admiralty who ordered church service every Sunday morning, otherwise Hornblower would have dispensed with it, as befitted a profound student of Gibbon. As it was, he had managed to evade having a chaplain on board – Hornblower hated parsons. He watched the men dragging up mess stools for themselves, and chairs for the officers. They were working diligently and cheerfully, although not with quite that disciplined purposefulness which characterized a fully trained crew. His coxswain Brown covered the compass box on the quarterdeck with a cloth, and laid on it, with due solemnity, Hornblower's Bible and prayer book. Hornblower disliked these services; there was always the chance that some devout member of his compulsory congregation might raise objections to having to attend – Catholic or Nonconformist. Religion was the only power which could ever pit itself against the bonds of discipline; Hornblower remembered a theologically minded master's mate who had once protested against his reading the Benediction, as though he, the King's representative at sea – God's representative, when all was said and done – could not read a Benediction if he chose!

He glowered at the men as they settled down, and began to read. As the thing had to be done, it might as well be done well, and, as ever, while he read he was struck once more by the beauty of Cranmer's prose and the deftness of his adaptation. Cranmer had been burned alive two hundred and fifty years before – did it benefit him at all to have his prayer book read now?

Bush read the lessons in a tuneless bellow as if he were hailing the foretop. Then Hornblower read the opening lines of the hymn, and Sullivan the fiddler played the first bars of the tune. Bush gave the signal for the singing to start – Hornblower could never bring himself to do that; he told himself he was neither a mountebank nor an Italian opera conductor – and the crew opened their throats and roared it out.

But even hymn singing had its advantages. A captain could often discover a good deal about the spirits of his crew by the way they sang their hymns. This morning either the hymn chosen was specially popular or the crew were happy in the new sunshine, for they were singing lustily, with Sullivan sawing away at an ecstatic obbligato on his fiddle. The Cornishmen among the crew apparently knew the hymn well, and fell upon it with a will, singing in parts to add a leavening of harmony to the tuneless bellowings of the others. It all meant nothing to Hornblower – one tune was the same as another to his tone-deaf ear, and the most beautiful music was to him no more than comparable with the noise of a cart along a gravel road. As he listened to the unmeaning din, and gazed at the hundreds of gaping mouths, he found himself wondering as usual whether or not there was any basis of fact in this legend of music – whether other people actually heard something more than mere noise, or whether he was the only person on board not guilty of wilful self-deception.

Then he saw a ship's boy in the front row. The hymn meant something to him, a least. He was weeping broken-heartedly, even while he tried to keep his back straight and to conceal his emotions, with the big tears running down his cheeks and his nose all beslobbered. The poor little devil had been touched in one way or another – some chord of memory had been struck. Perhaps the last time he had heard that hymn was in the little church at home, beside his mother and brothers. He was homesick and heartbroken now. Hornblower was glad for his sake as well as for his own when the hymn came to an end; the next ceremony would steady the boy again.

He took up the Articles of War and began to read them as the Lords

Commissioners of the Admiralty had ordained should be done each Sunday in every one of His Britannic Majesty's Ships. He knew the solemn sentences by heart at this, his five hundredth reading, every cadence, every turn of phrase, and he read them well. This was better than any vague religious service or Thirty Nine Articles. Here was a code in black and white, a stern, unemotional call to duty pure and simple. Some Admiralty clerk or pettifogging lawyer had had a gift of phrasing just as felicitous as Cranmer's. There was no trumpet-call about it, no clap-trap appeal to sentiment; there was merely the cold logic of the code which kept the British Navy at sea, and which had guarded England during seventeen years of a struggle for life. He could tell by the death-like stillness of his audience as he read that their attention had been caught and held, and when he folded the paper away and looked up he could see solemn, set faces. The ship's boy in the front row had forgotten his tears. There was a far away look in his eyes; obviously he was making good resolutions to attend more strictly to his duty in future. Or perhaps he was dreaming wild dreams of the time to come when he could be a captain in a gold-laced coat commanding a seventy- four, or of brave deeds which he would do.

In a sudden revulsion of feeling Hornblower wondered if lofty sentiment would armour the boy against cannon shot – he remembered another ship's boy who had been smashed into a red jam before his eyes by a shot from the *Natividad.*

from *A Ship of the Line* by C. S. Forester (1938)

Mutiny on the High Seas

The events surrounding the Captain of HMS *Bounty* being cast adrift with nineteen men in a 23-foot sailing launch off Tofoa in the Friendly Islands in April 1789 have been the subject of more controversy and conflicting evidence in print than any other milestone in the Royal Navy's history. Unfortunately, artistic licence has distorted the general view of the episode's central character, Captain Bligh, casting him as a brutal tyrant of the worst extreme, administering summary justice while in command of a private ship (one on independent service, far from the overriding authority of a Flag Officer). Both Charles Laughton and Trevor Howard have played him in films as a sadistic monster who gets what he deserves by provoking the mutiny led by Fletcher Christian, his Master's Mate (assistant navigator and watchkeeping officer).

Serious historians, however, have now put the record straight. By the standards of the day, they maintain, Bligh, if anything, erred on the soft side in administering punishments. This view seems to be borne out by the court-martials of the *Bounty* mutineers held in September 1792, presided over by Admiral Lord Hood, Commander-in-Chief of the Fleet at Spithead. Of the ten men who went on trial for their lives, four were acquitted outright and two recommended for the Royal Mercy, which was promptly given. During the trial, Bligh was portrayed as a mean, inhumane captain, not over-concerned with the welfare of his men, given to *ad hoc* restrictions on food rations, aided and abetted by his swindling clerk, John Samuel. A sign of his unpredictable moods was that he was forever wrongly accusing his men of petty theft and other more serious misdemeanours. At no point, however, was the defence entered that the mutiny had been triggered off by the sort of sadistic behaviour attributed to Bligh in the two feature films and in the novel that inspired them.

Mutiny on the Bounty was written in 1932 by Charles Nordhoff and James Norman Hall, who had been Army comrades in the First World War and who were both contributors to the American magazine *Atlantic Monthly*. In the 1920s they had retreated to live in Tahiti, where they wrote their classic book – clearly under the same seductive allure of the islands and their attractive inhabitants which they reasoned to have underlain the mutineers' impulsive action. This assumption predicated a few serious departures from historical fact – but who can say that their tale is not the better for it?

The element of fiction immediately becomes apparent when one compares the *Bounty*'s crew-list in the novel with those who actually served under Bligh. Although there is only one substitution, it is an important one. The authors introduced a fictional hero, Roger Byam, in place of Midshipman Peter Heywood. The latter was one of the two against whom the evidence – including being seen with a cutlass in his hand on the day of the mutiny – was inconclusive enough to enable him to come out of the Spithead court-martial with a Royal Pardon. He went on to attain command in the Royal Navy, and carried to the grave a dark secret, variously thought to have been that there was a homosexual relationship between Bligh and Fletcher Christian, or that the latter had syphilis. The Hays Office was not ready for such seamy matters in 1932, so Heywood was dropped from the novel and Nordhoff and Hall rewrote history by introducing the fictional Byam. The inclusion of a new hero allowed them scope for the additional box-office attraction of his skinny-dipping with the chieftain's daughter – and all that inevitably followed in the fragrant moonlight – after Bligh had put him ashore to compile an English dictionary of the local language. He is the hero of this exciting yarn about life in a ship in the largely uncharted Pacific while Nelson was kicking his heels on half-pay in Norfolk.

Here is Roger Byam's first-hand account of the irrevocable steps taken by the mutineers towards becoming fugitives from the long arm of the Royal Navy:

'That's it! Seize him up! Give him a taste of his own poison!'

'Flay the hide off him!'

'Silence!' Christian called, sternly; and then, to Bligh: 'We'll give you justice, sir, which is more than you have ever given us. We'll take you in irons to England . . .'

A dozen protesting voices interrupted him.

'To England? Never! We won't have it, Mr Christian!'

Immediately the deck was again in an uproar, all the mutineers clamouring against Christian's proposal. Never was the situation with respect to Bligh so critical as at that moment, and it was to his credit that he showed no sign of flinching. The men were in a savage mood, and it was touch and go as to whether he would be shot where he stood; but he glared at each of them in turn as though challenging them to do so. Luckily a diversion was created when Ellison came dashing up flourishing a bayonet. There was no real harm in this lad, but he loved mischief better than his dinner, and, being thoughtless and high-spirited, he could be counted upon to get himself into trouble whenever the opportunity presented itself. Evidently he considered joining in a mutiny nothing more than a fine lark, and he now came dancing up to Bligh with such a comical expression upon his face that the tension was relieved at once. The men broke into cheers. 'Hooray, Tommy! Are you with us, lad?'

'Let me guard him, Mr Christian!' he cried. 'I'll watch him like a cat!' He skipped up and down in front of Bligh, brandishing his weapon. 'Oh, you rogue! You old villain! You'd flog us, would you? You'd stop our grog, would you? You'd make us eat grass, would you?'

The men cheered him wildly. 'Lay on, lad!' they shouted. 'We'll back you! Give him a jab in the guts!'

'You and your Mr Samuel! A pair of swindlers, that's what you are! Cheating us out of our food! You've made a pretty penny between you! You old thief! You should be a bumboat man. I'll lay you'd make your fortune in no time!'

It was a bitter experience for Bligh to be baited thus by the least of his seamen, but as a matter of fact nothing more fortunate for him could have happened. His life at that moment hung in the balance, and Ellison, in giving vent to his feelings, relieved the pent-up emotions of men who were not glib of speech and could express their hatred of Bligh only in action. Christian realized this, I think, and permitted Ellison to speak his mind, but he soon cut him short and put him in his place.

'Clear the cutter!' he called. 'Mr Churchill!'

'Aye, aye, sir!'

'Fetch up Mr Fryer and Mr Purcell! Burkitt!'

'Here, sir!'

'You and Sumner and Mills and Martin – stand guard here over Mr Bligh!'

Burkitt took the end of the line in one of his huge hairy fists.

'We'll mind him, sir! I'll lay to that!'

'What's your plan, Mr Christian? We've a right to know,' said Sumner. Christian turned quickly and looked at him. 'Mind what you're about, Sumner!' he said quietly. 'I'm master of this ship! Lively, men, with the cutter.'

Several men climbed into the boat to clear out the yams, sweet potatoes, and other ship's stores which were kept there, while others unlashed it and got ready the tackle for hoisting it over the side. Burkitt stood directly in front of Captain Bligh, holding the point of a bayonet within an inch of his breast. Sumner stood behind him with his musket at ready, and the other men on either side. Thompson excepted, they were the hardest characters among the sailors, and Bligh wisely said nothing to arouse them further. Others of the mutineers were stationed about the decks, and there were three at each of the ladderways. I wondered how the affair had been so well and secretly planned. I searched my memory, but could recall no incident of a character in the least suspicious.

I had been so intent in watching the scene of which Bligh was the centre that I had forgotten Stewart. We had become separated, and while I was searching for him Christian saw me for the first time. He came at once to where I was standing. His voice was calm, but I could see that he was labouring under great excitement.

'Byam, this is my affair,' he said. 'Not a man shall be hurt, but if any take part against us it will be at the peril of the entire ship's company. Act as you think best.'

'What do you mean to do?' I asked.

'I would have carried Bligh to England as a prisoner. That is impossible; the men won't have it. He shall have the cutter to go where he chooses. Mr Fryer, Hayward, Hallet, and Samuel shall go with him.'

There was no time for further talk. Churchill came up with the master and Purcell. The carpenter, as usual, was surly and taciturn. Both he and Fryer were horror-stricken at what had happened, but they were entirely self-possessed. Christian well knew that these two men would seize the first opportunity, if one presented itself, for retaking the ship, and he had them well guarded.

'Mr Byam, surely you are not concerned in this?' Fryer asked.

'No more than yourself, sir,' I replied.

'Mr Byam has nothing to do with it,' said Christian. 'Mr Purcell . . .'

Fryer interrupted him.

'In God's name, Mr Christian! What is it you do? Do you realize that this means the ruin of everything? Give up this madness, and I promise that we shall all make your interest our own. Only let us reach England . . .'

'It is too late, Mr Fryer,' he replied, coldly. 'I have been in hell for weeks past, and I mean to stand it no longer.'

'Your difficulties with Captain Bligh give you no right to bring ruin upon the rest of us.'

'Hold your tongue, sir,' said Christian. 'Mr Purcell, have your men fetch up the thwarts, knees, and gear bolts for the large cutter. Churchill, let the carpenter go below to see to this. Send a guard with him.'

Purcell and Churchill went down the forward ladderway.

'Do you mean to set us adrift?' Fryer asked.

'We are no more than nine leagues from the land here,' Christian replied. 'In so calm a sea Mr Bligh will have no difficulty in making it.'

'I will stay with the ship.'

'No, Mr Fryer; you will go with Captain Bligh. Williams! Take the master to his cabin while he collects his clothes. He is to be kept there until I send word.'

Fryer requested earnestly to be allowed to remain with the vessel, but Christian well knew his reason for desiring this and would not hear to the proposal. He put an end to the matter by sending the master below.

Purcell now returned, followed by Norman and McIntosh, his mates, carrying the gear for the cutter. Purcell came up to me at once.

'Mr Byam, I know that you have no hand in this business. But you are, or have been, a friend to Mr Christian. Beg him to give Captain Bligh the launch. The cutter is rotten and will never swim to the land.'

This, I knew, was the case. The cutter was riddled with worms and leaked so badly as to be almost useless. The carpenters were to have started repairing her that same morning. Purcell would not come with me to speak of the matter, giving as a reason Christian's dislike of him. 'He would not care to grant any request of mine,' he said. 'If the cutter is hoisted out, it will be almost certain death for Captain Bligh and all who are permitted to go with him.'

I wasted no time, but went to Christian at once. Several of the mutineers gathered round to hear what I had to say. Christian agreed at once. 'He shall have the launch,' he said. 'Tell the carpenter to have his men fit her.' He then called, 'Leave off with the cutter, my lads! Clear the launch.'

There were immediate protests, led by Churchill, against this new arrangement.

'The launch, Mr Christian?'

'Don't let him have it, sir! The old fox'll get home in her!'

'She's too bloody good for him!'

There was an argument over the matter, but Christian forced his will upon the others. In fact, they made no determined stand. All were eager to be rid of the captain, and they had little reason to fear that he would ever see England again.

The mutineers were in such complete control of the situation that Christian now gave orders for the rest of those who were not of his party to be brought on deck. Samuel, Bligh's clerk, was among the first to appear. He was anything but a favourite with the ship's company, and was greeted with jeers and threats by his particular enemies. I had supposed that he would make a poor showing in such a situation. On the contrary, he acted with spirit and determination. Disregarding the insults of the sailors, he went directly to Captain Bligh to receive his orders. He was permitted to go to Bligh's cabin with John Smith, the captain's servant, to fetch up his clothes. They helped him on with his boots and trousers and laid his coat over his shoulders.

I saw Hayward and Hallet standing aft by the rail. Hallet was crying, and both of them were in a state of great alarm. Someone touched my shoulder and I found Mr Nelson standing beside me.

'Well, Byam, I'm afraid that we're even farther from home than we thought. Do you know what they plan to do with us?'

I told him the little I knew. He smiled ruefully, glancing toward the island of Tofoa, now a faint blur on the horizon.

'I suppose that Captain Bligh will take us there,' he said. 'I don't much relish the prospect of meeting any more Friendly Islanders. Their friendliness is of a kind that we can well dispense with.'

The carpenter appeared at the ladderway, followed by Robert Lamb, the butcher, who was helping to bring up his tool chest.

'Mr Nelson,' he said, 'we know whom we have to thank for this.'

'Yes, Mr Purcell, our unlucky stars,' Nelson replied.

'No sir! We have Captain Bligh to thank for it, and him alone! He has brought it upon us all by his damnable behaviour!'

Purcell had the deepest hatred for Bligh, which was returned with interest. The two men had not spoken for months save when absolutely necessary. Nevertheless, when Mr Nelson suggested that he might be permitted to stay with the ship if he chose, the carpenter was horrified.

'Stop aboard? With rogues and pirates? Never, sir! I shall follow my commander.'

At this moment Churchill, who was everywhere about the decks, caught sight of us.

'What are you about there, Purcell? Damn your blood! You'd steal our tools, would you?'

'Your tools, you scoundrel? They're mine, and they go where I go!'

'You shan't take a nail from the ship if I have my way,' Churchill replied. He then called out to Christian, and there was another argument, not only with respect to the tool chest, but as to the carpenter himself. Christian was partly in the mind to keep him on the vessel, knowing his value as a craftsman, but all the others urged against it. Purcell had a violent temper and was regarded by the men as a tyrant second only to Bligh.

'He's a damned old villain, sir!'

'Keep the carpenter's mates, Mr Christian. They're the men for us.'

'Make him go in the boat!'

'Make me go, you pirates?' he cried. 'I'd like to see the man who'll *stop* me!'

Unfortunately, Purcell was as thick-headed as he was fearless, and he now so far forgot the interest of Bligh's party as to boast of what we would do as soon as we should be clear of the mutineers.

'Mark my word, you rogues! We'll bring every man of you to justice! We'll build a vessel to carry us home . . .'

'So he will, Mr Christian, if we give him his tools,' several men shouted.

'The old fox could build a ship with a clasp knife!'

Purcell realized too late what he had done. I believe that Christian would have given him many of his tools, of which there were duplicates on board, but having been reminded of what he might do with them, he now ordered the tool chest to be taken below, and Purcell was permitted to have nothing but a hand saw, a small axe, a hammer, and a bag of nails. Bligh, who had overheard all that was said, could contain himself no longer. 'You infernal idiot!' he roared at Purcell, and was prevented from saying more by Burkitt, who place a bayonet at his throat.

The decks were now filled with people, but Christian took good care that those not of his party should be prevented from coming together in any numbers. As soon as the launch had been cleared, he ordered the boatswain to swing her out. 'And mind yourself, Mr Cole! If you spring a yard or carry anything away it will go hard with you!' Fifteen or more of us were ordered to assist him, for the mutineers were too canny to lay aside their arms and bear a hand.

'Foresail and mainsail there! All ready?'

'Aye, aye, sir!'

'Let go sheets and tacks!'

'All clear, sir!'

'Clew garnets – up with the clews!'

The breeze was still so light as barely to fill the sails, and the clews of the mainsail and foresail went smoothly up to the quarters of the yards. The yards were now squared and the braces made fast, and with half a dozen men holding the launch inboard she was hoisted, swung out over the bulwarks, and lowered away.

One of the first men ordered into her was Samuel. Hayward and Hallet followed next. Both were shedding tears and crying for mercy, and they were half carried to the gangway. Hayward turned to Christian, clasping his hands imploringly.

'Mr Christian, what have I ever done that you should treat me so?' he exclaimed. 'In God's name, permit me to stay with the ship!'

'We can dispense with your services here,' Christian replied, grimly. 'Into the boat, the pair of you!'

Purcell went next. He required no urging. I think he would have died rather than remain in the ship now that she had been seized by mutineers. His few tools were handed down to him by the boatswain, who followed. Christian ordered Bligh to be brought to the gangway, and his hands were freed.

'Now, Mr Bligh, there is your boat, and you are fortunate to have the launch and not the cutter. Go into her at once, sir!'

'Mr Christian,' said Bligh, 'for the last time I beg you to reflect! I'll pawn my honour – I pledge you my word never to think of this again if you will desist. Consider my wife and family!'

'No, Mr Bligh. You should have thought of your family long before this, and we well know what your honour is worth. Go into the boat, sir!'

Seeing that all pleading was useless, Bligh obeyed, and was followed by Mr Peckover and Norton, the quartermaster. Christian then handed down a sextant and a book of nautical tables.

'You have your compass, sir. This book is sufficient for every purpose, and the sextant is my own. You know it to be a good one.'

*

Coleman and I sought out Christian, who was standing by one of the cabin gratings, out of sight of the launch. We begged him to let Bligh have some muskets and ammunition.

'Never!' he said. 'They shall have no firearms.'

'Then give them some cutlasses at least, Mr Christian,' Coleman urged, 'unless you wish them to be murdered the moment they set foot on shore. Think of our experience at Namuka!'

Christian consented to this. He ordered Churchill to fetch some cutlasses from the arms chest, and a moment later he returned with four, which were handed into the boat. Meanwhile, Morrison had taken advantage of this opportunity to run below for some additional provisions for the launch. He and John Millward brought up a mess kid filled with pieces of salt pork, several calabashes of water, and some additional bottles of wine and spirits, which they lowered into the boat.

'You cowards!' Purcell shouted, as the cutlasses were handed in. 'Will you give us nothing but these?'

'Shall we lower the arms chest, carpenter?' William Brown asked, jeeringly. McCoy threatened him with his musket. 'You'll get a bellyful of lead in a minute,' he shouted.

'Bear off and turn one of the swivels on 'em!' someone else called. 'Give 'em a whiff of grape!'

Burkitt now raised his musket and pointed it at Bligh. Alexander Smith, who was standing beside him, seized the barrel of the musket and thrust it up. I am convinced that Burkitt meant to shoot Bligh, but Christian, observing this, ordered him to be dragged back, deprived of his arms, and placed under guard. He made a terrific struggle, and it required four men to disarm him.

Meanwhile, Fryer and others were urging Bligh to cast off lest they should all be murdered. This Bligh now ordered to be done, and the launch dropped slowly astern. The oars were gotten out, and the boat, so low in the water that she seemed on the point of foundering, was headed toward the island of Tofoa, which bore northeast, about ten leagues distant. Twelve men made a good load for the launch. She now carried nineteen, to say nothing of the food and water and the gear of the men.

'Thank God we were too late to go with her, Byam!'

Morrison was standing beside me.

'Do you mean that?' I asked.

He was silent for a moment, as though considering the matter carefully. Then he said, 'No, I don't. I would willingly have taken my chance in her – but it's a slim chance indeed. They'll never see England again.'

Tinkler was sitting on a thwart. Mr Nelson, and Peckover, the gunner, and Elphinstone, the master's mate, and all of the others – they were as good as dead – more than a thousand leagues from any port where they might expect help. About them were islands filled with the cruellest of savages, who could be held at bay only by men well armed. Granted that some might escape death at the hands of the Indians, what chance had so tiny a boat, so appallingly loaded, to reach any civilized port? The possibility was so remote as to be not worth considering.

Sick at heart, I turned away from the sight of the frail craft, looking so small, so helpless, on that great waste of waters. There had been a cheer from some of the mutineers: 'Huzza for Tahiti!' as Christian had ordered, 'Get sail on her!' Ellison, McCoy, and Williams had run aloft to loose the fore-topgallant sail. Afterward a silence had fallen over the ship, and the men stood by the bulwarks, gazing at the launch growing smaller and smaller as we drew away from her. Christian, too, was watching, standing where I had last seen him, by the cabin grating. What his thoughts were at this time it would be impossible to say. His sense of the wrongs he had suffered at Bligh's hands was so deep and overpowering as to dominate, I believe, every other feeling. In the course of a long life I have met no others of his kind. I knew him, I suppose, as well as anyone could be said to know him, and yet I never felt that I truly understood the workings of his mind and heart. Men of such passionate nature, when goaded by injustice into action, lose all sense of anything save their own misery. They neither know nor care, until it is too late, what ruin they make of the lives of others.

It was getting on toward eight o'clock when the launch had been cast off. Shortly afterward the breeze, from the northeast, freshened, and the *Bounty* gathered way quietly, slipping through the water with a slight hiss of foam. The launch became a mere speck, seen momentarily as she rose to the swell or as the sunlight flashed from her oars. Within half an hour she had vanished as though swallowed up by the sea. Our course was west-northwest.

from *Mutiny on the Bounty* by Charles Nordhoff and James Norman Hall (1932)

Nordhoff and Hall saved the famous 3,600-mile trip in the open boat to Timor for a follow-up novel, *Men Against the Sea*.

The Hardest Man in the Sealing Trade

The opening chapter of *The Sea-Wolf*, Jack London's 1904 classic about seal-hunters in the Bering Sea, bears some resemblance to Rudyard Kipling's *Captains Courageous*, first published seven years previously. In Kipling's tale a railroad baron's young Ivy League son falls overboard from a transatlantic liner after smoking a cigar too strong for his unaccustomed stomach and his sense of balance. His rescue in fog by a Grand Banks fishing schooner, and the ensuing weeks spent as an involuntary member of her crew, make a man of him.

So it is in London's novel with Humphrey Van Weyden, a thirty-five-year-old intellectual, critic and lecturer, returning to San Francisco in the ferry-boat from Sausalito after a regular summer weekend with another literary dilettante. When a thick fog descends, the ferry is abruptly run down and sunk. Our hero is picked up by the 90-foot seal-hunting schooner *Ghost*, outward-bound for Japanese waters under the command of the notorious Wolf Larsen, a Nietzschean super-brute who thinks nothing of snuffing out a life in the process of keeping his crew in line. That morning he has killed his mate for returning unfit for duty after a last debauch on shore and is consequently rewriting the Watch Bill by *ad hoc* promotions. Van Weyden – 'Hump', as Larsen calls him – is impressed as cabin-boy to working under the odious Cockney cook, Tom Mugridge, as servant to those who mess aft with the Captain.

Wolf Larsen soon reveals an unexpected side to his nature. A self-taught, well-read man, he enjoys obtuse philosophical arguments with the new cabin-boy in between bouts of enforcing discipline through his terrifying paroxysms of rage. After one such fury, the new mate disappears overboard, and Van Weyden finds himself in his shoes.

Once they reach the seal herds north of Japan, all six boats are launched every day, each manned by a hunter and two others, leaving *Ghost* with just the Captain, her unqualified Mate and useless cook on board. An abrupt change in the weather could mean trouble.

> I remember one beautiful day, when the boats left early and the reports of the hunters' guns grew dim and distant and died away as they scattered far and wide over the sea. There was just the faintest wind from the westward; but it breathed its last by the time we managed to get to leeward of the last lee boat. One by one – I was at the masthead and saw – the six boats disappeared over the bulge of the earth as they followed the seal into the west. We lay, scarcely

rolling on the placid sea, unable to follow. Wolf Larsen was apprehensive. The barometer was down, and the sky to the east did not please him. He studied it with unceasing vigilance.

'If she comes out of there,' he said, 'hard and snappy, putting us to windward of the boats, it's likely there'll be empty bunks in steerage and fo'c'sle.'

By eleven o'clock the sea had become glass. By midday, though we were well up in the northerly latitudes, the heat was sickening. There was no freshness in the air. It was sultry and oppressive, reminding me of what the old Californians term 'earthquake weather'. There was something ominous about it, and in intangible ways one was made to feel that the worst was about to come. Slowly the whole eastern sky filled with clouds that over-towered us like some black sierra of the infernal regions. So clearly could one see cañon, gorge, and precipice, and the shadows that lie therein, that one looked unconsciously for the white surf-line and bellowing caverns where the sea charges on the land. And still we rocked gently, and there was no wind.

'It's no squall,' Wolf Larsen said. 'Old Mother Nature's going to get up on her hind legs and howl for all that's in her, and it'll keep us jumping, Hump, to pull through with half our boats. You'd better run up and loosen the topsails.'

'But if it's going to howl, and there are only two of us?' I asked, a note of protest in my voice.

'Why we've got to make the best of the first of it and run down to our boats before our canvas is ripped out of us. After that I don't give a rap what happens. The sticks'll stand it, and you and I will have to, though we've plenty cut out for us.'

Still the calm continued. We ate dinner, a hurried and anxious meal for me with eighteen men abroad on the sea and beyond the bulge of the earth, and with that heaven-rolling mountain range of clouds moving slowly down upon us. Wolf Larsen did not seem affected, however; though I noticed, when we returned to the deck, a slight twitching of the nostrils, a perceptible quickness of movement. His face was stern, the lines of it had grown hard, and yet in his eyes – blue, clear blue this day – there was a strange brilliancy, a bright scintillating light. It struck me that he was joyous, in a ferocious sort of way; that he was glad there was an impending struggle; that he was thrilled and upborne with knowledge that one of the great moments of living, when the tide of life surges up in flood, was upon him.

Once, and unwitting that he did so or that I saw, he laughed aloud, mockingly and defiantly, at the advancing storm. I see him yet standing there like a pygmy out of the *Arabian Nights* before the huge front of some malignant genie. He was daring destiny, and he was unafraid.

He walked to the galley. 'Cooky, by the time you've finished pots and pans you'll be wanted on deck. Stand ready for a call.'

'Hump,' he said, becoming cognizant of the fascinated gaze I bent upon him, 'this beats whisky and is where your Omar Khayyám misses. I think he only half lived after all.'

The western half of the sky had by now grown murky. The sun had dimmed and faded out of sight. It was two in the afternoon, and a ghostly twilight, shot through by wandering purplish lights, had descended upon us. In their purplish light Wolf Larsen's face glowed and glowed, and to my excited fancy he appeared encircled by a halo. We lay in the midst of an unearthly quiet, while all about us were signs and omens of oncoming sound and movement. The sultry heat had become unendurable. The sweat was standing on my forehead, and I could feel it trickling down my nose. I felt as though I should faint, and reached out to the rail for support.

And then, just then, the faintest possible whisper of air passed by. It was from the east, and like a whisper it came and went. The drooping canvas was not stirred, and yet my face had felt the air and been cooled.

'Cooky,' Wolf Larsen called in a low voice. Thomas Mugridge turned a pitiable scared face. 'Let go that foreboom tackle and pass it across, and when she's willing let go the sheet and come in snug with the tackle. And if you make a mess of it, it will be the last you ever make. Understand?

'Mr Van Weyden, stand by to pass the head-sails over. Then jump for the topsails and spread them as quick as God'll let you – the quicker you do it the easier you'll find it. As for Cooky, if he isn't lively bat him between the eyes.'

I was aware of the compliment and pleased, in that no threat had accompanied my instructions. We were lying head to north-west, and it was his intention to jibe over all with the first puff.

'We'll have the breeze on our quarter,' he explained to me. 'By the last guns the boats were bearing away slightly to the south'ard.'

He turned and walked aft to the wheel. I went forward and took my station at the jibs. Another whisper of wind, and another, passed by. The canvas flapped lazily.

'Thank Gawd she's not comin' all of a bunch, Mr Van Weyden,' was the Cockney's fervent ejaculation.

And I was indeed thankful, for I had by this time learned enough to know, with all our canvas spread, what disaster in such event awaited us. The whispers of wind became puffs, the sails filled, the *Ghost* moved. Wolf Larsen put the wheel hard up, to port, and we began to pay off. The wind was now dead astern, muttering and puffing stronger and stronger, and my head-sails were pounding lustily. I did not see what went on elsewhere, though I felt the sudden surge and heel of the schooner as the wind-pressures changed to the jibing of the fore- and main-sails. My hands were full with the flying-jib, jib, and staysail; and by the time this part of my task was accomplished the *Ghost* was leaping into the southwest, the wind on her quarter and all her sheets to starboard. Without pausing for breath, though my heart was beating like a trip-hammer from my exertions, I sprang to the topsails, and before the wind had become too strong we had them fairly set and were coiling down. Then I went aft for orders.

Wolf Larsen nodded approval and relinquished the wheel to me. The wind was strengthening steadily and the sea rising. For an hour I steered, each moment becoming more difficult. I had not the experience to steer at the gait we were going on a quartering course.

'Now take a run up with the glasses and raise some of the boats. We've made at least ten knots, and we're going twelve or thirteen now. The old girl knows how to walk.'

I contented myself with the fore crosstrees, some seventy feet above the deck. As I searched the vacant stretch of water before me, I comprehended thoroughly the need for haste if we were to recover any of our men. Indeed, as I gazed at the heavy sea through which we were running, I doubted that there was a boat afloat. It did not seem possible that such frail craft could survive such stress of wind and water.

I could not feel the full force of the wind, for we were running with it; but from my lofty perch I looked down as though outside the *Ghost* and apart from her, and saw the shape of her outlined sharply against the foaming sea as she tore along instinct with life. Sometimes she would lift and send across some great wave, burying her starboard-rail from view, and covering her deck to the hatches with the boiling ocean. At such moments, starting from a windward roll, I would go flying through the air with dizzying swiftness, as though I clung to the end of a huge, inverted pendulum, the arc of which, between the greater rolls, must have been seventy feet or more. Once, the terror of this giddy sweep overpowered me, and for a while I clung on, hand and foot, weak and trembling, unable to search the sea for the missing boats or to behold aught of the sea but that which roared beneath and strove to overwhelm the *Ghost*.

But the thought of the men in the midst of it steadied me, and in my quest for them I forgot myself. For an hour I saw nothing but the naked, desolate sea. And then where a vagrant shaft of sunlight struck the ocean and turned its surface to wrathful silver, I caught a small black speck thrust skyward for an instant and swallowed up. I waited patiently. Again the tiny point of black projected itself through the wrathful blaze a couple of points off our port-bow. I did not attempt to shout, but communicated the news to Wolf Larsen by waving my arm. He changed the course, and I signalled affirmation when the speck showed dead ahead.

It grew larger, and so swiftly that for the first time I fully appreciated the speed of our flight. Wolf Larsen motioned for me to come down, and when I stood beside him at the wheel gave me instructions for heaving to.

'Expect all hell to break loose,' he cautioned me, 'but don't mind it. Yours is to do your own work and to have Cooky stand by the fore-sheet.'

I managed to make my way forward, but there was little choice of sides, for the weather-rail seemed buried as often as the lee. Having instructed Thomas Mugridge as to what he was to do, I clambered into the fore-rigging a few feet. The boat was now very close, and I could make out plainly that it was lying head to wind and sea and dragging on its mast and sail, which had been thrown overboard and made to serve as a sea-anchor. The three men were bailing. Each rolling mountain whelmed them from view, and I would wait with sickening anxiety, fearing that they would never appear again. Then, and with black suddenness, the boat would shoot clear through the foaming crest, bow pointed to the sky, and the whole length of her bottom showing, wet and dark, till she seemed on end. There would be a fleeting glimpse of the three men flinging water in frantic haste, when she would topple over and fall into the yawning valley, bow down and showing her full inside length to the stern upreared almost directly above the bow. Each time that she reappeared was a miracle.

The *Ghost* suddenly changed her course, keeping away, and it came to me with a shock that Wolf Larsen was giving up the rescue as impossible. Then I realized that he was preparing to heave to, and dropped to the deck to be in readiness. We were now dead before the wind, the boat far away and abreast of us. I felt an abrupt easing of the schooner, a loss for the moment of all strain and pressure, coupled with a swift acceleration of speed. She was rushing around on her heel into the wind.

As she arrived at right angles to the sea, the full force of the wind (from which we had hitherto run away) caught us. I was unfortunately and ignorantly facing it. It stood up against me like a wall, filling my lungs with air which I could not expel. And as I choked and strangled, and as the *Ghost* wallowed for an instant, broadside on and rolling straight over and far into the wind, I beheld a huge sea rise far above my head. I turned aside, caught my breath, and looked again. The wave overtopped the *Ghost* and I gazed sheer up and into it. A shaft of sunlight smote the over-curl, and I caught a glimpse of translucent, rushing green, backed by a milky smother of foam.

Then it descended, pandemonium broke loose, everything happened at once. I was struck a crushing, stunning blow, nowhere in particular and yet everywhere. My hold had been broken loose, I was under water, and the thought passed through my mind that this was the terrible thing of which I had heard, the being swept in the trough of the sea. My body struck and pounded as it was dashed helplessly along and turned over and over, and when I could hold my breath no longer, I breathed the stinging salt water into my lungs. But through it all I clung to the one idea – *I must get the jib backed over to windward.* I had no fear of death. I had no doubt that I should come through somehow. And as this idea of fulfilling Wolf Larsen's order persisted in my dazed consciousness, I seemed to see him standing at the wheel in the midst of the wild welter, pitting his will against the will of the storm and defying it.

I brought up violently against what I took to be the rail, breathed, and breathed the sweet air again. I tried to rise, but struck my head and was knocked back on hands and knees. By some freak of the waters I had been swept clear under the forecastle-head and into the eyes. As I scrambled out on all fours, I passed over the body of Thomas Mugridge, who lay in a groaning heap. There was no time to investigate. I must get the jib backed over.

When I emerged on deck it seemed that the end of everything had come. On all sides there was a rending and crashing of wood and steel and canvas. The *Ghost* was being wrenched and torn to fragments. The foresail and fore-topsail, emptied of the wind by the manoeuvre, and with no one to bring in the sheet in time, were thundering into ribbons, the heavy boom threshing and splintering from rail to rail. The air was thick with flying wreckage, detached ropes and stays were hissing and coiling like snakes, and down through it all crashed the gaff of the foresail.

The spar could not have missed me by many inches, while it spurred me to action. Perhaps the situation was not hopeless. I remembered Wolf Larsen's caution. He had expected all hell to break loose, and here it was. And where was he? I caught sight of him toiling at the main-sheet, heaving it in and flat with his tremendous muscles, the stern of the schooner lifted high in the air and his body outlined against a white surge of sea sweeping past. All this, and more, – a whole world of chaos and wreck, – in possibly fifteen seconds I had seen and heard and grasped.

I did not stop to see what had become of the small boat, but sprang to the jib-sheet. The jib itself was beginning to slap, partially filling and emptying with sharp reports; but with a turn of the sheet and the application of my whole strength each time it slapped, I slowly backed it. This I know: I did my best. I pulled till I burst open the ends of all my fingers; and while I pulled, the flying-jib and staysail split their cloths apart and thundered into nothingness.

Still I pulled, holding what I gained each time with a double turn until the next slap gave me more. Then the sheet gave with greater ease, and Wolf Larsen was beside me, heaving in alone while I was busied taking up the slack.

'Make fast!' he shouted. 'And come on!'

As I followed him, I noted that in spite of rack and ruin a rough order obtained. The *Ghost* was hove to. She was still in working order, and she was still working. Though the rest of her sails were gone, the jib, backed to windward, and the mainsail hauled down flat, were themselves holding, and holding her bow to the furious sea as well.

I looked for the boat, and while Wolf Larsen cleared the boat-tackles, saw it lift to leeward on a big sea and not a score of feet away. And, so nicely had he made his calculation, we drifted fairly down upon it, so that nothing remained to do but hook the tackles to either end and hoist it aboard. But this was not done so easily as it was written.

In the bow was Kerfoot, Oofty-Oofty in the stern, and Kelly amidships. As we drifted closer the boat would rise on a wave while we sank in the trough, till almost straight above me I could see the heads of the three men craned overside and looking down. Then, the next moment, we would lift and soar upwards while they sank far down beneath us. It seemed incredible that the next surge should not crush the *Ghost* down upon the tiny eggshell.

But, at the right moment, I passed the tackle to the Kanaka, while Wolf Larsen did the same thing forward to Kerfoot. Both tackles were hooked in a trice, and the three men, deftly timing the roll, made a simultaneous leap aboard the schooner. As the *Ghost* rolled her side out of water, the boat was lifted snugly against her, and before the return roll came, we had heaved it in over the side and turned it bottom up on the deck.

When the storm has blown itself out the rest of the fleet is found, along with two more of *Ghost's* boats, which have been rescued by other schooners. After hi-jacking a boat and crew from his equally diabolical brother's steam sealing ship, Wolf ends up only four men short of his original complement.

Later, *Ghost* picks up five survivors from a sunken mailboat, including the disturbingly beautiful poetess Maud Brewster, to whom the Captain is instantly attracted. When his intentions towards her become apparent, she has cause to realise that Hump is her most reliable – indeed only – protector.

The chagrin Wolf Larsen felt from being ignored by Maud Brewster and me in the conversation at table had to express itself in some fashion, and it fell to Thomas Mugridge to be the victim. He had not mended his ways nor his shirt, though the latter he contended he had changed. The garment itself did not bear out the assertion, nor did the accumulations of grease on stove and pot and pan attest a general cleanliness.

'I've given you warning, Cooky,' Wolf Larsen said, 'and now you've got to take your medicine.'

Mugridge's face turned white under its sooty veneer, and when Wolf Larsen called for a rope and a couple of men, the miserable Cockney fled wildly out of the galley and dodged and ducked about the deck with the grinning crew in pursuit. Few things could have been more to their liking than to give him a tow over the side, for to the forecastle he had sent messes and concoctions of the vilest order. Conditions favoured the undertaking. The *Ghost* was slipping through the water at no more than three miles an hour, and the sea was fairly calm. But Mugridge had little stomach for a dip in it. Possibly he had seen men towed before. Besides, the water was frightfully cold, and his was anything but a rugged constitution.

As usual, the watches below and the hunters turned out for what promised sport. Mugridge seemed to be in rabid fear of the water, and he exhibited a nimbleness and speed we did not dream he possessed. Cornered in the right-angle of the poop and galley, he sprang like a cat to the top of the cabin and ran aft. But his pursuers forestalling him, he doubled back across the cabin, passed over the galley, and gained the deck by means of the steerage-scuttle. Straight forward he raced, the boat-puller Harrison at his heels and gaining on him. But Mugridge, leaping suddenly, caught the jib-boom-lift. It happened in an instant. Holding his weight by his arms, and in mid-air doubling his body at the hips, he let fly with both feet. The oncoming Harrison caught the kick squarely in the pit of the stomach, groaned involuntarily, and doubled up and sank backward to the deck.

Hand-clapping and roars of laughter from the hunters greeted the exploit, while Mugridge, eluding half of his pursuers at the foremost, ran aft and through the remainder like a runner on the football field. Straight aft he held, to the poop and along the poop to the stern. So great was his speed that as he curved past the corner of the cabin he slipped and fell. Nilson was standing at the wheel, and the Cockney's hurtling body struck his legs. Both went down together, but

Mugridge alone arose. By some freak of pressures, his frail body had snapped the strong man's leg like a pipe-stem.

Parsons took the wheel, and the pursuit continued. Round and round the decks they went, Mugridge sick with fear, the sailors hallooing and shouting directions to one another, and the hunters bellowing encouragement and laughter. Mugridge went down on the fore-hatch under three men; but he emerged from the mass like an eel, bleeding at the mouth, the offending shirt ripped into tatters, and sprang for the mainrigging. Up he went, clear up, beyond the ratlines, to the very masthead.

Half-a-dozen sailors swarmed to the crosstrees after him, where they clustered and waited while two of their number, Oofty-Oofty and Black (who was Latimer's boat-steerer), continued up the thin steel stays, lifting their bodies higher and higher by means of their arms.

It was a perilous undertaking, for, at a height of over a hundred feet from the deck, holding on by their hands, they were not in the best position to protect themselves from Mugridge's feet. And Mugridge kicked savagely, till the Kanaka, hanging on with one hand, seized the Cockney's foot with the other. Black duplicated the performance a moment later with the other foot. Then the three writhed together in a swaying tangle, struggling, sliding, and falling into the arms of their mates on the crosstrees.

The aërial battle was over, and Thomas Mugridge, whining and gibbering, his mouth flecked with bloody foam, was brought down to deck. Wolf Larsen rove a bowline in a piece of rope and slipped it under his shoulders. Then he was carried aft and flung into the sea. Forty, – fifty, – sixty feet of line ran out, when Wolf Larsen cried 'Belay!' Oofty-Oofty took a turn on a bitt, the rope tautened, and the Ghost, lunging onwards, jerked the cook to the surface.

It was a pitiful spectacle. Though he could not drown, and was nine-lived in addition, he was suffering all the agonies of half-drowning. The Ghost was going very slowly, and when her stern lifted on a wave and she slipped forward she pulled the wretch to the surface and gave him a moment in which to breathe; but between each lift the stern fell, and while the bow lazily climbed the next wave the line slacked and he sank beneath.

I had forgotten the existence of Maud Brewster, and I remembered her with a start as she stepped lightly beside me. It was her first time on deck since she had come aboard. A dead silence greeted her appearance.

'What is the cause of the merriment?' she asked.

'Ask Captain Larsen,' I answered composedly and coldly, though inwardly my blood was boiling at the thought that she should be witness to such brutality.

She took my advice and was turning to put it into execution, when her eyes lighted on Oofty-Oofty, immediately before her, his body instinct with alertness and grace as he held the turn of the rope.

'Are you fishing?' she asked him.

He made no reply. His eyes, fixed intently on the sea astern, suddenly flashed.

'Shark ho, sir!' he cried.

'Heave in! Lively! All hands tail on!' Wolf Larsen shouted, springing himself to the rope in advance of the quickest.

Mugridge had heard the Kanaka's warning cry and was screaming madly. I could see a black fin cutting the water and making for him with greater swiftness than he was being pulled aboard. It was an even toss whether the shark or we would get him, and it was a matter of moments. When Mugridge was directly beneath us, the stern descended the slope of a passing wave, thus giving the advantage to the shark. The fin disappeared. The belly flashed white in the swift upward rush. Almost equally swift, but not quite, was Wolf Larsen. He threw his strength into one tremendous jerk. The Cockney's body left the water; so did part of the shark's. He drew up his legs, and the man-eater seemed no more than barely to touch one foot, sinking back into the water with a splash. But at the moment of contact Thomas Mugridge cried out. Then he came in like a fresh-caught fish on a line, clearing the rail generously and striking the deck in a heap, on hands and knees, and rolling over.

But a fountain of blood was gushing forth. The right foot was missing, amputated neatly at the ankle. I looked instantly to Maud Brewster. Her face was white, her eyes dilated with horror. She was gazing, not at Thomas Mugridge, but at Wolf Larsen. And he was aware of it, for he said, with one of his short laughs:

'Man-play, Miss Brewster. Somewhat rougher, I warrant, than what you have been used to, but still – man-play. The shark was not in the reckoning.'

from *The Sea-Wolf* by Jack London (1904)

All ends happily for Maud and Hump, but not before they have been driven to escape from the schooner in one of her longboats one dark night. They fetch up on an uninhabited island, where they dig in for a long winter. No reader of Jack London will be surprised to learn that one morning they look out from their sealskin hut and find *Ghost* aground in their cove, her masts and rigging hanging over the side in terminal disarray. There are no ship's boats on board; all have been taken by the crew, who have abandoned their maniac skipper to his fate. Larsen is found alive, showing symptoms of a stroke or a brainstorm, with intermittent moments of treacherous lucidity. His armour-clad constitution prolongs the final agony. When it comes, the lovers overcome all the practical difficulties of setting up a jury rig, under which they sail towards Japan and rescue by a chance encounter with a revenue cutter.

Galley-slaves and a Royal Toothache

The closing decades of the tenth century saw England, under Ethelred the Unready, enjoying peace and freedom from plundering Vikings. King Alfred had forced Ragnar Hairy-breeks to come to terms, but across the Channel Charles the Simple had not been so fortunate: he had been obliged to buy peace by ceding part of his kingdom to the wild men from Scandinavia. It is known as Normandy to this day.

Always searching for land that would provide a secure base from which they could sail away to sack other countries while their families managed the farms, the Vikings pushed ever further west of their homeland, colonising Iceland in AD 860 and Greenland a century later. It was then that they reached Newfoundland, albeit 400 years after St Brendan and his monks from the west of Ireland were reputed to have got there.

Frans Bengtsson, the Swedish poet and historian, wrote extensively about the Vikings of those heroic years. In the early 1950s he published his epic novel *The Long Ships*, about Red Orm, son of Asa and the legendary sailor Toste, who regarded the west of Ireland as his private hunting-ground. They had five sons, of whom only two survived.

The eldest of them had come to grief at a wedding, when, merry with ale, he had attempted to prove that he could ride bareback on a bull; and the next one had been washed overboard on his first voyage. But the unluckiest of all had been their fourth son, who was called Are; for, one summer, when he was nineteen years old, he had got two of their neighbours' wives with child while their husbands were abroad, which had been instance of much trouble and sly jibing, and had put Toste to considerable expense when the husbands returned home. This dejected Are's spirits and made him shy; then he killed a man who had chaffed him overlong for his dexterity, and had to flee the country. It was rumoured that he had sold himself to Swedish merchants and had sailed with them to the east, so that he might meet no more people who knew of his misfortune, but nothing had been heard of him since. Asa, however, had dreamed of a black horse with blood on its shoulders, and knew by this that he was dead.

So after that, Asa and Toste had only two sons left. The leader of these was called Odd. He was a short youth, coarsely built and bowlegged, but strong and horny-handed, and of a reflective temper; he was soon accompanying Toste on his voyages, and showed himself to be a skilful shipman, as well as a hard fighter. At home, though, he was often contrary in his behaviour, for he found the long winters tedious, and Asa and he bickered continually. He was sometimes heard to say that he would rather be eating rancid salt-meat on board ship than Yuletide joints at home; but Asa remarked that he never seemed to take less than anyone else of the food she set before them. He dozed so much every day that he would often complain that he had slept poorly during the night; it did not even seem to help, he would say, when he took one of the servant-girls into the bed-straw with him. Asa did not like his sleeping with her servants; she said it might give them too high an opinion of themselves, and make them impudent towards their mistress; she observed that it would be more satisfactory if Odd acquired a wife. But Odd replied that there was no hurry about that; in any case, the women that suited his taste best were the ones in Ireland, and he could not very well bring any of them home with him, for, if he did, Asa and they would soon be going for one another tooth and nail. At this, Asa became angry and asked whether this could be her own son who addressed her thus, and expressed the wish that she might shortly die; to which Odd retorted that she might live or die as she chose, and he would not presume to advise her which state to choose, but would endure with resignation whatever might befall.

Although he was slow of speech, Asa did not always succeed in having the last word, and she used to say that it was in truth a hard thing for her to have lost three good sons and to have been left with the one whom she could most easily have spared.

Odd got on better with his father, however, and, as soon as the spring came, and the smell of tar began to drift across from the boat-house to the jetty, his humour would improve, and sometimes he would even try, though he had little talent for the craft, to compose a verse or two of how the auk's meadow was now ripe for ploughing; or how the horses of the sea would shortly waft him to the summer land.

But he never won himself any great name as a bard, least of all among those daughters of neighbouring thanes who were of marriageable age; and he was seldom observed to turn his head as he sailed away.

His brother was the youngest of all Toste's children, and the jewel of his mother's eye. His name was Orm. He grew quickly, becoming long and scatter-limbed, and distressing Asa by his lack of flesh; so that whenever he failed to eat a good deal more than any of the grown men, she would become convinced that she would soon lose him, and often said that his poor appetite would assuredly be his downfall. Orm was, in fact, fond of food, and did not grudge his mother her anxiety regarding his appetite; but Toste and Odd were some-times driven to protest that she reserved all the tit-bits for him. In his childhood, Orm had once or twice fallen sick, ever since when Asa had been convinced that his health was fragile, so that she was continually fussing over him with solicitous admonitions, making him believe that he was racked with dangerous cramps and in urgent need of sacred onions, witches' incantations and hot clay platters, when the only real trouble was that he had overeaten himself on corn porridge and pork.

As he grew up, Asa's worries increased. It was her hope that he would, in time, become a famous man and a chieftain; and she expressed to Toste her delight that Orm was shaping into a big, strong lad, wise in his discourse, in every respect a worthy scion of his mother's line. She was, though, very fearful of all the perils that he might encounter on the highway of manhood, and reminded him often of the disasters that had overtaken his brothers, making him promise always to beware of bulls, to be careful on board ship, and never to lie with other men's wives; but, apart from these dangers, there was so much else that might befall him that she hardly knew where to begin to counsel him.

Red Orm joins the afterguard of the flagship of a chieftain called Krok, along with his friend Toke Gormssen. They range far and wide in search of booty. One voyage takes them to Ramiro's kingdom (Spain), where they have the misfortune to be overwhelmed by boats of the Caliph of Cordova's fleet and are impressed as galley-slaves – not the sort of duty assigned to an unsuspecting blond in a modern yacht; nor would the conditions of employment suit today's National Union of Seamen.

The ship was manned by fifty soldiers, and the galley-slaves numbered seventy-two; for there were eighteen pairs of oars. From bench to bench they would often murmur of the possibility of working themselves free from their chains, overpowering the soldiers, and so winning their freedom; but the chains were strong, and were carefully watched, and guards were always posted when the ship was lying at anchor. Even when they engaged an enemy ship, some of the soldiers were always detailed to keep an eye on the slaves, with orders to kill any that showed signs of restlessness. When they were led ashore in any of the Caliph's great military harbours, they were shut up in a slavehouse until the ship was ready to depart again, being kept all the time under strict surveillance, and were never allowed to be together in large numbers; so that there seemed to be no future for them but to row for as long as life remained in their bodies, or until some enemy ship might chance to conquer their own and set them at liberty. But the Caliph's ships were many, and always outnumbered their enemies, so that this eventuality was scarcely to be reckoned with. Such of them as showed themselves refractory, or relieved their hatred with curses, were flogged to death or thrown overboard alive; though, occasionally, when the culprit was a strong oarsman, he was merely castrated and set again to his oar, which, although the slaves were never permitted a woman, they held to be the worst punishment of all.

When, in his old age, Orm used to tell of his years as a galley-slave, he still remembered all the positions that his fellow Vikings occupied in the ship, as well as those of most of the other slaves; and, as he told his story, he would take his listeners from oar to oar, describing what sort of man sat at each, and which among them died, and how other came to take their places, and which of them received the most whippings. He said that it was not difficult for him to remember these things, for in his dreams he often returned to the slave-ship, and saw the wealed backs straining before his eyes, and heard the men groaning with the terrible labour of their rowing, and, always, the feet of the overseer approaching behind him. His bed needed all the good craftsmanship that had gone into its making to keep it from splitting asunder as he would grip one of its beams to heave at the oar of his sleep; and he often said that there was no happiness in the world to compare with that of awakening from such a dream and finding it to be only a dream.

Three oars in front of Orm, also on the larboard side, sat Krok; and he was now a much changed man. Orm and the others knew that being a galley-slave fell harder on him than on the rest of them, because he was a man accustomed to command, and one who had always believed himself to be lucky. He was very silent, seldom replying when his neighbours addressed him; and although, with his great strength, he found no difficulty in doing the work required of him, he rowed always as though half asleep and deep in reflection on other matters. His stroke would gradually become slower, and his oar would fall out of time, and he would be savagely lashed by the overseer; but none of them ever heard him utter any cry as he received his punishment, or even mumble a curse. He would pull hard on his oar, and take up the stroke again; but his gaze would follow the overseer's back thoughtfully as the latter move forward, as a man watches a troublesome wasp that he cannot lay his hands on.

Krok shared his oar with a man called Gunne, who complained loudly of the many whippings he received on Krok's account; but Krok paid little heed to his lamentations. At length, on one occasion, when the overseer had flogged them both cruelly and Gunne's complaints were louder and his resentment greater than usual, Krok turned his eyes towards him, as though noticing his presence for the first time, and said 'Be patient, Gunne. You will not have to endure my company for much longer. I am a chieftain, and was not born to serve other men; but I have one task yet to accomplish, if only my luck will stretch sufficiently to allow me to do what I have to do.'

He said no more, and what task it was that he had to perform, Gunne could not wring from him.

Just in front of Orm there sat two men named Halle and Ögmund. They spoke often of the good days that they had spent in the past, of the food and the ale and the fine girls at home in the north, and conjured up various fitting deaths for the overseer; but they could never think of a way to bring any of them about. Orm himself was seated with a dark-brown foreigner who, for some misdemeanour, had had his tongue cut out. He was a good oarsman, and seldom needed the whip, but Orm would have preferred to be next to one of his own countrymen, or at any rate somebody able to talk. The worst of it, as far as Orm was concerned, was that the tongueless man, though unable to talk, was able all the more to cough, and his cough was more frightful than any that Orm had ever heard; when he coughed, he became grey in the face and gulped like a landed fish, and altogether wore such a wretched and woebegone appearance that it seemed impossible that he could live much longer. This made Orm anxious concerning his own health. He did not prize the life of a galley-slave very highly, but he was unwilling to be carried off by a cough; the tongueless man's performance made him certain in his mind of that. The more he reflected on the possibility of his dying like this, the more it dejected his spirits, and he wished that Toke had been seated nearer to him.

Toke was placed several oars behind Orm, so that they seldom had a chance to speak to one another, only, indeed, while they were being led ashore or back to the ship; for, in the slave-house, they were tethered together in groups of four in tiny cells, according to their places in the ship. Toke had, by now, regained something of his former humour, and could still manage to find something to laugh at, though he was usually at loggerheads with the man who shared his oar, whose name was Tume and who, in Toke's view, did less than his share of the rowing and ate more than his share of the rations. Toke composed abusive lampoons, some about Tume and some about the overseer, and sang them as shanties while he rowed, so that Orm and the others could hear them.

Most of the time, however, he occupied his thoughts with trying to plan some method of escape. The first time that Orm and he had a chance to speak to each other, he whispered that he had a good plan almost worked out. All he needed was a small bit of iron. With this, he could prise open one of the links in his ankle-chain, one dark night, when the ship was in port and everybody except the watchmen would be asleep. Having done this, he would pass the iron on to the other Vikings, each of whom would quietly break his chain. When they had all freed themselves, they would throttle the watchmen in the dark, without making a noise, and steal their weapons; then, once ashore, they would be able to fend for themselves.

Orm said that this would be a fine idea, if only it was practicable; and he would be glad to lend a hand in throttling the guards, if they got that far, which he rather doubted. Where, though, could they find a suitable piece of iron, and how could naked men, who were always under close observation, manage to smuggle it aboard without being detected? Toke sighed, and admitted that these were difficulties that would require careful consideration; but he could not think of any better plan, and said they would merely have to bide their time until an opportunity should present itself.

He succeeded in having a surreptitious word with Krok, too, and told him of his plan; but Krok listened to him abstractedly, and showed little interest or enthusiasm.

Not long afterwards, the ship was put into dry dock in one of the Caliph's shipyards to be scraped and pitched. Many of the slaves were detailed to assist with the work, chained in pairs; and the Northmen who knew the ways of ships, were among these. Armed guards kept watch over them; and the overseer walked his rounds with his whip, to speed the work, two guards, armed with swords and bows, following him everywhere he went to protect him. Close to the ship, there stood a large cauldron full of simmering pitch, next to which was a barrel containing drinking water for the slaves.

Krok and Gunne were drinking from this barrel when one of the slaves approached supporting his oar-companion, who had lost his foothold while engaged on the work and had so injured his foot that he was unable to stand on it. He was lowered to the ground, and had begun to drink, when the overseer came up to see what was afoot. The injured man was lying on his side, groaning; whereupon, the overseer, thinking that the man was shamming, gave him a cut with his whip to bring him to his feet. The man, however, remained where he was, with everybody's eyes fixed upon him.

Krok was standing a few paces behind them, on the far side of the barrel. He shifted towards them, dragging Gunne with him; and suddenly it seemed as though all his previous apathy had dropped away from him. When he was close enough, and saw that there was sufficient slack in the chain, he sprang forward, seized the overseer by the belt and the neck and lifted him above his head. The overseer cried out in terror, and the nearest of the guards turned and ran his sword through Krok's body. Krok seemed not to feel the blow. Taking two sideward paces, he flung the overseer head downwards into the boiling pitch, as the other guard's sword bit into his head. Krok tottered, but he kept his eyes fixed on what could be seen of the overseer. Then, he gave a laugh, and said: 'Now my luck has turned again,' and fell to the ground and died.

All the slaves raised a great shout of joy, to see the overseer meet such an end; but the gladness of the Vikings was mingled with grief, and in the months that followed they often recalled Krok's deed and the last words that he had uttered. They all agreed that he had died in a manner befitting a chieftain; and they expressed the hope that the overseer had lived long enough in the cauldron to get a good feel of the pitch.

*

When they rowed out to sea again, they had a new overseer to supervise their labours; but he seemed to have taken note of the fate of his predecessor, for he was somewhat sparing in the use of his whip.

The Vikings later acquire privileged status as part of the bodyguard of Almansur, the regent who has usurped power. After four years as trustees, they are able to hi-jack a merchantman, complete with its own galley-slaves, and make good their escape by way of a stopover on St Finnian's Isle off the Ring of Kerry.

When they reach the Skaw, they find King Harold Bluetooth suffering agonies from an abcess under one of his molars. The voyagers have brought with them a massive silver bell looted from St James's tomb in Asturias, with which they had hoped to please the King, a recent convert to Christianity. As a holy relic it might even help alleviate his toothache, although the King's ungovernable temper when in pain sometimes makes him forget the respect due to such relics. His principal monk, Brother Willibald, is almost sent to join the martyrs after being hit on the head by a big crucifix which his royal master wields like a battle-axe.

When the time comes to administer treatment, Brother Willibald hedges his bets:

So they turned the bell on to its side, and Brother Matthias swabbed its interior with a cloth dipped in holy water, which he then wrung out into a bowl. There was a lot of old dust in the bell, so that the water he wrung out of the cloth was quite black, which greatly delighted Brother Willibald. Then Brother Willibald set to work mixing his medicines, which he kept in a big leather chest, all the while delivering an instructive discourse to such of the company as were curious to know what he was attempting to do.

'The ancient prescription of St Gregory is the most efficacious in cases such as this,' he said. 'It is a simple formula, and there are no secrets about its preparation. Juice of sloe, boar's gall, saltpetre and bull's-blood, a pinch of horse-radish and a few drops of juniper-water, all mixed with an equal quantity of holy water in which some sacred relic has been washed. The mixture to be kept in the mouth while three verses from the psalms are sung; this procedure to be repeated thrice. This is the surest medicine against the toothache that we who practise the craft of healing know: and it never fails, provided that the sacred relic is sufficiently strong. The Apulian doctors of the old Emperor Otto fancied frog's blood to be more efficacious than bull's-blood, but few physicians are of that opinion nowadays; which is a fortunate thing, for frog's-blood is not easy to procure in winter.'

He took from his chest two small metal bottles, uncorked them, smelt them, shook his head, and sent a servant to the kitchen to fetch fresh galls and fresh bull's-blood.

'Only the best will suffice in a case such as this,' he said; 'and, when the relic is as powerful as the one we have here, great care must be taken over the other ingredients.'

All this had occupied several minutes, and King Harold now seemed to be less troubled by his pain. He turned his gaze towards Orm and Toke, evidently puzzled at seeing strangers clad in foreign armour; for they still wore the red cloaks and engraved shields of Almansur, and their helmets had nose-pieces and descended low down over their cheeks and necks. He beckoned to them to come nearer.

'Whose men are you?' he said.

'We are your men, King Harold,' replied Orm. 'But we have come hither from Andalusia, where we served Almansur, the great Lord of Cordova, until blood came between us and him. Krok of Lister was our chieftain when we first set forth, sailing in three ships. But he was killed, and many others with him. I am Orm, the son of Toste, of the Mound in Skania, chieftain of such as remain; and we have come to you with this bell. We thought it would be a good gift for you, O King, when we heard that you had become a Christian. Of its potency in countering the toothache I know nothing, but at sea it has been a powerful ally to us. It was the largest of all the bells over St James's grave in Asturia, where many marvellous things were found; we went there with our master, Almansur, who treasured this bell most dearly.'

from *The Long Ships* by Frans Bengtsson (English trans. 1954)

THE DARK SIDE

Gales and Calms

Embayed and Wrecked on a Lee Shore

Inevitably it is Shakespeare who has left us with one of the earliest authentic accounts in English literature of a shipwreck on a lee shore during a terrible storm. The opening lines of his last play, *The Tempest*, were probably inspired by eye-witness accounts of the wrecks of Sir George Somers' flagship on what is now Bermuda while on passage to the Virginia colonies in 1609. Shakespeare sets his scene on an uninhabited island, but transfers the action to a Mediterranean setting. The play was first performed in 1611 as part of the ceremonies in Whitehall marking the betrothal of the Princess Elizabeth to Frederick, the Elector Palatine of the Rhine. Her father, King James I, had seen his Authorized Version of the Bible published in the same year.

The curtain rises on a 'tempestuous noise of thunder and lightning. The waist of the ship is seen, seas breaking over it.' The Master and his Boatswain attempt to rally the crew and take urgent action to claw out of a situation dreaded more than any other by those under sail – being embayed on a lee shore. The King of Naples (Alonso), his brother (Sebastian), others of his family and the faithful old councillor Gonzalo are getting in the way of the crew's last-ditch efforts. Subsequent events are described with the economy of words and technical mastery which Shakespeare demonstrated in any setting. The crew are ordered to bestir themselves and lower the topsails 'yarely' (at the rush, or roundly, in the language of today's seamen), then to trim both 'courses' (mainsails, up to the present day) and to avoid the rocks by sailing 'a-hold' (close-hauled) into safer water. Anyone who has been caught in a sudden Gulf Stream storm will recognize the description of lightning as 'fireballs'.

When all else fails, the Boatswain takes to the bottle – not an unprecedented reaction in such a situation.

A SHIP-MASTER: A BOATSWAIN

Master [from the poop-deck]. Bos'n!
Boatswain [in the waist]. Here, master: what cheer?
Master. Good: speak to th' mariners: fall to't – yarely – or we run ourselves aground. Bestir, bestir.   [*he returns to the helm*

Master's whistle heard. Mariners come aft.

Boatswain. Heigh my hearts! cheerly, cheerly my hearts . . . yare, yare . . . take in the topsail . . . tend to th' Master's whistle . . . [*to the gale*] Blow till thou burst thy wind – if room enough!

ALONZO, SEBASTIAN, ANTONIO, FERDINAND, GONZALO, *and others come on deck.*

Alonso. Good boatswain have care . . . Where is the master? Play the men.

Boatswain. I pray now, keep below.

Antonio. Where is the master, bos'n?

Boatswain. Do you not hear him? You mar our labour. Keep your cabins: you do assist the storm.

Gonzalo. Nay, good, be patient.

Boatswain.   When the sea is . . . Hence! What care these roarers for the name of king? To cabin . . . silence . . . trouble us not!

Gonzalo. Good, yet remember whom thou hast aboard.

Boatswain. None that I more love than myself . . . You are a Councillor – if you can command these elements to silence, and work the peace of the present, we will not hand a rope more. Use your authority . . . If you cannot, give thanks you have lived so long, and make yourself ready in your cabin for the mischance of the hour, if it so hap . . .

Cheerly, good hearts . . . Out of our way, I say.   [*he runs forward*

Gonzalo [*his speech interrupted as the ship pitches*]. I have great comfort from this fellow . . . Methinks he hath no drowning mark upon him, his complexion is perfect gallows . . . Stand fast, good Fate, to his hanging, make the rope of his destiny our cable, for our own doth little advantage . . . If he be not born to be hanged, our case is miserable.

BOATSWAIN *comes aft: courtiers retreat before him to their cabins.*

Boatswain. Down with the topmast . . . yare, lower, lower! bring her to try with main course . . . ['*A cry' is heard below*]. A plague upon this howling . . . They are louder than the weather, or our office . . .

SEBASTIAN, ANTONIO *and* GONZALO *return.*

Yet again? What do you here? Shall we give o'er and drown? Have you a mind to sink?

Sebastian. A pox o' your throat, you bawling, blasphemous, incharitable dog!

Boatswain. Work you, then.   [*he turns from them*]

Antonio. Hang, cur, hang, you whoreson, insolent noise-maker! we are less afraid to be drowned than thou art.

Gonzalo. I'll warrant him for drowning, though the ship were no stronger than a nutshell, and as leaky as an unstaunched wench.

Boatswain [*shouting*]. Lay her a-hold, a-hold! Set her two courses. Off to sea again! [*in despair*] lay her off!

The ship strikes. Fireballs flame along the rigging and from beak to stern. Enter mariners wet.

Mariners. All lost! to prayers, to prayers! all lost!

Boatswain [*stupefied, slowly pulling out a bottle*]. What, must our mouths be cold?
Gonzalo. The king and prince at prayers. Let's assist them,
For our case is as theirs.
Sebastian. I am out of patience
Antonio. We are merely cheated of our lives by drunkards –
This wide-chopped rascal – would thou mightst lie drowning
The washing of ten tides!
Gonzalo. He'll be hanged yet,
Though every drop of water swear against it,
And gape at wid'st to glut him.
A confused noise below Mercy on us! –
We split, we split! Farewell, my wife and children! –
Farewell, brother! – We split, we split, we split!
Antonio. Let's all sink with' king.
Sebastian. Let's take leave of him. [*they go below*
Gonzalo. Now would I give a thousand furlongs of sea – for an acre of barren
ground . . . long heath, brown firs, any thing . . . The wills above be done, but
I would fain die a dry death!

*A crowd bursts upon deck, making for the ship's side, in the glare of the fireballs. Of a
sudden these are quenched. A loud cry of many voices.*

from *The Tempest* by William Shakespeare (1611)

Foundering Off the Scillies

Captain Billy Booth, the hero of Henry Fielding's novel *Amelia* (based on
the life and character of his wife, who also featured as Sophia in *Tom Jones*),
is not a seafaring man – nor was the author. Like Fielding, Booth has some
experience of corrupt 'trading Justices' as a member of the bench and having
gambled away all the money he can raise, including by hocking his wife's
jewellery, he finds himself in Newgate prison for no better reason than his
inability to bribe his way out of it. He is finally sprung out and gets a
commission in the army.

Much of the book is as he recounts it to Miss Mathews, a high-priced
courtesan with whom he shares a luxury she alone can afford in prison –
the privacy of a relatively clean cell. The following account of his voyage
in a troopship to join his regiment in Gibraltar betrays his lack of seagoing
experience, especially when he tells how his ship, the *Lovely Peggy* is apparently threatened with being wrecked on the Scillies from a position 40 miles
to the west of the islands by a north-easterly gale! After being rescued by
the escorting man-o'-war, Booth soon encounters the low esteem which

soldiers of any rank are held by a typically autocratic naval Captain – an attitude not unknown two centuries later.

'At length we embarked aboard a Transport, and sailed for *Gibraltar*; but the Wind, which was at first fair, soon chopped about; so that we were obliged, for several Days, to beat to Windward, as the sea phrase is. During this time the taste which I had of a Sea-faring Life did not appear extremely agreeable. We rolled up and down in a little narrow Cabbin, in which were three Officers, all of us extremely Sea-sick; our Sickness being much aggravated by the Motion of the Ship, by the View of each other, and by the Stench of the Men. But this was but a little Taste indeed of the Misery which was to follow: for we were got about six Leagues to the Westward of *Scilly*, when a violent storm arose at northeast, which soon raised the Waves to the Height of Mountains. The Horror of this is not to be adequately described to those who have never seen the like. The Storm began in the Evening, and as the Clouds brought on the Night apace, it was soon entirely dark; nor had we during many Hours any other Light than what was caused by the jarring Elements, which frequently sent forth Flashes, or rather Streams of Fire; and whilst these presented the most dreadful Objects to our Eyes, the roaring of the Winds, the dashing of the Waves against the Ship and each other, formed a Sound altogether as horrible for our Ears; while our Ship, sometimes lifted up as it were to the Skies, and sometimes swept away at once as into the lowest Abyss, seemed to be the Sport of the Winds and Seas. The Captain himself almost gave all for lost, and exprest his Apprehension of being inevitably cast on the rocks of *Scilly*, and beat to Pieces. And now, while some on board were addressing themselves to the Supreme Being, and others applying for Comfort to strong Liquors, my whole Thoughts were entirely engaged by my *Amelia*. A thousand tender Ideas crowded into my Mind. I can truly say, that I had not a single Consideration about myself, in which she was not concerned. Dying to me was leaving her, and the Fear of never seeing her more was a Dagger stuck in my Heart. Again, all the Terrors with which this Storm, if it reached her Ears, must fill her gentle Mind on my Account, and the Agonies which she must undergo, when she heard of my Fate, gave me such intolerable Pangs, that I now repented my Resolution, and wished, I own I wished, that I had taken her Advice and preferred Love and a Cottage to all the dazzling Charms of Honour.

'While I was tormenting myself with those Meditations, and had concluded myself as certainly lost, the Master came into the Cabbin and with a chearful Voice, assured us that we had escaped the Danger and that we had certainly passed to the Westward of the Rock. This was comfortable News to all present; and my Captain, who had been some time on his Knees, leaped suddenly up and testified his Joy with a great Oath.

A Person unused to the Sea would have been astonished at the Satisfaction which now discovered itself in the Master or in any on board: for the Storm still raged with great Violence, and the Day-light which now appeared, presented us with Sights of Horror sufficient to terrify Minds which were not absolute Slaves to the Passion of Fear; but so great is the Force of Habit, that what inspires a Landman with the highest Apprehension of Danger, gives not the least Concern to a Sailor, to whom Rocks and Quick-sands are almost the only Objects of Terror.

'The Master, however, was a little mistaken in the present Instance; for he had not left the Cabin above an Hour, before my Man came running to me, and acquainted me that the ship was half full of Water, that the Sailors were going to hoist out the Boat and save themselves, and begged me to come that Moment along with him, as I tendered my Preservation. With this Account, which was conveyed to me in a Whisper, I acquainted both the Captain and Ensign; and we all together immediately mounted the Deck, where we found the Master making use of all his Oratory to persuade the Sailors that the Ship was in no Danger; and at the same time employing all his Authority to set the Pumps a-going, which he assured them would keep the Water under and save his dear *Lovely Peggy*, (for that was the Name of the Ship) which he swore he loved as dearly as his own Soul.

'Indeed this sufficiently appeared; for the Leak was so great, and the Water flowed in so plentifully that his *Lovely Peggy* was half filled, before he could be brought to think of quitting her; but now the Boat was brought along-side the Ship and the Master himself, notwithstanding all his Love for her, quitted his Ship; and leaped into the Boat. Every Man present attempted to follow his Example, when I heard the voice of my Servant roaring forth my Name in a Kind of Agony. I made directly to the Ship Side, but was too late for the Boat being already overladen put directly off. And now, Madam, I am going to relate to you an Instance of heroic Affection in a poor Fellow towards his Master to which Love itself, even among Persons of superior Education, can produce but few similar Instances. My poor Man being unable to get me with him into the Boat, leaped suddenly into the Sea and swam back to the Ship; and when I gently rebuked him for his Rashness, he answered, he chose rather to die with me, than to live to carry the Account of my death to my *Amelia*; at the same time bursting into a Flood of Tears, he cried, "Good Heavens! what will that poor Lady feel when she hears of this!" This tender Concern for my dear Love endeared the poor Fellow more to me than the gallant Instance which he had just before given of his Affection towards myself.

'And now, Madam, my Eyes were shocked with a Sight, the Horror of which can scarce be imagined, for the Boat had scarce got four hundred Yards from the Ship, when it was swallowed up by the merciless Waves, which now ran so high, that out of the Number of Persons which were in the boat none recovered the Ship; tho' many of them we saw miserably perish before our Eyes, some of them very near us, without any Possibility of giving them the least Assistance.

'But whatever we felt for them, we felt, I believe, more for ourselves, expecting every Minute when we should share the same Fate. Among the rest one of our Officers appeared quite stupified with Fear. I never indeed saw a more miserable Example of the great Power of that Passion: I must not, however, omit doing him Justice by saying that I afterwards saw the same Man behave well in an

Engagement in which he was wounded. Tho' there likewise he was said to have betrayed the same Passion of Fear in his Countenance.

'The other of our Officers was no less stupified (if I may so express myself) with Fool-hardiness, and seemed almost insensible of his Danger. To say the Truth, I have, from this and some other Instances which I have seen, been almost inclined to think, that the Courage as well as Cowardice of Fools proceeds from not knowing what is or what is not the proper Object of Fear: Indeed, we may account for the extreme Hardiness of some Men, in the same Manner as for the Terrors of Children at a Bugbear. The Child knows not but that the Bugbear is the proper Object of Fear, the Block-head knows not that a Cannon Ball is so.

'As to the remaining Part of the Ship's Crew, and the Soldiery, most of them were dead drunk and the rest were endeavouring, as far as they could, to prepare for Death in the same Manner.

In this dreadful Situation we were taught that no human Condition should inspire Men with absolute Despair, for as the Storm had ceased for some time, the Swelling of the Sea began considerably to abate and we now perceived the Man of War which convoyed us, at no great Distance a-Stern. Those aboard her easily perceived our Distress and made towards us. When they came pretty near, they hoisted out two Boats to our Assistance. These no sooner approached the Ship, than they were instantaneously filled, and I myself got a Place in one of them, chiefly by the Aid of my honest Servant, of whose Fidelity to me on all Occasions I cannot speak or think too highly. Indeed I got into the Boat so much the more easily as a great Number on board the Ship were rendered by Drink incapable of taking any Care for themselves. There was time, however, for the Boat to pass and repass, so that when we came to call over Names, three only, of all that remained in the Ship, after the Loss of her own Boat, were missing.

'The Captain, Ensign and myself were received with many Congratulations by our Officers on board the Man of War. – The Sea Officers too, all except the Captain, paid us their Compliments, tho' these were of the rougher Kind, and not without several Jokes on our Escape. As for the Captain himself, we scarce saw him during many Hours; and when he appeared he presented a View of Majesty beyond any that I had ever seen. The Dignity which he preserved, did indeed give me rather the idea of a *Mogul* or a *Turkish* Emperor, than of any of the Monarchs of Christendom. To say the Truth, I could resemble his Walk on the Deck to nothing but to the image of Captain *Gulliver* strutting among the *Lilliputians*; he seemed to think himself a Being of an Order superior to all around him, and more especially to us of the Land Service. Nay such was the Behaviour of all the Sea Officers and Sailors to us and our Soldiers that instead of appearing to be Subjects of the same Prince, engaged in one Quarrel and joined to support one Cause, we Land-Men rather seemed to be Captives on board an Enemy's Vessel. This is a grievous Misfortune, and often proves so fatal to the Service, that it is a great pity some means could not be found of curing it.

from *Amelia* by Henry Fielding (1751)

Wrecked on St Kilda

It is generally believed by laymen that the most savage seas occur in the Southern Ocean. They are inaccurately referred to as the 'Roaring Forties', but in fact the worst of them are concentrated nearer the 50th parallel of latitude south, where the great seas have a clear fetch right around the world. Survivors of wartime convoys to Murmansk, however, speak with greater awe of the seas encountered between the Denmark Straits and the North Cape. It is also a fact that some of the most destructive waves ever observed were first recorded by Robert Louis Stevenson's father, Thomas, who used his wave dynamometer to record some terrifying specimens around the Orkneys and the Western Isles of Scotland. The language of the Admiralty Pilots, for all their traditional understatement, should have alerted sailors in small craft to think twice before venturing out in midwinter in those notorious Shipping Forecast areas Rockall and Bailey. They may sound like a firm of family solicitors in a market town, but more often than not they lie in the track of treacherous killer gales, many of which persist for several days. The Pilot describes them thus: 'In the terrific gales which usually occur four or five times in every year all distinction between air and water is lost; the nearest objects are obscured by spray, and everything seems enveloped in thick smoke. Upon the open coast [lee shore] the sea rises at once, and striking upon rocky shores rises in foam for several hundred feet . . .' When such conditions hit a rocky shore the deadly encounter of gale-driven combers and fierce tidal streams set the scene for catastrophe.

Since the days of the *Iliad*, all great writers about the sea have written a gale into their plots. They may not all achieve the chilling realism of the anonymous author of the Admiralty Pilot quoted above, but in *Atlantic Fury*, first published in 1962, Hammond Innes clearly knew from personal experience what he was writing about.

The scene is set in the waters west of the Hebrides, 100 miles out in the Atlantic, in the days when the Army had a tracking-station at the western extremity of its guided-missile range. A decision is handed down to evacuate most of the equipment and men from the small outcrop of Laerg (St Kilda, thinly disguised) to avoid the problems of resupplying the unit left there throughout the darkness and foul weather of winter in 58°N. The ships used are two Army-manned tank-landing craft (LCTs), 225 feet overall, shallow-draft, slab-sided functional ships with retractable bow loading-ramps for use on an open beach. At the best of times they pose manoeuvring problems, with their great windage and low power, but, caught on a lee shore in a gale, their stern kedge hawsers do not have the power to pull them off. In such circumstances they are frankly expendable.

Before the planned evacuation of the island can be completed, a local depression of great intensity suddenly appears, unnoticed by all except Cliff Morgan, the enthusiastic met. man attached to the base unit on Uist. (Such local variations on the big picture of oceanic synoptic charts are now accepted as part of the risks which sailors have to face. In tropical ocean areas far from the nearest land, local storms of great ferocity often go unnoticed by forecasters. A different but even more devastating weather phenomenon which got past the met. men at Bracknell until too late was the gale that hit the 1979 Fastnet race claiming fifteen competing yachtsmen's lives. It featured local winds and sea states over twice those forecast at the time Low 'Yankee' hit the racing fleet. The most credible explanation is that the isobars on the synoptic chart at the Bracknell Weather Centre were faired off as neat concentric lines but were in reality pinched together between recorded data points, thus disguising hurricane-force winds.) Just as Innes' met. man realizes what is about to happen, the LCT is ordered to disembark its cargo to gain sufficient extra buoyancy to get clear as soon as possible on the rising tide.

Captain Stratton, the young officer in command of the LCT, is sceptical about the warning from his base meteorologist, which clearly conflicts with the scheduled broadcast forecasts.

'But it's all so damned unofficial. Coastal Command don't know anything about it. All they could give me was what we've got right now – wind northerly, force nine, maybe more. They're checking with Bracknell. But I bet they don't know anything about it. Read that.' He reached out with his fingers and flipped the message form across to me. A polar air depression. That's Morgan's interpretation. And all based on contact with a single trawler whose skipper may be blind drunk for all I know.'

The message was impersonal, almost coldly factual considering the desperate information it contained: *GM3 CMX to LCTs* 8610 *and* 4400. *Urgent. Suspect polar air depression Laerg area imminent. Advise you be prepared winds hurricane force within next few hours. Probable direction between south and west. Interpretation based on contact* Viking Fisher 23.47. *Trawler about 60 miles S of Iceland reports wind speed 80 knots plus, south-westerly, mountainous seas, visibility virtually nil in heavy rain and sleet. Barometric pressure* 963, *still falling – a drop of* 16 *millibars in* 1 *hour. Endeavouring re-establish contact. Interpretation unofficial, repeat unofficial, but I believe it to be correct. C. Morgan, Met. Officer, Northton.*

I didn't say anything for a moment. I had a mental picture of Cliff sitting in that room with his earphones glued to his head and his thumb resting on the key, and that big Icelandic trawler almost four hundred miles to the north of us being tossed about like a toy. I thought there wouldn't be much chance of re-establishing contact until the storm centre had passed over, supposing there was anything left to contact by then. A polar air depression. I'd heard of such things, but never having sailed in these waters before, I'd no experience of it. But I knew the theory. The theory was very simple.

Here was a big mass of air being funnelled through the gap between the big Low over Norway and the High over Greenland, a great streaming weight of wind thrusting southwards. And then suddenly a little weakness develops, a slightly lower pressure. The winds are sucked into it, curve right round it, are suddenly a vortex, forcing the pressure down and down, increasing the speed and size of this whirligig until it's like an enormous high speed drill, an aerial whirlpool of staggering intensity. And because it would be a part of the bigger pattern of the polar air stream itself, it was bound to come whirling its way south, and the speed of its advance would be fast, fast as the winds themselves.

'Well?' Stratton was staring at me.

'He had other contacts,' I said. 'Those two trawlers . . .'

'But nothing on the forecast. Nothing official.' He was staring at me and I could read the strain in his eyes. No fear. That might come later. But the strain. He knew what the message meant – if Cliff's interpretation was correct; knew what it would be like if that thing caught us while we were still grounded. The wind might come from any direction then. The northerly air stream from which we were so nicely sheltered might be swung through 180°. And if that happened and the wind came in from the south . . . I felt my scalp move and an icy touch on my spine. My stomach was suddenly chill and there was sweat on my forehead as I said, 'How long before you get off?'

He didn't give me an answer straight off. He worked it out for me so that I could check the timing myself. They had beached at nine-forty-eight, two and three-quarter hours after high water. Next high water was at seven-twenty. Deduct two and three-quarter hours, less say half an hour to allow for the amount the ship had ridden up the beach . . . It couldn't be an exact calculation, but as far as he could estimate it we should be off shortly after five. I glanced at my watch. It was twenty minutes to one now. We still had nearly four and a half hours to wait. Four and a half solid bloody hours just sitting here, waiting for the wind to change – praying it wouldn't before we got off, knowing the ship was a dead duck if it did. 'No way of getting out earlier, I suppose?'

He shook his head.

The story is told through the eyes of Donald Ross, a wartime sailor and descendant of crofters on Laerg. He has hitched a ride to the island in the army LCT in the hope of unravelling the mystery of his brother Iain, whom he believes to have been washed ashore on a life-raft from a torpedoed troopship during the war. Ross is in the radio compartment of LCT 8610 when Cliff Morgan comes through again.

[Stratton] passed me the earphones. Faint and metallic I heard Cliff's voice calling me. And when I answered him, he said, '*Now listen, man. You're on board Eight-six-one-o, are you?*' I told him I was.

'*And You're beached – correct?*'

'Yes'

'*Well, you've got to get off that beach just as soon as you can. This could be very bad.*'

'We're unloading now,' I said. 'To lighten the ship'.

'*Tell the Captain he's got to get off – fast. If this thing hits you before you're off . . .*' I lost the rest in a crackle of static.

'How long have we got?' I asked. His voice came back, but too faint for me to hear. 'How long have we got?' I repeated.

'*. . . barometric pressure?*' And then his voice came in again loud and clear. '*Repeat, what is your barometric pressure reading now?*'

'Nine-seven-six,' I told him. 'A drop of three millibars within the last hour.'

'*Then it's not far away. You can expect an almost vertical fall in pressure, right down to around nine-six-o. Watch the wind. When it goes round . . .*' His voice faded and I lost the rest.

*

Then Cliff crashed net frequency to announce contact with Faeroes and weather ship *India. Faeroes report wind southerly force* 10. *Barometer* 968 *rising. W/S India: wind north-westerly force* 9 *or* 10. *Barometer* 969, *falling rapidly. Very big seas.*

CCN again with a supplementary forecast from the Meteorological Office: *Sea areas Hebrides, Bailey, Faeroes, South-East Iceland – Probability that small, very intense depression may have formed to give wind speeds of hurricane force locally for short duration. Storm area will move southwards with the main northerly airstream, gradually losing intensity.*

The outside world stirring in its sleep and taking an interest in us. Stratton passed the messages to Pinney without comment, standing at the chart table in the wheelhouse. Pinney read them and then placed them on top of the log book. He didn't say anything. There wasn't anything to say. The moment for getting the men ashore was gone half an hour ago. Waves were breaking up by the bows and occasionally a tremor ran through the ship, the first awakening as the stern responded to the buoyancy of water deep enough to float her. And in the wheelhouse there was an air of expectancy, a man at the wheel and the engine-room telegraph at stand-by.

The time was twelve minutes after four.

Just when her CO thinks he will be able to haul his unwieldy craft clear while still under a lee, the worst happens. The wind abruptly backs through 120°.

Stratton went to the door on the port side and flung it open again. No wind came in. The air around the ship was strangely still. But we could hear it, roaring overhead. The first grey light of dawn showed broken masses of cloud pouring towards us across the high back of Keava. The moon shone through ragged gaps. It was a wild, grey-black sky, ugly and threatening. Stratton stood there for a moment, staring up at it, and then he came back into the wheelhouse,

154

slamming the door behind him. 'When did it start backing? When did you first notice it?'

'About ten minutes ago. I wasn't certain at first. Then the swell began to . . .'

'Well, get back to the after-deck, Number One. If it goes round into the south . . .' He hesitated. 'If it does that, it'll come very quickly now. Another ten minutes, quarter of an hour. We'll know by then. And if it does – then you'll have to play her on the kedge like a tunny fish. That hawser mustn't break. Understand?, I'll back her off on the engines. it'll be too much for the winch. Your job is to see she doesn't slew. Slack off when you have to. But for Christ's sake don't let her stern swing towards the beach.'

Finally the LCT floats off and heads away from the rocks of what has suddenly become a dead lee shore. Both stern hawsers have to be cut adrift to avoid overrunning them and getting them wrapped around the screws.

We were round with Laerg at the bottom of the radar screen, the two sheltering arms running up each side, and the top all blank – the open sea for which we were headed. Steaming into it, we felt the full force of the wind now. It came in great battering gusts that shook the wheelhouse. Spray beat against the steel plates, solid as shot, and the bows reared crazily, twisting as though in agony, the steel creaking and groaning,. And when they plunged the lights showed water pouring green over the sides, the tank deck filled like a swimming pool.

'Half ahead together. Ten-fifty revolutions.'

Gods knows what it was blowing. And it had come up so fast. I'd never known anything like this – so sudden, so violent. The seas were shaggy hills, their tops beaten flat, yet still they contrived to curve and break as they found the shallower water of the bay. They showed as a blur beyond the bows in moments when the wind whipped the porthole glass clean as polished crystal. The barometer at 965 was still falling. Hundreds of tons of water sloshed around in the tank deck and the ship was sluggish like an overladen barge.

*

It was just on five-thirty then and dawn had come; a cold grey glimmer in the murk.

Darkness would have been preferable. I would rather not have seen the storm. It was enough to hear it, to feel it in the tortured motion of the ship. The picture then was imaginary, and imagination, lacking a basis of experience, fell short of actuality. But dawn added sight to the other senses and the full majesty of the appalling chaos that surrounded us was revealed.

I had seen pictures of storms where sea and rock seemed so exaggerated that not even artistic licence could justify such violent, fantastic use of paint. But no picture I had ever seen measured up to the reality of that morning. Fortunately, the full realization of what we faced came gradually – a slow exposure taking shape, the creeping dawn imprinting it in on the retina of our eyes like a developing agent working on a black and white print. There was no colour; just black through all shades of grey to white, the white predominating, all the surface of the sea streaked with it. The waves, like heaped-up ranges, were beaten down at the top and streaming spray – not smoking as in an ordinary gale, but the water whipped from their shaggy crests in flat, horizontal sheets, thin layers like razor blades cutting down-wind with indescribable force. Above these layers foam flew thick as snow, lifted from the seething tops of the broken waves and flung pell-mell through the air, flakes as big as gulls, dirty white against the uniform grey of the overcast.

Close on the starboard bow the skerry rocks of Sgeir Mhor lifted grey molars streaming water, the waves exploding against them in plumes of white like an endless succession of depth charges. And beyond Sgeir Mhor, running away to our right, the sheer cliffs of Keava were a black wall disappearing into a tearing wrack of cloud, the whole base of this rampart cascading white as wave after wave attacked and then receded to meet the next and smash it to pieces, heaping masses of water hundreds of feet into the air. Not Milton even, describing Hell, has matched in words the frightful, chaotic spectacle my eyes recorded in the dawn; the Atlantic in the full fury of a storm that had lifted the wind right to the top of the Beaufort scale.

That the landing craft wasn't immediately overwhelmed was due to the almost unbelievable velocity of the wind. The waves were torn to shreds as they broke so that their force was dissipated, their height diminished. The odd thing was I felt no fear.

But the LCT is slowly beaten into submission. First she loses her port engines when sea-water gets into the fuel header-tank. Then the steering motor shorts out when the tiller flat floods through an unsecured hatch. The time taken to engage emergency hand-steering is just enough for the storm to deliver its knock-out punch by broaching the ship on her beam ends. She is driven remorselessly towards the rocks.

It was six-ten by the clock above the chart table when we came abreast of Sgeir Mhor and for a full six minutes we were butting our bows into a welter of foaming surf with the last rock showing naked in the backwash of each trough less than a hundred yards on our starboard side. Every moment I expected to feel the rending of her bottom plates as some submerged rock cut into her like a knife gutting a fish. But the echo-sounder clicking merrily away recorded nothing less than 40 fathoms, and at six-sixteen we were clear, clawing our way seaward out of reach, I thought, at last.

North-westward of us now the sheer rock coast of Laerg was opening up, a rampart wall cascading water, its top vanishing into swirling masses of cloud. We were in deeper water then and Stratton was on the phone to the engine-room again, cutting the revolutions until the ship was stationary, just holding her own against the wind. 'If the old girl can just stay in one piece,' he yelled in my ear. I didn't need to be told what he planned to do; it was what I would have done in his shoes. He was reckoning that the storm centre would pass right over us and he was going to butt the wind until it did. Nothing else he could do, for he couldn't turn. When we were into the eye of the storm there would be a period of calm. He'd get the ship round then and tuck himself tight under those towering cliffs. We'd be all right then. As the centre passed, the wind would swing round into the east or north-east. We'd be under the lee of Laerg then. But how long before that happened – an hour, two hours? Out here in the deeper water the waves no longer built up in range of moving hills; they lay flat, cowed by the wind which seemed to be scooping the whole surface of the sea into the air. The noise was shattering, spray hitting the wheelhouse in solid sheets. Visibility was nil, except for brief glimpses of the chaos when a gust died. And then a squall blotting everything out and the Quartermaster quietly announcing that the wind had caught her and she wasn't answering.

*

The ship heeled further and further and as she came broadside-on to wind and sea we were spilled like cattle down the sloping deck to fetch up half-lying along the port wall of the wheelhouse. 'Any chance,' I gasped. 'of getting the other engines going?' And Stratton looking at me, the sweat shining under the stubble of his beard: 'How can they possibly do anything down there?' I realised then what it must be like in the engine-room, cooped up with that mass of machinery, hot oil spilling and their cased-in world turning on its side. 'We're in God's hands now,' he breathed. And a moment later, as though God himself had heard and was denying us even that faint hope, I felt the beat of those two remaining engines stagger, felt it through my whole body as I lay against the sloped steel of the wall.

I have said that panic is a nerve storm, an instinctive, uncontrollable reaction of the nervous system. I had experienced fear before, but not panic. Now, with the pulse of the engines dying, something quite uncontrollable leapt in my throat, my limbs seemed to dissolve and my whole body froze with apprehension. My mouth opened to scream a warning, but no sound came; and then, like a man fighting to stay sober after too much drink, I managed to get a grip of myself. It was a conscious effort of will and I had only just succeeded when the beat of the engines ceased altogether and I felt the ship dead under me. A glance at the radar showed the screen blank, half white, half black, as the sweep light continued to circle as if nothing had happened. We were heeled so far over that all the radar recorded was the sea below us, the sky above.

It was only the fact that we had such a weight of water on board that saved us. If the ship had been riding high, fully buoyant, she'd have turned right over. It was that and the terrific weight of the wind that held the seas flat.

The time was seven twenty-eight and Sgeir Mhor much less than a mile away now, the wind blowing us broadside towards it. Engines and steering gone. There was nothing we could do now and I watched as Stratton fought his way up the slope of the deck, struggling to reach the radio shack. In less than two minutes the operator was calling Mayday. But what the hell was the good of that? In those two minutes the velocity of the wind had blown us almost quarter of a mile. And it wasn't a case of the ship herself being blown – the whole surface of the sea was moving down-wind, scooped up and flung north-eastward by the pressure of the air.

157

Mayday, Mayday, Mayday.

I, too, had scrambled up the slope and into the alleyway. Through the open door of the radio shack I saw the operator clinging to his equipment, could hear him saying that word over and over again into the mike. And then he was in, contact, reporting to the world at large that our engines had packed up and we were being driven down on to the southernmost tip of Laerg, on to the rocks of Sgeir Mhor.

*

When we struck, the ship would roll over. That's what I figured, anyway. There was only one place to be then – out in the open. In the open there was just a chance. Wentworth had seen that, too. With two of the crew he was struggling to force the door to the deck open. I moved to help him, others with me, and under our combined efforts it fell back with a crash, and a blast of salt air, thick with spray, hit us. The Quartermaster was the first through. 'You next.' Wentworth pushed me through, calling to the men behind him.

Out on the side deck I saw at a glance that we were only just in time. Sgeir Mhor was very close now; grey heaps of rock with the sea slamming against them.

*

A big sea struck the ship and burst right over us. It tore one man from the rail and I saw him sail through the air as though he was a gull. And then we went on, working our way out above the tank deck. Only two men followed us. The rest clung in a huddle against the bridge.

Another sea and then another; two in quick succession and all the breath knocked out of me. I remember clinging there, gasping for air. I was about halfway along the ship. I can see her still, lying over with water streaming from her decks, the sea roaring in the tilted tank hold and all her port side submerged. And broadside to her canted hull, Sgeir Mhor looming jagged and black and wet, an island of broken rock in a sea of foam with the waves breaking, curved green backs that smoked spray and crashed like gunfire exploding salt water fragments high into the air.

And then she struck. It was a light blow, a mere slap, but deep down she shuddered. Another wave lifted her. She tilted, port-side buried in foam, and Sgeir Mhor rushed towards us, lifted skywards, towering black.

from *Atlantic Fury* by R. Hammond Innes (1962)

Only Donald Ross and the Quartermaster have reached the bows when the ship breaks in half. They are thrown on to the beach, from which they are later able to direct the rescuing tug to Sgeir Mhor where twenty-three others cling with seemingly no hope. Fifty-three lives have been lost.

Oil on Tumultuous Seas in the Southern Ocean

By the final volume of William Golding's trilogy, Captain Anderson's second-rater carrying passengers to Australia has already survived more near-disasters than the author may have dreamed possible during his time in command of a rocket-firing tank-landing ship during the Second World War. She has lost her fore-topmast when taken aback, has narrowly averted T-boning an iceberg in fog and has to have her ominously creaking hull held together by anchor cables passed under it in the manner of a girdle for an elephant with a suspect hernia. Now she is south of the Roaring Forties and must contend with ugly following seas threatening to overwhelm her at any time. Edmund Talbot first realizes that seamanlike precautions are being taken when he is interrupted with his pants down as he squats over a cold open hole above the starboard quarter just off the gangway to the wardroom. A burly petty officer bursts in and insists on passing a long line through the hold; it is then hauled up to the taffrail above. Miss Granham, the prissy governess from a cloistered home in a cathedral city, is likewise caught unawares in the female 'offices of necessity' on the port side. On deck, both lines are secured to swollen sacks the size of stranded seals. Later their purpose is demonstrated.

Now at last I did begin to understand about the Southern Ocean. We had no more than a scrap of sail set. Our roll seemed slower. I laboured up the stairs against the wind, and when we came into the open space of the quarterdeck I experienced what I should not have thought possible. The wind, which on other occasions I had thought severe enough in seeking to blow my mouth open, now did the same to my eyes, and no matter how I screwed up the lids the wind forced them open a crack, through which I could see nothing but blurred light. I got into the lee of the poop and learned how to make a shade of my hands, which enabled me to see more or less clearly.

'Up on the poop. Are you man enough?'

He laboured up the stairs with me behind him. Now this was the open air. The very lanterns on their painted ironwork vibrated. We crept round the rail and then with eyes blasted open turned sideways and squinted for glimpses but could see nothing. It was not surprising. There seemed nothing to distinguish wind from water, spray from foam, cloud from light, small shot from rain! I bent my head and examined my body. I had a shadow. But this was not the absence or diminution of light, it was the absence of mist, of rain, of spray. Charles had the same shadow; and now as I looked sideways across the wind I saw that every element in the rail, the turned uprights, the rail itself, had the same shadow.

'Why are we here? There is nothing to see! Is not the middle enough!'

He did not turn nor reply but made a dismissive and perhaps irritable gesture.

The seamen were dragging and lifting those same curious, wobbling sacks that had looked so much like bodies in the semi-darkness. Now I saw that they were full of liquid and attached to ropes. Charles had a large sailmaker's needle in his hands which he stabbed into the bags several times.

'Over with them!'

The men toppled the bags over the rail and into the sea. A wave rose up, a whole plateau of moving water. A secondary wave appeared on its surface, was torn off by the droning wind and hurled at us like a storm of shot.

'Belay!'

I turned and looked forward in time to see the bows slide back down from the plateau which had outsped us. I felt our stern rise. I turned to see other plateaux following us, the one partly hiding the next, a monstrous procession marching endlessly round the world and creating a place which surely was not for men!

'What have you done?'

'Look'

I followed his pointing finger. A plateau had heaved up slowly with every complication of tormented water on its surface as shot to strike us. Then, at the very farthest edge of what was visible, I saw a gleam of silver. It was spreading, drawing out into a kind of path astern of us not unlike that path of light which we see in water beneath the moon or sun. But this was very mild silver, glossy and unblemished. It was definite as a lane in chalk country. It shone beneath the fits and whirls of spray, the waves on waves which flew into the air like nightmare birds.

'Oil!'

A place for no man: for sea gods perhaps; for that great and ultimate power which surely must support the visible universe and before which men can do no more than mouth the life-defining and controlling words of the experience of living.

'Oil on troubled waters.'

from *Fire Down Below* by William Golding (1989)

A Slave-ship Trapped in the Doldrums

For an unwieldy sailing-ship to be caught in a prolonged calm could be a terrifying prospect, incomprehensible to any but sailors who have wallowed without steerage way in a molten swell. A ship might be lost with all hands by being swept by current on to a sheer cliff rising straight out of deep water in the South Atlantic. Eyewitnesses have reported seeing a fully rigged ship which has not taken the precaution of striking down her heavy cross-yards set up a rhythmic roll in the swell, finally capsizing and going straight down with her ensign hanging limp from her gaff.

But in 1860 – so John Hearne's novel *The Sure Salvation* relates – the barque of that name, under Captain William Hogarth, is trapped for nineteen days in the Doldrums. Although she and her illicit cargo of 500 slaves heading from Brazil never stop moving slowly westwards on the Equatorial Current, the sea around her moves as well, so she is beset in her own excrement as surely as if she lay in a dockyard basin or small harbour with no water circulating through sluice-gates.

By the tenth day, the barque was ringed by the unbroken crust of its own garbage. And the refuse itself had discharged a contour of dully iridescent grease which seemed to have been painted onto the sea with one stroke of a broad brush.

By the fifteenth day, even the most insensitive of the five hundred and sixteen souls aboard tried not to see this clinging evidence of their corruption, which the water would not swallow and the sun could not burn. Occasionally a small shark rushed, avidly from the depths, seized a jettisoned fragment and vanished on a turn. Otherwise the ship was the still centre of a huge stillness: pasted to the middle of a glazed plate that was the sea, exactly under the dome of a gigantic and impenetrable cover-lid.

It was now, as the calm entered its third week, that a vague and debilitating panic began to gnaw at the crew. A curious sense of expectancy attended any group of seated men. Abrupt and unnecessary labour was invented by the sailors before any direction from the officers. And these bursts of activity were succeeded by periods of quiet, mournful tenseness, as if each man were trying to fashion for himself some memory of the world's tumult.

In this prison of unyielding silence and immobility their only proofs of being were the writhing edge of the sun and the nightly fattening of the moon. They were tantalized by the conviction that immediately beyond the walls of opaque blue – on the horizon's edge, if only they could get there – they would find waves running before the wind, curling at their crests with a hiss of spray, and a sky loud with swooping birds that shrieked beautiful and reassuring discords.

*

In the cabin behind the wheel of the poop deck, Hogarth raised his eyes from the meticulous copperplate of his noon entry: at a distance, the words and figures could have been mistaken for print.

For a little while, etching them with such precision, Hogarth had been happy. It was not often at sea that he could experience the dutiful pleasure of fashioning letters as he had been taught. Too often the shudder of the barque as it lunged into a wave would mar the smooth hook that should have completed an *a*, or the bows would toss briskly, forcing the table up against his hand and squashing the perfect curve at the top of the *9*. Now, in this calm, the deck steady as the floor of a room, his fist returned effortlessly to its first lesson. Almost as if that other, loving hand in the long-ago rectory of his boyhood had closed around his and guided the pen.

*

Hogarth leaned back in his chair. Now that his entry was complete, he could feel the impotent quiet of the ship settle on him again like a useless burden to

161

be shouldered up a hill. There was no comfort now in the disciplined achievement of the two lines of writing that headed the fresh page of the log. Behind them were fourteen, no fifteen, nearly identical entries. With each entry he recorded the progress of a battle that must end in his defeat. For a moment he tensed in his chair, as if gathering his energy to hurl it against the bright stillness beyond the cabin. Then, slowly, he relaxed and closed his log on the lines that read:

Noon, May 17, 1860 – Lat 1° 14' S, Long 32° 16' W. No distance. Calm continues. Full sails set. Cargo in prime condition because of our special care.

*

Price, the boatswain, turned the key in the second of the two padlocks which, passed through stout rings, secured the grating to the hatchway. He opened the clasp, slid it out of the ring screwed into the grating, clicked it shut again around the ring sunk into the lip of the hatchway, straightened and nodded as he stepped back. Short and fair and thick, with cut-off bandy legs, he had an oblong torso that gave the appearance of being the same width from his hips to his shoulders and a slab of dough-coloured face that seemed to begin, without the bridge of a neck, immediately above his thorax.

On his nod, Dunn, Calder and the old Portuguese bent and heaved on the portside of the hatch cover. Fore and aft of the cover, six to an end, twelve more of the Portuguese heaved in unison. The grating lifted from the hatchway, was swung across the opening and laid flat on the deck. The smells of sweat and heavy sleep, like a coma, of faeces, menstrual blood, baby's vomit, of closely packed flesh thickened in the air above the hold, diffused slowly about the decks, sharpened by the ammoniac scent of stale urine. And with the smells came a sudden babble of voices, the sounds of untidy movement, and the dull brutal notes of iron on iron.

'By God,' Bullen said complacently to Reynolds, the second officer, 'they make a right stench, don't they?'

'They do indeed, Mister Bullen,' Reynolds replied. 'Filthy brutes. And when you consider how commodiously we house them. D'you think anything will ever civilize the animals?'

*

From the poop above them, Hogarth said harshly: 'Mister Bullen! Mister Reynolds! Bring the blacks on deck, if you please.'

Bullen jumped as Hogarth's rasp snatched him from his mesmerized contemplation of Reynolds' antic display. He glared at the little grinning man with the glum fury of a child caught in the consequences of another's mischief.

'Immediately, sir,' Reynolds answered with precise mimicry, drew the American Navy Colt .44 thrust into his belt, cocked it, said over his shoulder to the boatswain, 'Ready, Price?' and dived into the shadows of the hold like a ferret. For a moment those on deck could hear only the frisky clatter of his boots on the ladder, and then his voice, lilting with that private savage hilarity, as he addressed the ship's unseen burden.

'Well, well, my black friends! Good day to you again. The calm continues, I am afraid. But put your trust in me. Reynolds will see you come to no harm . . .'

Price jerked his great blunt head in silent command to the waiting men and moved to the open hatch, his thick, top-heavy body wallowing stolidly on the truncated legs, a ring of keys dangling from his fist.

Dunn, Calder, the old Portuguese and three of the others followed him. On the deck beside the hatch was a large box, its lid flung back; and from this each man as he passed on his way to the hold drew a stubby-handled whip, a cat-o'-nine-tails, with tightly, shrunken knots beading the thongs. And each man's face as he was swallowed by the dark yawn of the hold seemed to assume, suddenly, the blank snout of a visor: a parody, at once diminished and absurd, of the subtle features beneath.

The confused and babbling commentary within the hold, which had stilled at Reynolds' descent, began again – as if the slaves comprehended instinctively that those who now came among them were, even if captors, men from the same dimensions of appetite and understanding as themselves.

Bullen moved to a position directly beneath Hogarth's on the poop. Behind the culverin, Dolan knelt with his forearms resting on the breech, his crumpled, monkey face bleak, with all its vivid lines now like creases, the lustrous dark eyes dulled with a sombre alertness. Beside him, one of the Portuguese stood, holding the linkstock, the brown hide of his chest oily with a film of sweat as the brazier of charcoal threw up hard waves of heat. The boy with the slim, flamenco dancer's body and the happily sensual mouth stood behind the grape-shot canisters. Along the starboard bulwark, eight of the Portuguese were ranged, carrying the Springfield carbines issued on mustering by Bullen and Reynolds. Four others, armed like them, were spaced along the forward lip of the hatch. They held themselves with the relaxed yet practised attention of sportsmen in their stands waiting for flushed birds.

Above them on the poop, Hogarth stood with widely planted feet, his hands resting in sculptured rigidity on the rail, his gaze absorbed and remote, as if the life that throbbed in those he commanded or had purchased was only the necessary but ignorant nourishment to the vibrant and superior purpose he represented.

Now from the dark square held in the frame of the hatch there began to filter decisive and functional sounds: the snapping of opened padlocks; the scrape of drawn bolts; the jangle and clash of shackles on wood; tense, harsh voices giving commands; an occasional astounded cry of pain; and a low melancholy buzz. A new wave of stinking air stirred by the moving bodies below rose sluggishly: the smells it carried seemed to catch in the nostrils like the droplets suspended in a warm mist. Among the concerted noise of pain, iron, despair and curt orders, Reynolds' jocular and authoritative voice hammered with the insistence of an untended pianola.

*

The slaves came from the hold and into the light slowly. The women and fourteen children between five and twelve emerged singly, unfettered, but the men were shackled left ankle to right in pairs. Each pair, as they put their heads above the lip of the hatchway, turned from side to side with dazed caution, blinking against the first glare, gave a listless heave onto the deck, and shambled a few paces in lock step before dragging to a halt like a grotesque music-hall team that had forgotten the routine. Four of the Portuguese moved among the pairs prodding them into motion again with the handles of their cat-o'-nines, moving them down the deck away from the hatch, uttering cries at once encouraging and peremptory, as a band of drovers might gentle into order the lurching confusion of an unwatered herd. Like the men, the women were naked, with shaven heads on which the first stubble was beginning to grow again: twenty-three of them were carrying babies, and sixteen were varyingly great with child.

'They look well, sir,' said Bullen.

'So they should, Mister Bullen,' Hogarth said flatly, not glancing down at Bullen. 'I feed them well.'

On the deck below, the melancholy protocol of seating was being completed: the women and children forward of the midshiphouse; the men in ranks three deep, port and starboard of the quarterdeck, under the culverin and the muzzles of the Springfields held by the eight sailors now spaced, four to each side, along the bulwarks. The male slaves squatted with thighs drawn up to their chest, arms round their shins, with foreheads sunk on their knees, or vacantly gazing across the narrow strip of open deck between the two front ranks. Among the women and children amidships, the sounds of one baby, then another, wailing, the smack of a hand on flesh and the soprano yelp of a small boy were followed by a rattle of intense, feminine voices raised in charge, countercharge and opinion.

John Hearne's description of the 'useless box' of a ship coming to life as the south-east Trades slowly assert themselves has an authentic ring. The final touch is to get the best helmsman on the wheel so as not to lose what may be only a fleeting opportunity to break clear of the dreadful flat spot. A century later it was the way to win an offshore race.

There is a tremor that runs through a long-becalmed ship when the first breath of wind begins to swell the foreroyal, upper fore-topgallant, the main royal and swing the spanker on its boom. As there is a sudden toss and dip to the bow as the flying jib feels the first hint of freshening.

They need be no more than movements so slight that a glass of water balanced on the rail would remain steady, without the surface of the liquid even tilting.

But they are registered as surely in the body of an old sailor as the sound and the coursing of its mother's heart and blood are felt by a baby in the womb.

They will bring him from the deepest, most exhausted sleep, the most troubled dream, as if you had plucked him from his hammock to the deck at the end of a rope.

Old Calder was the first man out of the forecastle on that twenty-first morning in the middle watch, just before six bells, at three o'clock when sleep is heaviest. He was dressed only in his drawers, and shouting exultantly to Mr Bullen and the men of the middle watch before even they, who had been awake and straining to discern any smallest sign of hope, realized what his sudden, extraordinary appearance meant.

But it was the boy Joshua who next appeared from among all off watch who were restoring themselves in their various sleeps.

Joshua was on deck, running towards Calder, his eyes alert and fierce as those of a rat, ready for any order from one who knew best what might ensure survival.

He was on deck and waiting beside Calder even before Reynolds, cursing and jumping into his trousers as he half-hopped, half-ran, appeared from the officers' cabins under the poop; and before Price seemed to materialize from his quarters like a *djinn* from the lamp, bawling for all hands on deck.

Joshua was out of his boy's sleep and his dream of the captain's lady, and standing beside old Calder in time to see Hogarth take over the wheel and hear Hogarth's voice, quietly, penetrate through even Price's roar. 'Well done, Joshua. There's a sixpence on your smartness when we are set steady . . .' And then, as the breeze began to strengthen and the canvas above them began to assume its own undirected potential life, he began to call his orders down to the filled deck.

He did not roar like Price, nor even seem to have to rise to Reynolds' urgent, brusque shouts. He called, simply, on a note, in tones, that sounded with a curious, metallic clarity: peremptory, brief and decisive as the declarations of a bugle in the contending turmoil of noise during a battle.

And as most of the men began to vanish aloft into the rigging, and adjusted yards and halyards turned sails into their most advantageous set, Hogarth ceased to call any orders at all. There was no need for it. There were those who could speak for him as he had taught them. Through the spokes of the wheel (which he turned slightly from time to time as the complex and incredibly rapid labour above him was performed twenty, forty, sixty feet above his head by unlettered men to whose skill and courage the wealth of the world was entrusted) he could feel life and purpose returning to his command. God's breath blown into a few square yards of dead cloth; his patiently learned knowledge, the craft of men he and others like him had nurtured – and this ship was no longer a useless box, however carefully designed and assembled: it was a creature more noble than any that had ever coursed these waters. Nobler because it could have life only when given into the care of those who understood how much it depended for its life on God's breath and had thanked Him for providing it.

'Mister Bullen,' he called. Bullen on deck at the end of a calm – under his eye – was a safer proposition than Bullen aloft.

'Sir,' Bullen called, and Hogarth watched with amusement the unnecessary, vigorous striding aft to the poop. He and Bullen could have quite easily conversed from where Bullen stood by the midshiphouse; but on such a morning, with a steadily freshening wind beginning to push his ship out of the waste and despair which had been accumulating around it for twenty-one days, he could find no place for irritation in his heart.

'Mister Bullen,' he said casually, 'be good enough to summon that old feller, Calder, from aloft. I know he is the best fore-topgallant man we have, but I do not think he will be much needed there now. We would appear to have a steady, manageable wind on our south-east quarter now; and I would like to have him at the wheel to make the best advantage of it.'

from *The Sure Salvation* by John Hearne (1981)

Captain Hogarth's problems do not end with breaking out of the Doldrums. First the half-caste cook Alexandre Defosse, carrying authentic documents to prove he is a free citizen of Louisiana, hijacks the ship and her cargo. He has no intention of cashing in on the street-value of the cargo (£50,000), but plans to set up a republic of freed slaves in the Amazon delta. His plans, however, are abruptly frustrated by the appearance of HMS *Beaver*, which has the unanswerable tactical advantage of auxiliary steam propulsion.

Lieutenant Honeyball in command takes possession of the slave-ship and hands the whole lot over to a bewildered local official in a small coastal settlement, to await the return of the Governor and his entourage from a trip upriver. *Faute de mieux*, Alexandre Defosse is appointed to keep the slaves in order while they dance in celebration. Whatever fate awaits them, it cannot be worse than the stinking hold of the *Sure Salvation*.

Fog

An East Coast Barge-tow in Wartime

Many authors have found the sea an ideal canvas on which to deploy their talents, not only as a medium for satisfying the limitless appetite of vicarious readers who are also hooked. An author writing a novel around a suburban community is as limited as a composer working from a penny-whistle. When he turns to the sea as his theme he finds himself sitting at the console of a mighty Wurlitzer with fifty stops and foot-pedals with which to weave his plots around the ocean's boundless moods, the diverse crews who face its dangers and the sort of ships they embark on. Writers like John Masefield were concerned mainly with those hard-driven thoroughbred clipper-ships; Conrad wrote during the period of transition to steam, most vividly about rusty old tramp-steamers in the Far East; C. S. Forester and a host of imitators rarely looked beyond the Royal Navy of Nelson's time.

It is not surprising that a Dutch writer should have set the scene of many of his novels in ocean-going tugs, in which a unique breed of sailors from the Maas have been pre-eminent since steam propulsion was first used. He does not write of fussy little harbour craft shepherding big ships without bow-thrusters into their assigned berths, but of huge, floating power-packs capable of towing floating docks to Singapore or oil rigs to the Gulf of Mexico, in between salvaging stricken cargo-ships with shifting cargoes. Jan de Hartog has had over two dozen of his books translated into English since the Second World War. *The Captain* is about a young tug-captain serving under a remote autocratic family fleet-owner who had all but cornered the lucrative market when Stukas screamed out of the skies over Rotterdam in May 1940. He escapes from the Dutch naval base Den Helder in a small old tug towing an assorted bunch of river-barges across the North Sea. He then finds that his company has committed itself to operating on the hazardous waters off the east coast of Britain as part of a deal with the Dutch government-in-exile in order to keep the family tugboat fleet intact and ready to resume business as usual when the war ends. He becomes a relief Captain, undertaking a variety of single voyages in tugs of uncertain handling characteristics manned by demoralized crews who are openly hostile to the unfamiliar young skipper on the bridge.

One such voyage takes him southwards through minefields laid by both sides, a sitting target for E-boats and the Luftwaffe. Hartog's description of the young relief Captain towing eight unmanoeuvrable barges out of South Shields in thick fog is chillingly evocative for anyone who has stood on a bridge without radar or electronic aids, feeling his way through uncertain cross-tides, suffering nail-biting anxiety while waiting for the next channel buoy to materialize.

My self-confidence lasted until late that afternoon, when we cast off to move upstream and pick up our tow for Tilbury. I had shot my bolt when I announced that I would tow it in single file against the current, so I had to leave at low tide. It was a grey windless day with low-hanging cloud; darkness would fall soon with that sky. I had no idea what type of barges to expect; as we steamed upriver towards the terminal where we were to pick them up, I gradually came to feel certain that the lot of them would be standard hundred-foot lighters which any tugboat captain would have lashed together, four abreast, and pushed out to sea regardless of the tide. The traffic in the mouth of the Tyne was heavy; immediately beyond the outer buoy lay the minefields; there was not much room to play with for a long, sluggish string of barges. The sooner I disentangled myself from the traffic of freighters, tankers and fishermen coming and going, the better it would be.

My luck held out; when I swung the *Anna Kwel* around in the current at the terminal, I saw moored to the dock a motley batch of small craft, most of them Dutch canal barges with leeboards. And as if that were not enough, I even discovered the long low alligator-like silhouette of a Thames barge among them, at least a hundred years old, with leeboards like the wings of a prehistoric saurian. I could have come to no other decision in this case than to tow these craft in single file, against the current, even if I had spent hours plotting the tow on paper. Old *Anna* handled surprisingly well, considering her size; I knew at once that she would not give me any trouble. One thing I had learned all right, during my year as the skipper of a harbour launch, and that was how to handle a vessel. I felt confident I would be able to thread a needle with this one.

We made fast alongside the Thames barge; I went to have a look at the ships and to decide on their sequence in the tow. On board the Dutch barges I was welcomed with the proud surliness typical of the waterman; they had all crossed the North Sea during that day in May when the Germans had been approaching the coast, a beautiful day, warm, calm and hazy. They had puttered across the glassy sea with their small auxiliary engines in complete safety; but although the east coast of England was safer for small craft than the west coast of Holland, they could not possibly operate in the coastal trade under their own power; they had to be towed. Their crews were mostly made up of man and wife, and, expert as the Dutch bargees might be of handling their craft, they had no notion of navigation. To let them blunder about in the narrow channels through the minefields up and down the coast of England in fog and rain and at dead of night would mean they would finish by blowing themselves up. As it was, those channels, though swept continuously by the Royal Navy, were beset by drifting mines.

I had no experience of the coastal run; I had no idea what I was in for. I did not realize, that day, that most of those taciturn bargees and their stolid wives were doomed to fall under the murderous cannon and machine-gun fire of German raiders. Tows like this one, ponderously crawling along the narrow lanes of the mine-swept channels, were perfect game for the young hunters of the Luftwaffe, and although the wheelhouses of the barges were protected by sandbags, they were pathetically vulnerable. Most of them had too few water-tight bulkheads anyhow, and all of them were so shallow that a direct hit of cannonshell would slam straight through their cargo and through their bottoms. Out of the hundreds of Dutch canal barges that had scurried across the hazy North Sea that day in May 1940, only a handful returned home after the war.

When I began to sort them out that afternoon, I found that they were just as mulish abroad as they had been at home. They argued about their place in the tow; all of them wanted to be the last in line, so as to save strain on their bollards; all of them dug in their heels when they were told to stop procrastinating and obey orders. The crew of the *Anna Kwel* followed my floundering tour of the barges with fascination. The taciturn mate sat smoking a pipe on the aft deck, calmly watching the young upstart getting snarled up in a monumental snafu.

When at last I had managed to make up the tow, almost two hours had been squandered in endless deliberations. The sky was getting lower; the smell of fog was in the air and, as far as I was concerned, the smell of fear. My self-confidence was almost gone by the time we finally set out; thirteen surly barges in single file connected by shortened hawsers. The hawsers would be payed out to their full length only after we had rounded the outer buoy and made the sharp starboard turn into the channel between the minefields. The tide was running fast and strong, traffic was heavy; I had to nose my way into midstream with such caution that we made little headway. The run from the terminal to the outer buoy was about five miles; at the speed I was going, I would barely make it before the tide turned. And I had better, for to be forced to stop or even slow down while running downstream with a string of craft like these, without power of their own and no steerage way to speak of, meant they would crowd in on me from behind. To have a tow piling up on my stern would be an unpropitious beginning, to say the least.

I paced the bridge with a nonchalance that would not have deceived a child. I knew that everybody on board the tug realized the potentialities of the situation. If they were praying, they probably prayed that I might find myself trussed by a knot of rudderless barges, drifting helplessly towards the minefields. The mate, on the bridge as I had so highhandedly requested, stood smoking his pipe in the lee of the wheelhouse with an air of complacency.

We already had the jetties of South Shields harbour entrance in sight when suddenly fog descended over us. It blotted out the world so thoroughly that I could barely discern the first barge of the tow astern. There was nothing for it;

I had to stop. I rang the engine down to Dead Slow and ordered the bosun to shoot the lead, not to find out the depth of the river but to check on our ground speed. We were still going too fast; I called the engine room through the voice pipe on the bridge, and when a raucous voice called back, 'Yeah,' I told him to ease the revolutions until we were barely ticking over. The mate, meanwhile, went on quietly smoking his pipe by the wheelhouse, enjoying himself. The ship seemed to be very quiet all at once; so quiet that the sound of footsteps behind me made me whip around. I saw a tall thin character with a big nose and small eyes amble onto the bridge with an expression of anticipation, as if he had been called out to see the nudes.

'Who are you?' I asked sharply.

'Strutter, Hendrik W., radio officer. At your service, Admiral,' the character said with a poker face. 'Do you mind if I stay to look?'

'Look at what?'

'The corrida,' he answered, with unnerving candour. 'I am an aficionado. What I love about bullfights is the moment of truth.'

'Fancy that,' I said icily; but it was no longer my self-confident, level-headed alter ego who spoke. It was my true self, the reckless boy in a jam, trying to bluff his way out, with a cracked voice, the fear of death closing the door on his composure.

We crawled on at a snail's pace for what seemed an eternity. The mate made our foghorn bray every two minutes, provoking the deep hoarse roar of freighters, the snarl of tugboats, the high idiotic whooping of a siren, the breathy goatlike 'Maa-aa' of a hand-operated Norwegian horn. From all directions a whole fleet seemed to be converging on us and yet I saw nothing, nothing at all, not a buoy, not a shadow, not a ship; it was as if some vindictive deity had blinded me with a swirling cloud, peopled with the pot-bellied, bird-beaked, surrealist monsters of the paintings by Hieronymus Bosch. I stood there, clutching the rail, trying to calm down the trembling of my calves and the banging of my heart. Any moment now, the tide would turn and we would start to drift sideways into the traffic lane or into the minefields out there in the fog.

And then, without warning, the way it had come down, the fog lifted. I discovered we had remained in the same place: the pierheads well in sight, the houses of South Shields blinking wetly in a pale diffused sunlight, the channel crowded with craft, all stopped, some of them athwart the tide. My tow was in fairly good shape, only the last two units had begun to drift out; I had to get out of there fast. It would be a matter of minutes before the tide turned; because of the delay with the barges at the terminal, I had not studied South Shields Approaches thoroughly enough on the chart. I cursed the war because it had suspended pilot services for small craft; if only I could have handed the responsibility to someone else! But there I was, Master after God of a string of barges half a mile long, about to be turned into a barrier across the channel. I took out the binoculars; they were so mouldy that I might as well have gazed through a kaleidoscope, but eventually I discerned the outer buoy. I rang down for full speed; the tow lined up on course; then I nipped into the wheelhouse to take a bearing across the compass of the outer buoy in the distance. I had just lined up when down came the fog again, this time with an acrid stench of factory smoke. I was committed now, I could no longer stop the tow as I had done last time, for the tide was turning, and if I stopped, my barges would soon be all over the place. Theoretically, the solution would have been to swing the whole string of them around 180 degrees and to head back into the current, waiting for the fog to lift, but thirteen barges, even on the short hawser, were too many to swing around in the channel. I had to carry on, putting all my chips on one card: the bearing I had taken on the outer buoy.

There was nothing left for me to do but to pace on the bridge and peer nervously into nothing. I went back into the wheelhouse to check the course again. As I stood staring at the compass, feeling a small rivulet of sweat wriggle down my back, the gleeful radio officer followed me into the wheelhouse and leaned against the wall just inside the door. I felt like yelling at him to get the hell out, but that would have destroyed the image of the calm, self-confident craftsman. After a while, I became too sick with apprehension to be bothered by his presence.

As I stood staring into the emptiness of the fog, listening to the barks, the bellows, the beeps and the bleats of all those ships around me, I had the sudden feeling that I was steering too low. I had no reasonable cause for that suspicion. I could not see a thing out there; for all I knew, the outer buoy might be too far over to starboard by now. But an odd, instinctive restlessness urged me to steer a couple of points higher.

I was so conscious of the fact that I had no concrete observation to justify this impulse that, for a few minutes, I stood there nervously swallowing, trying to hide sick little burps of fear. Then the high, mischievous voice of the wireless operator said, 'That old compass is not too reliable, you know. it's kind of sluggish in the northeast quadrant, I understand.'

It was so obvious that he intended to rattle me that I suddenly found the strength to say, 'Thank you, I wondered about that.' I turned to the man at the wheel and said, 'Take her up a point.'

'Up a point,' the calm voice of the helmsman echoed.

'Steady as you go.'

'Steady as you go.'

We ploughed on into the fog at top speed, our foghorn braying with gulps of hot water and a hiss of steam. As the minutes ticked by, everybody on that bridge began to realize that this was serious. The mate still stood in the corner, but his pipe had gone out and I could sense his apprehension. The wireless operator stood quite still, staring fixedly ahead into the fog. We must have left the pierheads behind us by now, but I could not see a thing. We were in the open, and if we missed that outer buoy we would find ourselves in the minefields within a matter of minutes. I cursed myself for having given in to that impulse to steer higher; why in the name of God hadn't I stuck to my observation and trusted the accuracy of my eye rather than some somnambulistic prompting? I saw the torso of a seaman in a duffel coat and a balaclava emerge on the fo'c'sle, peering into the fog. Of course, I should have ordered a lookout! How damn stupid, why had I forgotten? The foredeck of the tug was so short that it did not make too much difference, but even so I should have thought of it. I suddenly realized that I had done everything wrong. I had, from the word go, guilelessly stumbled into one trap after the other until now I was barrelling down at a speed of five knots straight for the minefields of the Dogger Bank with a tow of thirteen barges.

I have no idea how long it took; all I remember is that at the depth of my dejection, when I was about to cover my face with my hands and to break down sobbing, the voice on the lookout yelled, surprisingly close, 'Thar she is! On the starboard bow!'

He pointed into the fog. With my heart in my throat, I gazed into the greyness. Out of that cotton-wool world emerged a dark bobbing object trailing shrouds of fog, turning in the swirling tide. It was the outer buoy. If I had been sailing with full visibility, I would have given it a wider berth; now I was so stunned by its appearance that I merely stood there, gaping at it, as it bobbed by. The swell was not strong enough to operate its bell, it drifted past silently, ghostlike, was lost in the swirling greyness astern; then it started to ring out as the wash of the tugboat rocked it.

I stood there, stunned by the realization that I had been saved by outrageous luck. I had to do something now, give my next order, but I just stood there, speechless, riveted to the spot; then I heard the wireless operator say, with a sudden sound of sincerity, 'Well, I'll be damned! Neat job, Skipper.'

That woke me up. That alter ego took over again and said, 'So glad you approve. How about stamping for some coffee?'

'Fair enough,' he said. 'Will do,' and he went out on the boatdeck. It had been exactly the right thing to say; only a skipper who was really experienced in the tugboat business would know that the sole person who could ask for coffee to be brought up was the wireless operator, who did so by stamping on the floor of his cabin, which was right over the galley. In the salvage business, he was not supposed to leave his listening post but to sit there for twenty-four hours a day, earphone on his head, his transmitter at the ready.

Meanwhile, I had subconsciously been listening to the tolling of the buoy each time the wash of a barge rocked it. When I finally said to the helmsman, 'All right, bring her round; course south southeast by south,' I had counted ten. It meant taking another risk, but not nearly as grave as the one I had taken when I headed full speed into the fog for an invisible buoy four miles away. If I gave my order to swing around too soon, the tail barge would hit the buoy, but I was sure it was the right moment, with that same, strange certainty that had prompted me to change course.

The tow swung around; I went out onto the bridge. Before long, the lookout reported the first marker of the mine-swept channel to starboard. The pregnant cook in the butcher's apron came up with the coffee; I was respectfully served first. As I stood sipping the hot sweet liquid, my eyes filming over with the steam, a voice muttered, 'It's lifting again.'

It was the mate. His pipe was lit once more. He stood beside me for a little while, stirring his coffee, then he said, 'Fog's the very devil on this coast. At every departure, you have to pass your driving test all over again.'

I appreciated the gesture, but all I could offer in response was a grunt. I took another sip, and I was sure everybody on that bridge heard my teeth clattering against the mug. It was the reaction. I was trembling so uncontrollably that I had to hold the mug with both hands.

I had no means of knowing that what had happened to me was a manifestation of the sixth sense possessed by every born sailor. You can train a man in navigation, seamanship, celestial observation and the computing of tide, current, speed, wind and drift, and yet he will never be a sailor unless, at the moment of truth when he is forced into a corner from which there is no way out except by instant intuitive action, he unerringly makes the right move.

It took me years to realize this; I certainly had no inkling of it that afternoon when I headed my first tow out to sea as Master, oceangoing tugboats.

from *The Captain* by Jan de Hartog (1968)

The rest of the book recounts Harinxma's promotion to the biggest tug in the fleet, which takes part in two of the worst Murmansk convoys after having guns and depth-charges added. In the end she is sunk by her own depth-charges; a handful of survivors is picked up by a British escort. The captain's morale is sapped by events and a creeping bout of conscientious objection, which leaves our hero where he started – in non-combatant tugs on the East Coast run.

Sabotage in an Ocean-racer

Sooner or later the cut-throat world of international offshore racing was bound to find its own Dick Francis, complete with the odds-on favourite being nobbled and hard men hired to cosh a double-dealing jockey in a dark mews. He has arrived in the shape of Sam Llewellyn, a young, experienced member of racing crews in those skimmed-out hi-tech sailing spacecraft, dependent on human ballast for their ability to carry maximum sail, their crews living on the weather rail throughout an ocean race. The money behind these state-of-the-art racing machines often comes from the very rich – men anxious to achieve in a tough world in which they are long since past playing any useful part. Rather like the 1-handicap member of a polo team made up of hired guns from the Argentine with handicaps in the 7-9 range. He takes the field at Smith's Lawn or Cowdray for no better reason than because he can afford to pick up the annual tab of at least £250,000 to campaign a polo team.

In the case of *Dead Reckoning*, Sam Llewellyn's first novel, set in the world of the Admiral's Cup, there are black motives behind the diabolical sabotaging of Charlie Agutter's top contender for the British team. The craft loses her rudder in mysterious circumstances; his brother is killed; and his growing reputation as the hottest young yacht designer in the game is all but ruined.

The description of the start and the first windward leg of an Olympic course will be familiar even to those who have experienced it only off Bembridge in sedate day-boats, excepting that the action and the reflexes are speeded up as though moving from go-karts to Formula One. In this extract, Charlie, after his new boat has been sabotaged, is obliged to take last year's model, hastily tuned-up, into the final trials.

Sorcerer was looking businesslike with her red and gold caduceus battle flag billowing from the forestay. I was the last aboard; I had timed it that way, because the crew was a good unit and I wanted them to feel at home together before I went aboard. Scotto was there, his bandages invisible under his bulky wet-gear. I said, 'How are you?' and he looked at me as if I was mad. If Scotto was not admitting any disabilities, he would not be acting disabled. It was as simple as that. 'Okay,' I said. 'Any problems?'

There were no problems. *Sorcerer* was in as good shape as she would ever be. 'Cast off,' I said. 'Flags, Scotto.'

Scotto went for the locker, plied the halyard, and the two flags went up the backstays – the Royal Ocean Racing Club Class I pennant, and below, the C flag flown by all Captain's Cup boats. They snapped and fluttered in the stiff breeze as we motored down the creek, past the ends of the jetties.

The creek widened. I said, 'Number two genoa.'

Ahead, the sea was grey, with the occasional white horse. The wind blew flat and hard along the coast. Nobody on the boat spoke, except me.

'Up main,' I said.

The grinders applied their colossal arms and shoulders to the Lewmar halyard winches, and the ochre-and-white Kevlar sail ran briskly up the mast.

'Up genoa.'

The trimmers squinted at the tell-tales, playing the sheets. *Sorcerer* leaned smoothly away from the wind and accelerated for the open grey horizon. Her crew arranged themselves in position; right aft, me at the wheel, and Doug the tactician with his clipboard. In the cockpit, Nick the trimmer, a mastman, a halyardsman and Crispin, the spare helmsman, on the mainsheet. Then there were the gorillas; Scotto in the cockpit and Dike, the foredeck hand. We all sat to weather, on the uphill side of the boat, and sucked glucose tablets. The crew gazed out at the grey sea and the far-off white triangles of sails by the tiny black shapes of the committee boats. It was cold and raw and peaceful. But I could feel the boat alive under the wheel. Doug the tactician flicked buttons on the digital readout by his seat, and peered through his binoculars at the distant white sails, and scribbled in waterproof pencil on his clipboard. The peace was purely temporary. This was the moment of drawing breath, before sailing became war.

We put in a couple of practice tacks, feeling our way through wind and water. At first we were overstrung; Nick the trimmer oversheeted the genoa, and I swore harder than was necessary. But after ten minutes or so, we began to quieten down as everyone found their groove of concentration. I was telling people to do things; adjust the backstays, ease sheets, shift their weight. But if you had asked me afterwards, I wouldn't have known what I was saying. I was part of the equipment.

'Coming up to five-minute gun,' said Doug. 'We'll take the right-hand end.'

The first leg of an Olympic triangle heads into the wind, which makes the pre-start manoeuvres complicated. The basic idea is to cross the line bang on the start-gun, travelling at maximum speed. In theory, it is a good idea to start at one end or the other, since the eyesight of the starters on the committee boat has been known to be unreliable. If you start at the right-hand end, close-hauled on the starboard tack, with the wind blowing over the starboard side of the boat, you have the right of way over other boats. If you start at the left-hand end of the line, away from the committee boat, you tend to have clearer water.

In practice, it is not as easy as that.

We sailed up to within fifty yards of the minesweeper that was doing duty as committee boat, picking our way through the dipping masts and gleaming hulls crowding the start area.

'Five minutes,' said Doug. As he spoke, one of the minesweeper's turrets boomed a puff of white smoke and the crowd of yachts bore away. I could see Archer, his close-cropped brown hair fluttering in the breeze at *Crystal*'s helm. He saw me, too; he gave no sign of recognition.

Race rules begin at the five-minute gun. Pre-start manoeuvres, are so complicated that they are governed by special right-of-way rules which are stretched to breaking-point at every start. Offensive sailing can leave the opposition miles away from the line at the start-gun, or push them over it before the gun, which is just as bad. So as Doug muttered a string of suggestions in my ear, I steered my way through the tangle of jockeying hulls, reaching away for position from which to make the run-in, watching the digital stopwatch readout, which was counting down in ten-second jumps.

At three minutes and ten seconds, Doug said 'Watch him.' I heard the clatter of waves on hull. Just behind my left shoulder, a silver bow was slicing the water. 'Can't tack across him,' said Doug. 'We'd hit.'

'Trying to force us off the line,' I muttered. 'Let's do him. Ready about!' I shouted.

A warning hail came down the wind from astern. I ignored it, pulling the wheel down until the luff of the mainsail shivered. The silver bow came on, shouting.

'Go!' I called. 'Go' was one of our codewords. It meant jibe; turn with the wind passing under the stern of the boat, not her head. The boom swung over. Two minutes, the readout said. We sagged away to starboard. After perhaps thirty seconds, I brought *Sorcerer*'s nose hard on the wind. The start-line on the committee boat's side was bang on the nose; there was clear water between us and it, and it was our right of way. Ahead and to port, the boat which had tried to ease us out had thought better of it, and was going down for the start. But she was going to be early, and too far down the line.

'No protest flag,' said Doug. 'Yet.'

'She didn't have to alter course. We're in the clear.'

'Correct. You were lucky, though. Go for it.'

The start boat came closer. She was long and grey and high. The wind would do funny things round her hull and upperworks; I didn't want to get too close.

'Look out,' said Doug.

I had seen. Down to port, a gaggle of five boats was approaching, close-hauled on the port tack. They were led by a green-and-orange hull that I recognized as *Crystal*. They were on a collision course.

'They'll tack,' I said. 'Hail.'

'Starboard,' yelled Scotto. Archer was perhaps a hundred and twenty feet away. He glanced over his right shoulder, then returned his eyes forward. The boats astern of him were tacking.

'Bastard,' said Doug. 'We'll cut him in half.'

As I looked down *Sorcerer*'s deck, I could see green-and-orange hull and ochre Kevlar where there should have been clear water. It was my right of way; Archer knew it. I could hear myself yelling, but I did not alter course. I could see the place where we would hit, felt *Sorcerer* falter as he took the wind momentarily from her sails as he crossed her.

I think it was that little falter that saved him. His transom went past *Sorcerer*'s nose with perhaps two inches to spare. The faces of his crew were round-eyed, except Johnny Forsyth. Johnny was grinning his hard, evil, racing grin.

'Bastards,' said Doug.

The green-and-orange hull turned in the water ten feet from the mine-sweeper's side. Boom and genoa came over. They were level with us and to windward, and we were getting dirty wind from them.

'Wait for it,' I said.

And it happened as it had to. The back-draughts from the minesweeper's sides bulged his genoa and main back the wrong way, and for a split second *Crystal* wallowed.

'Zero,' said Doug.

Above our heads the start-gun boomed, and we were away, ahead and upwind of the fleet on the starboard tack, with Archer's nose a couple of feet aft of our stern. When I glanced back I could see his foredeck man at the hatch, his crew out on the weather deck and above them, the flicker of back-draughts in his luffs as they in their turn caught the dirty wind deflected by *Sorcerer*'s main. Behind him and to leeward, the rest of the fleet jostled, a chaos of sails and hulls.

'He'll have to tack,' said Doug.

'Never mind him,' I said. 'Let's get to the mark.'

The windward mark lay a couple of miles southwest of Beggarman's Head, at the western end of Pulteney Bay. It was slack water, so tide was not a factor until the beginning of the ebb. By that time, we should be round the mark. I could see the buoy, a big orange inflatable against the dark cliffs of the headland. Doug and I knew what we were going to do. I looked to port. The remaining eleven yachts were tightly bunched, masts bristling from the pack. The best of them was ten seconds behind us; two of the last boats had protest flags fluttering on their backstays. *Crystal* was a quarter of a mile away, on the port tack. As I watched, she tacked again onto starboard. We were well clear of her.

'Tack now,' said Doug.

We tacked, and tacked again. Now we were on the starboard tack, to starboard of the rhumb line, the direct line between the committee boat and the buoy. *Crystal* lay a hundred yards to leeward. We were still clear of her. The rest of the fleet seemed in no hurry to follow.

'And again,' said Doug.

I waited, just to make sure. It was a short tack, this one, and it had to be in the right place. To leeward, there was activity on Archer's foredeck. He was setting his number one genoa. In my humble opinion, Archer was too far to leeward; he had miscalculated. I kept my eye on the wind-speed and direction readout. When I saw what I was looking for I said, 'Ready about. Helm's a-lee.'

I saw Archer look up and across. It was a struggle not to wave at him, because what we had done was sail into a wind-bend, where the westerly was bent southwards by the face of Beggarmen's Head, so that instead of making the mark with another tack, we had enough of a lift to make it on this one. The nice thing about wind-bends is that they operate in a small area; this one had not yet affected anyone else in the fleet. Then I saw Archer's bow come up; he had got it too, but his wind was lighter than mine because he was too far over, in the shadow of the distant headland.

We stayed in that narrow corridor of sou'westerly breeze for perhaps five minutes. During those five minutes, the rest of the fleet fell back. Only Archer managed to stay in touch, and he was a good twenty seconds behind now.

We came round the first mark clean as a whistle, and the tri-radial popped up like a balloon. We settled down for the first reaching leg. There wasn't quite enough wind for *Sorcerer* to get out of the water and start tobogganing, but she dragged her old bones through the swell well enough, and I was able to relax a bit – but not too much; the first windward leg is always hard work, and there's a temptation to slacken off on the reach.

I had just checked astern. The fleet was round the mark, with Archer well out in front, but too far away to interfere with us. My eyes ran up to the hard curve of the mainsail with the huge swell of spinnaker beyond it, then caught on something. At first I didn't know what it was; it was merely a hangnail of the mind, something out of place. So I ran my eye back over it. And as so often happens, it chose the moment to do what it was going to do.

What I had seen was high at the masthead; a thread fluttering where the starboard backstay joined the masthead casting. I had time to say, 'Look out,' and then there was a bang and the boat lurched heavily. The tri-radial collapsed and the boom whacked across. I had to force myself not to shut my eyes, because if you were to choose the best way of losing your mast overboard, that would probably be it.

We lay head to wind, sail flapping. What had happened was that the starboard backstay had broken. The backstay is there to support the mast from astern, and to put the right degree of bend into it. Scotto stood on the transom, staring at the line trailing in the water.

'Move,' I said; he had been there all of two seconds.

'Get some headsail on her,' he said.

I yelled for the genoa, praying that he knew what he was doing, because if he didn't the mast was going to be a useful corkscrew. The fleet was on us now. The genoa went up and filled. When I dared look at the backstay, instead of double cables converging on the masthead blocks from the slope of the transom, there was only one. But at its base, the single cable forked, with a tackle leading to each of the chainplates of the original double backstay.

'Tri-radial!' I yelled, and pushed the wheel.

What has happened does not become apparent until the next offshore race, with the heavy sponsor Sir Alec Breen smoking his Romeo y Julieta against the taffrail.

All this time, I had been dimly aware that Breen was not behaving like an owner. Normally, owners fall into two types. One is the exaggeratedly helpful, who gets in the way hurling himself after loose sheets. The other is the Big Smiler, who sits as far back as he can, out of the way, and grins like a Cheshire Cat at anyone whose eye he can catch. Breen was sitting still, but he was not smiling.

He pulled me back and said, 'Did you re-rig the mast after the last race?'

'No,' I said.

'I got a bill for a backstay.'

'Yes,' I said. 'We bust one. So we made a modification, put on a single instead of a double.'

Breen said, 'Well, if I was going to sabotage a boat, I'd go for some brand-new equipment. How would you sabotage a backstay?'

The bow plunged into a wave, and spray flew aft. It caught Breen full in the face, but he didn't even blink.

'I'd slack it off,' I said. 'Then I'd put a kink in. Then I'd crank up the purchase till it straightened. That way you'd have a stay about as strong as button-thread. It'd take about five minutes.'

'Well?' said Breen.

'Well,' I said, tracing with my eye the taut wire that ran from the transom, through the high, rushing air, to the masthead casting seventy feet above us. 'And why the hell not?'

I beckoned Scotto. 'We need a volunteer,' I said. 'And some of your spares.' Scotto went to fetch. I said to Breen, 'It's not necessarily the backstay. Are you sure you don't want to retire?'

'Balls,' said Breen, with sudden and terrifying vigour. 'This is the first time I've been away from a telephone in five years. Fix that stay, and if we lose the mast we lose the damn mast.'

'All right,' I said, slightly awed. 'You're the owner.'

Sorcerer's crew might not have been together long, but they showed no signs of it now. Within three minutes, Dike the foredeck man was walking up the mast like an orang-outang, while Al the mastman applied his gigantic shoulders to the halyard winch.

'If you needed proof that man was descended from apes, you'd have it right here,' said Doug. Breen turned and glared at him. Then, surprisingly, he laughed.

It was the first time I had heard Breen laugh. It seemed likely that it was the first time anybody had heard him laugh. It made me like him, a lot; after all, it was his money at risk, and there was even a certain amount of danger about the situation – though the danger was mostly for Dike.

Dike did not, however, seem to mind. He sang noisily as he shackled the jury backstay to the masthead casting. He yelled insults at Scotto as Scotto effected a temporary junction between jury backstay and chainplate, and took the strain. And he sang again, obscenely, as he lowered the old backstay to the deck. On the way down the mast, *Sorcerer* hit a seventh wave and stopped dead. He looped out into space like a spider on its web, and crashed into the sail. Al the mastman lowered him with a run, and he unclipped and shambled aft on his prehensile Docksiders.

'Nice work,' said Breen.

from *Dead Reckoning* by Sam Llewellyn (1987)

THE LIGHTER SIDE

French Newspaper Report of Trafalgar

No doubt the editor of the leading French newspaper in 1805, *Le Moniteur*, would never have suspected that his correspondent's report from Cadiz after the Battle of Trafalgar would one day be included in an anthology of fiction about the sea. But not until Josef Goebbels launched his frequent premature reports of the sinking of HMS *Ark Royal* during the Second World War was combat reportage matched by such indiscriminate exaggeration in sublime disregard of the facts.

FIRST BULLETIN OF THE GRAND NAVAL ARMY
[FROM THE MONITEUR]
As it appeared in the HERALD
BATTLE OF TRAFALGAR

Head Quarters, Cadiz, Oct. 25.

THE operations of the grand naval army second in the Atlantic those of the grand imperial army in Germany. – The English fleet is annihilated! – Nelson is no more! – Indignant at being inactive in port, whilst our brave brethren in arms were gaining laurels in Germany, Admirals Villeneuve and Gravina resolved to put to sea, and give the English battle. They were superior in number, forty-five to our thirty-three; but what is superiority of numbers to men determined to conquer? Admiral Nelson did everything to avoid a battle; he attempted to get into the Mediterranean, but we pursued, and came up with him off Trafalgar. The French and Spaniards vied with each other who should first get into action. Admirals Villeneuve and Gravina were both anxious to lay their Ships alongside the Victory, the English Admiral's Ship. Fortune, so constant always to the Emperor, did not favour either of them – the Santissima Trinidada was the fortunate Ship. In vain did the English Admiral try to evade an action: the Spanish Admiral Oliva prevented his escape and lashed his Vessel to the British Admiral. The English Ship was one of 136 guns; the Santissima Trinidada was but a 74. – Lord Nelson adopted a new system: afraid of combating us in the old way, in which he knows we have a superiority of skill, as was proved by our victory over Sir Robert Calder, he attempted a new mode of fighting. For a short time they disconcerted us; but what can long disconcert his Imperial Majesty's arms? We fought yard-arm to yard-arm, gun to gun. Three hours did we fight in this manner: the English began to be dismayed – they found it impossible to resist us; but our brave sailors were tired of this slow means of gaining a victory; they wished to board; the cry was, *à la bordage!* Their impetuosity was irresistible. At that moment two Ships, one French and one Spanish, boarded the Temeraire: the English fell back in astonishment and affright – we rushed to the flag-staff – struck the colours – and all were so anxious to be the bearer of the intelligence to their own Ship, that *they jumped overboard*; and the English Ship, by this unfortunate impetuosity of our brave sailors and their allies, was able, by the assistance of two more Ships that came to her assistance, to make her escape in a sinking state. Meanwhile Nelson still resisted us. It was now who should first board, and have the honour of taking him, French or Spaniard – two Admirals on each side disputed the honour – they boarded his Ship at the same moment – Villeneuve flew to the quarter-deck – with the usual *generosity* of the French, he carried a brace of pistols in his hands, for he knew the Admiral had lost his arm, and could not use his sword – he offered one to Nelson: they fought, and at the second fire Nelson fell; he was immediately carried below. Oliva, Gravina, and Villeneuve, attended him with the accustomed French humanity. Meanwhile, fifteen of the English Ships of the line had struck – four more were obliged to follow their example – another blew up. Our victory was now complete, and we prepared to take possession of our prizes; but the elements were this time unfavourable to us; a dreadful storm came on – Gravina made his escape to his own Ship at the beginning of it – the Commander in Chief, Villeneuve, and a Spanish Admiral, were unable, and *remained on board the Victory* – The storm was long and dreadful; our Ships being so well manoeuvred, rode out the gale; the English being so much more damaged, were driven ashore, and many of them wrecked. At length, when the gale abated, thirteen sail of the French and Spanish line got safe to Cadiz; – the other twenty have, no doubt, *gone to some other part, and will soon be heard of.* We shall repair our damages as speedily as possible, go again in pursuit of the enemy, and afford them another proof of our determination to wrest from them the empire of the seas, and to comply with his Imperial Majesty's demand of *Ships, Colonies,* and *Commerce.* Our loss was trifling, that of the English was immense. We have, however, to lament the *absence* of Admiral Villeneuve, whose ardour carried him beyond the strict bounds of prudence, and, by compelling him to board the English Admiral's Ship, prevented him from returning to his own. After having acquired so decisive a victory, we wait with impatience the Emperor's order to sail to the enemy's shore, annihilate the rest of his navy, and thus complete the triumphant work we have so brilliantly begun.

from *Le Moniteur* (October 1805)

For nearly 200 years historians have credited a sniper in the main-top of the French ship *Redoubtable* with having killed Nelson. Not so, it seems: the fearless Admiral Villeneuve offered a pistol duel, which he won.

In fact, the opposing fleets joined battle with thirty-three ships-of-the-line in the combined French and Spanish squadrons. Somehow they counted eighteen more HM ships than were present at the action; they probably seemed more like forty-five to the French. Eighteen of the enemy were sunk or captured; 6,000 of their sailors perished, while another 23,000 were shipped home as prisoners to help build Portland breakwater and make warship models out of fishbones. Admiral Villeneuve went to England as a prisoner, but was released soon afterwards and committed suicide in a coaching-inn at Rennes on his way home.

Every HM ship which took part in the action lived to fight again, although 1,700 of our sailors were lost. Unless naval historians have got it all wrong, the victory off Trafalgar assured British naval supremacy for 100 years and put paid to any lingering plans Bonaparte may have had to invading England.

Mal de Mer

Amongst the Beautiful People

Many readers may find it almost as surprising to discover Evelyn Waugh in this anthology of fiction-writers about the sea as to see P. G. Wodehouse described as a science-fiction writer. But Waugh's description in the opening chapters of *Vile Bodies* of a rough voyage in an unventilated cross-Channel ferry in the days before stabilizers will be sharply evocative to any who have suffered such an experience. The behaviour of the ship and its mixed bag of passengers could scarcely have been better described by Conrad. Here we meet many of the dotty characters who brought Waugh early literary fame, sharing their ordeal at sea with a diverse supporting cast. As in the much larger, more sedate ferries of today, their reactions to ship-motion range from being prostrated in their bunks, awaiting a merciful end, to the studied bravado of cigar-smoking seasoned travellers who make it business as usual for the bar-steward, adding the noise of breaking glasses to the creaks, groans and thumps of the ship herself.

It was clearly going to be a bad crossing.

With Asiatic resignation Father Rothschild SJ put down his suitcase in the corner of the bar and went on deck. (It was a small suitcase of imitation crocodile hide. The initials stamped on it in Gothic characters were not Father Rothschild's, for he had borrowed it that morning from the *valet-de-chambre* of his hotel. It contained some rudimentary underclothes, six important new books in six languages, a false beard and a school atlas and gazetteer heavily annotated.) Standing on the deck Father Rothschild leant his elbows on the rail, rested his chin in his hands and surveyed the procession of passengers coming up the gangway, each face eloquent of polite misgiving.

*

High above his head swung Mrs Melrose Ape's travel-worn Packard car, bearing the dust of three continents, against the darkening sky, and up the companion-way at the head of her angels strode Mrs Melrose Ape, the woman evangelist.

'Faith.'

'Here, Mrs Ape,'

'Charity.'

'Here, Mrs Ape.'

'Fortitude.'

'Here, Mrs Ape.'

'Chastity . . . Where is Chastity?'

'Chastity didn't feel well, Mrs Ape. She went below.'

'That girl's more trouble than she's worth. Whenever there's any packing to be done, Chastity doesn't feel well. Are all the rest here – Humility, Prudence, Divine Discontent, Mercy, Justice and Creative Endeavour?'

'Creative Endeavour lost her wings, Mrs Ape. She got talking to a gentleman in the train . . . Oh, there she is.'

'Got 'em?' asked Mrs Ape.

Too breathless to speak, Creative Endeavour nodded. (Each of the angels carried her wings in a little black box like a violin case.)

'Right,' said Mrs Ape, 'and just you hold on to 'em tight and not so much talking to gentlemen in trains. You're angels, not a panto, see?

The angels crowded together disconsolately. It was awful when Mrs Ape was like this. My, how they would pinch Chastity and Creative Endeavour when they got them alone in their nightshirts. It was bad enough their going to be so sick without that they had Mrs Ape pitching into them too.

Seeing their discomfort, Mrs Ape softened and smiled. She was nothing if not 'magnetic'.

'Well, girls,' she said, 'I must be getting along. They say it's going to be rough, but don't you believe it. If you have peace in your hearts your stomach will look after itself, and remember if you *do* feel queer – *sing*. There's nothing like it.'

'Good-bye, Mrs Ape, and thank you,' said the angels; they bobbed prettily, turned about and trooped aft to the second-class part of the ship. Mrs Ape watched them benignly, then, squaring her shoulders and looking (except that she had really no beard to speak of) every inch a sailor, strode resolutely forward to the first-class bar.

Other prominent people were embarking, all very unhappy about the weather; to avert the terrors of sea-sickness they had indulged in every kind of civilized witchcraft, but they were lacking in faith.

Miss Runcible was there, and Miles Malpractice, and all the Younger Set. They had spent a jolly morning strapping each other's tummies with sticking plaster (how Miss Runcible had wriggled).

The Right Honourable Walter Outrage, MP, last week's Prime Minister, was there. Before breakfast that morning (which had suffered in consequence) Mr Outrage had taken twice the maximum dose of a patent preparation of chloral, and losing heart later had finished the bottle in the train. He moved in an uneasy trance, closely escorted by the most public-looking detective sergeants. These men had been with Mr Outrage in Paris, and what they did not know about his goings on was not worth knowing, at least from a novelist's point of view. (When they spoke about him to each other they called him 'the Right Honourable Rape', but that was more by way of being a pun about his name than a criticism of the conduct of his love affairs, in which, if the truth were known, he displayed a notable diffidence and the liability to panic.)

Lady Throbbing and Mrs Blackwater, those twin sisters whose portrait by

Millais auctioned recently at Christie's made a record in rock-bottom prices, were sitting on one of the teak benches eating apples and drinking what Lady Throbbing, with late Victorian *chic*, called 'a bottle of pop', and Mrs Blackwater, more exotically, called '*champagne*', pronouncing it as though it were French.

'Surely, Kitty, that is Mr Outrage, last week's Prime Minister.'

'Nonsense, Fanny, where?'

'Just in front of the two men with bowler hats, next to the clergyman.'

'It is certainly like his photographs. How strange he looks.'

'Just like poor Throbbing . . . all that last year.'

'. . . And none of us even suspected . . . until they found the bottles under the board in his dressing-room . . . and we all used to think it was drink . . .'

'I don't think one finds *quite* the same class as Prime Minister nowadays, do you think?'

'They say that only one person has any influence with Mr Outrage . . .'

'At the Japanese Embassy . . .'

'Of course, dear, not so loud. But tell me, Fanny, seriously, do you think really and truly Mr Outrage has IT?'

'He has a very nice figure for a man of his age.'

'Yes, but *his* age, and the bull-like type is so often disappointing. Another glass? You will be grateful for it when the ship begins to move.'

'I quite thought we *were* moving.'

'How absurd you are, Fanny, and yet I can't help laughing.'

So arm in arm and shaken by little giggles the two tipsy old ladies went down to their cabin.

Of the other passengers, some had filled their ears with cotton wool, others wore smoked glasses, while several ate dry captain's biscuits from paper bags, as Red Indians are said to eat snake's flesh to make them cunning. Mrs Hoop repeated feverishly over and over again a formula she had learned from a yogi in New York City. A few 'good sailors', whose luggage bore the labels of many voyages, strode aggressively about smoking small, foul pipes and trying to get up a four of bridge.

Two minutes before the advertised time of departure, while the first admonitory whistling and shouting was going on, a young man came on board carrying his bag. There was nothing particularly remarkable about his appearance. He looked exactly as young men like him do look; he was carrying his own bag, which was disagreeably heavy, because he had no money left in francs and very little left in anything else. He had been two months in Paris writing a book and was coming home because, in the course of his correspondence, he had got engaged to be married. His name was Adam Fenwick-Symes.

Father Rothschild smiled at him in a kindly manner.

*

Then he was gone again, and almost at once the boat began to slip away from the quay towards the mouth of the harbour.

Sometimes the ship pitched and sometimes she rolled and sometimes she stood quite still and shivered all over, poised above an abyss of dark water;

then she would go swooping down like a scenic railway train into a windless hollow and up again with a rush into the gale; sometimes she would burrow her path, with convulsive nosings and scramblings like a terrier in a rabbit hole; and sometimes she would drop dead like a lift. It was this last movement that caused the most havoc among the passengers.

'Oh,' said the Bright Young People. 'Oh, oh oh.'

'It's just exactly like being inside a cocktail shaker,' said Miles Malpractice, 'Darling, your face – eau de Nil.'

'Too, too sick-making,' said Miss Runcible, with one of her rare flashes of accuracy.

Kitty Blackwater and Fanny Throbbing lay one above the other in their bunks rigid from wig to toe.

'I wonder, do you think the *champagne* . . . ?'

'Kitty.'

'Yes, Fanny, dear.'

'Kitty, I think, in fact, I am sure I have some sal volatile . . . Kitty, I thought that perhaps as you are nearer . . . it would really hardly be safe for me to try and descend . . . I might break a leg.'

'Not after *champagne*, Fanny, do you think?'

'But I need it. Of course, dear, *if it's too much trouble?*'

'Nothing is too much trouble, darling, you know that. But now I come to think of it, I remember, quite clearly, for a fact, that you did *not* pack the sal volatile.'

*

To Father Rothschild no passage was worse than any other. He thought of the sufferings of the saints, the mutability of human nature, the Four Last Things, and between whiles repeated snatches of the penitential psalms.

The Leader of His Majesty's Opposition lay sunk in a rather glorious coma, made splendid by dreams of Oriental imagery – of painted paper houses; of golden dragons and gardens of almond blossom; of golden limbs and almond eyes, humble and caressing; of very small golden feet among almond blossoms; of little painted cups full of golden tea; of a golden voice singing behind a painted paper screen; of humble, caressing little golden hands and eyes shaped like almonds and the colour of night.

Outside his door two very limp detective sergeants had deserted their posts.

'The bloke as could make trouble on a ship like this 'ere deserves to get away with it,' they said.

The ship creaked in every plate, doors slammed, trunks fell about, the wind howled; the screw, now out of the water, now in, raced and churned, shaking down hat-boxes like ripe apples; but above all the roar and clatter there rose from the second-class ladies' saloon the despairing voices of Mrs Ape's angels, in frequently broken unison, singing, singing, wildly, desperately, as though their hearts would break in the effort and their minds lose their reason, Mrs Ape's famous hymn, *There ain't no flies on the Lamb of God.*

The Captain and the Chief Officer sat on the bridge engrossed in a crossword puzzle.

'Looks like we may get some heavy weather if the wind gets up,' he said. 'Shouldn't wonder if there wasn't a bit of a sea running to-night.'

'Well, we can't always have it quiet like this,' said the Chief Officer. 'Word of eighteen letters meaning carnivorous mammal. Search me if I know how they do think of these things.'

Adam Fenwick-Symes sat among the good sailors in the smoking-room drinking his third Irish whisky and wondering how soon he would feel definitely ill. Already there was a vague depression gathering at the top of his head. There were thirty-five minutes more, probably longer with the head wind keeping them back.

Opposite him sat a much-travelled and chatty journalist telling him smutty stories. From time to time Adam interposed some more or less appropriate comment, 'No, I say that's a good one,' or, 'I must remember that,' or just 'Ha, Ha, Ha,' but his mind was not really in a receptive condition.

Up went the ship, up, up, up, paused and then plunged down with a sidelong slither. Adam caught at his glass and saved it. Then, shut his eyes.

'Now I'll tell you a drawing-room one,' said the journalist.

Behind them a game of cards was in progress among the commercial gents. At first they had rather a jolly time about it, saying, 'What ho, she bumps,' or 'Steady, the Buffs,' when the cards and glasses and ash-tray were thrown on to the floor, but in the last ten minutes they were growing notably quieter. It was rather a nasty kind of hush.

'. . . And forty aces and two-fifty for the rubber. Shall we cut again or stay as we are?'

'How about knocking off for a bit? Makes me tired – table moving about all the time.'

''Why, Arthur, you ain't feeling ill, surely?'

'Course I ain't feeling ill, only tired.'

*

'D'you know, I think I shall go on deck for a minute. A bit stuffy in here, don't you think?'

'You can't do that. The sea's coming right over it all the time. Not feeling queer, are you?'

'No, of course I'm not feeling queer. I only thought a little fresh air. Christ, why won't the damn thing stop?'

'Steady, old boy. I wouldn't go trying to walk about, not if I were you. Much better stay put where you are. What you want's a spot of whisky.'

'Not feeling ill, you know. Just stuffy.'

'That's all right, old boy. Trust Auntie.'

The bridge party was not being a success.

*

It was at this time, when things were at their lowest, that Mrs Ape reappeared in the smoking-room. She stood for a second or two in the entrance balanced between swinging door and swinging door-post; then as the ship momentarily righted itself, she strode to the bar, her feet well apart, her hands in the pockets of her tweed coat.

'Double rum,' she said and smiled magnetically at the miserable little collection of men seated about the room. 'Why, boys,' she said, 'But you're looking terrible put out over something. What's it all about? Is it your souls that's wrong or is it that the ship won't keep still? Rough? 'Course it's rough. But let me ask you this. If you're put out this way over just an hour's sea-sickness' ('Not sea-sick, ventilation,' said Mr Henderson mechanically), 'what are you going to be like when you make the mighty big journey that's waiting for us all? Are you right with God?' said Mrs Ape. 'Are you prepared for death?'

'Oh, am I not?' said Arthur. 'I 'aven't thought of nothing else for the last half hour.'

'Now, boys, I'll tell you what we're going to do. We're going to sing a song together, you and me.' ('Oh, God,' said Adam.) 'You may not know it, but you are. You'll feel better for it body *and* soul. It's a song of Hope. You don't hear much about Hope these days, do you? Plenty about Faith, plenty about Charity. They've forgotten all about Hope. There's only one great evil in the world to-day. Despair. I know all about England, and I tell you straight, boys, I've got the goods for you. Hope's what you want and Hope's what I got. Here, steward, hand round these leaflets. There's the song on the back. Now all together, sing. Five bob for you, steward, if you can shout me down. Splendid, all together, boys.'

In a rich, very audible voice Mrs Ape led the singing. Her arms rose, fell and fluttered with the rhythm of the song. The bar steward was hers already – inaccurate sometimes in his reading of the words, but with a sustained power in the low notes that defied competition. The journalist joined in next and Arthur set up a little hum. Soon they were all at it, singing like blazes, and it is undoubtedly true that they felt the better for it.

Father Rothschild heard it and turned his face to the wall.

Kitty Blackwater heard it.

'Fanny.'

'Well.'

'Fanny, dear, do you hear singing?'

'Yes, dear, thank you.'

'Fanny, dear, I hope they aren't holding a service. I mean, dear, it sounds so like a hymn. Do you think, possibly, we are in *danger*? Fanny, are we going to be wrecked?'

'I should be neither surprised nor sorry.'

'Darling, how can you? . . . We should have heard it, shouldn't we, if we had actually *hit* anything? . . . Fanny, dear, if you like I will have a look for your sal volatile.'

'I hardly think that would be any help, dear, since you *saw* it on my dressing-table.'

'I may have been mistaken.'

'You *said* you *saw* it.'

The captain heard it. 'All the time I been at sea,' he said, 'I never could stand for missionaries.'

'Word of six letters beginning with ZB,' said the chief officer, 'meaning "used in astronomic calculation".'

'Z can't be right,' said the captain after a few minutes' thought.

The Bright Young People heard it. 'So like one's first parties,' said Miss Runcible, 'being sick with other people singing.'

Mrs Hoop heard it. 'Well,' she thought, 'I'm through with theosophy after this journey. Reckon I'll give the Catholics the once over.'

Aft, in the second-class saloon, where the screw was doing its worst, the angels heard it. It was some time since they had given up singing.

'Her again,' said Divine Discontent.

Mr Outrage alone lay happily undisturbed, his mind absorbed in lovely dream sequences of a world of little cooing voices, so caressing, so humble; and dark eyes, night-coloured, the shape of almonds over painted paper screens, little golden bodies, so flexible, so firm, so surprising in the positions they assumed.

They were still singing in the smoking room when, in very little more than her usual time, the ship came into the harbour at Dover. Then Mrs Ape, as was her invariable rule, took round the hat and collected nearly two pounds, not counting her own five shillings which she got back from the bar steward. 'Salvation doesn't do them the same good if they think it's free,' was her favourite axiom.

from *Vile Bodies* by Evelyn Waugh (1930)

Hornblower a Sufferer

Evelyn Waugh's bizarre characters were neither the first nor the only ones to suffer from seasickness in the English Channel. Lord Nelson himself was afflicted. His fictional biographer, C. S. Forester, tells how Horatio Hornblower, sailing from Plymouth, has to beat a hasty retreat to the privacy of his cabin in the 74-gun HMS *Sutherland* after watching his new crop of pressed men ('straight out of the haystacks') struck down when they clear the lee of the land off Rame Head.

They were well out to sea now, with the Eddystone in sight from the deck, and under the pressure of the increased sail the *Sutherland* was growing lively. She met her first big roller, and heaved as it reached her bow, rolled corkscrew fashion, as it passed under her, and then pitched dizzily as it went away astern. There was a wail of despair from the waist.

'Off the decks, there, blast you!' raved Harrison. 'Keep it off the decks!'

Men were being seasick already, with the freedom of men taken completely by surprise. Hornblower saw a dozen pale forms staggering and lurching towards the lee rails. One or two men had sat down abruptly on the deck, their hands to their temples. The ship heaved and corkscrewed again, soaring up and then sinking down again as if she would never stop, and the shuddering wail from the waist was repeated. With fixed and fascinated eyes Hornblower watched a wretched yokel vomiting into the scuppers. His stomach heaved in sympathy, and he found himself swallowing hard. There was sweat on his face although he suddenly felt bitterly cold.

He was going to be sick, too, and that very soon. He wanted to be alone, to vomit in discreet privacy, away from the amused glances of the crowd on the quarterdeck. He braced himself to speak with his usual stern indifference, but his ear told him that he was only achieving an unsuccessful perkiness.

'Carry on, Mr Bush,' he said. 'Call me if necessary.'

He had lost his sea legs, too, during this stay in harbour – he reeled as he crossed the deck, and he had to cling with both hands to the rail of the companion. He reached the halfdeck safely and lurched to the after cabin door, stumbling over the coaming. Polwheal was laying dinner at the table.

'Get out!' snarled Hornblower, breathlessly. 'Get out!'

Polwheal vanished, and Hornblower reeled out into the stern gallery, fetching up against the rail, leaning his head over towards the foaming wake. He hated the indignity of seasickness as much as he hated the misery of it. It was of no avail to tell himself, as he did, despairingly, while he clutched the rail, that Nelson was always seasick, too, at the beginning of a voyage. Nor was it any help to point out to himself the unfortunate coincidence that voyages always began when he was so tired with excitement and mental and physical exertion that he was ready to be sick anyway. It was true, but he found no comfort in it as he leaned groaning against the rail with the wind whipping round him.

He was shivering with cold now as the nor-easter blew; his heavy jacket was in his sleeping cabin, but he felt he could neither face the effort of going to fetch it, nor could he call Polwheal to bring it. And this, he told himself with bitter irony, was the calm solitude for which he had been yearning while entangled in the complications of the shore. Beneath him the pintles of the rudder were groaning in the gudgeons, and the sea was seething yeastily in white foam under the counter. The glass had been falling since yesterday, he remembered, and the weather was obviously working up into a nor'easterly gale. Hounded before it, across the Bay of Biscay he could see no respite before him for days, at this moment when he felt he could give everything he had in the world for the calm of the Hamoaze again.

His officers were never sick, he thought resentfully, or if they were they were just sick and did not experience this agonizing misery. And forward two hundred seasick landsmen were being driven pitilessly to their tasks by overbearing petty officers. It did a man good to be driven to work despite his seasickness, always provided that discipline was not imperilled thereby as it would be in his case. And he was quite, quite sure that not a soul on board felt as miserable as he did, or even half as miserable. He leaned against the rail again, moaning and blaspheming. Experience told him that in three days he would be over all this and feeling as well as ever in his life, but at the moment the prospect of three days of this was just the same as the prospect of an eternity of it. And the timbers creaked and the rudder groaned and the wind whistled and the sea hissed, everything blending into an inferno of noise as he clung shuddering to the rail.

from *A Ship of the Line* by C. S. Forester (1938)

Para Handy and the Clyde Puffers –
an Ocean Tragedy

It can be hard to find humour in tales told in a vernacular which is sometimes incomprehensible to outsiders. Phonetic spelling can complicate matters further. None the less, there is a case for preserving the lore of the sea in the language spoken by Thames bargemen, Grand Banks fishermen, Swedish Cape Horners, Caribbean schoonermen or the crews of Mexican shrimp boats.

While Popeye and Tug-boat Annie are reasonably easy to understand, Neil Munro's West of Scotland Para Handy stories call for a few decoding footnotes of the 'hoot mon' variety. It needs to be explained that the 'Gleska polis' refers to law-enforcement officers in Glasgow, while words pronounced in standard English with a 'j' or soft 'g' appear in print as 'ch': 'chust as I said, yon's a pairfect chentleman'.

These basic rules may help the reader to follow the misadventures of the *Vital Spark*, one of the fleet of shoal-draught Clyde puffers, the rather scruffy crews of which lived a unique life. Each puffer was distinguished by its characteristic profile, with a high straight stem, a mast with a derrick right forward and a small deckhouse abaft the single funnel, belching smoke from its vertical boiler to provide the power to butt against choppy seas at 5 knots – or maybe 6 if hurrying to catch the pub at Tarbert before closing time. They carried timber, coal, spare parts for farm machinery and the general merchandise needed to support the small, scattered communities in the harbours and lochs of the Clyde Approaches and the Western Highlands which were not served by the MacBrayne ferry network.

Para Handy (Gaelic for 'Son of Peter') is the nickname of the red-bearded Captain Peter Macfarlane, Master Mariner in casual command, supported by Dougie the Mate; the engineer Macphail, whose gaze occasionally turns from the pages of lurid pulp romances to the steam-gauges; and a variety of deck-hands, from Sunny Jim to Hurricane Jack. All share their skipper's eye for the main chance, a free dram or any way of outwitting longshoremen found in a waterfront pub. Neil Munro, a native of Inverary on Loch Fyne, rose to be editor of a Glasgow evening paper in the 1920s. For many years his typewriter added weekly instalments to the legend of Para Handy, little realizing that they would be preserved on film and TV, enshrined as history.

George IV, being a sovereign of imagination, was so much impressed by stories of Waterloo that he began to say he had been there himself, and had taken part in it. He brought so much imagination to the narrative that he ended by believing it – an interesting example of the strange psychology of the liar. Quite as remarkable is the case of Para Handy, whose singular delusion of Sunday fortnight last is the subject of much hilarity now among seamen of the minor coasting-trade.

The first of the storm on Saturday night found the *Vital Spark* off Toward on her way up-channel, timber-laden, and without a single light, for Sunny Jim, who had been sent ashore for oil at Tarbert, had brought back a jar of beer instead by an error that might naturally occur with any honest seaman.

When the lights of other ships were showing dangerously close the mate stood at the bow and lit matches, which, of course, were blown out instantly.

'It's not what might be called a cheneral illumination,' he remarked, 'but it's an imitation of the Gantock Light, and it's no' workin' proper, and you'll see them big fellows will give us plenty o' elbow-room.'

Thanks to the matches and a bar of iron which Macphail had hung on the lever of the steam-whistle, so that it lamented ceaselessly through the tempest like a soul in pain, the *Vital Spark* escaped collision, and some time after midnight got into Cardwell Bay with nothing lost except the jar, a bucket, and the mate's sou'-wester.

'A dirty night! It's us that iss weel out of it,' said Para Handy gratefully, when he had got his anchor down.

The storm was at its worst when the Captain went ashore on Sunday to get the train for Glasgow on a visit to his wife, the farther progress of his vessel up the river for another day at least being obviously impossible. It was only then he realized that he had weathered one of the great gales that make history. At Gourock pierhead shellbacks of experience swore they had never seen the like of it; there were solemn bodings about the fate of vessels that had to face it. Para Handy, as a ship's commander who had struggled through it, found himself regarded as a hero, and was plied with the most flattering inquiries. On any other day the homage of the shellbacks might have aroused suspicion, but its disinterested nature could not be called in question, seeing all the public-houses were shut.

'Never saw anything like it in aal my born days,' he said. 'I wass the length wan time of puttin' off my sluppers and windin' up my watch for the Day of Chudgement. Wan moment the boat wass up in the air like a flyin'-machine, and the next she wass scrapin' the cockles off the bottom o' the deep. Mountains high – chust mountains high! And no' wee mountains neither, but the very bens of Skye! The seas was wearin' through us fore and aft like yon mysterious river rides that used to be at the Scenic Exhibeetion, and the noise o' the cups and saucers clatterin' doon below wass terrible, terrible! If Dougie wass here he could tell you.'

'A dog's life, boys!' said the shellbacks. 'He would be ill-advised that would sell a farm and go to sea. Anything carried away, Captain?'

A jar, a bucket, and a sou'-wester seemed too trivial a loss for such a great occasion. Para Handy hurriedly sketched a vision of bursting hatches, shattered bulwarks, a mate with a broken leg, and himself for hours lashed to the wheel.

It was annoying to find that these experiences were not regarded by the shellbacks as impressive. They seemed to think that nothing short of tragedy would do justice to a storm of such unusual magnitutde.

Para Handy got into the train, and found himself in the company of some Paisley people, who seemed as proud of the superior nature of the sotrm as if they had themselves arranged it.

'Nothing like it in history, chentlemen,' said Para Handy, after borrowing a match. 'It's me that should ken, for I wass in it, ten mortal hours, battlin' wi' the tempest. A small boat carried away and a cargo o' feather bonnets on the deck we were carryin' for the Territorials. My boat was shaved clean doon to the water-line till she looked like wan o' them timber-ponds at the Port – not an article left standin'! A crank-shaft smashed on us, and the helm wass jammed. The enchineer – a man Macphail belongin' to Motherwell – had a couple of ribs stove in, and the mate got a pair o' broken legs; at least there's wan o' them broken and the other's a nesty stave. I kept her on her coorse mysel' for five hours, and the watter up to my very muddle. Every sea was smashin' on me, but I never mudged. My George, no! Macfarlane never mudged!'

The Paisley passengers were intensely moved, and produced a consoling bottle.

'Best respects, chentlemen!' said Para Handy. 'It's me that would give a lot for the like o' that a three o'clock this mornin'. I'm sittin' here withoot a rag but what I have on me. A fine sea-kist, split new, wi' fancy grommets, all my clothes, my whole month's wages, and presents for the wife in't – it's lyin' yonder somewhere off Innellan . . . It's a terrible thing the sea.'

At Greenock two other passengers came into the compartment, brimful of admiration for a storm they seemed to think peculiarly British in its devastating character – a kind of vindication of the island's imperial pride.

'They've naething like it on the Continent,' said one of them. 'They're a' richt there wi' their volcanic eruptions and earthquakes and the like, but when it comes to the naitural elements—' He was incapable of expressing exactly what he thought of British dominance in respect of the natural elements.

'Here's a poor chap that was oot in his ship in the worst o't,' said the Paisley passengers. Para Handy ducked his head in polite acknowledgment of the newcomers' flattering scrutiny, and was induced to repeat his story, to which he added some fresh sensational details.

He gave a vivid picture of the *Vital Spark* wallowing helplessly on the very edge of the Gantock rocks; of the fallen mast beating against the vessel's side and driving holes in her; of the funnel flying through the air, with cases of feather bonnets ('cost ten pounds apiece, chentlemen, to the War Office'); of Sunny Jim incessantly toiling at the pump; the engineer unconscious and delirious; himself, tenacious and unconquered, at the wheel, lashed to it with innumerable strands of the best Manila cordage.

'I have seen storms in every part of the world,' he said; 'I have even seen yon terrible monsoons that's namely oot about Australia, but never in my born life did I come through what I came through last night.'

Another application of the consolatory bottle seemed to brighten his recollection of details.

'I had a lot o' sky-rockets,' he explained. 'We always have them on the best ships, and fired them off wi' the wan hand, holdin' the wheel wi' the other. Signals o' distress, chentlemem. Some use cannons, but I aye believe in the sky-rockets: you can both hear and see them. It makes a difference.'

'I kent a chap that did that for a day and a nicht aff the Mull o' Kintyre, and it never brung oot a single lifeboat,' said one of the Paisley men.

It was obvious to Para Handy that his tragedy of the sea was pitched on too low a key to stir some people; he breathed deeply and shook a melancholy head.

'You'll never get lifeboats when you want them, chentlemen,' he remarked. 'They keep them aal laid up in Gleska for them Lifeboat Setturday processions. But it was too late for the lifeboat anyway for the *Fital Spark*. The smertest boat in the tred, too.'

'Good Lord! She didna sink?' said the Paisley men, unprepared for such a dénouement.

'Nothing above the water at three o'clock this mornin' but the winch,' said the Captain. 'We managed to make our way ashore on a couple o' herrin'-boxes . . . Poor Macphail! A great man for perusin' them novelles, but still-and-on a fellow of much agility. The very last words he said when he heaved his breath – and him, poor sowl, withoot a word o' Gaelic in his heid – wass, "There's nobody can say but what you did your duty, Peter." That wass me.'

'Do ye mean to say he was drooned?' asked the Paisley men with genuine emotion.

'Not drooned,' said Para Handy; 'he simply passed away.'

'Isn't that deplorable! And whit came over the mate?'

'His name wass Dougald,' said the Captain sadly, 'a native of Lochaline, and ass cheery a man ass ever you met across a dram. Chust that very mornin' he said to me, "The 5th of November, Peter; this hass been a terrible New Year, and the next wan will be on us in a chiffy."'

By the time the consolatory bottle was finished the loss of the *Vital Spark* had assumed the importance of the loss of the *Royal George*, and the Paisley men suggested that the obvious thing to do was to start a small subscription for the sole survivor.

For a moment the conscience-stricken Captain hesitated. He had scarcely thought his story quite so moving, but a moment of reflection found him quite incapable of recalling what was true and what imaginary of the tale he told them. With seven-and-sixpence in his pocket, wrung by the charm of pure imagination from his fellow-passengers, he arrived in Glasgow and went home.

He went in with a haggard countenance.

'What's the matter wi' ye, Peter?' asked his wife.

'Desperate news for you, Mery. Desperate news! The *Fital Spark* is sunk.'

'As long's the crew o' her are right that doesna matter,' said the plucky little woman.

'Every mortal man o' them drooned except mysel,' said Para Handy, and the tears streaming down his cheeks. 'Nothing but her winch above the water. They died like Brutain's hardy sons.'

'And what are you doing here?' said his indignant wife. 'As lang as the winch is standin' there ye should be on her. Call yoursel' a sailor and a Hielan'man!'

For a moment he was staggered.

'Perhaps there's no' a word o' truth in it,' he suggested. 'Maybe the thing's exaggerated. Anything could happen in such a desperate storm.'

'Whether it's exaggerated or no' ye'll go back the night and stick beside the boat. I'll make a cup o' tea and boil an egg for ye. A bonny-like thing for me to go up and tell Dougie's wife her husband's deid and my man snug at home at a tousy tea! . . . Forbye, they'll maybe salve the boat, and she'll be needin' a captain.'

With a train that left the Central some hours later Para Handy returned in great anxiety to Gourock. The tragedy of his imagination was now exceedingly real to him. He took a boat and rowed out to the *Vital Spark*, which he was astonished to see intact at anchor, not a feature of her changed.

Dougie was on deck to receive him.

'Holy smoke, Dougie, iss that yoursel'?' the Captain asked incredulously. 'What way are you keepin'?'

'Fine,' said Dougie. 'What way's the mistress?'

The Captain seized him by the arm and felt it carefully.

'Chust yoursel', Dougie, and nobody else. It's me that's prood to see you. I hope there's nothing wrong wi' your legs?'

'Not a drop,' said Dougie.

'And what way's Macphail?' inquired the Captain anxiously.

'He's in his bed wi' "Lady Audley",' said the mate.

'Still deleerious?' said the Captain with apprehension.

'The duvvle was never anyting else,' said Dougie.

'Did we lose anything in the storm last night?' asked Para Handy.

'A jar, and a bucket, and your own sou'-wester,' answered Dougie.

'My Chove!' said Para Handy, much relieved. 'Things iss terribly exaggerated up in Gleska.'

from Para Handy Tales by Neil Munro (1955)

Tug-boat Annie and Horatio Bullwinkle

Para Handy and his kind inspired many stories, usually ending with a twist abruptly giving the skipper of a Clyde puffer the best of the bargain. It was the same among the tugboat community operating out of Puget Sound near Seattle, competing for jackpot salvage opportunities whenever ocean-going ships piled on to the rocky shores of the Straits of San Juan da Fica in thick fog and fierce, unpredictable cross-currents. Former merchant seaman turned film-scriptwriter Norman Reilly Raine set his immortal yarns of Tug-boat Annie in the late 1920s, when the lack of radar, hyperbolic aids or even radio voice-sets meant that navigation depended on dead-reckoning and a lot of local knowledge. Played by Marie Dressler in the 1933 film, Annie gets the better of even the most case-hardened old skippers, like the one played by Wallace Beery, when it comes to getting a tow-line on board a ship as its last chance of survival.

A wild half-gale, aftermath of a week of blizzards, wailed down the strait of Georgia and churned the waters of Puget Sound to a lather of foam and spouting grey seas. The deepwater tug *Narcissus*, her upper works white with snow and frozen brine, plunged wildly through the last little stretch of clamorous water to the shelter of Secoma Harbour.

Tug-boat Annie Brennan, the tug's skipper, and senior master of the Secoma Deep-Sea Towing and Salvage Company, lifted the back of her chilblained hand to rub her eyes, inflamed and rheumy from lack of sleep and the strain of peering ahead through the tumultuous and snow-blanketed sea miles, and looked through the wheel-house window at the welcoming lights shining through the winter evening from Secoma's hilly streets. She patted the tug's wheel and spoke to Peter, the paunchy, slope-shouldered mate, phlegmatically chewing behind her.

'Well, she done it again, the dirty old tramp!'

'There was times I doubted if we'd get through, Annie,' Peter replied. 'It's been a long drag down from the outside of the island, but we didn't lose a log.'

'Course not! Don't talk such hodge-podge,' said Annie indignantly. 'The *Narcissus* never fell down on a job yet.'

She put the wheel expertly over and brought the *Narcissus* around the pierhead and into her place beside her wharf. Ahead and astern of her the other tugs of the company fleet – *Asphodel, Daisy, Pansy* and others – rose and fell on the swell that came in from the turmoil of the outer harbour.

Tug-boat Annie shivered slightly in her old sweater, and blinked the snow from her lashes as she lumbered across the wharf to the company office to report. She climbed the stairs and flung open the office door, letting in a swirl

of snow and icy air, then stood grinning in the doorway and rubbing her hands. She boomed:

'Hello, folks! Here I am!'

'Keep quiet, Annie,' the dispatcher told her sharply, 'and shut that door!'

Tug-boat Annie gazed about her in mild surprise. There was tenseness among the office staff; and in the taut silence she could hear the voice of Alec Severn, her employer, telephoning behind the glass partition of his office. She knew immediately, from his tone, that the occasion was unusual.

She closed the door with such care that only the windows rattled, then tiptoed elephantinely to the centre of the main office and presented her generous stern to the comforting rays of the old-fashioned pot-bellied stove.

Clearly something big was afoot. Annie brushed aside her boss's suggestion that a fresh relief-skipper should take her *Narcissus* to sea for the operation.

Severn accepted the inevitable and sat back, his red, good-humoured face intent.

'The steamer *Utgard*, with a large general cargo from the Orient, is piled up on the rocks at La Push, below Cape Flattery. She went ashore in the blizzard this afternoon about two o'clock. And her underwriters have given us the job of getting her off.'

'What's there in it for us?'

'A hundred and ten thousand – if we salvage her.'

Annie nodded.

'And nothing if we don't, o' course. How bad has she struck?'

'Her pumps are taking care of the water that's coming in, so the radio message said; but the great danger is that the weather might get bad again, and she'd break up. So you'll have to hurry, Annie. Take the *Pansy* and the *Buttercup* —'

Annie shook her head.

'No use, Alec. They ain't big enough for a job like this, especially if the sea kicks up.'

'But we have nothing bigger. And the *Narcissus* can't do it alone.'

'Why didn't they call on that big salvage tug, the *Salvage Prince*, at Victoria. She's closer, and —'

'She's laid up in dry dock. What other tug can we get, Annie? I don't want to lose this business.'

Tug-boat Annie's mastiff face went into a furrowed knot as she cogitated; then her red-rimmed eyes took on an angry glitter.

'It certainly boils me up to admit it, Alec – but we'll have to share the job wid that boatload o' colic across the slip!'

'You mean —?'

'Yeah – Bullwinkle! His *Salamander* is the only other tug in Secoma powerful enough and fast enough to be any use. Guess I'd better see him and talk terms. He's sure to hold me up, too.'

Severn reluctantly agreed.

'Be careful how you handle him, and get the best terms you can. He doesn't like us, remember.'

'I'll be the soul o' tack, Alec.'

She clumped hastily down the stairs, and after pausing at the *Narcissus* to tell her sea-weary crew to stand by, she barged across to the opposite side of the slipe to enlist the aid of the *Narcissus'* most bitter business rival, the big and able tug *Salamander*, Horatio Bullwinkle, master.

Mr Bullwinkle was reclining on the settee in his snug cabin, scanning the evening paper, when Tug-boat Annie, after a jocose rat-a-tat, thrust her head in at the door.

'Hello there, Bullwinkle, ye old haddock,' she greeted him, diplomatically jovial. 'What – don't tell me ye know how to read?'

The master of the *Salamander*, knowing that his is the only suitable tug available, drives a hard bargain.

Presently he held in his hand her signed agreement, that upon the successful salvage of the steamer *Utgard*, the proceeds were to be divided: forty per cent to the Secoma Deep-Sea Towing and Salvage Company, and to Horatio Bullwinkle sixty per cent. He folded the paper and placed it in his pocket.

'People finds things like you,' Annie commented bitterly, 'when they turns up a wet plank.'

Harsh daybreak in the strait of Juan de Fuca found the *Narcissus* and the *Salamander* battling with a stiff head wind. When they had rounded, with generous clearance, the fog signal of Cape Flattery, Tug-boat Annie awakened from a three-hour snooze. She rubbed the sleep from her eyes, then raised her stiff and aching body from the bunk.

*

When she reached the deck the tugs were proceeding cautiously down the coast. Tug-boat Annie took her post in front of the wheel-house, listening intently for the *Utgard's* answer to the *Narcissus'* hoarse and frequent whistle blasts.

At length, muffled by the fog, she heard an answering '*Whoo-up!*' from the estimated locality of the Indian hamlet of La Push. She signalled Shiftless, the deckhand, who was at the wheel, and he gave several sharp hoots of the whistle, echoed by the *Salamander*, which was buffeting her way, a diluted shadow in the fog, about two hundred yards astern.

Both tugs swung in towards the shore, and soon, through the mist and steadily falling snow, the stranded steamer became visible. And as the *Narcissus* steamed alongside, stokers and seamen with huddled shoulders and beads on their nose-ends, blew on their frozen fingers and gazed woodenly down at her. The two tugs ranged opposite the steamer's waist, and Annie was about to megaphone up, when the captain appeared. He was tall, and thin-faced, and his eyes, dark-rimmed with worry, held the look of a beaten man. He addressed the *Salamander*.

'I am Captain Hall,' he said, in a high almost piping voice. 'Are you the tugs the underwriters sent?'

'Sure we are,' Annie shouted up. 'Looks like ye're in kind of a conundrum, Captain. How bad are ye damaged?'

'You run away back to your galley, cookie,' replied the shipmaster tolerantly, 'and let me talk to your skipper.'

At this, a raucous laugh from the *Salamander* focused attention upon Mr Horatio Bullwinkle, who, with a flaming red tippet around his thick neck, and his strong, bandy legs braced, stood on the forward deck of his tug. 'That's a good one, Annie!' chortled Mr Bullwinkle. 'Haw, haw haw!'

'That's jest a voice from the stockyards – don't pay no attention to him, Captain!' Annie told the startled shipmaster. 'I'm the skipper o' this tug. And that queer-looking contraption over there's the *Salamander*, what I brought along to save her master from starvin' to death. Now what damage have ye got?'

'For God's sake,' piped the outraged shipmaster, 'don't tell me they sent a woman off to do this job?'

'They did!' answered Annie grimly. 'And I'll mebbe do as good a job o' salvage as you done gettin' your vessel safe to port! Come on – let's get goin'!'

'We might have been all right if the weather didn't blow up stronger, but she's hard aground,' returned Captain Hall dubiously. 'The pumps will take care of what water comes in when we are free, and I'll give you what help I can with my engines and anchors and such to drag us off. It shouldn't be hard.'

'Ye're a kind of a optimist, Captain,' Tug-boat Annie told him. 'Anyways, we'll put our hind foot foremost.'

There was further question and answer, in the course of which Captain Hall had occasion to revise his estimate of Annie's fitness for the job; and when the palaver was over the tugs efficiently made their preparations. And with the arrival of high tide the work commenced.

The two powerful tugs, aided by the steamer, toiled heart-breakingly through the day, but without avail. After nightfall the rising sea added to their difficulties. Heavy steel towing wires parted under the terrific strain, and the towboatmen dodged the back-springing coils, cheating death by the blink of an eyelash, then set to work in the darkness and icy spray, with numb and bleeding fingers, only to have them snap again under the tremendous tension of the panting tugs. After the tide had ebbed agains the tugs stood by, diving and pitching in the breaking seas that threatened time and again to wash them out.

Tug-boat Annie remained on deck until dawn, her heavy eyelids kept apart only by sheer, indomitable will-power. She was worn out, not alone with physical fatigue, but through the anxiety of realizing that if they did not succeed in releasing the steamer by the next flood tide it might be too late. If the wind shifted, their utmost skill would be useless, and she must be pounded to pieces by the white-crested combers.

Slowly, like a damp, white ghost, daylight dissolved the darkness. Through all of the ensuing period of high water she and Bullwinkle, their animosity submerged in the stress of a common task, brought to bear upon their problem all the tricks and ingenious makeshifts by which, through decades of tug-boat and salvage work, Tug-boat Annie had managed to wrest success from disaster.

And then, when it seemed that achievement was farthest from their grasp, the *Utgard* shifted slightly, and a tremor ran through her frame. A sea battered the stricken steamer, and the tugs held on; another sea, and the tugs, with the wires humming like dynamos under the appalling strain, made a final gigantic effort; and the *Utgard*, as though suddenly tired of the fight, moved again, forward, scraped her plates over the shelf of rock on which she had rested, slid clear of her bed, and floated serenely free into deep water, and was towed safely off-shore.

*

The *Narcissus*, plunging triumphantly through the seas, ran alongside the *Utgard*, from which a pilot ladder was lowered, and Tug-boat Annie, standing on her short forward deck, drenched in spray and beating snow, watched her chance. Grasping the ladder at the proper moment she mounted, heavily but with agility extraordinary in one of her bulk, to the steamer's deck.

'You did a good job, missus,' Captain Hall told her, forcing his drawn lips into a smile.

'I know it!' said Annie, with a complacent grin that turned unexpectedly into a yawn. 'Though it was kinda nip and touch, wasn't it? And yon Bullwinkle done his part noble, too – the long-eared baboon! Now what about towing' ye into port? Damaged the way ye are, it might be dangerous under your own steam.'

'N-no—' said Captain Hall, indecisively, 'I think I'll be able to manage all right.'

'It'll be kinda ticklish, gettin' through the strait in the thicker weather – and ye said ye ain't familiar with these waters.'

'I'll be able to manage now, all right.' With his vessel once more afloat the shipmaster seemed to have regained something of confidence.

'Okay, then. And I'll thank ye for a receipt for the work we done.'

In his cabin Captain Hall gave her the receipt – a signed acknowledgment that she had performed the salvage and had delivered the *Utgard* to her master, free of the rocks of La Push, and ready to proceed to port. Tug-boat Annie tucked the receipt away, and Captain Hall accompanied her as far as the waist. She halted and looked out into the fog and driving snow; and when she turned back to Captain Hall her face was troubled.

Annie left the refloated *Utgard* with Horatio Bullwinkle still haggling with her master over a further contract to tow her into port. She then slipped away into the fog and headed inshore, where she used her dinghy to land through the surf and make a telephone call to head office, before setting course for home.

Once more the *Narcissus* struck her old nose into the seas, homeward bound. The wind had slacked off considerably, but the weather was still thick, and the hooting of two fog-enshrouded vessels ahead of her announced that the steamer

204

Utgard and her escort, the triumphant *Salamander*, were sloshing their way to port.

'Not that I care, ye saucy rogue,' Tug-boat Annie in her cabin muttered, her eyes, with their red and swollen lids, fixed upon the blarneying grin of her late husband. 'I've made a good sum for the company, wid the salvage, even if it is the short end of the horn. And if Bullwinkle wants to cackle over makin' a bit extra on the towin', he can do it and welcome – the scut! Hmmph! I didn't want to do it, anyway.'

Bracing herself against the wide rolling of the tug, she removed her sea-boots and prepared, with a luxurious yawn, to turn in to her bunk.

There was a rap on the door.

'Oh, drat – who is it?'

'It's me, Annie.' Peter inserted his red and dripping face.

'What's the matter – fog gettin' thicker?'

'Can't hardly see the nose on your face.'

'All right. Keep the whistle goin'. I'll be right out.'

Once again drawing on her cold, damp boots and a heavy coat, and jamming her old felt hat over her eyes, she passed with slatting laces to the heaving deck. The balance of the long day, grey and dense and with a rawness that penetrated every corner of the tug, passed slowly into night; and through the long anxious hours, while the *Narcissus* rounded the invisible headland of Flattery and crept cautiously along the strait of Juan de Fuca towards Puget Sound, Tug-boat Annie dozed on a stool in the wheel-house, and went out on deck at intervals to whip her exhausted body into a semblance of life and wakefulness under the wet lash of the night.

Off Port Townsend she is intercepted by a local tug, who hails her with the message that *Utgard* has piled ashore again in the fog.

'I knowed it! That ape, Bullwinkle—'

'To say she was piled up ashore again in the fog. She struck near Clallam Bay.'

'Is she ashore hard?'

'She's prob'ly a total loss.'

For a leaden second Annie's mind shrank from decision. After all, her salvage job was done – she had the master's receipt in her pocket – and she had earned her reward. She needed sleep, and then a hot, unhurried meal, and more sleep. In the pause of indecision the grooves of weariness about her mouth and eyes were etched perceptibly deeper. Then her jaws closed, and her palm came down with a smack on the *Narcissus'* rail.

'Okay – thanks, Harvey!' she called to the master of the *May Dillon*, and vanished from the wheel-house. A quick jingle rang in the *Narcissus'* bowels, the big tug came about in a swirl of foam, her broad stern squatted down to it, and with the water marbling under her counter she spun the broad, white thread of her wake through the strait along the way they had come.

The *Utgard* was piled up with a broken back. Like a huge grey stricken animal she loomed out of the fog, her bow well on the beach, where the receding tide had left her, and her stern sagging down in the deeper water until the letters of her port of registry were submerged. It needed only the brief inspection that Tug-boat Annie gave her as the *Narcissus* swept out of the fog and past her stern, to know that her case was hopeless beyond salvage. But near the pilot ladder, let down from the after-well deck, the *Salamander* floated, unharmed.

'Tug-boat man, huh?' Annie rasped for Mr Bullwinkle's benefit; but her sarcasm was wasted, for that gentleman was on the bridge of the *Utgard*, as she discovered when she had climbed the pilot ladder to the steamer's deck. As she neared the top of the bridge ladder she heard the voices of Captain Hall and Mr Bullwinkle raised in angry recrimination. They were standing outside the chart-room, glaring at each other, their faces blue with cold, and garments mottled by the freshly falling snow; and the appearance of Tug-boat Annie's untidy head and wet, brick-red features, gave fresh impetus to their dispute.

'You cast my line adrift—'

'And you put another on board me, to try to drag us off here after we struck, thereby resuming your job. It's all one sequence, I tell you.'

'Wait a minute, Captain,' Tug-boat Annie growled. 'It wasn't Bullwinkle here – it was my company – what the underwriters employed to savage your ship. He made that towin' arrangement on his own hook. But when we dragged your vessel off the La Push rocks that constituted a complete and successful salvage. What's more' – she fumbled in her pocket. 'I got your receipt to prove it!' – and she produced the receipt.

'You see?' shouted Mr Bullwinkle exultantly. 'By golly, Annie, ye ain't so stupid as you look.'

Captain Hall shook his head with the febrile stubbornness of the weak man unjustly assailed.

'That receipt doesn't mean a thing. It hasn't meant a thing since he put a line on board my ship at La Push to tow me in. And I'll prove it with one question.'

'What's the question?' asked Annie uneasily.

'Wasn't this man your assistant – your employee – in the salvage operations?'

Tug-boat Annie recognized the fatal significance of the question; but being by nature truthful, she did not avoid it.

'Yes,' she answered simply.

'There you are, then. As the principal, you are legally responsible for the acts of your employee; and since he continued the salvage after you left, and failed to complete it, your company cannot legally claim the salvage fee.'

'Oh – so that's how it stands, is it?' said Tug-boat Annie quietly.

There was a short silence. Captain Hall's thin face was chalk-white with strain, and worry had painted dark circles around his deep-set eyes; but his rather weak mouth was set in a stubborn line. Bullwinkle, square-set, husky and formidable, his face red with passion, watched him warily.

The silence was broken by Captain Hall. He held out his hand to Tug-boat Annie.

'I'll ask you to give me back that receipt,' he said.

'Don't you give it to him, Annie old pal,' said Mr Bullwinkle quickly.

Tug-boat Annie turned on him savagely.

'You keep out o' this, ye hairy alligator! You've did damage enough!' She turned to the shipmaster, and asked quietly: 'Suppose I don't give it to ye? What's it to you? Your job's gone, anyway.'

Captain Hall's thin shoulders braced, in a vain attempt at jauntiness. But a lump worked visibly in his throat.

'You're right, of course,' he said huskily. 'It is nothing to me personally, for I'll lose my berth, and probably my certificate through this. But – well, it's still my duty to protect the underwriters. The ship's a total loss, now, and they'll have to pay my owners for full value of vessel and cargo, which runs well over a million dollars. So it's hardly fair to expect them to pay your company an additional $110,000 for an unsuccessful salvage, is it?'

It was a brave effort, and Tug-boat Annie admired his stand. She noted the upflung head, and the discouraged eyes that longed to plead, yet would not. Her own eyes misted with quick compassion.

'No,' she said deeply, 'that'd hardly be fair. Mind, I'm not sayin' that if Bullwinkle hadn't acted like a dirty dog, I wouldn't hang on to this receipt. But – well, us Puget Sound tow-boat men don't do business that way. So—'

She proffered the receipt; but before the grateful shipmaster could take it, Mr Bullwinkle forcibly intervened.

'Have you gone crazy, Annie?' he bellowed. 'Throwin' away $110,000 like that? What about my rights?'

'If you had your rights,' she told him, 'ye'd be buryin' beef bones in somebody's back yard!'

'Annie, listen,' he pleaded. 'You keep that receipt, and I'll go fifty–fifty on the salvage with ye, instead of sixty-forty. No,' as he saw her jaw tighten, 'I'll take the forty, and you keep the sixty!'

'Beginning' to crawl now, are ye? Here, Captain—'

'Here, you!' shouted Mr Bullwinkle, 'I'll not let ye give it to him.'

'Well, in that case' – began Annie. She stepped back a pace or two, deliberately tore the paper into tiny flakes, and with an elaborate flip of her hand threw them in the air. The cold and vagrant breeze caught them, and they fluttered away, lost in the whirling snow.

Thinking he has lost his share of the spoils, Horatio Bullwinkle only too readily settles for a promissory note from Annie for $5,000 for his time and labour in lieu of the salvage fee.

She descended the ladder to her tug. As her tug left the *Utgard's* side and set a course for home, the *Salamander* also gathered way and ran parallel, a few yards distant. Mr Bullwinkle thrust his uncouth head out of the pilot-house window.

'Hey – Annie!' he hailed.

Annie opened the door and stepped on deck. 'What – ain't you dead yet?' she began, but Mr Bullwinkle interrupted.

'Annie, you was an awful sap to give me that five thousand.'

'I know it!' said Annie tartly. 'But if ye'd had manners enough to keep yer trap shut a while back, ye'd have got $44,000 instead o' five – less the premium, o' course.'

'What do you mean?' he asked uneasily.

'I tried to tell ye, back on the *Utgard*,' replied Tug-boat Annie complacently, 'but, oh, no! – you wouldn't listen. I was goin' to give ye a full forty per cent share o' the *Utgard*'s salvage fee, but well, it's too late now.'

'Sa-ay – what are you getting at?' demanded Mr Bullwinkle, now thoroughly alarmed.

'It's so simple that even you might understand it,' said Annie patiently. 'When you went off in charge o' the *Utgard* I rowed ashore at La Push, and telephoned Alec Severn to insure our salvage fee for the full amount. Then, no matter what happened to the *Utgard*, we'd still be sure o' that $110,000. So I could well afford to give you $5,000, instead of the sixty per cent ye'd have got if ye'd hung on to that agreement, or the forty per cent I'd have gave ye if ye'd let me talk to ye. What's that?'

Mr Bullwinkle's reply was interesting but unprintable.

'Oh, my!' Annie cried, covering her ears in pretended horror. 'Ain't ye ashamed to use language the like o' that? By the way, the Secoma waterfront'll still have its laugh – on'y the laugh'll be on the other foot, now!'

She shut the door, and with a tired but happy sigh stretched herself on the wheel-house settee, and looked at Shiftless with one drowsy eye.

''Ome, James!' she said.

from The Last Laugh by Norman Reilly Raine

On Dropping a Jam Sandwich

The term Sod's Law is now as firmly established in the English language as Murphy's Law is in the United States. It was first used in 1977 in the following unforgettable form: 'Sod's Law is a well-know theorem which proclaims that a slice of bread buttered and jammed aspect up will, if dropped, land on the rug aspect down.' Its authors were two amiably eccentric offshore sailors, Bill Lucas and Andrew Spedding, in an era when there were still boats sailing with wire sheets, towed logs, Highfield levers and chain check stoppers to take the load whilst transferring a heavy line from one cleat to another. They developed their one-line proposition with a sequence of cumulative misfortunes consequent on dropping the jam sandwich:

> At sea it also lands aspect DOWN, but also at sea an inverted bottom and legs indicate that the top end of that person is hanging down through the open floor cover over the engine trying to stop the shaft turning. A lurch from the boat divorces the slice of bread from the adhesive sticking it to the floor: the bread slides past the engineer. As it goes past his right ear he tries to grab it, misses, swears, and drops the spanner in the sump and swears harder.
>
> The cussing from the engine alarms the cook out of the galley space; she steps on, and slides with, the remaining butter and jam. On deck the crew are handing the spinnaker which they hurl down the hatch on top of the jam, the engineer, the cook and the pot full of greasy stew she had been holding prior to the incident. A keen young foredeck hand rushes down to the saloon to get out a new headsail. As he clambers over the heap of red nylon he does not notice that it conceals two muttering fellow crew members, or for that matter the open engine cover. He falls and helps push the mess into the engine space where the exhaust pipe, still hot from a battery charge, burns a hole in the spinnaker. The coaming edge claims a slice of his shin. Someone on deck shouts 'Now the workers have got the kite off, how about some grub?'
>
> It takes some time to sort out the shambles in the saloon, and in the process the bread that slid into the bilge is forgotten. Four hours later the new watch pump the bilge, and the offending slice is turned into bread paste and jams the outlet valve on the pump. The engine hatch is again lifted to attend to the pump when someone coming off watch carves himself a thick wad of bread, butters it, and spreads half a pot of strawberry jam over the top, then . . .

Nowadays most lightweight diesels have been properly marinized and will start at the touch of a button, always assuming the batteries have enough amps left and that they have not been squandered on such irrelevancies as navigation lights and what we laughingly call the Hotel Load (water pumps, hot showers and the audio tape-deck). Even at this point the skipper has few worries. An engine so fitted can be swung into action by any passing prop forward who happens to catch the compression stroke off guard. Make sure there are plenty of Band-aids nearby, for the gorilla is certain to have laid bare his knuckles on an adjacent piece of furniture as he hits the crank as though it were his opposite number in the Welsh pack.

The situation does not arise with engines let deep into the garboards as part of the keel structure. Nor did it matter in some hot international offshore racing rule-cheaters whose engines were installed only as ballast and had had their pistons removed and cylinders filled with molten lead.

In an extract headed 'Yottingineering', Lucas and Spedding recount how you must learn to live with your boat's engine.

The two aspects of marine engines which most affect boats are: (1) Companies who build marine engines are sited deep in dry farming country or well away from nasty salt water in the heart of the industrial Midlands. The official reasons for this are their need to concentrate on their main line of trade to make truck or tractor engines. The real reason is so that they can remain aloof from the concept that their product will start becoming rusty at its first brush with salt air, and that the process will continue on subsequent meetings. The owners will spend the next twenty years trying to keep this at bay. (2) Designers and builders who plan or build marine engines into yachts have a masochistic wish to place them in the most incredibly difficult places: if they can, at the back of a slot between two bulkheads under the cockpit or in an impossibly difficult space under the floor of the saloon. Indeed, if you go into a production boatyard you will see that operation one is to pull the fibreglass hull out of the mould; operation two is to put the engine into this vast open space; and operations three to twenty-six to build bulkheads, lockers and a lid all round the engine making any subsequent work on it a feat worthy of a limbo dancer or a small animal able to put 25 ft-lbs on a torque wrench.

However, once in the boat marine engines have to start swaying about and adjusting to their surroundings. Anyone who knows Rudyard Kipling's poem about a new ship where the various parts have to live with each other's stresses will understand that the thing has to 'tune' in, and marine engines will acquire an individual Character (note the capital C). It is this which the Yottingineer needs to understand.

The manual for the engine will say, for instance:

'Changing the filter is a simple operation; remove the retaining nut at the top, drop down the filter bowl, change the XYZ cartridge and replace taking care to see the retaining gasket is properly seated.'

To do this in your boat means taking up the cockpit floor, and then finding you cannot squeeze down the hole – in desperation you hire the small boy from the boat on the outboard end of the trot. Give him a Coke and lower him down the hole with simple instructions. The wing nut on the top does not give up easily, but after you have adjusted the Mole Grips several times he gets it loose and takes off the filter without difficulty.

Unfortunately he drops the wing nut down the sump. You spend half an hour fishing from the front of the engine with a magnet tied to a stick trying to retrieve it, before the helpful neighbour tells you that that is the only non-ferrous part of these particular engines. You charm your slim helper with promises of funds for the fun fair to keep him down the hole trying spare nuts you have in the tool kit. After another half hour your friendly neighbour comes back to tell you that those engines are all Universal threads . . . you have a selection of Whitworth and metric. You bodge the whole thing up with boat tape for that weekend, and the boatyard charges you £27.30 to fit a new filter unit. When this sort of thing doesn't happen you are becoming in sympathy with the character of your engine.

from *Sod's Law of the Sea* by Bill Lucas and Andrew Spedding (1977)

A Monkey at Sea

John Masefield (1878–1967) ended his days as Poet Laureate. He began as an apprentice in a Cape Horner in 1893, but ill-health forced him to give up a seafaring life. He became a journalist on the *Manchester Guardian* and for nearly sixty years wrote a succession of narrative ballads and novels about the sea. His most famous novel was *Bird of Dawning* (1933), a fictionalized account of the great tea-clipper race from Foochow to London in 1863 between *Taeping, Serica* and *Aeriel*, when they all finished on the same tide. However, it was Masefield's first collection of short stories, *A Mainsail Haul* (1905), that marked him out as a front-ranking writer about the sea. There is much in these tales about Caribbean pirates, beautiful princesses and sea-serpents. One lovely yarn concerns a massive Able Seaman who, before sailing homewards from Panama, blows his last silver dollar on a pet monkey. Masefield's eye for evocative detail, which he later used so effectively in listing the general cargo in his famous poem 'Dirty British Coaster', is shown here in the inventory of goods on display in the Panama water front store:

'Once upon a time there was a clipper ship called the *Mary*, and she was lying in Panama waiting for a freight. It was hot, and it was calm, and it was hazy, and the men aboard her were dead sick of the sight of her. They had been lying there all the summer, having nothing to do but to wash her down, and scrape the royal masts with glass, and make the chain cables bright. And aboard of her was a big AB from Liverpool, with a tattooed chest on him and an arm like a spar. And this man's name was Bill.

'Now, one day, while the captain of this clipper was sunning in the club, there came a merchant to him offering him a fine freight home and "despatch" in loading. So the old man went aboard that evening in a merry temper, and bade the mates rastle the hands aft. He told them that they could go ashore the next morning for a "liberty-day" of four-and-twenty hours, with twenty dollars pay to blue, and no questions asked if they came aboard drunk. So forward goes all hands merrily, to rout out their go-ashore things, their red handkerchiefs, and "sombre-airers", for to astonish the Dons. And ashore they goes the next morning, after breakfast, with their silver dollars in their fists, and the jolly-boat to take them. And ashore they steps, and "So long" they says to the young fellows in the boat, and so up the Mole to the beautiful town of Panama.

'Now the next morning that fellow Bill I told you of was tacking down the city to the boat, singing some song or another. And when he got near to the jetty he went fumbling in his pocket for his pipe, and what should he find but a silver dollar that had slipped away and been saved. So he thinks, "If I go aboard with this dollar, why the hands'll laugh at me; besides, it's a wasting of it not to spend it." So he cast about for some place where he could blue it in.

'Now close by where he stood there was a sort of a great store, kept by a Johnny Dago. And if I were to tell you of the things they had in it, I would need nine tongues and an oiled hinge to each of them. But Billy walked into this store, into the space inside, into like the 'tween decks, for to have a look about him before buying. And there were great bunches of bananas a-ripening against the wall. And stacks of dried raisins, and bags of dried figs, and melon seeds, and pomegranates enough to sink you. Then there were cotton bales, and calico, and silk of Persia. And rum in puncheons, and bottled ale. And all manner of sweets, and a power of a lot of chemicals. And anchors gone rusty, fished up from the bay after the ships were gone. And spare cables, all ranged for letting go. And ropes, and sails, and balls of marline stuff. Then there was blocks of all kinds, wood and iron. Dunnage there was, and scantling, likewise sea-chests with pictures on them. And casks of beef and pork, and paint, and peas, and petrolium. But for not one of these things did Billy care a handful of bilge.

'Then there were medical comforts, such as ginger and calavances. And plug tobacco, and coil tobacco, and tobacco leaf, and tobacco clippings. And such a power of a lot of bulls' hides as you never saw. Likewise there was tinned things like cocoa, and boxed things like China tea. And any quantity of blankets, and rugs, and donkeys' breakfasts. And oilskins there was, and rubber sea-boots, and shore shoes, and Crimee shirts. Also Dungarees, and soap, and matches, so many as you never heard tell. But no, not for one of these things was Bill going for to bargain.

'Then there were lamps and candles, and knives and nutmeg-graters, and things made of bright tin and saucers of red clay; and rolls of coloured cloth, made in the hills by the Indians. Bowls there were, painted with twisty-whirls by the folk of old time. And flutes from the tombs (of the Incas), and whistles that looked like flower-pots. Also fiddles and beautiful melodeons. Then there were paper roses for ornament, and false white flowers for graves; also paint-brushes and coir-brooms. There were cages full of parrots, both green and grey; and white cockatoos on perches a-nodding their red crests; and Java lovebirds a-billing, and parrakeets a-screaming, and little kittens for the ships with rats. And at the last of all there was a little monkey, chained to a sack of jib-hanks, who sat upon his tail a-grinning.

'Now Bill he sees this monkey, and he thinks he never see a cuter little beast, not never. And then he thinks of something, and he pipes up to the old Johnny Dago, and he says, pointing to the monkey:

' "Hey-a Johnny! How much-a take-a little munk?"

'So the old Johnny Dago looks at Bill a spell, and then says:

' "I take-a five-a doll' that-a little munk."

'So Billy planks down his silver dollar, and says:

' "I give-a one doll', you cross-eyed Dago."

'Then the old man unchained the monkey, and handed him to Bill without another word. And away the pair of them went, down the Mole to where the boats lay, where a lanchero took them off to the *Mary*.

'Now when they got aboard all hands came around Bill, saying: "Why, Bill, whatever are you going to do with that there little monkey?" And Bill he said: "You shut your heads about that there little monkey. I'm going to teach that little monkey how to speak. And when he can speak I'm going to sell him to a museum. And then I'll buy a farm. I won't come to sea any more." So they just laugh at Bill, and by and by the *Mary* loaded, and got her hatches on, and sailed south-away, on the road home to Liverpool.

'Well, every evening, in the dog-watch, after supper, while the decks were drying from the washing-down, Bill used to take the monkey on to the fo'c's'le head, and set him on the capstan. "Well, ye little divvle," he used to say, "will ye speak? Are ye going to speak, hey?" and the monkey would just grin and chatter back at Billy, but never no Christian speech came in front of them teeth of his. And this game went on until they were up with the Horn, in bitter cold weather, running east like a stag, with a great sea piling up astern. And then one night, at eight bells, Billy came on deck for the first watch, bringing the monkey with him. It was blowing like sin, stiff and cold, and the *Mary* was butting through, and dipping her fo'c's'le under. So Bill takes the monkey, and lashes him down good and snug on the drum of the capstan, on the fo'c's'le head. "Now, you little divvle," he said, "will you speak? Will you speak, eh?" But the monkey just grinned at him.

'At the end of the first hour he came again. "Are ye going to speak, ye little beggar?" he says, and the monkey sits and shivers, but never a word does the little beggar say. And it was the same at four bells, when the look-out man was relieved. But at six bells Billy came again, and the monkey looked mighty cold, and it was a wet perch where he was roosting, and his teeth chattered; yet he didn't speak, not so much as a cat. So just before eight bells, when the watch was nearly out, Billy went forward for the last time. "If he don't speak now," says Billy, "overboard he goes for a dumb animal."

'Well, the cold green seas had pretty nearly drowned that little monkey. And the sprays had frozen him over like a jacket of ice, and right blue his lips were, and an icicle was a-dangling from his chin, and he was shivering like he had an ague. "Well, ye little divvle," says Billy, "for the last time will ye speak? Are ye going to speak, hey?" And the monkey spoke. "*Speak* is it? *Speak* is it?" he says. "It's so cold it's enough to make a little fellow *swear*."

'It's the solemn gospel truth that story is.'

from *Mainsail Haul* by John Masefield (1905)

SHIPS IN PEACETIME

An East-coast Collier

In C. J. Cutliffe Hyne's *The Paradise Coal-boat*, Ezra Pollard is a typical east-coast sailor, pushed off to sea from his South Shields home at the age of ten. He does not get his first command – the 900-ton collier *Paradise* – until he is forty-four, having been bullied into taking navigation classes and his necessary tickets by his socially ambitious barmaid wife. The courtesy title of his rank apart, he bears no resemblance to those well-spoken skippers of passenger-liners with 'RNR' after their signatures; nor can he claim a baronet or shipowner for second cousin.

Reporting back after his first trip, he is abruptly fired. His tight-fisted owner Mr Gedge has not been impressed by Ezra's having reduced to half speed in thick fog – as Board of Trade regulations demanded – and then having lost more time punching head seas on the homeward voyage in ballast.

After a month on the beach, however, Ezra begs for a second chance and gets one, with an equivocal briefing from the owner:

> Ezra mopped his face with a white pocket handkerchief. 'I've a wife and kids, Mr Gedge, and I've got to think of them first. I don't think you'd find a master anywhere to drive your steamboat harder than me.'
>
> 'You think you could push her along if you had a second try at the job, eh?'
>
> 'By God,' said Ezra. 'I'd go round no corners that weren't land! I'd stick on my course and not budge from it for a battleship. I'd drive her full ahead through any weather that is sent down to cover the sea, and if there's others gets in my road it's their look-out. I neither shift my hellum nor slow down for anything that swims.'
>
> Gedge glanced at the man queerly. 'That's the right principle; only don't you go away with any reckless idea that I want you to blunder along, and run vessels down, and – bring – the crews back here – to make claims on me.'
>
> Ezra mopped with the handkerchief. 'I'd like you to make it bit clearer, sir. I don't think I quite—'
>
> 'What I have said is sufficiently clear already. I intend to have my steamers driven. I don't want accidents. And I won't have accidents that they can call me to account for afterwards. Now, it's no use saying you don't understand. There's the berth waiting for you, and you know what's required. Take it or leave it; only don't take it and handle the boat as you did before, or you'll get no third chance from me, and I don't think my recommendation will go far to find you another billet anywhere else.'

That Captain Ezra Pollard did accept the post, and did understand what was required of him, may be gathered from the statement that when the *Paradise* ran down an unknown smack, just south of the Spurn, Captain Ezra was in command. The air that night was thick with driving rain and sprindrift; the sea was thick with homing smacks and the other traffic; and the collier, under two black trysails and a full head of steam, was going through it at the best of her speed. The skipper was not on the upper bridge at the time, but he rushed out of the charthouse at the shock of the collision, and rated his mate most violently for daring to ring off the engines without orders. With his own hand he telegraphed for 'full speed ahead', and called the mate a liar for suggesting that cries of help were coming up through the darkness. The mate retorted by calling him a murderer, and in the subsequent scuffle most of the crew took part. But in the meanwhile the grimy collier had been surging southward across Humber mouth at nine knots, and by the time the matter had been fought through the cries had died out in the wet, windy night, and though wild threats of reporting were made in the heat of the moment, these were forgotten whilst the steamer waddled up the muddy waters of London river. A sailor-man at sea speaks big about the law; on shore he avoids it as much as may be.

Captain Ezra Pollard, however, did not forget the incident; in fact the memory of it stayed by him so persistently that it took all the sweetness out of his life, and he called himself much worse names as a daily exercise than his mate had called him in the heat of the moment. But he did not desist from driving the *Paradise* at her accustomed pace (which was as hard as she would go on a given coal consumption), come sunshine, come fog. He had four reasons for doing this, and they all dwelt in a small house in South Shields. And he was quite satisfied that one deviation from the course he had set down would cause the excellent Mr Gedge to dismiss him without mercy, and plunge the household in the Tyneside town into destitution. He did not blame Gedge, because he quite understood that a shipowner who has a living to make cannot afford, under any circumstances, to run coal-boats at a loss . . .

*

But meanwhile the *Paradise* kept him ferrying coals from the Tyne to London river, between which places there exists one of the best used steam-lanes in the world; and his owner decreed that he should not slow down for even the thickest fog that the weather-fiends could spin. Ezra never left port without a sinking feeling beneath his waistcoat and a sense of impending misfortune in every grain of his person. And on thick nights the voices of the smacksmen he had run down off Humber mouth (and not carried home to claim damages) came and chatted to him out of the sea-smoke which drove from the wave-crests.

But though he had many close shaves – some of them desperately close – on the wild, thick nights along that crowded sea-road, for the next six years Ezra managed to keep out of actual collision; and so valuable a servant did he prove, that Gedge increased his pay by one pound a month, making it now eleven pounds in all; on the strength of which Mrs Pollard clanked whole sixpences into the plate at chapel, and bought a gilt clock with a glass shade for the best room.

Still, the evil fates could not let so promising a chance slip by for always. A night came, a bleak December night, thick with snow and heavy with gale. The iron lower decks of the *Paradise* were a mask of ice. On the upper bridge, ashes were strewn twice a watch to give foothold, and the canvas dodgers were thick glistening walls. Captain Pollard, who looked like a barrel of clothes, stumped athwart the bridge beating together his fingerless woollen gloves, and behind him the steam siren did its best to hoot above the booming of the gale and the clash of the racing seas. It was not much use looking ahead. With difficulty one could make out the loom of the foremast, and beyond that was a blanket of drifting snow and driving sea-smoke. Ezra had not picked up a light since he left the Tyne pier-heads, and his dead reckoning told him that he would have to port his helm soon to hit off London river. When he got in there and picked up his pilot, then for the first time since leaving home he would be able to go below and turn in.

Of a sudden a row of white lights shone out through the snow clouds, a green light dimly showing above them, a single white light topping all. Then the outline of a great steamer loomed out, and then *Crash!* and a noise as of ten thousand boiler-riveters all working at once.

The helm of the *Paradise* had been shoved hard-a-port, the stranger's to hard-a-starboard; the engines of each ship had been rung off, but not yet reversed. The time was too short. The stranger took the *Paradise*'s stem little aft of 'midships, and when the two ships broke apart from that horrible wrestle, there was a big passenger liner sinking rapidly in a freezing North Sea gale.

The *Paradise* backed off and lay to, rolling like a black drainpipe in the trough, and drifting rapidly to leeward. She carried no carpenter, but the skipper himself went forward to inspect, and found that, saving for a few plates bent, no damage had been done. It was a wonderful escape and it need never be reported. The skipper returned to deck with a grim, set face. If he steamed on to the river, he could slip into dock, and no questions would be asked. The crew could be easily silenced. But if he went back to the assistance of the other steamer, everything would be known; there would be a Board of Trade inquiry; Gedge would be mulcted in damages; he (Ezra) would probably 'lose his ticket', and certainly lose his berth for good and always. And of course, Mrs Pollard and the children would taste their due share of the disaster by being permitted either to starve or go to the deuce.

The ghosts of the smacksmen he had drowned off Humber mouth gave him advice from the darkness. 'A man can only be damned once,' they said, 'and you've been damned for us already. Think of the missis and the kids, you fool, and shove her for Gravesend at once. You've lost sight of the other steamer already, and you'll never find her again in a devil of a night like this. Besides, she's probably gone down by now.'

A dead rocket-stick dropped down like an arrow out of the night above, and fell on the ice of the upper bridge at his feet.

Ezra apostrophized the absent Gedge. 'No,' he said, 'curse you, I can't do it this time. A smack's different; there's only old sailors on her, who are made to be drowned. But there's women on that blasted steamer, and kids, who have lived soft all their lives and wanted for nothing; and I don't believe even you could leave them yourself.' He rung on his engines to 'full ahead' once more, and gave the quartermaster a course. And then he indulged in fluent profanity, because he was merely the master of a coasting collier, and expected to lose his only means of livelihood; and also because he saw in imagination his wife and children first shunned by the congregation of the chapel, and then begging crumbs in the public streets of South Shields.

The siren of the other steamer sent over the charging seas a sound like the bellow of a wounded bull, and Ezra followed it up with a new eagerness. ' "One may as well be hanged for a sheep as a lamb," says the proverb; and,' said Ezra to himself, 'If I'm going to crack myself up for good over pulling a parcel of petticoats out of the mess, hang me if I mightn't just as well take off the sailormen, yes, and even the brutes in the stokehold whilst I'm about it.' So he exhorted the weak crew of the collier in a language which they entirely understood, and swung his boat-davits outboard as he steamed through the snowy darkness.

The story of the actual rescuing of the three hundred human lives need not be retold here, as it was printed quite recently, with riotous amplitude of details, by all the newspapers of the civilized globe. Parliament was not sitting at the time; the world was gnawing for a sensation; and they had the story of the rescue served up to them in double-leaded type, with all the unpicturesque details and swear-words omitted. They learnt how by savage effort and reckless daring the master of an undermanned coal-boat had saved every soul on a swamping liner during a gale which had already made itself historical for casualties. All, that is, excepting the few who out of sheer contrariness, chose to die from exposure to the bitter cold. Two of the *Paradise*'s men were killed during the transhipment, and one got injured for life; but these received only trivial mention. It was Ezra whom the freakish public in its never to-be-reckoned-on way, set up for its week's hero; and Ezra, when he grasped the fact that ruin might be evaded after all, saw the one chance of his life ahead, and used all the small wit which God had given him to squeeze profit out of it to the uttermost ooze.

He could have laughed aloud at the fuss which was being made over the fact that he had risked his life – he who had risked life a thousand times before without comment. But he remembered Mrs Pollard, and the children, and the chapel, and he did not laugh. He posed as the massive, modest, guileless shipmaster, and made what he could out of the situation. The passengers he had picked up gave him a purse of two hundred guineas (showing that they were folks of no pride by assessing themselves low); the owners of the liner, by way of making a suitable present, gave him a watch which was worth his year's income; the dreaded Board of Trade let him off with flying colours; and, last of all, Gedge did not turn him adrift. On the contrary, he advanced him. The excellent Gedge had recently made a new investment. He had bought (by help of a mortgage) one of those delightful colliers that they build by the mile in the

Tyneside yards, and cut off by the fathom as they are wanted; and (on selling the original of that name to a Norwegian) he christened her the *Paradise*, and put Ezra in command at the unheard-of wage of thirteen pounds a month. Mr Gedge knew luck when he saw it, and had a theory that fortunes are made by backing luck or buying its influence when it comes in one's way.

But Mrs Pollard had less of an eye for details than results. Her increased affluence suggested so many possibilities. She was able to take a tray now when the chapel gave tea-parties, and on Sunday nights she was frequently in a position to ask the minister in for supper, to the envy of her neighbours. She now also could afford to pay the premium for her eldest daughter to the genteelest milliner in all South Shields. She had, moreover, the satisfaction of hearing Ezra spoken of (by everyone who did not undestand the true inwardness of the business) as the smartest coal-boat skipper who ever went out of Tyne pier-heads.

Still Ezra himself was not entirely happy. The new *Paradise* is a ten-knot boat, and has to be driven as such whatever weather may betide. Moreover, when loaded, there are two thousand tons of her altogether, so that her momentum is large, and the blow she could strike correspondingly heavy. The ambitious Mr Gedge will hear of extension of time between ports for no reason whatever, come fog come gale; and Ezra frequently spends fifty consecutive hours on the bridge, so as to be ready to act as circumstances should direct, should another of those unavoidable collisions be thrust upon him. Gedge warned him on the subject.

'Better not shove luck too hard, Captain,' he said, as he handed him over the new command. 'It's dangerous having those collisions at all; but it's a heap more dangerous to bring survivors home. Don't get nervous about driving her through. She's well insured.'

So the *Paradise* coal-boat still exists as a danger to navigators along certain tracks in the North Sea, and probably in the due course of events she will some day furnish the newspapers with another 'shipping disaster'. I only hope I am not in the other craft, that is all. I do not fancy Ezra is the man to stop and pick up human flotsam a second time. Mrs Pollard has such an assured position in the chapel circle now, that Ezra quite understands it would be death to her for him to lose his berth and pay.

from *The Paradise Coal-boat* by C. J. Cutliffe Hyne (1897)

Majestic Liners on the North Atlantic

During the first half of the twentieth century, before non-stop airliners put them out of business, majestic ocean-liners held sway on the North Atlantic routes, and new generations of passengers crossed the seas in stabilized, air-conditioned comfort with little awareness of the ocean around them. They would neither spare a thought for nor envisage what it must be like for the crews of deep-sea-trawlers or weather-ships in the same latitudes. If they met bad weather it was seldom for long. On an east–west crossing the speed of those Cunarders and their rivals was such that, during the time it took black-tie passengers to dine and play a couple of rubbers of bridge, an entire cyclonic low-pressure weather pattern could be traversed, from the moment when the barometer started to fall, signalling the advent of a warm front, until the ship broke out into moderating seas and clear skies beyond the associated cold front where the isobars were once again well spaced-out.

As a boy, H. M. Tomlinson, son of a London docker, was spellbound by the ships from all over the world which he watched locking in and out from the Thames to work cargoes. Thereafter he spent as much of his life travelling the seven seas as his job as a reporter and magazine editor permitted. He is best known for his award-winning *Gallion's Reach*, but a lesser-known work, published just after the First World War, perfectly captures the contrast between the passengers on a luxury liner and those dangerously exposed to the perils of the sea as part of their daily business.

In a tramp steamer, which was overloaded, and in midwinter, I had crossed to America for the first time. What we experienced of the western ocean during that passage gave me so much respect for it that the prospect of the return journey, three thousand miles of those seas between me and home, was already the gloom of augury.

The shipping posters of New York, showing stately liners too lofty even to notice the Atlantic, were arguments good enough for steerage passengers, who do, I know, reckon a steamer's worth by the number of its funnels; but the pictures did nothing to lessen my regard for that dark outer world I knew. And having no experience of ships installed with racquet courts, Parisian *cafés*, swimming baths, and pergolas, I was naturally puzzled by the inconsequential behaviour of the first-class passengers at the hotel. They were leaving by the liner which was to take me, and, I gathered, were going to cross a bridge to England in the morning. Of course, this might have been merely the innocent profanity of the simple-minded.

Embarking at the quay next day, I could not see that our ship had either a beginning or an end. There was a blank wall which ran out of sight to the right and left. How far it went, and what it enclosed, were beyond me. Hundreds of us in a slow procession mounted stairs to the upper floor of a warehouse, and from thence a bridge led us to a door in the wall half-way in its height. No funnels could be seen. Looking straight up from the embarkation gangway, along what seemed the parapet of the wall was a row of far-off indistinguishable faces peering straight down at us. There was no evidence that this building we were entering, of which the high black wall was a part, was not an important and permanent feature of the city. It was in keeping with the magnitude of New York's skyscrapers, which this planet's occasionally irritable skin permits to stand there to afford man an apparent reason to be gratified with his own capacity and daring.

But with the knowledge that this wall must be afloat there came no sense of security when, going through that little opening in its altitude, I found myself in a spacious decorated interior which hinted nothing of a ship, for I was puzzled as to direction. My last ship could be surveyed in two glances; she looked, and was, a comprehensible ship, no more than a manageable handful for an able master. In that ship you could see at once where you were and what to do. But in this liner you could not see where you were, and would never know which way to take unless you had a good memory. No understanding came to me in that hall of a measured and shapely body, designed with a cunning informed by ages of sea-lore to move buoyantly and surely among the ranging seas, to balance delicately, a quick and sensitive being, to every precarious slope, to recover a lost poise easily and with the grace natural to a quick creature controlled by an alert mind.

There was no shape at all to this structure. I could see no line the run of which gave me warrant that it was comprised in the rondure of a ship. The lines were all of straight corridors, which, for all I knew, might have ended blindly on open space, as streets which traverse a city and are bare in vacancy beyond the dwellings. It was possible we were encompassed by walls, but only one wall was visible. There we idled, all strangers, and to remain strangers, in a large hall roofed by a dome of coloured glass. Quite properly, palms stood beneath. There were offices and doors everywhere. On a broad staircase a multitude of us wandered aimlessly up and down. Each side of the stairway were electric lifts, intermittent and brilliant apparitions. I began to understand why the saloon passengers thought nothing of the voyage. They were encountering nothing unfamiliar. They had but come to another hotel for a few days.

I attempted to find my cabin, but failed. A uniformed guide took care of me. But my cabin, curtained, upholstered, and warm, with mirrors and plated ware, sunk somewhere deeply among carpeted and silent streets down each of which the perspective of glow-lamps looked interminable, left me still questioning. The long walk had given me a fear that I was remote from important affairs which might be happening beyond. My address was 323. The street door – I was down a side turning, though – bore that number. A visitor could make no mistake, supposing he could find the street and my side turning. That was it.

There was a very great deal in this place for everybody to remember, and most of us were strangers. No doubt, however, we were afloat, if the lifebelts in the rack meant anything. Yet the cabin, insulated from all noise, was not soothing, but disturbing. I had been used to a ship in which you could guess all that was happening even when in your bunk; a sensitive and communicative ship.

A steward appeared at my door, a stranger out of nowhere, and asked whether I had seen a bag not mine in the cabin. He might have been created merely to put that question, for I never saw him again on the voyage. This liner was a large province having irregular and shifting bounds, permitting incontinent entrance and disappearance. All this should have inspired me with an idea of our vastness and importance, but it did not. I felt I was one of a multitude included in a nebulous mass too vague to hold together unless we were constantly wary.

In the saloon there was the solid furniture of rare woods, the ornate decorations, and the light and shadows making vague its limits and giving it an appearance of immensity, to keep the mind from the thought of our real circumstances. At dinner we had valentine music, dreamy stuff to accord with the shaded lamps which displayed the tables in a lower rosy light. It helped to extend the mysterious and romantic shadows. The pale, disembodied masks of the waiters swam in the dusk above the tinted light. I had for a companion a vivacious American lady from the Middle West, and she looked round that prospect we had of an expensive café, and said, 'Well, but I am disappointed. Why, I've been looking forward to seeing the ocean, you know. And it isn't here.'

'Smooth passage,' remarked a man on the other side. 'No sea at all worth mentioning.' Actually, I know there was a heavy beam sea running before a half-gale. I could guess the officer in charge somewhere on the exposed roof might have another mind about it; but it made no difference to us in our circle of rosy intimate light bound by those vague shadows which were alive with ready servitude.

'And I've been reading *Captains Courageous* with this voyage in view. Isn't this the month when the forties roar? I want to hear them roar, just once, you know, and as gently as any sucking dove.' We all laughed. 'We can't even tell we're in a ship.'

She began to discuss Kipling's book. 'There's some fine seas in that. Have you read it? But I'd like to know where that ocean is he pretends to have seen. I do believe the realists are no more reliable than the romanticists. Here we are a thousand miles out, and none of us have seen the sea yet. Tell me, does not a realist have to magnify his awful billows just to get them into his reader's view?'

I murmured something feeble and sociable. I saw then why sailors never talk directly of the sea. I, for instance, could not find my key at that moment – it was in another pocket somewhere – so I had no iron to touch. Talking largely of the sea is something like the knowing talk of young men about women; and what is a simple sailor man that he should open his mouth on mysteries?

Only on the liner's boat-deck, where you could watch her four funnels against the sky, could you see to what extent the liner was rolling. The arc seemed to be considerable then, but slowly described. But the roll made little difference to the promenaders below. Sometimes they walked a short distance on the edges of their boots, leaning over as they did so, and swerving from the straight, as though they had turned giddy. The shadows formed by the weak sunlight moved slowly out of ambush across the white deck, but often moved indecisively, as though uncertain of a need to go; and then slowly went into hiding again. The sea whirling and leaping past was far below our wall side. It was like peering dizzily over a precipice when watching those green and white cataracts.

The passengers, wrapped and comfortable on the lee deck, chatted as blithely as at a garden-party, while the band played medleys of national airs to suit our varied complexions. The stewards came round with loaded trays. A diminutive and wrinkled dame in costly furs frowned through her golden spectacles at her book, while her maid sat attentively by. An American actress was the centre of an eager group of grinning young men; she was unseen, but her voice was distinct. The two Vanderbilts took their brisk constitutional among us as though the liner had but two real passengers though many invisible nobodies.

The children, who had not ceased laughing and playing since we left New York, waited for the slope of the deck to reach its greatest, and then ran down towards the bulwarks precipitously. The children, happy and innocent, completed for us the feeling of comfortable indifference and security which we found when we saw there was more ship than ocean. The liner's deck canted slowly to leeward, went over more and more, beyond what it had done yet, and a pretty little girl with dark curls riotous from under her red tam-o'-shanter, ran down, and brought up against us violently with both hands, laughing heartily. We laughed too. Looking seawards, I saw receding the broad green hill, snow-capped, which had lifted us and let us down. The sea was getting up.

Near sunset, when the billows were mounting express along our run, sometimes to leap and snatch at our upper structure, and were rocking us with some ease, there was a commotion forward. Books and shawls went anywhere as the passengers ran. Something strange was to be seen upon the waters.

It looked like a big log out there ahead, over the starboard bow. It was not easy to make out. The light was failing. We overhauled it rapidly, and it began to shape as a ship's boat. 'Oh, it's gone,' exclaimed someone then. But the forlorn object lifted high again, and sank once more. Whenever it was glimpsed it was set in a patch of foam.

That flotsam, whatever it was, was of man. As we watched it intently, and before it was quite plain, we knew intuitively that hope was not there, that we were watching something past its doom. It drew abeam, and we saw what it was, a derelict sailing ship, mastless and awash. The alien wilderness was around us now, and we saw a sky that was overcast and driven, and seas that were uplifted, which had grown incredibly huge, swift, and perilous, and they had colder and more sombre hues.

The derelict was a schooner, a lifeless and soddened hulk, so heavy and uncontesting that its foundering seemed at hand. The waters poured back and forth at her waist, as though holding her body captive for the assaults of the active seas which came over her broken bulwarks, and plunged ruthlessly about.

There was something ironic in the indifference of her defenceless body to these unending attacks. It mocked this white and raging post-mortem brutality, and gave her a dignity that was cold and superior to all the eternal powers could now do. She pitched helplessly head first into a hollow, and a door flew open under the break of her poop; it surprised and shocked us, for the dead might have signed to us then. She went astern of us fast, and a great comber ran at her, as if it had but just spied her, and thought she was escaping. There was a high white flash; we heard that blow. She had gone. But she appeared again far away, forlorn on a summit in desolation, black against the sunset. The stump of her bowsprit, the accusatory finger of the dead, pointed at the sky.

I turned, and there beside me was the lady who had wanted to find the sea. She was gazing at the place where the wreck was last seen, her eyes fixed, her mouth a little open in awe and horror.

from *Old Junk* by H. M. Tomlinson (1918)

A Neglected Ship

F. Tennyson Jesse's best-known novel about the sea (*Moonraker*: see p. 297) owes most of its fame to its having been adapted as a film. But the author's true mastery of the genre is to be found in *Tom Fool*, in which she demonstrates a deep understanding of the character of ships and those who sailed in them.

In the early days of the emigrant trade to Australia, Tom Foulds runs away to sea at the age of fourteen and ships in the full-rigged *Berinthia*. Her Captain's sizeable financial stake in the ship sacrifices maintenance and all possible running costs in the interest of making fast passages, regardless of the consequences for the wretched crew. Homeward bound from Chile with a cargo of nitrate, her skipper, who is at best bordering on insanity, finally snaps, driven mad by the Doldrums.

Tom had expected the rounding of the dreaded Cape Stiff to be the most exciting period of his career as a sailor, but all he saw was a mist-wreathed headland, black and low, amidst the scurrying whiteness, and the *Berinthia* passed the Horn with too fair a wind and too far from her frowning heights for Tom not to feel that, after the great gale, this was rather a tame business.

The mutterings on board the *Berinthia* had now risen to a height. Although a British ship, she was not properly provisioned with lime-juice, and scurvy broke out amongst the men. Cockney and the man who had made an attempt to escape with him had, owing to being kept to the last moment in the guard-house at Callao, been able to buy no adequate clothing against the rigours of the Cape Horn weather; for the skipper had none in his slop chest. Cockney was swept overboard one night when his frozen fingers could no longer cling to the rigging.

The *Berinthia* ran into another gale off the Plate, and then into ten days of a dead muzzler, during which the Old Man used language fit to wake the dead. In the tropic of Capricorn they got into the south-east trades, and frozen limbs recovered, and half-starved frames absorbed the sun thankfully. In the Doldrums a calm took hold of them as though with a mighty hand, and, in the mysterious fashion of calms, ships drifted into view all over the circle of shining water that lay about them. Men were kept busy scraping and painting, but the skipper cursed on the quarter-deck, and kept his eyes glued to the glasses in the endeavour to find out how many of the Chincha guano fleet were lying within sight. Day after day passed.

One noon, when the sun burnt like a shield of brass in the heavens, the Old Man came on deck to take his needless observations, and, after doing so, put down his sextant and remained staring, in an odd fashion, out to sea. He was quite silent, but Tom, warned by that sudden feeling he always had when something was going to happen, watched him, and saw that his face and neck were growing crimson and the veins were standing out as they did when he was in a passion. A strange tenseness suddenly seemed to hold everyone, even the *Berinthia* herself.

Suddenly, his face suffused with a dreadful purple, the Old Man tore off his cap, and, flinging it upon the deck at his feet, called out, in a voice so thick with rage that even in his ship no one had heard the like:

'Great God Almighty . . . if You're half the man You think Yourself, come down on my quarter-deck and I'll fight You for ten dollars a side and a wind . . . so help me, Satan!'

There was a horrified silence. The Old Man rocked a little on his feet and then fell forwards, lying stiffly upon the white planking. It was a second before anyone moved to his side.

He never regained consciousness, but died that night, just as a fair wind sprang up and the water began to talk at the *Berinthia*'s bows. Apoplexy, said Mr Glass, who became acting master. The Judgement of God, said the boatswain. Tom did not know what to think; he could not help feeling that, had his passion been less overpowering, the skipper might have uttered his blasphemy, and still not been striken upon his quarter-deck, and what would the boatswain have said then? But he felt, too that it was somehow supremely satisfying that the skipper had been so stricken, and that John would have felt it so, too, though he would have refused to believe the boatswain . . . or said he refused.

The *Berinthia* picked up her pilot in the Channel without the usual haggling over the price, and once again Tom saw the low green shores of London River slipping past him, this time as he was towed up-stream. The guano had been brought safely to port, but the skipper and part-owner of the *Berinthia* would gain no profit from that cargo which had been won with so much blood and sorrow.

from *Tom Fool* by F. Tennyson Jesse (1926)

A year later the sadly neglected ship falls apart in a pampero off the Plate and flounders.

Habitability Factors

A second extract from F. Tennyson Jesse's *Tom Fool* tells how, during the earlier part of the voyage, Tom makes a valuable friend of John Masters, the son of one of the Liverpool aristocracy of shipowners under whose patronage Tom steadily climbs the ranks to command. But he has to respect Old Masters's characteristic prejudices against innovations in ship design and construction during the transitional era from sail to steam.

Old Masters, though he utterly refused to have anything to do with steam, had yielded to the innovation of iron ships, and the *Happy Return*, an iron ship some six months old, had steel lower masts, and lower rigging of steel wire. She carried very square yards and double topsail yards, and her lines were as beautiful as those of the crack tea-clippers of a decade earlier.

'But I'll never love 'em like I have the wooden ships,' Old Masters told Tom, when he was taking him over the sister ship of the *Happy Return* – the *Under Providence*. 'We shall never beat oak or Malabar teak. I tell you, boy, a man had to know his business when he built a ship only a few years ago. He had to choose good natural oak crooks for the knees and aprons and good square timber for the frames. Then he had to keep it till it was well seasoned. None of this modern hustle then! Elm for the sheathings, pine for the decks – all had to be kept, and kept until it was ready for use. Many's the time I've searched over and over piles of timber as big as a house to find just the right pieces for floors and futtocks, to find wood as near as possible to the curve I required. We built for strength in those days. None of your tin biscuit boxes! 'Tween-deck beams, main-deck beams, shelfs, knees, strakes and everything – all were as perfect as they could be. I don't say my iron ships aren't as sound as they can be, but they're not like the old days of wood. Do you hear me boy?'

And Tom would agree, partly because he genuinely liked and admired the hard-headed old man, partly because he, too, had a love for wooden ships, though, when he joined the *Happy Return*, he felt he would not have changed her even for his last ship – always such a perfect vessel in the eyes of a sailor.

All ships were uncomfortable, either wood or iron. Neither Tom nor any other sailor expected them to be anything else. Wooden ships leaked like a basket, bilge-water rotted the timbers so that the stench was often unbearable. Ventilation was an impossibility. Warmth, except the warmth produced by herding men close together in a small space, was unobtainable; in both wooden and iron ships, hawse-pipes passed through the fo'c'sle carrying the cables, filthy and stinking with mud, to the chain locker. The paint-room and the privy added their odours to that of mud and bilge-water and human sweat and half-dried clothes; and perhaps an evil-smelling cargo laid another burden on the heavy air.

In iron ships the iron sweated in cold weather till the water ran off their sides into the men's bunks. Skippers drove iron ships into head-seas simply because the fabric would stand it, until the men were worn out with the noise and the perpetual knocking about. Iron ships always had foul bottoms and they were always wet ships, because of the driving. Wood or iron both had their disadvantages and fo'c'sles were always hell – that was the long and the short of it – and there were many ships where the afterguard was not much better off. Yet men stuck to the sea; he had stuck to it. It gave him something that no other life ever could.

In the end it all comes down to the men:

'I don't know,' said Tom gravely. 'I think that perhaps sailors are better than landsmen – they grumble like the devil, but they're the finest men in the world. And when I see what they put up with and how they give you of their best, I feel jolly proud I began with my hands in the tar-bucket instead of in the pockets of a brass-bound uniform. You've got to bully them and drive them, but you get more out of them, and with all their grumbling they're the most uncomplaining devils, when it really gets down to rock-bottom, of any race in the world. They go on till they drop and do their duty when they're half-dead already. There can't be much wrong with human nature while that's still the case, can there?'

'You must have sailed with some pretty fair brutes, too,' observed John.

'I have – but mostly in the afterguard. I only served one voyage in a Yankee Down-Easter. God! how she could sail, and what gorgeous seamen her afterguard were! But I never want to do it again, though, by God, they do feed you well! No scrimping – but the men are treated worse than brutes. You get just as rigid discipline in the Blue-nose craft, but nothing like as much brutality just for brutality's sake. That's the worst and the best of the sea, John – you're always coming up against examples of unselfishness and courage that make you feel a worm, and the next moment against cruelties that you wouldn't think possible.'

from *Tom Fool* by F. Tennyson Jesse (1926)

SHIPS AT WAR

With Nelson at Trafalgar

Nicholas Ramage, heir to Admiral the Earl of Blazey, served his time as a junior officer in the Royal Navy without using his proper style as Lord Ramage for fear of up staging his untitled senior officers. On his way to the Senior Captain's List he had acquired rich estates and the hand of the beautiful daughter of an influential member of the House of Lords. Unlike his hero, Horatio Nelson, he was born to privilege and had an assured future in the Service without having to over-indulge his outrageous talent for dashing leadership afloat – which was just as well, for he shared with Nelson a resolute disregard of senior officers' orders whenever the opportunity for independent aggressive action against the enemy arose.

Like other fictional early nineteenth-century sea-captains of those days created by twentieth-century authors – Hornblower, Bolitho and Aubrey – there is no Ramage to be found in the Navy Lists of Nelson's day or for the next century, although the US Navy is proud of one who won the Congressional Medal of Honour (VC) as a submariner in the Second World War. Nevertheless, the exploits and personalities of these fictional heroes and the ships in which they served are entirely credible.

Dudley Pope's hero features in sixteen novels, mostly written while the author cruised in Caribbean waters in his 37-foot yacht *Ramage*. There he also found the inspiration for his biography *Harry Morgan's Way*, winner of the 1977 Best Book of the Sea Award. Four years later came *Life in Nelson's Navy*, marking him out as an authoritative naval historian of considerable importance.

Writing of *Ramage at Trafalgar*, Pope claims that 'all the facts concerning Nelson and the Battle are true; only the events surrounding Ramage are fiction.' The grey zone between fact and fiction is so finely drawn that I felt obliged to check some of his exploits in the ex-French frigate *Calypso* which he had earlier taken as a prize. In September 1805 he is torn from the arms of his wife Sarah to get his ship out of a refit at Chatham Dockyard and join the frigates blockading Cadiz.

After a fast passage across the Bay of Biscay, Ramage soon finds himself holding the key inshore billet on the chain of frigates stretching from the shoal waters in the entrance to Cadiz to where Nelson and his battlefleet lie in waiting far beyond the western horizon. At last the enemy fleet breaks out its anchors and slowly emerges, one by one, each movement relayed by flag-hoists to the quarterdeck of the flagship *Victory*.

Nor can I find any record of ships in Villeneuve's fleet whose part in the action match those ascribed with a ring of authenticity to *Le Brave* and *Le Hazard*, ships not listed by any historian as taking part in the battle.

Nevertheless the story loses nothing by Dudley Pope's variations and is wholly credible.

How long would the French admiral allow a British frigate to sail back and forth in the lee of the Castillo de San Sebastián? But a moment later a hail from the masthead was drowned by a shout from Orsini: 'One of them is turning towards us!'

Ramage looked across to the entrance to Cadiz and saw that a 74-gun ship was turning to larboard and either heading for the *Calypso* or making a bolt for the open sea. Which? Anyway it did not matter: she was a mile and a half away now and even if heading for the open sea (why? none of the others was) would pass within half a mile of the *Calypso*, which would be trapped against the land if she too did not make a bolt seaward.

'We'll get under way, go about and then steer west, if you please Mr Aitken,' Ramage snapped. 'Mr Orsini – go to the guns and make sure all the crews are ready; wet and sand the decks; make sure they're all loaded with roundshot.'

He watched Aitken bellowing orders using the speaking trumpet and slowly, sails flapping, the thick rope of the sheets flogging like snakes held by the tail, the frigate turned, the yards were braced sharp up and the sails were sheeted home.

Ramage looked astern at the 74. French. Plum-coloured hull with two black strakes in way of the gunports. And in addition to topsails and courses she was now letting fall her topgallants . . . she was after the *Calypso*, not making a bolt for it: there was no one to stop her going off into the Atlantic; reaching out there, courses and topsails would be enough. But topgallants if you were in a hurry . . .

A 74 – and Villeneuve probably gave the order to a fast one. Eighteen- and 24-pounders. Thirty-seven of them on a broadside, quite apart from carronades, which were not counted. Against them, sixteen 12-pounders. Might as well pelt her with oranges, Ramage thought.

'She's moving fast,' Southwick commented. 'Just her wind, from the look of it, sir.' He gave one of his gigantic sniffs. 'She'll overhaul us.'

Ramage turned to Aitken. 'We'll have topgallants and royals, Mr Aitken. Then go below and change into silk stockings: those woollen ones are no good for going into action: more work for the surgeon with wool fluff if you get a leg wound.'

He turned to Southwick, his eyes flickering to the *Calypso*'s wake. Already the frigate was heeling as she came clear of the lee formed by the headland on which stood the *castillo*.

'We can't outrun him, that's for sure, so we've got to outmanoeuvre him, Mr Southwick.'

'We could turn north and try stunsails,' Southwick offered.

'And so could the Frenchman,' Ramage said. 'We have only one advantage over him, and we'd better make the best of it.'

Southwick took off his hat and scratched his head. 'Blessed if I can see what it is,' the master admitted.

'Tacking,' Ramage said cryptically and since Aitken had hurried below he picked up the speaking trumpet and shouted: 'I'll have another swig on those topsail sheets, and stand by headsail sheets: once we're abreast this headland we'll be hard on the wind.'

Southwick sniffed again. 'Once he's finished with us he'll go after the *Euryalus* and then the *Sirius*,' Southwick said gloomily. 'This damned French admiral wants to stop Lord Nelson finding out what's going on.'

'He's left it too late,' Ramage commented. 'His Lordship already knows the Combined Fleet is putting to sea, and that's what really matters.'

By now the *Calypso* was rolling and pitching her way round the headland, seeming excited at the idea of a hard flog to windward after days spent hove-to or just jogging along while officers and lookouts eyed the Combined Fleet at anchor. 'Don't forget that isolated rock off this headland, sir,' Southwick cautioned.

'Laja del Norte, you mean? It's a couple of hundred yards south-west of the end of the headland, isn't it?'

Southwick nodded. 'Couple of fathoms of water over it. Enough to hole us but too deep for the sea to break on it.'

Again Ramage looked astern: he could just see the trucks of the French ship's masts as she reached along the other side of the headland. She would be tacking in two or three minutes, just as the *Calypso* came into sight tacking southwards along the coast.

The idea was bold enough – maybe even stupid enough. He had thought of it several days ago while shaving, anticipating that the French admiral would try to drive the frigates off. The only mistake so far was that Villeneuve should have done it several days ago, before the Combined Fleet started to sail.

He had taken Southwick's chart (the one passed on by the *Victory*'s master) and carefully taken off the bearings of the Fuerte de La Cortadura, and then measured the distances. There was a ten-foot rise of water at the top of the springs, so if the French admiral sent out a couple of frigates *and* the wind was south *and* it was the top of the tide *and* they were Spanish and knew this coast well, then the plan would fail. But a French ship of the line at low water (which it was now) and the wind south and her captain not knowing this stretch of the coast . . . well, it was all a gamble and he always reckoned he was not a gambling man. Not standing or sitting round a table watching the roll of a dice or turn of a card, anyway. But losing at dice or cards did not lead to the risk of a roundshot lopping off your head, which was what this particular gamble had as a stake . . .

'We're clear of the Laja del Norte now,' he said to Southwick and then, seeing Aitken hurry back on deck, said to him: 'I want you to get us due south of the point: I want to pass a point exactly two miles west of the fort at the end of the city.'

He pointed to the slate. 'Write down this bearing and distance. I want you to tack exactly there.'

Southwick was frowning and shaking his head, puzzled by Ramage's instructions.

'Bajos de León,' Ramage said cryptically, and turned to look astern.

'Here she comes,' he said, taking a telescope from the binnacle box drawer. 'Pitching just nicely. Yes, fairly clean bottom. She's one of the ships that joined Villeneuve from Brest; that copper sheathing hasn't spent weeks in the Mediterranean and then crossed the Atlantic twice. Going to be a race, gentlemen.'

Now, as the *Calypso* plunged south, spray beginning to sweep across the deck (Ramage noticed gun captains fitting the canvas aprons over the flintlocks to protect them), the frigate on this tack was steering straight for the San José church, the wind now brisk on her starboard side as she heeled under the press of canvas.

Ramage stared ahead over the frigate's bow. Yes, she was steering straight for the church, a mile ahead. The water shallowed half a mile out from the beach, so they would tack *there*. He walked over to the binnacle. And as soon as they tacked they would be steering . . . well, just right.

Now he looked astern at the French 74. She too was shouldering up the spray – but was she catching up fast enough? Ramage thought not.

'Ease the topsail and t'gallant sheets a little – I want to lose a knot or two,' Ramage told Aitken.

The Scotsman did not question the order but Ramage saw him give Southwick a puzzled glance.

The frigate slowed and Jackson had to let her pay off a little to keep the sails drawing. The best he could steer was slightly to the north of the San José church.

Ramage looked astern at the Frenchman and nodded. The 74 was now steering exactly in the *Calypso*'s wake. He would have to tack the *Calypso* along the four-fathom line, otherwise the Frenchman might lose his nerve and tack too soon.

'Have the leadsman start singing out the moment it starts shoaling from four fathoms,' he told Aitken, 'and we tack immediately.'

Aitken was going to protest that they could go on to the three-fathom line because the beach shoaled gently, but the look of concentration on Ramage's face made him stay silent.

The leadsman's chant was monotonous: five fathoms . . . five fathoms . . . five fathoms . . . four and a half . . . four and a half . . . four.

Ramage looked at Aitken, who snapped an order to Jackson and started shouting sail orders through his speaking trumpet.

As soon as the flapping of canvas stopped, Ramage reminded Aitken: 'Sou'-west by south, Mr Aitken, and make a note of the time.'

Yes, a cast of the log would be useful, but he was dealing with a mile and a half, and by the time the log was reeled in . . .

He turned and watched the Frenchman. No, the luffs of his sails were not shivering yet. The Frenchman, too, was relying on his leadsman. On he went, until he was almost directly astern of the frigate and in line with the San José church. Then the 74 tacked – tacked smartly, Ramage had to admit. And now she was exactly in the *Calypso*'s wake and . . . yes, she was beginning to overhaul the frigate. Ramage imagined himself on the quarterdeck of the 74. Yes, overhaul her noticeably: they must be confident that in three or four more tacks they would be ranging up alongside the English frigate . . . yes, the French would reckon to finish the job in a couple of broadsides, although one should be enough.

*

In line astern of the 74 is the San José church. The men at the wheel of the 74 are not doing a very good job: not just the surging of the seas, when one leaves the wheel alone, knowing that the ship will come back on course by herself. No, the Frenchmen are sawing the wheel from one side to the other so that she shoots off half a point one way, then swings back half the other. The 74's wake must look like a demented snake.

But for all that she is overhauling the *Calypso*, which is what matters. The French captain must be well satisfied: he has the Englishman at his mercy. Whichever way he tries to escape (and he is cut off by the land from going east or north) the 74 has the advantage of speed: one needs patience, *mes braves*.

Ramage walked to the binnacle, glanced down at the weather side compass, and then at the Cortadura fort. Yes, one and a half miles away. And the bearing was correct. But that damned 74 was making faster time than he anticipated. *A lot faster time.*

*

'She's fast to windward: perhaps she doesn't reach or run so well,' Southwick said hopefully.

'Going to windward is *our* fastest point of sailing,' Ramage reminded him. 'She's French-built, just like us.'

'True, true,' Southwick admitted, lifting his quadrant again and balancing himself against the *Calypso*'s roll.

Ramage looked again at the compass and then at the Cortadura Fort. He caught Jackson's eye. 'Steer small,' he said sharply.

*

Jackson glanced astern and immediately wished he had not: five hundred yards away? No more. Close enough that they would soon fire a round or two from their bowchasers, trying the range. And it would be just their luck that a round from a bowchaser would bring down the mizzen – or skitter across the quarterdeck and smash the wheel.

Jackson looked back at the binnacle and turned to the two men at the wheel. 'Steer small, blast you!' he snarled, and felt better for it. The lubber line was precisely on the 'SW x W' mark on the compass card, but Jackson thought, for the first time for many years, that he wanted to live. The point had not arisen with such urgency for a long time. Always Mr Ramage had a plan and it was easy to see what it was: easy to see, in other words, that one would live to fight another day. Not this time, though: there was no arguing that 74s were faster than frigates.

He glanced astern again. Three hundred yards, and already the blasted Frenchman was hauling out to starboard so that he could range alongside instead of poking his jibboom through the *Calypso*'s sternlights.

Ramage looked at Aitken. The Scot was pale under his tan, but holding the speaking trumpet as casually as though he was going to give a routine order: a tweak on a sheet, maybe. And Southwick? The master was gripping his quadrant as though it was a charm that would protect him from the 74's roundshot.

Once again Ramage looked down at the compass, and then back at the Cortadura Fort. One and a half or two miles. Split the difference and that made it one and three quarters. And on course. Now he turned and looked astern. Feet apart to balance against the roll; hands clasped behind his back; a confident look on his face. So that the ship's company thought he was going to wave at the 74 as it came up alongside, each gun captain sighting, trigger line taut in his right hand, kneeling on the right knee, with the left leg flung out to one side to maintain balance . . . At least Ramage could not hear the bellow of *Ça Ira* against the moan of the wind!

A hundred yards? Less, perhaps. No, he had timed this wrong; there was no confused flurry of sea now, no rolling of the water, no darker patches, just that damned 74 slicing along. She did look rather splendid: he was prepared to admit that. And deadly and menacing, too; there was no denying that.

'If we tacked . . .?' Aitken said, as though talking to himself.

Ramage shook his head: he had started them off on this dance and they had to complete all the steps: tacking now would mean the 74 would tack as well – and, if she was quick enough, get in a raking broadside, and just one raking broadside might be enough for the *Calypso*.

He watched as a spurt of smoke was quickly carried away by the wind from one of the enemy's bowchase guns. There was no thud of the shot hitting the *Calypso*. The 74 caught a strong puff of wind that missed the frigate and surged ahead, sails straining.

Fifty yards. Another lucky puff like that and she will be alongside and the *Calypso*'s decks will be swept by roundshot and grape; masts will collapse over the side as rigging parts; the wheel and binnacle will be smashed; there will not be a man left alive on deck. All because I underestimated a French 74, Ramage thought bitterly. He found he was not afraid. Deathly cold, but not actually afraid. Sarah would never know how it happened, and suddenly he wanted her to understand, understand that he had made a genuine mistake. Just one mistake that would leave Sarah a widow in – well, about a minute, and Aldington without a master. Still, Sarah would live there and she would—

He blinked: the 74 had suddenly stopped and slowly, as though they were tired, one mast after another toppled forward across the bow with yards and sails. She began to slew round as the heavy canvas fell over the side, acting as an anchor. Two guns went off, smoke spurting through the ports, as gun captains were sent sprawling by the shock. An anchor came adrift and fell into the sea with a splash, and the ship settled in the water like a broody hen on her nest.

'What happened?' Southwick gasped. 'What caused all that?'

Ramage fought off a desire to giggle with relief. 'The Bajos de León,' he said. 'Three scattered shoals. At this state of the tide they have just enough water for a frigate to get across, but not enough for a 74.'

from *Ramage at Trafalgar* by Dudley Pope (1986)

A Light Cruiser on a Murmansk Convoy

Alistair MacLean was born and brought up in the Highlands, the son of a
Scottish minister. He served the last four years of the Second World War
as a torpedo-man on east-coast convoys, seeing plenty of action against E-
boats, dive-bombers and mines of growing sophistication. After the war he
became a schoolmaster, writing in his spare time. The fact that his world-
wide bestsellers, many of them made into feature films, include several set
against the background of Murmansk convoys owes much to his brother,
who was a master mariner in the Merchant Navy. He knew only too well
the odds facing anyone who risked his life delivering much-needed war
materials to our seemingly ungrateful allies. Anyone on such a mission
would be haunted by twin nightmares, never knowing which was most to
be feared – the weather or the enemy.

HMS *Ulysses* is a 5.25-inch-gun light cruiser of the 'Dido' Class, wearing
the flag of Rear-Admiral Tyndall, commanding the 14th Aircraft Carrier
Squadron of four escort 'carriers with a mixed screen of destroyers, frigates
and corvettes. Having been over three months without shore leave and come
through a succession of the heaviest battles ever fought in the Arctic, she is
abruptly ordered to sail again from Scapa Flow to rendezvous in the
Denmark Strait with an important Halifax–Murmansk convoy (FR 77).

The story of how *Ulysses* finally runs out of the luck for which she is
renowned is an amalgam of all the horror stories of Russian convoys. Only
Tirpitz does not get into close action, but her threat is enough to contain
most of the heavy metal of the Home Fleet, including their strike 'carriers,
so that they are unable to reach FR 77 in its last desperate hours of need.

There are few quibbles with the way in which Alistair MacLean observes
the ship and her company, excepting only his persistent use of 'poop-deck'
to describe the quarterdeck of an HM ship. No one who has ever sailed the
route in winter will accuse him of over-dramatizing the gale.

> It was the worst storm of the war. Beyond all doubt, had the records been
> preserved for Admiralty inspection, that would have proved to be incomparably
> the greatest storm, the most tremendous convulsion of nature since these record-
> ings began. Living memory aboard the *Ulysses* that night, a vast accumulation
> of experience in every corner of the globe, could certainly recall nothing even
> remotely like it, nothing that would even begin to bear comparison as a parallel
> or precedent.
>
> At ten o'clock, with all doors and hatches battened shut, with all traffic

prohibited on the upper deck, with all crews withdrawn from gun-turrets and magazines and all normal deck watchkeeping stopped for the first time since her commissioning, even the taciturn Carrington admitted that the Caribbean hurricanes of the autumns of '34 and '37 – when he'd run out of sea-room, been forced to heave-to in the dangerous right-hand quadrant of both these murderous cyclones – had been no worse than this. But the two ships he had taken through these – a 3,000-ton tramp and a superannuated tanker on the New York asphalt run – had not been in the same class for seaworthiness as the *Ulysses*. He had little doubt as to her ability to survive. But what the First Lieutenant did not know, what nobody had any means of guessing, was that this howling gale was still only the deadly overture. Like some mindless and dreadful beast from an ancient and other world, the Polar monster crouched on its own doorstep, waiting. At 2230, the *Ulysses* crossed the Arctic Circle. The monster struck.

It struck with a feral ferocity, with an appalling savagery that smashed minds and bodies into a stunned unknowingness. Its claws were hurtling rapiers of ice that slashed across a man's face and left it welling red: its teeth were that sub-zero wind, gusting over 120 knots, that ripped and tore through the tissue paper of Arctic clothing and sunk home to the bone: its voice was the devil's orchestra, the roar of a great wind mingled with the banshee shrieking of tortured rigging, a requiem for fiends: its weight was the crushing power of the hurricane wind that pinned a man helplessly to a bulkhead, fighting for breath, or flung him off his feet to crash in some distant corner, broken-limbed and senseless. Baulked of prey in its 500-mile sweep across the frozen wastes of the Greenland ice-cap, it goaded the cruel sea into homicidal alliance and flung itself, titanic in its energy, ravenous in its howling, upon the cockleshell that was the *Ulysses*.

The *Ulysses* should have died then. Nothing built by man could ever have hoped to survive. She should have been pressed under to destruction, or turned turtle, or had her back broken, or disintegrated under those mighty hammer-blows of wind and sea. But she did none of these things.

How she ever survived the insensate fury of that first attack, God only knew. The great wind caught her on the bow and flung her round in a 45° arc and pressed her far over on her side as she fell – literally fell – forty heart-stopping feet over and down the precipitous walls of a giant trough. She crashed into the valley with a tremendous concussion that jarred every plate, every Clyde-built rivet in her hull. The vibration lasted an eternity as overstressed metal fought to re-adjust itself, as steel compressed and stretched far beyond specified breaking loads. Miraculously she held, but the sands were running out. She lay far over on her starboard side, the gunwales dipping: half a mile away, towering high above the mast-top, a great wall of water was roaring down on the helpless ship.

The 'Dude' saved the day. The 'Dude', alternatively known as 'Persil' but officially known as Engineer-Commander Dodson, immaculately clad as usual in overalls of the most dazzling white, had been at his control position in the engine-room when that tremendous gust had struck. He had no means of knowing what had happened. He had no means of knowing that the ship was not under command, that no one on the bridge had as yet recovered from that first shattering impact: he had no means of knowing that the quartermaster had been thrown unconscious into a corner of the wheelhouse, that his mate, almost a child in years, was too panic-stricken to dive for the madly-spinning wheel. But he did know that the *Ulysses* was listing crazily, almost broadside on, and he suspected the cause.

His shouts on the bridge tube brought no reply. He pointed to the port controls, roared 'Slow' in the ear of the Engineer WO – then leapt quickly for the starboard wheel.

Fifteen seconds later and it would have been too late. As it was, the accelerating starboard screw brought her round just far enough to take that roaring mountain of water under her bows, to dig her stern in to the level of the depth-charge rails, till forty feet of her airborne keel lay poised above the abyss below. When she plunged down, again that same shuddering vibration enveloped the entire hull. The fo'c'sle disappeared far below the surface, the sea flowing over and past the armoured side of 'A' turret. But she was bows on again. At once the 'Dude' signalled his WO for more revolutions, cut back the starboard engine.

Below decks, everything was an unspeakable shambles. On the mess-decks, steel lockers in their scores had broken adrift, been thrown in a dozen different directions, bursting hasps and locks, spilling their contents everywhere. Hammocks had been catapulted from their racks, smashed crockery littered the decks: tables were twisted and smashed, broken stools stuck up at crazy angles, books, papers, teapots, kettles and crockery were scattered in insane profusion. And amidst this jumbled, sliding wreckage, hundreds of shouting, cursing, frightened and exhausted men struggling to their feet, or knelt, or sat or just lay still.

Surgeon-Commander Brooks and Lieutenant Nicholls, with an inspired, untiring padre as good as a third doctor, were worked off their feet. The veteran Leading SBA Johnson, oddly enough, was almost useless – he was violently sick much of the time, seemed to have lost all heart: no one knew why – it was just one of these things and he had taken all he could.

Men were brought in to the Sick Bay in their dozens, in their scores, a constant trek that continued all night long as the *Ulysses* fought for her life, a trek that soon overcrowded the meagre space available and turned the wardroom into an emergency hospital. Bruises, cuts, dislocations, concussion, fractures – the exhausted doctor experienced everything that night. Serious injuries were fortunately rare, and inside three hours there were only nine bed-patients in the Sick Bay, including AB Ferry, his already mangled arm smashed in two places – a bitterly protesting Riley and his fellow-mutineers had been unceremoniously turfed out to make room for the more seriously injured.

*

The *Ulysses* did not die. Time and again that night, hove to with the wind fine on her starboard bow, as her bows crashed into and under the far shoulder of a trough, it seemed that she could never shake free from the great press of water. But time and again she did just that, shuddering, quivering under the fantastic strain. A thousand times before dawn officers and men blessed the genius of the Clyde shipyard that had made her: a thousand times they cursed the blind malevolence of that great storm that put the *Ulysses* on the rack.

Perhaps 'blind' was not the right word. The storm wielded its wild hate with an almost human cunning. Shortly after the first onslaught, the wind had veered quickly, incredibly so and in defiance of all the laws, back almost to the north again. The *Ulysses* was on a lee shore, forced to keep pounding into gigantic seas.

Gigantic – and cunning also. Roaring by the *Ulysses*, a huge comber would suddenly whip round and crash on deck, smashing a boat to smithereens. Inside an hour, the barge, motor-boat and two whalers were gone, their shattered timbers swept away in the boiling caudron. Carley rafts were broken off by the sudden hammer-blows of the same cunning waves, swept over the side and gone for ever: four of the Balsa floats went the same way.

No one who has ever stood on a bridge in rapidly deteriorating conditions will forget the moments leading up to prudent seamanship dictating a 180° turn in order to run off dead before the storm, or nearly so. In the same weather as *Ulysses* experienced, I once watched a County Class cruiser execute such a turn 3 cables ahead of us. Not only were we able to look down her three tall stacks, but we saw her whole lee gunwhale 60 feet above the waterline disappear into the seas: I made that a roll of over 60°.

It was dawn now, a wild and terrible dawn, fit epilogue for a nightmare. Strange, trailing bands of misty-white vapour swept by barely at mast-top level, but high above the sky was clear. The seas, still gigantic, were shorter now, much shorter, and even steeper: the *Ulysses* was slowed right down, with barely enough steerage way to keep her head up – and even then, taking severe punishment in the precipitous head seas. The wind had dropped to a steady fifty knots – gale force: even at that, it seared like fire in Nicholls's lungs as he stepped out on the flag-deck, blinded him with ice and cold. Hastily he wrapped scarves over his entire face, clambered up to the bridge by touch and instinct. The Kapok Kid followed with the glass. As they climbed, they heard the loudspeakers crackling some unintelligible message.

Turner and Carrington were alone on the twilit bridge, swathed like mummies. Not even their eyes were visible – they wore goggles.

'Morning, Nicholls,' boomed the Commander. 'It *is* Nicholls, isn't? 'He pulled off his goggles, his back turned to the bitter wind, threw them away in disgust. 'Can't see damn all through these bloody things . . . Ah, Number One, he's got the glass.'

Nicholls crouched in the for'ard lee of the compass platform. In a corner, the duckboards were littered with goggles, eye-shields and gas-masks. He jerked his head towards them.

'What's this – a clearance sale?'

'We're turning round, Doc.' It was Carrington who answered, his voice calm and precise as ever, without a trace of exhaustion. 'But we've got to see where we're going, and as the Commander says all these damn' things there are useless – mist up immediately they're put on – it's too cold. If you'll just hold it – so – and if you would wipe it, Andy?'

Nicholls looked at the great seas. He shuddered.

'Excuse my ignorance, but why turn round at all?'

'Because it will be impossible very shortly,' Carrington answered briefly. Then he chuckled. 'This is going to make me the most unpopular man in the ship. We've just broadcast a warning. Ready, sir?'

'Stand by, engine-room: stand by, wheelhouse. Ready, Number One.'

For thirty seconds, forty-five, a whole minute, Carrington stared steadily, unblinkingly through the glass. Nicholls's hands froze. The Kapok Kid rubbed industriously. Then:

'Half-ahead, port!'

'Half-ahead, port!' Turner echoed.

'Starboard 20!'

'Starboard 20!'

Nicholls risked a glance over his shoulder. In the split second before his eyes blinded, filled with tears, he saw a huge wave bearing down on them, the bows already swinging diagonally away from it. Good God! Why hadn't Carrington waited until that was past?

The great wave flung the bows up, pushed the *Ulysses* far over to starboard, then passed under. The *Ulysses* staggered over the top, corkscrewed wickedly down the other side, her masts, great gleaming tree trunks thick and heavy with ice, swinging in a great arc as she rolled over, burying her port rails in the rising shoulder of the next sea.

'Full ahead port!'

'Full ahead port!'

'Starboard 30!'

'Starboard 30!'

The next sea, passing beneath, merely straightened the *Ulysses* up. And then, at last, Nicholls understood. Incredibly, because it had been impossible to see so far ahead, Carrington had known that two opposing wave systems were due to interlock in an area of comparative calm: how he had sensed it, no one knew, would ever know, not even Carrington himself: but he was a great seaman, and he had known. For fifteen, twenty seconds, the sea was a seething white mass of violently disturbed, conflicting waves of the type usually found, on a small scale, in tidal races and overfalls – and the *Ulysses* curved gratefully through. And then another great sea, towering almost to bridge height, caught her on the far turn of the quarter circle. It struck the entire length of the *Ulysses* – for the first time that night – with tremendous weight. It threw her far over on her side, the Ice rails vanishing. Nicholls was flung off his feet, crashed heavily in the side of the bridge, the glass shattering. He could have sworn he heard Carrington laughing. He clawed his way back to the middle of the compass platform.

And still the great wave had not passed. It towered high above the trough into which the *Ulysses*, now heeled far over to 40°, had been so contemptuously flung, bore down remorselessly from above and sought, in a lethal silence and with an almost animistic savagery, to press her under. The inclinometer swung relentlessly over – 45°, 50°, 53°, and hung there an eternity, while men stood on the side of the ship, braced with their hands on the deck, numbed minds barely grasping the inevitable. This was the end. The *Ulysses* could never come back.

A lifetime ticked agonizingly by. Nicholls and Carpenter looked at each other, blank-faced, expressionless. Tilted at that crazy angle, the bridge was sheltered from the wind. Carrington's voice, calm, conversational, carried with amazing clarity.

'She'd go to 65° and still come back,' he said matter-of-factly. 'Hang on to your hats, gentlemen. This is going to be interesting.'

Just as he finished, the *Ulysses* shuddered, then imperceptibly, then slowly, then with vicious speed lurched back and whipped through an arc of 90°, then back again. Once more Nicholls found himself in the corner of the bridge. But the *Ulysses* was almost round.

The Kapok Kid, grinning with relief, picked himself up and tapped Carrington on the shoulder.

'Don't look now, sir, but we have lost our mainmast.'

It was a slight exaggeration, but the top fifteen feet, which had carried the after radar scanner, were undoubtedly gone. That wicked, double ship-lash, with the weight of the ice, had been too much.

'Slow ahead both! Midships!'

'Slow ahead both! Midships!'

'Steady as she goes!'

The *Ulysses* was round.

The Kapok Kid caught Nicholls's eye, nodded at the First Lieutenant.

'See what I mean, Johnny?'

'Yes.' Nicholls was very quiet. 'Yes, I see what you mean.' Then he grinned suddenly. 'Next time you make a statement, I'll just take your word for it, if you don't mind. These demonstrations of proof take too damn' much out of a person!'

Running straight before the heavy stern sea, the *Ulysses* was amazingly steady. The wind, too, was dead astern now, the bridge in magical shelter. The scudding mist overhead had thinned out, was almost gone. Far away to the south-east a dazzling white sun climbed up above a cloudless horizon. The long night was over.

An hour later, with the wind down to thirty knots, radar reported contacts to the west. After another hour, with the wind almost gone and only a heavy swell running, smoke plumes tufted above the horizon. At 1030, in position, on time, the *Ulysses* rendezvoused with the convoy from Halifax.

from *HMS Ulysses* by Alistair MacLean (1955)

Hereafter it is the enemy who become the greater and more decisive threat. Co-ordinated attacks from the air and U-boat packs pick off the convoy one by one before the heavy cruiser *Hipper* joins action. The story ends with *Ulysses* steaming full speed at the German cruiser, her largest White Ensign streaming from the mast, when her forward magazine explodes and sends her to the bottom of the Arctic Ocean.

A USN Frigate in the Third World War

In his first novel, *The Hunt for Red October*, Tom Clancy startled the top brass in the Pentagon by his in-depth technical knowledge of submarine operations and the high technology of weapons and electronics which make them possible. Unbelievable as it seems, the author had no career experience at sea but culled his details from information freely available to any member of the public who knew where to look in the era of the Freedom of Information Laws. His second book, *Red Storm Rising*, enacts the opening days of the Third World War as it might have been in the North Atlantic had not Mikhail Gorbachev secured himself the Nobel Peace Prize.

The battle is seen in turn by those fighting over, under and on the seas between the North Cape and the Caribbean. I have selected Captain Ed Morris in the anti-submarine frigate USS *Pharris* to step into the breach left forty years earlier by HMS *Ulysses*.

The day before open hostilities break out, *Pharris* sails from Delaware Bay as one of the escorts for the initial resupply convoy needed to get the heavy logistic back-up materials to north-western Europe. A third of the convoy is sunk for the loss of three Soviet submarines, before the rest are turned over to NATO escorts in exchange for a west-bound convoy of ships in ballast. Stormy weather gives the escorts a temporary tactical edge and some much-needed relief.

The spray stung his face, and Morris loved it. The convoy of ballasted ships was steaming into the teeth of a forty-knot gale. The sea was an ugly, foam-whipped shade of green, droplets of seawater tearing off the whitecaps to fly horizontally through the air. His frigate climbed up the steep face of endless twenty-foot swells, then crashed down again in a succession that had lasted six hours. The ship's motion was brutal. Each time the bow nosed down it was as though the brakes had been slammed on a car. Men held on to stanchions and stood with their feet wide apart to compensate for the continuous motion. Those in the open like Morris wore life preservers and hooded jackets. A number of his young crewmen would be suffering from this, ordinarily – even professional sailormen wanted to avoid this sort of weather – but now mainly they slept. *Pharris* was back to normal Condition-3 steaming, and that allowed the men to catch up on their rest.

Weather like this made combat nearly impossible. Submarines were mainly a one-sensor platform. For the most part, they detected targets on sonar and the crashing sea noise tended to blanket the ship sounds submarines listened for. A really militant sub skipper could try running at periscope depth to operate

247

his search radar, but that meant running the risk of broaching and momentarily losing control of his boat, not something a nuclear submarine officer looked kindly upon. A submarine would practically have to ram a ship to detect it, and the odds against that were slim. Not did they have to worry about air attacks for the present. The sea's crenellated surface would surely confuse the seeker head of a Russian missile.

For their own part, their bow-mounted sonar was useless, as it heaved up and down in a twenty-foot arc, sometimes rising completely clear of the water. Their towed-array sonar trailed in the placid waters a few hundred feet below the surface, and so could theoretically function fairly well, but in practice, a submarine had to be moving at high speed to stand out from the violent surface noise, and even then engaging a target under these conditions was no simple matter. His helicopter was grounded. Taking off might have been possible, but landing was a flat impossibility under these conditions. A submarine would have to be within ASROC torpedo range – five miles – to be in danger from the frigate, but even that was a slim possibility. They could always call in a P-3 Orion – two were operating with the convoy at present – but Morris did not envy their crews a bit, as they buffeted through the clouds at under a thousand feet.

For everyone a storm meant time off from battle, for both sides to rest up for the next round. The Russians would have it easier. Their long-range aircraft would be down for needed maintenance, and their submarines, cruising four hundred feet down, could keep their sonar watches in comfort.

When the storm abates the enemy moves in. The 'chaff' mentioned is a radar decoy, composed of foil strips launched like a smoke-screen to thwart an attack by radar-guided weapons.

The calm sea meant that *Pharris* was back on port-and-starboard steaming. Half the crew was always on duty as the frigate held her station north of the convoy. The towed sonar was streamed aft. and the helicopter sat ready on the flight deck, its crew dozing in the hangar. Morris slept also, snoring away in his leather bridge chair, to the amusement of his crewmen. So, officers did it, too. The crew accommodations often sounded like a convention of chainsaws.

'Captain, message from CINCLANTFLT.'

Morris looked up at the yeoman and signed for the message form. An eastbound convoy one hundred fifty miles north of them was under attack. He walked back to the chart table to check distances. The submarines there were not a threat to him. That was that. He had his own concerns, and his world had shrunk to include them only. Another forty hours to Norfolk, where they would refuel, replace expended ordnance, and sail again within twenty-four hours.

'What the hell's that?' a sailor said loudly. He pointed to a low-lying trail of white smoke.

'That's a missile,' answered the officer of the deck. 'General quarters! Captain, that was a cruise missile southbound a mile ahead of us.'

Morris snapped upright in his seat and blinked his eyes clear. 'Signal the convoy. Energize the radar. Fire the chaff.' Morris ran to the ladder to CIC. The ship's alarm was sounding its strident note before he got there. Aft, two Super-RBOC chaff rockets leaped into the sky and exploded, surrounding the frigate with a cloud of aluminium foil.

'I count five inbounds,' a radar operator was saying. 'One's heading toward us. Bearing zero-zero-eight, range seven miles, speed five hundred knots.'

'Bridge, come right full rudder to zero-zero-eight,' the tactical action officer ordered. 'Stand by to fire off more chaff. Air action forward, weapons free.'

The five-inch gun swiveled slightly and loosed several rounds, none of which came near the incoming missile.

'Range two miles and closing,' reported the radarman.

'Fire four more Super-RBOCs.'

Morris heard the rockets launch. The radar showed their chaff as an opaque cloud that enveloped the ship.

'CIC,' called a lookout. 'I see it. Starboard bow, inbound – it's gonna miss, I got a bearing change. There – there it goes, passing aft. Missed us by a couple hundred yards.'

The missile was confused by the chaff. Had its brain had the capacity to think, it would have been surprised that it struck nothing. Instead, on coming back to a clear sky, the radar seeker merely looked for another target. It found one, fifteen miles ahead, and altered course toward it.

'Sonar,' Morris ordered, check bearing zero-zero-eight. There's a missile-armed sub out there.'

'Looking now, sir. Nothing shows on that bearing.'

'A five-hundred-knot sea-skimmer. That's a Charlie-class sub, maybe thirty miles out,' Morris said. 'Get the helo out there. I'm going topside.'

The captain reached the bridge just in time to see the explosion on the horizon. That was no freighter. The fireball could only mean a warship had had her magazines exploded by a missile, perhaps the one that had just missed them. Why hadn't they been able to stop it? Three more explosions followed. Slowly the noise traveled across the sea toward them, reaching *Pharris* as the deep sound of an enormous bass drum. The frigate's Sea Sprite helicopter was just lifting off, racing north in the hope of catching the Soviet sub near the surface. Morris ordered his ship to slow to five knots in the hope that the lower speed would allow his sonar to perform just a little better. Still nothing. He returned to CIC.

The helicopter's crew dropped a dozen sonobuoys. Two showed something, but the contact faded, and was not reestablished. Soon an Orion showed up and carried on the search, but the submarine had escaped cleanly, her missiles having killed a destroyer and two merchantmen. *Just like that*. Morris thought. *No warning at all.*

The next alarm comes when a periscope feather is sighted immediately before torpedoes are launched at the frigate.

'Hydrophone effects – torpedoes inbound, bearing three-five-one!'

Instantly the weapons officer ordered the launch of an antisubmarine torpedo down the same bearing in the hope that it would disturb the attacking submarine. If the Russian's torpedoes were wire-guided, he'd have to cut the wires free to maneuver the sub clear of the American return shot.

Morris raced up the ladder to the bridge. Somehow the submarine had broken contact and maneuvered into firing position. The frigate changed course and speed in an attempt to ruin the submarine's fire-control solution.

'I see one!' the XO said, pointing over the bow. The Soviet torpedo left a visible white trail on the surface. Morris noted it, something he had not expected. The frigate turned rapidly.

'Bridge, I show two torpedoes, bearing constant three-five-zero and decreasing range,' the tactical action officer said rapidly.

'Both are pinging at us. The Nixie is operating.'

Morris lifted a phone. 'Report the situation to the escort commander.'

'Done, skipper. Two more helos are heading this way.'

Pharris was now doing twenty knots and accelerating, turning her stern to the torpedoes. Her helicopter was now aft of the beam, frantically making runs with its magnetic anomaly detector, trying to locate the Soviet sub.

The torpedo's wake crossed past the frigate's bow as Morris's ship kept her helm over. There was an explosion aft. White water leaped a hundred feet into the air as the first Russian 'fish' collided with the nixie torpedo decoy. But they had only one nixie deployed. There was another torpedo out there.

'Left full rudder!' Morris told the quartermaster. 'Combat, what about the contact?' The frigate was now doing twenty-five knots.

'Not sure, sir. The sonobuoys have our torp but nothing else.'

'We're gonna take a hit,' the XO said. He pointed to a white trail on the water, less than two hundred yards away. It must have missed the frigate on its first try, then turned for another. Homing torpedoes kept looking until they ran out of fuel.

There was nothing Morris could do. The torpedo was approaching on his port bow. If he turned right, it would only give the fish a larger target. Below him the ASROC launcher swung left toward the probable location of the submarine, but without an order to fire, all the operator could do was train it out. The white wake kept getting closer. Morris leaned over the rail, staring at it with mute rage as it extended like a finger toward his bow. It couldn't possibly miss now.

'That's not real smart, Cap'n.' Bosun Clarke's hand grabbed Morris's shoulder and yanked him down to the deck. He was just grabbing for the executive officer when it hit.

The impact lifted Morris a foot off the steel deck. He didn't hear the explosion, but an instant after he had bounced off the steel a second time, he was deluged with a sheet of white water that washed him against a stanchion. His first thought was that he'd been thrown overboard. He rose to see his executive officer – headless, slumped against the pilothouse door. The bridge wing was torn apart, the stout metal shielding ripped by fragments. The pilothouse windows were gone. What he saw next was worse.

The torpedo had struck the frigate just aft of the bow-mounted sonar. Already the bow had collapsed, the keel sundered by the explosion. The foc's'l was awash, and the horrible groaning of metal told him that the bow was being ripped off his ship. Morris staggered into the bridge and yanked the annunciator handle to All Stop, failing to notice that the engineers had already stopped engines. The ship's momentum pushed her forward. As Morris watched, the bow twisted to starboard, ten degrees off true, and the forward gunmount became awash, its crew trying to head aft. Below the mount were other men. Morris knew that they were dead, hoped that they had died instantly, and were not drowning, trapped in a sinking steel cage. His men. How many had their battle stations forward of the ASROC launcher?

Then the bow tore away. A hundred feet of the ship left the remainder to the accompaniment of screeching metal. It turned as he watched, colliding with the afterpart of the ship as it rotated in the water like a small berg. There was movement at an exposed watertight door. He saw a man try to get free, and succeed, the figure jumping into the water and swimming away from the wallowing bow.

The bridge crew was alive, all cut by flying glass but at their posts. Chief Clarke tooke a quick look at the pilothouse, then ran below to assist with damage control. The damage-control parties were already racing forward with fire hoses and welding gear, and at damage-control central the men examined the trouble board to see how severe the flooding was. Morris lifted a sound-powered phone and twisted the dial to this compartment.

'Damage-control report!'

'Flooding aft to frame thirty-six, but I think she'll float – for a little while anyway. No fires. Waiting for reports now.'

Morris switched settings on the phone. 'Combat, radio the screen commander that we've taken a hit and need assistance.'

'Done, sir. *Gallery*'s heading out this way. Looks like the sub got away. They're still searching for her. We have some shock damage here. All the radars are down. Bow sonar is out. ASROC is out. The tail is still working, though, and the Mark-32 mounts still work. Wait – screen commander's sending us a tug, sir.'

'Okay, you have the conn. I'm going below to look at the damage.' *You have the conn*, Morris though. How do you conn a ship that ain't moving? A minute later he was at a bulkhead, watching men trying to shore it up with lumber.

'This one's fairly solid, sir, the next one forward's leaking like a damn sieve, no way we'll patch it all. When the bow let go, it must have twisted everything loose.' The officer grabbed a seaman by the shouder. 'Go to the after D/C locker and get more four-by-fours!'

'Will this one hold?'

'I don't know. Clarke is checking the bottom out now. We'll have to weld in some patches and stiffeners. Give me about ten minutes and I'll tell you if she'll float or not.'

Clarke appeared. He was breathing heavily. 'The bulkhead's sprung at the tank tops, and there's a small crack, too. Leaking pretty good. The pumps are on, and just about keeping even. I think we can shore it up, but we have to hustle.'

The damage-control officer led the welders below at once. Two men appeared with a portable pump. Morris ordered them below.

'How many men missing?' Morris asked Chief Clarke. He was holding his arm strangely.

'All the guys made it out of the five-inch mount, but I haven't seen anybody from belowdecks. Shit, I think I broke something myself.' Clarke looked at his right arm and shook his head angrily. 'I don't think many guys made it outa the bow, sir. The watertight doors are twisted some, they gotta be jammed tight.'

'Get that arm looked at,' Morris ordered.

'Oh, fuck the arm, skipper! You need me.' The man was right. Morris went back topside with Clarke behind him.

On reaching the bridge, Morris dialed up engineering. The noise on the phone answered his first question.

The engineer spoke over the hiss of escaping steam. 'Shock damage, Captain. We got some ruptured steam pipes on the number one boiler. I think number two will still work, but I've popped the safeties on both just in case. The diesel generators are on line. I got some hurt men here. I'm sending them out. I – okay, okay. We just did a check of number two boiler. A few minor leaks, but we can fix 'em quick. Otherwise everything looks pretty tight. I can have it back on line in fifteen minutes.'

'We need it.' Morris hung up.

Pharris lay dead in the water. With the safety valves opened, steam vented onto the massive stack structure, giving off a dreadful rasping sound that seemed like the ship's own cry of pain. The frigate's sleek clipper bow had been replaced by a flat face of torn metal and hanging wires. The water around the ship was foul with oil from ruptured fuel tanks. For the first time Morris noticed that the ship was down by the stern; when he stood straight, the ship was misaligned. He knew he had to wait for another damage-control report. As with an accident victim, the prognosis depended on the work of surgeons, and they could not be rushed or disturbed. He lifted the phone to CIC.

'Combat, Bridge. What's the status of that submarine contact?'

'*Gallery*'s helo dropped on it, but the torp ran dry without hitting anything. Looks like he ran northeast, but we haven't had anything for about five minutes. There's an Orion in the area now.'

'Tell them to check inside of us. This character isn't going to run away unless he has to. He might be running in, not out. Tell the screen commander.'

'Aye, Cap'n.'

He hadn't hung the phone up when it buzzed.

'Captain speaking.'

'She'll float, sir.' the damage-control officer said at once. 'We're patching the bulkhead now. It won't be tight, but the pumps can handle the leakage. Unless something else goes bad on us, we'll get her home. They sending the tug out to us?'

'Yes.'

'If we get a tow, sir, it better be sternfirst. I don't want to think about trying to run this one into a seaway.'

'Right'. Morris looked at Clarke. 'Get a gang of men aft. We'll be taking the tow at the stern, rig it up. Have them launch the whaleboat to look for survivors. I saw at least one man in the water. And get a sling on that arm.'

'You got it, Cap'n.' Clarke moved aft.

Morris went to CIC and found a working radio.

'X-Ray Alfa, this is *Pharris*.' Morris called to the screen commander. 'State your condition.'

'We took one hit forward, the bow is gone all the way to the ASROC launcher. We cannot maneuver. I can keep her afloat if we hit some bad weather. Both boilers currently down, but we should have power back in less than ten minutes. We have casualties, but I don't know how many or how bad yet.

'Commodore, we got hit by a nuke boat, probably a Victor. Unless I miss my guess, he's headed your way.'

'We lost him, but he was heading out,' the Commodore said.

'Start looking inside, sir,' Morris urged. 'This fellow got to knife-fighting range and pulled a beautiful number on us. This one isn't going to run away for long, he's too damned good for that.'

The Commodore thought that one over briefly. 'Okay, I'll keep that in mind. *Gallery*'s en route to you. What other assistance do you need?'

'You need *Gallery* more than we do. Just send us the tug,' Morris answered. He knew that the submarine wouldn't be coming back to finish the kill. He'd accomplished that part of his mission. Next, he'd try to kill some merchants.

'Roger that. Let me know if you need anything else. Good luck, Ed.'

'Thank you, sir. Out.'

Morris ordered his helo to drop a double ring of sonobuoys around his ship just in case. Then Sea Sprite found three men in the water, one of them dead. The whaleboat recovered them, allowing the helo to rejoin the convoy. It was assigned to *Gallery*, which took *Pharris*'s station as the convoy angled south.

Below, welders worked their gear in waist-deep saltwater as they struggled to seal off the breaks in the frigate's watertight bulkheads. The task lasted nine hours, then the pumps drained the water from the flooded compartments.

Before they had finished, the fleet tug *Papago* pulled alongside the frigate's square stern. Chief Clarke supervised as a stout towing wire was passed across and secured. An hour later, the tug was pulling the frigate on an easterly course at four knots, backwards to protect the damaged bow. Morris ordered his towed-array sonar to be strung over the bow, trailing it out behind to give them some small defense capability. Several extra lookouts were posted to watch for periscopes. It would be a slow, dangerous trip back home.

*

There were only two bodies to bury. Another fourteen men were missing and presumed dead, but for all that, Morris counted himself fortunate. Twenty sailors were injured to one extent or another. Clark's broken forearm, a number of broken ankles from the shock of the torpedo impact, and a half-dozen bad scaldings from rupture steam pipes. That didn't count minor cuts from flying glass.

Morris read through the ceremony in the manual, his voice emotionless as he went through the words about the sure and certain hope of how the sea will one day give up her dead . . . On command the seamen tilted up the mess tables. The bodies wrapped in plastic bags and weighted with steel slid out from under the flags, dropping straight into the water. It was ten thousand feet deep here, a long last trip for his executive officer and a third-class gunner's mate from Detroit. The rifle salute followed, but not taps. There was no one aboard who could play a trumpet, and the tape recorder was broken. Morris closed the book.

'Secure and carry on.'

The flags were folded properly and taken to the sail locker. The mess tables were carried below and the stanchions were replaced to support the lifelines. And USS *Pharris* was still only half a ship, fit only to be broken up for scrap, Morris knew.

Morris nurses what is left of his first command safely back to port. After calling on as many as possible of the next-of-kin of his fallen shipmates, he is ordered at short notice to relieve the ailing Captain of USS *Reuben James*, a larger and better-equipped platform on which to continue the battle for the supremacy of the North Atlantic sea-lanes. His first voyage is a short one along the eastern seabord of the United States. This is his first encounter with a Royal Navy escort assigned to work with him by SACLANT. They get off to a good start, and go on to co-operate effectively in the face of an enemy growing in agressive confidence.

HMS *Battleaxe* was already out there, three miles ahead, a subtly different shade on her hull, and the White Ensign fluttering at her mast. A signal light started blinking at them.

WHAT THE DEVIL IS A REUBEN JAMES, *Battleaxe* wanted to know.

'How do you want to answer that, sir?' a signalman asked.

Morris laughed, the ominous spell broken. 'Signal, "At least we don't name warships for our mother-in-law."'

'All right!' The petty officer loved it.

from Red Storm Rising by Tom Clancy (1986)

The war ends suddenly, after an internal putsch in the Kremlin. There is a hastily agreed armistice, just as Ed Morris brings *Reuben James* alongside in Norfolk, Virginia, at the end of his last operational voyage.

A Type VIIC U-boat's Fight for Survival

One of the greatest books about war at sea is *U-boat*, a fictionalized story of one long patrol from La Pallice, the port of La Rochelle and home-base of the 3rd U-boat Flotilla from 1940 onwards. In fact, it is made up of experiences recorded by a war correspondent on three patrols – in itself a remarkable achievement since the statistical life-expectancy of any U-boat was 1.6 patrols. Post-war records show that only one boat (U.953) returned safely from her eighth patrol; another 785 were sunk long before, 203 of them on their first patrol, in all taking down with them 27,000 men out of a total force of 40,000. Yet when the war ended there were 100 new submarines nearing completion, with sufficient crews to man all of them – an astonishing tribute to the way in which those men wearing white cap covers (the exclusive privilege of a U-boat commander) sustained morale.

Lothar-Günther Buchheim's classic is a fitting memorial to those incredibly brave men. It was made into a cult movie (*Das Boot*) which faithfully observed the feelings of men enduring conditions of unimaginable squalor for months on end in a 16-foot-diameter steel tube 2 centimetres thick. Most of the time they were on the surface in the North Atlantic in all weathers, resigned to weeks of fruitless searching, never knowing where they stood in the ever-changing technological battle of weapons against counter-measures.

The novel was faithfully translated by J. Maxwell Brownjohn, who commented that 'many features of life in a U-boat – notably the dangers and discomforts, sense of comradeship and relationships between officers and men – will strike a chord with all who served in submarines'. He might have added that the uninhibited language and outrageous behaviour between one patrol and another is equally credible to British and German submariners.

In the novel, the U-boat *U-A*, a Type VIIC, spends a month reaching her assigned patrol area in the western Atlantic. Apart from having to dive to escape aircraft several times while clearing the Bay of Biscay, no contact is made with the enemy. For days on end the weather is the crew's main preoccupation.

> I went on the bridge as often as I could. To stand there was like standing on a small treeless island. Sea and sky were visible in their entirety, uninterrupted by superstructure, masts or yards.
> The sky attired itself in a different colour each morning. There were skies of

vitriol and pistachio green, skies of a green as astringent as lime-juice held to the light, or dull as the greenish froth from a boiled-over saucepan of spinach, or ice-cold as a cobalt green shading to Naples yellow.

The vault of heaven had many yellows to offer. A frequent morning shade was pale chrome yellow, whereas the evening skies were a rich colour like brass, cadmium or Indian yellow. Sometimes the whole sky became enveloped in yellow flame. The clouds, too, could turn a dirty sulphurous shade of yellow. The radiant aureoles of sunset varied from greenish golden-yellow to cold golden-yellow and an iridescent orange version of the same.

For sheer splendour, the red skies were unsurpassed. Morning and evening alike, the atmosphere could be flooded with red light of the utmost intensity. The reds seemed to be the richest and most varied shades of all, ranging from a faint pink flush to delicate opaline rose or deep purple, from hazy mallow-red to harsh hydrant-red. Between these lay mother-of-pearl red, geranium-red and scarlet, and between red and yellow lay infinite gradations of orange.

Violet infernos in the sky were rarer than red. The diffuse and fugitive violets, which swiftly dulled to grey, were reminiscent of worn taffeta, but the blackish, turbid blue-violets looked malign and menacing. There were also evenings steeped in purple-violets so gaudy that no painter would have dared to reproduce them.

The grey skies had tonal nuances without number. They could be warm or chill, mingled with umber, dark ochre or burnt Sienna. Velasquez grey, dove-grey – vivid greys of this kind alternated with totally inexpressive greys like concrete or steel.

Apart from grey, blue was the sky's principal colour. Most splendid of all was deep blue seen above a turbulent sea whipped high by angry gusts of wind: a cobalt blue infinity bare of storm clouds. Sometimes the blue was as rich as indigo dissolved in water, and greenish cerulean blue had a rarity which made it all the more exquisite.

The colours of the sea were as variable as those of the sky – steamy crepuscular grey, black and bottle-green, violet and white and as manifold as its own ever-changing textures: silky, matt, ribbed, ruffled, splintered, choppy, corrugated, undulant.

U-A was still freighted with fourteen torpedoes and 120 rounds for the 88mm. Test firings had made minor inroads into the anti-aircraft ammunition, and a sizeable quantity of our 114 tons of oil had been used. We were also lighter by a considerable proportion of our supplies.

So far, we were a dud investment on the part of Germany's Supreme Commander. We had failed to inflict the slightest damage on the enemy. We had still to cover ourselves in glory, break Albion's stranglehold, add a new leaf to the laurels of the German U-boat arm, etcetera . . .

We had merely stood watches, eaten and digested, inhaled bad smells and produced some of our own.

We hadn't fired a single torpedo. Misses would at least have made more room in the fore-ends, but every fish was still in residence, lovingly tended, carefully greased and regularly maintained.

As the sky darkened, so the rags of water that fluttered from the jumping-wire at every dip of the bow turned as grey as laundry washed in wartime soap. Soon, nothing could be seen in any direction but grey on grey. The grey of the sea merged without a break into the grey of the sky.

We were bludgeoning our way into a head sea. The submarine pitched like a rocking-horse, up and down. The strain of peering through binoculars became a torment. It was all I could do not to be overwhelmed by my wan and cheerless surroundings and subside into apathy.

The grey light seemed to press upon my eyelids through a gauze filter. The grey soup contained nothing solid for the eye to apprehend, and fine spindrift made the grey still more opaque.

If only something would happen! I longed for a brief spurt at full power – anything that would make *U-A* cleave the waves instead of lurching into them at this soul-destroying jog-trot.

*

Hours trickled by, and still we received no signal addressed to *U-A*. The Captain sat huddled in the corner of his bunk and busied himself with an assortment of coloured folders containing pamphlets of every description, confidential and secret instructions, tactical rules, flotilla orders and other directives. In view of his well-known aversion to official bumf in all its forms, he could only have been masking an excitement like ours.

At 1700 another signal came in. The Captain raised his eyebrows. His whole face seemed to blossom. A signal addressed to us! He read it and gloom descended once more. Almost absently, he shoved the slip across to me. It was a request for a weather report.

The quartermaster drafted one and gave it to the Captain to sign. 'Barometer 1005 rising, air temperature 5 degrees, sea 7 degrees, wind north-west 6, sea and swell 5-6, 4-eighths cloud, cirro-stratus, visibility 7 miles, position KM.'

At last comes the order from U-boat headquarters to move against a known convoy. In high seas and poor visibility, *U-A* makes her first contact of the patrol.

A mast, no doubt about it, but a mast without an accompanying plume of smoke. Just a single hairline of a mast? Strain my eyes as I would, nothing showed but this pig's bristle which seemed to climb above the skyline as I watched.

Every merchantman trailed a plume of smoke which betrayed her presence long before her masts showed above the horizon. Ergo, this was no merchantman.

A minute went by. I kept my eyes glued to the pig's bristle and felt my throat throb with mounting excitement.

All doubt had vanished. The mast was growing steadily taller, so the destroyer must be heading our way. There was no possibility of evasion on the surface, not with our engines.

'They must have spotted us – damn and blast!' The Captain hardly raised his voice as he gave the alarm.

I reached the upper lid in a single bound. My boots hit the deck-plates with a metallic thud. The Captain gave the order to open all main vents even before he had fully secured the upper lid.

'Periscope depth,' he called down to the control-room. The Chief restored trim. The needle of the depth-gauge halted, then travelled slowly back across the dial. Dufte stood panting beside me in his wet oilskins. Zeitler and Böckstiegel, the two planesmen, were seated at their push-button controls, intently watching the water-level in the Papenberg. The first lieutenant inclined his head and let the rainwater drip off the brim of his sou'wester.

Nobody spoke. The only sound was a gentle electric hum which seemed to come from behind padded doors.

The silence was eventually broken by the Captain's voice. 'Depth?'

'Twenty metres,' reported the Chief.

'Periscope depth.'

The water in the Papenberg slowly sank. The submarine rose until the periscope broke surface.

We were not levelled off yet, so the Chief pumped aft from the forward trimming tank. U-A gradually returned to the horizontal but did not lie still. The waves nudged her in all directions, heaving, pulling, shoving. Periscope observation would be difficult.

I was listening for the Captain's voice when the hydrophone operator reported propeller noises on the starboard beam.

I passed the report to the conning-tower.

'Very good,' replied the Captain. Then, just as drily: 'Action stations.'

The hydrophone operator was leaning out of his cubby-hole into the passage. His unseeing eyes were dilated. Seen from the front, his face was a flat mask with two holes for a nose. Apart from the Captain, he was the only man aboard whose senses extended to the world outside our steel shell: the Captain could see the enemy, the hydrophone operator could hear him. The rest of us were blind and deaf. 'Propeller noises increasing,' he reported. 'Drawing slowly aft.'

The Captain's voice was muted. 'Flood tubes 1 to 4.'

I thought so. The Old Man planned to take on the destroyer – he had his sights on a red pennant. He needed a destroyer to complete his collection, I knew it as soon as I heard him order us to periscope depth.

Another order from the conning-tower: 'Captain to control-room – Chief, accurate depth, please.'

A tall order, in this sea. The muscles in the Chief's lean face tautened and relaxed spasmodically as though his jaws were busy with chewing-gum. Woe to him if the boat rose too far, if she broke surface and betrayed us to the enemy . . .

The Captain was sitting astride his saddle in the cramped space between the periscope shaft and the conning-tower casing, head clamped to the rubber eye-pieces and splayed thighs gripping the massive shaft. His feet rested on the pedals which enabled him to rotate the shaft swiftly and silently through 360 degrees, saddle and all. His right hand gripped the lever which extended and retracted it.

The periscope motor hummed. He had slightly withdrawn the periscope head so as to keep it as close to the surface as he possibly could.

The Chief was standing utterly motionless behind the two look-outs, who were now operating the hydroplanes. His eyes, too, were fixed on the Papenberg. The column of water slowly rose and fell, each rise and fall corresponding to the height of the waves on the surface.

Subdued murmurs. The hum of the periscope motor sounded as if it had been passed through a fine filter. It started, stopped, started again. The Captain was extending the look-stick for seconds at a time, then letting the sea wash over it. The destroyer must be quite close now.

'Flood No. 5 tube,' came a whisper from above.

The order was quietly passed to the stern torpedo compartment. We were in action.

I sat down on the sill of the bulkhead door. A whispered report from aft: 'No. 5 tube ready, bow-cap shut.'

*

It was extremely difficult to hit a destroyer, with its shallow draught and high degree of manoeuvrability. Once hit, however, it vanished like a puff of thistledown. An explosion, a geyser of water and fragmented steel, and finis – nothing remained.

The Captain's steady voice came from above. 'Open bow-caps, tubes 1 and 2. Enemy speed fifteen. Angle on the bow, four zero left. Range one thousand.'

The second lieutenant set the values on the calculator. The fore-ends reported bow-caps open. The first lieutenant passed the word, quietly but distinctly: 'Tubes 1 and 2 ready, sir.'

With his hand on the firing-lever, the Captain waited for the enemy to cross the hairline.

I longed to see.

Silence lent wings to my imagination. Baneful pictures took shape: a British destroyer bearing down on us at point-blank range. A ship's bow with its creaming bow-wave – a bird of prey with a white bone in its beak – loomed over us, about to ram. Dilated eyes, a rending of metal, jagged steel plates, a torrent of green water pouring into our torn hull.

The Captain's voice rang out, sharp as a whiplash. 'Flood Q. Sixty metres. Shut all bow-caps.'

The Chief, a fraction of a second later: 'Planes hard-a-dive, full ahead both. All hands forward!'

A babble of voices. I flung myself to one side, feet scrabbling the deck-plates. The first man dived through the after bulkhead, tripped, regained his footing and hurried on forward past the wireless office at a crouching run.

I caught a series of wide-eyed inquiring looks as more men passed me, slipping and stumbling. Two bottles of fruit-juice rolled down the passage from the POs' mess and smashed against the control-room bulkhead.

All hydroplanes were still hard-a-dive. The submarine was already at a steep bow-down angle, but still the men kept coming. They slid through the tilted control-room like skiers. One of them swore sibilantly as he fell headlong.

Only the engine-room watch remained aft now. I lost my footing but managed to grab the shaft of the search periscope just in time. The sausages seemed to be almost parallel with the deckhead. I heard the Captain's voice superimposed on a slither and thud of boots: 'Any time now.' It sounded quite casual, like a passing remark.

He climbed slowly down the ladder with the exaggerated deliberation of someone demonstrating a drill movement, ascended the incline and propped one buttock on the chart-stowage. His right hand encircled a pipe for support.

The Chief brought us slowly up by the head and ordered all hands back to diving stations. The men who had hurried forward worked their way aft again, hand over hand.

Using the sausages as a rough-and-ready inclinometer, I estimated that we were still thirty degrees bow-down.

RRABUMM! RRUMM! RRUMM!

I was jolted by three resounding blows like axe-strokes. Half-stunned, I heard a muffled roar. Icy fingers palpated my heart. What was the roaring sound? Then I realized: it was water rushing back into the submarine cavities created by the explosions.

Two more colossal thuds.

The control-room PO had retracted his head like a tortoise. The new control-room hand, the Vicar, swayed and clung to the chart-table.

Another detonation, louder than the rest.

The lights went out, leaving us in Stygian gloom.

'Secondary lighting's failed!' I heard someone shout.

The Chief's orders seemed to come from far away. Cones of torch light drilled yellowish holes in the darkness. A voice demanded fuses. The captains of stations made their reports by voice-pipe: 'Fore-ends well.' – 'Motor-room well.' – 'Engine-room well.'

'No leaks reported, sir,' said the quartermaster. His voice sounded quite as unemotional as the Captain's.

A moment later the deck-plates danced to the impact of two double detonations.

'Blow Q.' The pump started up with an incisive noise. As soon as the sound of the detonations had died away, it was stopped again to prevent the enemy's hydrophone from getting a bearing.

'Bring up the bow,' the Chief ordered his planesmen. Then, to the Captain: 'Boat trimmed, sir.'

'There'll be more to come,' the Captain said. 'They actually spotted the periscope, damn them. Almost incredible, in a sea like that.'

He looked round without a trace of dismay. I even detected a note of mockery in his voice. 'Psychological warfare, gentlemen, that's all.'

Nothing happened for the next ten minutes. Then a violent detonation shook the hull. More thuds followed in quick succession. The U-boat quaked and groaned.

'Fifteen,' counted the quartermaster, 'sixteen, seventeen. Eighteen, nineteen.'

The Chief was staring at the needle of the depth-gauge, which jumped a line or two at every concussion. His eye were wide and looked even darker than usual. The Captain's eyes were shut in concentration: own course, enemy course, avoiding couse. His reactions had to be instantaneous. Alone of us all, he was fighting a battle. Our lives depended on the accuracy of his decisions.

*

The hydrophone operator murmured: 'Getting louder.'

The Captain detached himself from the periscope shaft and walked over to me on tiptoe. 'Bearing?'

'Bearing steady at two-six-zero, sir.'

Four explosions in quick succession. Before the roar and gurgle of their aftermath had died away the Captain said in an undertone: 'She was handsomely painted. An oldish ship with a heavily raked forecastle, but otherwise flush-decked.'

I was jolted by another explosion. The deck-plates rattled.

'Twenty-seven, twenty-eight,' counted the quartermaster, emulating the Captain's studiously offhand tone.

A bucket rolled across the deck.

'Quiet, blast it!'

This time it sounded as if someone had put the gravel in a tin can and shaken it to and fro, once in each direction. The Asdic was overlaid by a brisk, intermittent chirping of a different kind: the throb of the corvette's propellers. They were clearly audible. I froze again as though the slightest movement, the smallest sound, would bring the propeller-beats nearer. Not a blink, not a flicker of the eye, not a breath, not a nervous twitch, not a change of expression, not a goose pimple.

Another five depth-charges for the quartermaster's tally. My face remained a frozen mask. The Captain raised his head. Articulating the words clearly, he dropped them into the dying echoes of the last explosion: 'Easy, everyone. It could be a lot worse.'

The calm in his voice was good to hear. It settled on my jangling nerves like balm.

Then we lurched under a single shattering blow which sounded like a gigantic club thrashing a sheet of iron. Two or three men staggered.

Wisps of blue smoke hung in the air. And again: BRUMM! BRUMM! RRABUMM!

'Thirty-five, thirty-six, thirty-seven.' This time the words came in a whisper.

The Captain said firmly: 'Never mind the noise – a few bangs never hurt anyone.' Then he reinterred himself in his course calculations. A deathly silence fell. After a while he murmured: 'How does she bear now?'

'Two-six-zero, sir, growing louder.'

The Captain's head lifted. He had reached a decision. 'Hard-a-starboard,' he ordered, then: 'Hydrophone operator, we're turning to starboard.'

*

He leant forward and addressed Herrmann. 'Check if she's going away.' Impatiently, he added: 'Well, any change?'

'Constant, sir,' Herrmann replied. After a while: 'Growing louder.'

'Bearing?'

'Bearing steady at two-two-zero, sir.'

At once the Captain went hard-a-starboard. We were doubling back on our tracks.

Both motors were ordered slow ahead.

Drops of condensation punctured the almost tangible silence at regular intervals: Plink, plonk – tip, tap – plip, plop.

A new series of concussions made the deck-plates dance and rattle. 'Forty-seven, forty-eight,' Kriechbaum counted. 'Forty-nine, fifty, fifty-one.'

I glanced at my wrist-watch: 1430. When had we dived? It must have been shortly after midday, so we had been under counter-attack for two hours.

*

'Propeller noises drawing aft,' reported Herrmann. Two more depth-charges exploded almost simultaneously, but the detonations were fainter and more muffled than their predecessors.

'Miles away,' said the Captain.

RRUMM, RRABUMM!

Still more muffed. The Captain reached for his cap. 'Dummy runs. They might as well go home and practise.'

Isenberg had already substituted some new glass tubes for the broken gauge-glasses, as though he realized that the sight of their shattered remains was bad for morale.

I stood up. My legs were stiff and numb. I extended a bloodless foot and felt as if I had stepped into a void. Grabbing the table for support, I looked down at the chart.

There was the pencil-line representing U-A's route, and there was the pencilled cross which marked our last fix. The line ended abruptly. I resolved to make a note of the grid reference if we got out alive.

Herrmann made a sweep through the full 360 degrees.

'Well?' asked the Captain, looking bored. His left cheek bulged as he rammed his tongue against it from the inside.

'Going away,' Herrmann replied.

The Captain looked round with an air of satisfaction. He even grinned. 'Well, that seems to be that.'

He stretched and shook himself. 'Quite instructive, really. In line for a red pennant one minute, clobbered the next.' He ducked stiffly through the bulkhead and vanished into his cubby-hole, calling for a piece of paper.

I wondered what he was drafting – something pithy for his patrol report or a signal to base. If I knew anything about him, it would be a handful of bone-dry words like 'Surprised by corvette in rainstorm. Counter-attacked three hours.'

Five minutes later he reappeared in the control-room. He exchanged a glance with the Chief, ordered us to periscope depth and climbed leisurely into the conning-tower.

The Chief gave a series of plane orders.

'Depth?' came the Captain's voice from above.

'Forty metres,' the Chief reported, then: 'Twenty metres, fifteen metres – periscope depth.'

I heard the periscope motor hum, stop, hum again. A minute went by. No word from above. We waited in vain for a sign of life.

'Something must be up . . .' murmured the control-room PO.

At last the Captain spoke. 'Take her down quick! 50 metres all – hands forward.'

I repeated the order and the hydrophone operator passed it on. The words travelled aft like a multiple echo. Men began to hurry forward through the control-room, grim-faced once more.

'Bloody hell,' muttered the Chief. The needle of the depth-gauge resumed its slow progress: 20 metres, 30, 40 . . .

The Captain's sea-boots appeared. He clambered slowly down the ladder. All eyes were fixed on his face, but he only gave a derisive grin. 'Slow ahead both. Steer zero-six-zero.' At last he enlightened us: 'The corvette's lying a thousand metres away. Stopped, by the look of her. The crafty sods were planning to jump us.' He bent over the chart. After a while he turned to me. 'Cunning bastards – you can't be too careful. We may as well dawdle west for a bit.'

'When's dusk?' he asked the quartermaster.

'1830, sir.'

'Good. We'll stay deep for the time being.'

from *U-Boat* by Lothar-Günther Buchheim (1974)

The next ten days are neutralized by severe gales precluding any offensive action by either side. When, during her seventh week out from La Pallice, the weather finally moderates, *U-A* finally gets in amongst a convoy. She sinks two merchantmen before being put down for another prolonged counter-attack lasting over eight hours.

A Stricken Frigate Just Makes It

Nicholas Monsarrat's fame rests largely on his classic novel about the Battle of the Atlantic, *The Cruel Sea*. It has tended to overshadow a book he wrote four years earlier, in 1947. Although no more than a long short story, for my money *HMS Marlborough Will Enter Harbour* is at least its equal.

Marlborough is a 1,200-ton Bird Class sloop, similar to HMS *Starling*, led by the legendary 2nd Escort Group Commander, Captain F. J. Walker, RN, who sank six U-boats on one voyage.

The old *Marlborough* . . . The Captain was not married, and if he had been it might not have made any difference: he was profoundly and exclusively in love with this ship, and the passion, fed especially on the dangers and ordeals of the past three war years, left no room for a rival. It had started in 1926, when she was brand new and he had commissioned her: it had been his first job as First Lieutenant, and his proudest so far. She had been the very latest in ships then – a new sloop, Clyde-built, twin turbines, two four-inch guns (the twin mountings came later) and a host of gadgets and items of novel equipment which were sharp on the palate . . . There had been other ships, of course, in the sixteen years between; his first command had been a river gunboat, his second a destroyer: but he had never forgotten *Marlborough*. He had kept an eye on her all the time, checking her movements as she transferred from the Home Fleet to the Mediterranean, thence to the China Station, then home again: looking up her officers in the Navy List and wondering if they were taking proper care of her: making a special trip up to Rosyth on one of his leaves, to have another look at her; and when, at the outbreak of war, he had been given command of her, it had been like coming home again, to someone dearly loved who was not yet past the honeymoon stage.

She was not, in point of fact, much of a command for a commander, even as the senior ship of an escort group, and he could have done better if he had wished. But he did not wish. Old-fashioned she might be, battered with much hard driving, none too comfortable, at least three knots slower than the job really demanded; but she could still show her teeth and she still ran as sweet as a sewing machine, and the last three years had been the happiest of his career. He was intensely jealous of her efficiency when contrasted with more up-to-date ships, and he went to endless trouble over this, intriguing for the fitting of new equipment 'for experimental purposes', demanding the replacement of officers or key-ratings if any weak point in the team began to show itself. In three years of North Atlantic convoy work he had spared neither himself nor his ship's company any of the intense strain which the job imposed; but *Marlborough* he had nursed continuously, so that the prodigious record of hours steamed and miles covered had cost the minimum of wear.

He knew her from end to end, not only with the efficient 'technical' eye of the man who had watched the last five months of her building, but with an added, intimate regard for every part of her, a loving admiration, an eye tenderly blind to her shortcomings

*

[She] was torpedoed at dusk on the last day of 1942 while on independent passage from Iceland to the Clyde. She was on her way home for refit, and for the leave that went with it, after a fourteen-month stretch of North Atlantic convoy escort with no break, except for routine boiler-cleaning. Three weeks' leave to each watch – that had been the buzz going round the ship's company when they left Reykjavik after taking in the last convoy; but many of them never found out how much truth there was in that buzz, for the torpedo struck at the worst moment, with two-thirds of the ship's company having tea below decks, and when it exploded under the forward mess-deck at least sixty of them were killed outright.

HMS *Marlborough* was an old ship, seventeen years old, and she took the outrage as an old lady of breeding should. At the noise and jar of the explosion a delicate shudder went all through her: then as her speed fell off there was stillness, while she seemed to be making an effort to ignore the whole thing: and then, brought face to face with the fury of this mortal attack, gradually and disdainfully she conceded the victory.

The deck plating of the fo'c'sle buckled and sagged, pulled downwards by the weight of the anchors and cables: all this deck indeed, crumpled as far as the four-inch gun mounting, which toppled forwards until the gun-muzzles were pointing foolishly to the sea; a big lurch tore loose many of the ammunition lockers and sent them cascading over the side. Until the way of her sixteen knots fell off, there were crunching noises as successive bulkheads took the weight of water, butted at it for a moment, and then gave in: and thus, after a space, she lay – motionless, cruelly hit, two hundred miles south-west of the Faeroes and five hundred miles from home.

So far it had been an affair of metal: now swiftly it became an affair of men. From forward came muffled shouting – screaming, some of it – borne on the wind down the whole length of the ship, to advertise the shambles buried below. The dazed gun's crew from 'A' gun, which had been directly over the explosion, climbed down from their sagging platform and drew off aft. There was a noise of trampling running feet from all over the ship: along alleyways, up ladders leading from the untouched spaces aft: confused voices, tossed to and fro by the wind, called as men tried to find out how bad the damage was, what the orders were, whether their friends had been caught or not.

On the upper deck, near the boats and at the foot of the bridge-ladders, the clatter and slur of feet and voices reached its climax. In the few moments before a firm hand was taken, with every light in the ship out and only the shock of the explosion as a guide to what had happened, there was confusion, noisy and urgent: the paramount need to move quickly clashed with indecision and doubt as to where that move could best be made. The dusk, the rising sea, the bitterly cold wind, which carried an acrid smell in sharp eddying puffs, were all part of this discordant aftermath; the iron trampling of those racing feet all over the ship bound it together, co-ordinating fear into a vast uneasy whole, a spur for panic if panic ever showed itself.

It never did show itself. The first disciplined reaction, one of many such small reassurances, to reach the bridge was the quartermaster's voice, admirably matter-of-fact, coming up the wheel-house voice-pipe: 'Gyro compass gone dead, sir!' The midshipman, who shared the watch with the First Lieutenant and was at that moment licking a lip split open on the edge of the glass dodger, looked round uncertainly, found he was the only officer on the bridge, and answered: 'Very good. Steer by magnetic,' before he realized the futility of this automatic order. Then he jerked his head sideways, level with another voice-pipe, the one leading to the Captain's cabin, and called: 'Captain, sir!'

There was no answer. Probably the Captain was on his way up already. God, suppose he'd been killed, though . . . The midshipman called again: 'Captain, sir!' and a voice behind him said: 'All right, Mid. I heard it.'

He turned round, to find the comforting bulk of the Captain's dufflecoat outlined against the dusk. It was not light enough to see the expression on his face, nor was there anything in his voice to give a clue to it. It did not occur to the midshipman to speculate about this, in any case: for him, this was simply the Captain, the man he had been waiting for, the man on whom every burden could now be squarely placed.

'Torpedo, sir.'

'Yes.'

The Captain, moving with purpose but without hurry, stepped up on to the central compass platform, glanced once round him – and sat down. There was something special in that act of sitting down, there in the middle of the noise and movement reaching the bridge from all over the ship, and everyone near him caught it. The Captain, on the bridge, sitting in the Captain's chair. Of course: that was what they had been waiting for . . . It was the beginning, the tiny tough centre, of control and order. Soon it would spread outwards.

'Which side was it from?'

'Port, sir. Just under "A" gun.'

'Tell the engine-room what's happened . . . Where is the First Lieutenant?'

He is engaged with fourteen ratings in trying to save the badly buckled foremost surviving bulkhead. On entering the compartment he shuts the watertight doors behind him and is soon added to the unknown numbers of damage-control parties who sacrificed their lives to give their ship and her survivors an outside chance.

Throughout the long winter night, HMS *Marlborough* lies dead in the water with no power for propulsion, auxiliaries or lighting. Her radio has been smashed beyond repair. Finally, the Captain decides to see for himself how shoring up the next bulkhead aft is progressing. It is now all that is keeping the ship afloat: her Captain agonizes over giving the order he dreads above all – to abandon ship.

The journey down, deck by deck, had the same element of compulsion in it as, in a nightmare, distinguishes the random lunatic journey which can only lead to some inescapable horror at its end. The boat-deck was crowded: two loaded stretchers lay near the whaler, the figures on them not more than vague impressions of pain in the gloom: Merrett was directing the unlashing of a raft near by: on the lee side of the funnel a dozen hands, staring out at the water, were singing 'Home on the Range', in low-pitched chorus. The small party – Captain, Chief, Adams, the quartermaster – made their way aft, past the figures grouped round 'X' gun, and down another ladder. At the iron-deck level, a few feet from the water, all was deserted. 'I sent the damage control party up, as soon as we'd finished, sir,' the Chief said, as he stepped through the canvas screen into the alleyway leading forward. 'There was nothing else for them to do.'

Under cover now, the four of them moved along the rocking passage: Chief's torch picking out the way, flicking from side to side of the hollow tunnel against which the water was already lapping. Under their stumbling scraping feet the slope led fatally downwards. The clanging toll seemed to advance to meet them. They passed the entrance to the engine-room: just within, feet straddled on the grating, stood a young stoker, the link with the outside world in case the bridge voice-pipe failed. To him, as they passed, the Chief said: 'No orders yet. I'll be coming back in a minute,' and the stoker drew back into the shadows to pass the message on. Then they came to a closed watertight door, and this they eased slowly open, a clip at a time, so that any pressure of water within would show immediately. But it was still dry . . . the door swung back, and they stepped inside the last watertight space that lay between floating and sinking.

It was dimly lit, by two battery lanterns clipped to overhead brackets: the light struck down on a tangle of joists and beams, heel-pieces, wedges, cross-battens – the work of the damage control party. The deck was wet underfoot, and as *Marlborough* rolled, some inches of dirty water slopped from side to side, carrying with it a scummy flotsam of caps, boots, and ditty-boxes. The Captain switched on his torch, ducked under a transverse beam, and stepped up close to the bulkhead. It was as the Chief had said, in bad shape; bulging towards him, strained and leaking all down one seam, responding to the ship's movements with a long-drawn-out, harsh creaking. For a single moment, as he watched it, he seemed to be looking through into the space beyond, where Number One and his fourteen damage control hands had been caught. The forbidden picture – forbidden in the strict scheme of his captaincy – gave place to another one, conjured up in its turn by the clanging which now sounded desperately loud and clear: the three flooded mess-decks underneath his feet, the sealed-off shambles of the explosion area. Then his mind swung back, guiltily, to the only part of it that mattered now, the shored-up section he was standing in, and he nodded to himself as he glanced round it once more. It confirmed what he had been expecting but had only now faced fairly and squarely: Chief had done a good job, but it just wasn't good enough.

He turned quickly. 'All right, Chief. Bring your engine-room party out on to the upper deck. Adams! Pipe "Hands to stations for—" '

The words 'Abandon ship' were cut off by a violent explosion above their heads.

For a moment the noise was so puzzling that he could not assign it to anything: it was just an interruption, almost supernatural, which had stopped him finishing that hated sentence. Then another piece of the pattern clicked into place, and he said: 'That was a shell, by God!' and made swiftly for the doorway.

Outside, he called back over his shoulder: 'Chief – see to the door again!' and then started to run. His footsteps rang in the confined space: he heard Adams following close behind him down the passageway, the noise echoing and clattering all round him, urging him on. Reaching the open air at last was like escaping from a nightmare into a sweating wakefulness which must somehow be instantly co-ordinated and controlled. As he went up the ladder to the boat-deck there was a brilliant flash and another explosion up on the bridge, followed by the sharp reek of the shell-burst. Damned good shooting from somewhere . . . something shot past his head and spun into a ventilator with a loud clang. He began to run again, brushing close by a figure making for 'X' gun shouting, 'Close up again! Load star-shell!' Guns, at least, had his part of it under control.

He passed the space between the two boats. It was here, he saw, that the first shell had struck: the motor-boat was damaged, one of the stretchers was overturned, and there were three separate groups of men bending over figures stretched out on deck. He wanted to stop and find out how bad the damage was, and, especially, how many men had been killed or hurt, but he could not: the bridge called him, and had prior claim.

It was while he was climbing quickly up the ladder that he realized that the moon had now risen, low in the sky, and that *Marlborough* must be cleanly silhouetted against the horizon. If no one on the upper deck had seen the flash of the submarine's firing, the moon ought to give them a line on her position. Guns would probably work that out for himself. But it would be better to make sure.

Now he was at the top of the ladder, his eyes grown accustomed to the gloom, his nostrils assailed by the acrid stink of the explosion. The shell he had seen land when he first came out on deck had caught the bridge fair and square, going through one wing and exploding against the chart-house. Only two men were still on their feet – the signalman and one of the look-outs: the other look-out was lying, headless, against his machine-gun mounting. Adams, at his shoulder, drew in his breath sharply at the sight, but the Captain's eyes had already moved farther on, to where three other figures – who must be Haines, the midshipman, and the messenger – had fallen in a curiously theatrical grouping round the compass platform. The light there was too dim to show any details: the dark shambles could only be guessed at. But one of the figures was still moving. It was the midshipman, clinging to a voice-pipe and trying to hoist himself upright.

He said quickly: 'Lie still, Mid,' and then: 'Signalman, give me the hailer,' and lastly, to Adams: 'Do what you can for them.' He caught sight of the young, shocked face of the other look-out staring at him, and called out sharply: 'Don't look in-board. Watch your proper arc. Use your glasses.' Then he switched on the microphone, and spoke into it:

'X gun, X gun – illuminate away from the moon – illuminate away from the moon.' He paused, then continued: 'Doctor or sick-berth attendant report to the bridge now – doctor or sick-berth attendant.'

Pity had inclined him to put the last order first: the instinct of command had told him otherwise. But almost before he stopped speaking, the sharp crack of 'X' gun came from aft, and the star-shell soared. Guns had had the same ideas as himself.

Adams, who was kneeling down and working away at a rough tourniquet, said over his shoulder:

'Shall I carry on with that pipe, sir?'

'No. Wait.'

The U-boat coming to the surface had altered everything. The ship was now only a platform for 'X' gun, and not to be abandoned while 'X' gun still had work to do.

As the star-shell burst and hung, lighting up the grey moving sea, the Captain raised his glasses and swept the arc of water that lay on their beam. Almost immediately he saw the U-boat, stopped on the surface, broadside on to them and not more than a mile away. Before he had time to speak over the hailer, or give any warning, there was a noise from aft as Guns shouted a fresh order; and then things happened very quickly.

'X' gun roared. A spout of water, luminous under the star-shell, leapt upwards, just beyond the U-boat and dead in line – a superb sighting shot. considering the suddenness of this new crisis. There was a pause, while the Captain's mind raced over the two possibilities now open – that the U-boat, guessing she had only a badly crippled ship to deal with, would fight it out on the surface, or that she would submerge to periscope depth and fire another torpedo. Then came the next shot, to settle all his doubts.

It came from both ships, and it was almost farcically conclusive. The flash of both guns was instantaneous. The U-boat's shell exploded aft, right on 'X' gun, ripping the whole platform to pieces; but from the U-boat herself a brilliant orange flash spurted suddenly, to be succeeded by the crump of an explosion. Then she disappeared completely.

'X' gun, mortally wounded itself, had made its last shot a mortal one for the enemy.

That leaves the Captain with just thirty fit survivors, including only two officers, the doctor and the engineer. The latter works miracles with his decimated staff: first the power is restored; then the bow-down trim is reduced by jettisoning anything that can be shifted for'ard. After a brief burial service for the nineteen bodies not trapped in flooded compartments, main propulsion is restored on one shaft. In constant fear of the leading bulkhead's collapsing, *Marlborough* makes her way gingerly at 3 knots towards a landfall on the Hebrides, 270 miles to the south-east. When the weather suddenly turns nasty, she is obliged to turn and proceed stern first. For the next five days she butts her way painfully into the seas, until she is obliged to risk heading into the seas again, because there is a danger of her bow sections being pulled off.

With only a badly shattered magnetic compass to steer by, it is not surprising that the landfall is 200 miles out when the red flashing light of Rathlin Island is seen fourteen days after they had been torpedoed. Somehow maritime patrol aircraft have failed to spot the crippled ship.

'Trawlers ahead, sir,' said the signalman, breaking in on his thoughts. 'Three of them. I think they're sweeping.'

Back to civilization: to lights, harbours, dawn mine-sweepers, patrolling aircraft, a guarded fairway.

'Call them up, signalman.'

But one of the trawlers was already flashing to them. The signalman acknowledged the message, and said: 'From the trawler, sir: "Can I help you?" '

'Make: "Thank you. Are you going to Londonderry?" '

A pause, while the lamps flickered. Then: 'Reply "Yes", sir!'

'Right. Make: "Will you pass a message to the Port War Signal Station for me, please?" '

Another pause. 'Reply, "Certainly", sir.'

The Captain drew a long breath, conscious deep within him of an enormous satisfaction. 'Write this down, and then send it to them. "To Flag Officer in Charge, Londonderry, v. *Marlborough*. HMS *Marlbourough* will enter harbour at 1300 today. Ship is severely damaged above and below waterline. Request pilot, tugs, dockyard assistance and burial arrangements for one officer and seventy-four ratings." Got that?'

from *HMS Marlborough Will Enter Harbour* by Nicholas Monsarrat (1947)

NAVIGATION

Polynesians from Bora Bora to Hawaii

At a time when Mediterranean navigators rarely ventured any distance out of sight of land, descendants of the Phoenecians who first populated the Polynesian islands in the South Pacific made many long trans-oceanic voyages in their catamaran canoes. They had no charts and sailed many centuries before the first magnetic compass was invented, yet unerringly they contrived to make some astonishing landfalls.

James A. Michener, a New Yorker still happily adding to his prodigious literary output, sprang to fame when Rogers and Hammerstein based their smash-hit musical *South Pacific* on his *Tales of the South Pacific*, written after his experiences in the US Navy in those waters. His novel *Hawaii* is a panoramic social history of how the islands were colonized over the centuries by waves of immigrants from widely scattered origins. But here we are concerned only with the first settlers and with how they got there across 4,000 miles of uncharted ocean from the Friendly Islands, of which Tahiti is the best known. A tribe from Bora Bora, under their King Tamatoa and his young brother Teroro, are driven to seek a new homeland where they can worship their hereditary god Tane, free from the savage priests of the 'wrong' god, Oro, with their constant demands for human sacrifices. Sickened, the tribe slips away in search of the legendary islands to the north, far beyond the outer limit of their navigable experience, heading first for Nuku Hiva in the Marquesas group, 800 miles to the north-east. The god Ta'aroa is acknowledged by all to be absolute ruler of the oceans.

Before their departure, Teroro makes a comparatively short trip in the royal canoe to the nearby island of Havaiki, where the High Priest has summoned a convocation to impose the god Oro on all the islands, thus posing a deadly threat to the King.

In silence and in spiritual exaltation, Teroro pulled away the last prop that bound his glorious canoe to land, and slowly it began to taste the lagoon, to dip its high-tiered stern into the gentle waves, and finally to ride upon the bosom of Ta'aroa, which was its home.

The young chiefs who would paddle the canoe that night now leaped into the two hulls and adjusted the movable seats that slid back and forth along the dugout sections. Teroro, grabbing his personal god-carved paddle, gave the canoe a mighty shove that sent it far into the lagoon, with him trailing his feet aft in the green waters. 'Hoist sail!' he cried. 'We'll test the wind.' And when a noonday breeze dropped down from the cliff, it caught the sail and began to move the great double-hulled canoe, and men paddled briskly, and soon with lightning speed *Wait-for-the-West-Wind* hurtled across its home lagoon.

It flew like a special albatross, just dipping into the waves. It went like the wind-caught leaf of a breadfruit tree, skimming the waters. It went like a young woman hurrying to meet her lover, like the essence of the god Ta'aroa majestically inspecting the ramparts of his ocean. It sped like the spirit of a warrior killed in battle, on its swift journey to the everlasting halls of Tane. And it flashed across the lagoon like what it was: a miraculous, slim, double-hulled craft of Bora Bora, the swiftest ship the world at that time had ever known, capable of doing thirty knots in bursts, ten knots for days at a time, hour after hour; a huge, massive craft seventy-nine feet long, with a tiered stern twenty-two feet high and a solid platform slung across the hulls on which forty men or the statues of forty gods could ride, with pigs and pandanus and water stowed safely in the hidden innards.

'Wait for the west wind,' the men who built the canoe had advised, 'for it blows strong and sure from the heart of the hurricane.' The north wind cannot be depended upon, and the east wind is no treasure, for it blows constantly, and the south wind brings nothing but irritating minor storms, never those that shake the earth, not storms that last for weeks at a time and which can be counted upon to drive a canoe to the farthest points of earth. Wait for the west wind! It blows from the heart of the hurricane. It is a wind to match this great canoe.

On this day, it was an ordinary eastern wind. Some of the world's sailors might even have counted it a considerable breeze, but to Bora Borans who longed for the westerly gale that could carry them even to distant Nuku Hiva, the day's wind was really nothing. But it did bear a hint of invitation, and so on the spur of the moment Teroro cried, 'Through the reef!'

Wait-for-the-West-Wind was already doing better than fifteen knots, and a prudent navigator usually took his craft through this perilous reef at slowest speed, but on this sun-swept day Teroro shot his precious craft directly at the small opening that marked the dividing line between the placid green waters of the lagoon and the thundering blue ocean which pounded outside.

The canoe seemed to anticipate the impending crash of giant waves, for it tensed in the wind, cut a little deeper into the lagoon, and leaped towards the passageway through the reef. For an instant the crew could glimpse cruel fingers of grey coral clutching at the defiant craft, but this danger was quickly forgotten, for ahead loomed the towering waves.

With a song crying from its sail, with vigour to match that of the young chiefs who manned it, the swift canoe shot into the combers, lost its nose in a great grey-blue wave, then rose triumphantly on to the crest and sped away into the very centre of the wind and the rousing waves and vast blue sea of Ta'aroa.

'What a canoe!' Teroro exulted, the spray whipping his black hair about his face.

Later the King decides to make good his escape, taking an awesome gamble on making a passage to the unknown which might last up to fifty days. He takes with him sixty men, fifteen women of child-bearing age, and a selection of animals and plants with which to start new farms. He also ships as extra navigator his wise old uncle Tupuna – the only tribesman conversant with all the details of the legends supporting the existence of the islands far to the north. He is allowed to bring along his creepy old wife Teura, an acknowledged expert in reading omens at sea. They are scheduled to make a stop for replenishment at Nuku Hiva.

As the canoe is launched from the beach the High Priest plants an effigy of the god Oro in its shrine, but, as soon as it is clear of the reefs, the effigy is ditched and sunk by a well-aimed spear.

And so the double canoe, *Wait-for-the-West-Wind*, loaded and creaking with king and slave, with contradictory gods and pigs, with hope and fear, set forth upon the unknown. At the prow stood Teroro, ill-named the wise one, but at this fateful moment he was wise enough not to look back at Bora Bora, for that would have been not only an evil omen but folly as well, for he would have seen Marama [his woman who was not chosen to colonize their new home], and that sight he could not have borne.

When *West Wind* reached the reef, and stood for a moment in its last stretch of easily navigable water, all in the canoe experienced a moment of awful dread, for outside the coral barrier roared the storm of slashing waves and tremendous deeps. Just for an instant Mato, lead paddle on the left, whispered, 'Great Tane! Such waves!' But with prodigious force he led the paddlers into a swift rhythm that bore them directly into the heart of the storm. The canoe rose high in the sea, teetered a moment with its shrouds whistling, then ripped down, down into the valley of the waves. Spray dashed across all heads and the two halves seemed as if they must tear apart. Pigs squealed in terror and dogs barked, while in the flooded grass house women thought: 'This is death.'

But instantly the powerful canoe cut into the waves, found itself, and rode high on to the crest of the ocean, away from Bora Bora of the muffled paddles, away from the comforting lagoon and on to the highway that led to nothingness.

In such weather King Tamatoa led his people into exile. They did not go in triumph or with banners flying; they fled at night, with no drums beating. They did not leave with riches and in panoply; they were rudely elbowed off their island with only enough food to sustain them precariously. Had they been more clever, they would have held their homeland; but they were not and they were forced to go. Had they perceived the deeper nature of gods, they would never have fallen prey to a savage deity who tormented them; but they were stubborn rather than wise, and the false god expelled them.

Later ages would depict these men as all-wise and heroic, great venturers seeking bright new lands; but such myths would be in error, for no man leaves where he is and seeks a distant place unless he is in some respect a failure; but having failed in one location and having been ejected, it is possible that in the next he will be a little wiser.

There was, however, one overriding characteristic that marked these defeated people as they swept into the storm: they did have courage. Only if they had been craven could they have swallowed their humiliation and remained on Bora Bora; this they would not do. It is true that they fled into the dusk, but each man carried as his most prized possession his own personal god of courage. For Teroro it was the mighty albatross that winged its way over distant seas. For King Tamatoa it was the wind that spoke to him in tempest. For Tupuna it was the spirit of the lagoon that brought fish. And for his ancient bleary-eyed wife, Teura, the keeper of omens, it was a god so powerful that she scarcely dared mention its name. But it followed her in the ocean, her great and sweet and powerful deity, her courage in the unknown.

*

Then it was that the wisdom of Tupuna in setting forth at dusk on the new day of the month became apparent, for there, rising in the eastern sky and with no bright moon in competition, sparkled the Seven Little Eyes. It was their first twilight appearance of the year, their reassuring return which proved that the world would continue for at least twelve more months. With what extraordinary joy the voyagers greeted the Little Eyes. From the grass house women came forth and filled their hearts with comfort. Those crew members who had to keep the canoe headed with the wind found new resilience in their tired muscles, and Teroro knew that he was on course.

Then, the miracle vouchsafed, Tane drew the clouds once more across the heavens, and the storm continued, but contentment beyond measure settled upon the canoe, for it was at last apparent that the company moved in accordance with divine laws. How sweet the roar of the wind that bore them on, how consoling the motion of the waves that carried them into the unknown; how appropriate the world, how well ordered and secure the heavens. On the canoe, that daring and insignificant bundle of wood lashed together by sennit and men's wills, all hearts were deep in peace, and the onwardness of their journey sang contentedly in all parts of the craft, so that when old Tupuna crawled back to his watching point abaft the gods' house he called softly to Teroro ahead, 'The king is content. The omen proves that Oro was caught by Ta'aroa and conveyed safely to Havaiki. All is well.' And the canoe moved on.

The most critical part of any twenty-four-hour period came in the half-hour just before dawn, for unless the navigator could catch a glimpse of some known star and thus check course he would have to proceed through an entire day with only the unreliable sun to steer by; for while it was true that master astronomers like Teroro and Tupuna could follow each movement of the sun and take from it their heading, they could not use it to determine their latitude. For that they depended upon the stars; their sailing directions reminded them which stars culminated over which islands, and to pass the last moments of night without seeing any constellations was not only an omen of bad luck in the future, it was also proof of present difficulty, which, if it persisted for several days, might develop into catastrophe.

For example, after their first fleeting glimpse of the Seven Little Eyes, Teroro and his uncle had waited anxiously for Three-in-a-Row, which other astronomers then living in distant deserts had already named Orion's Belt, for the sailing directions said that these stars hung over Nuku Hiva, their replenishment point. But Three-in-a-Row had not appeared during the night watch and Teroro had been unable to determine his latitude. Now the conspicuous stars were setting without having been seen, and the navigator was worried.

He had, however, observed on earlier trips that it was a peculiarity of his ocean that in the last few minutes of morning twilight some star, as if determined to aid mariners, pushed clouds aside and showed itself, and he thought there was still time for this to happen.

'Three-in-a-Row will appear there,' Tupuna announced confidently, but Teroro wondered if the night's strong wind might not have blown the canoe rather farther north than his uncle suspected.

'Maybe they will be closer to that cloud,' Teroro suggested. The difference of opinion was not to be resolved, for clouds continued to streak out of the west to meet the sun rising on the other side of the ocean. On this day dawn was neither inspiring nor refreshing, for the sun straggled reluctantly up behind many layers of cloud, half illuminated the ocean with dull grey and proved to the voyagers that they did not know where they were.

Teroro and Tupuna, having accomplished all they could, fell into immediate sleep in the stormy daylight; and it was then that the latter's wife, wizened, red-eyed old Teura, paid for her passage. She climbed out of the grass house, splattered sea water over her wrinkled face, rubbed her bleary eyes, threw her head back and started studying the omens. In nearly two-thirds of a century of living with the gods, she had unravelled many of their tricky ways. Now she watched how Ta'aroa moved the waves, how the spume rose, how the tips fell away and in what manner they tumbled back into the troughs. She marked the colour of the sea and the construction of the basic swells that underlay the more conspicuous waves.

At mid-morning she saw a land bird, possibly from Bora Bora itself, winging its way out to sea, and from its flight she was able to determine the bird's estimate of how long the storm would continue, and it confirmed her own. A bit of bark, washed out to sea days before from Havaiki, was of particular interest to the old woman, for it proved that the ocean had a northerly set, which was not apparent from the wind, which blew more towards the northeast.

But most of all the rheumy-eyed old seer studied the sun, for although it was well masked behind layers of cloud, her practised eye could mark its motion. 'Star men like Tupuna and Teroro don't think much of the sun,' she snorted, but when she placed her observations of its course beside the deductions she had made from earlier omens she concluded: 'Those men don't know where they are! We're far to the north of our course!'

A storm lasting a week apparently distorts some of the omens, so they decided to forget about Nuku Hiva and press on northwards. Finally they are rewarded by a sight of the Big Dipper (Ursa Major in nautical almanacs) pointing towards a new and disturbing star on the northern horizon. The fact that it does not move is considered to be an omen of terrible significance. The King believes that the god Tane has placed a fixed barrier in his path; but second thoughts prevail, sustaining them through the gruelling ordeal of crossing the Doldrums.

'It would seem so,' Teura said. 'Else why would the star be set there, like a rock?'

Apprehension gripped them, for if Tane was against this voyage all must perish. They could not go back now. 'And yet,' Tupuna recalled, 'the chant says that when the west wind dies, we are to paddle across the sea of no wind towards the new star. Is this not the new star, fixed there for us to use?'

For many minutes the group discussed this hopeful concept and concluded that it might have merit. They decided, therefore, that this should be done: continue for the coming day along the course set by the westerly wind and consult again at dusk, weighing all omens. The four went to their appointed places and discharged their various tasks, but in the remaining moments of the night Teroro stood alone in the prow studying the new star, and gradually a new idea germinated in his brain, tentatively at first, like a drum beating in the far distance, and then with compelling intensity.

He began softly: 'If this new star is fixed . . . Suppose it actually does hang there night after night and at all hours . . . Let's say that every star in the new heavens can be associated with it in known patterns . . .' He lost the thread of some compelling thought and started over again.

'If this star is immovable, it must hang at a known distance above the horizon . . . No, that's not right. What I mean is, for every island, this fixed star must hang at a known distance . . . Start with Tahiti. We know exactly what stars hang directly over Tahiti at each hour of the night for each night of the year. Now if this fixed star . . .'

Again he was unable to draw together the threads of his thought, but he sensed that some grand design of the gods was making itself manifest, so he wrapped one arm around the mast of Tane and concentrated his entire being upon the new star. 'If it hangs there for ever, then every island must stand in some relationship to it. Therefore, once you see how high that star is, you know exactly how far north or south you must sail in order to find your island. If you can see the star, you will know! You will know!'

Suddenly, and with dazzling clarity, Teroro saw an entirely new system of navigation based on Tane's gift, the fixed star, and he thought: 'Life must be sweet indeed for sailors in these waters!' For he knew that northern sailors had what southerners did not: a star which could tell them, at a single glance, their latitude. 'The heavens are fixed!' he cried to himself. 'And I shall be free to move beneath them.' He looked happily to the west where the Little Eyes blinked at him prior to dawn, and he whispered to them, 'The new land you lead us to must be sweet indeed if it exists in such an ordered ocean beneath such an ordered sky.'

And for the rest of the voyage, through the terrible days that lay ahead, Teroro alone, of all the canoe, knew no fear. He was sure.

For many anxious days they run before an easterly wind, with the Pole Star remaining at the same height above the horizon.

It was old Teura, however, who saw the first substantial sign; on the twenty-seventh morning she saw a small piece of driftwood, torn away from some distant tree, and Teroro avidly directed the canoe towards it. When it was pulled aboard it was found to contain four land worms, which were fed to the astonished chickens.

'It has been in the ocean less than ten days,' Teura announced. Since the canoe could travel five or six times faster than a drifting branch, it seemed likely that land lay somewhere near; and old Teura entered into a period of intense concentration, clutching at omens and interpreting them hopefully by means of old prayers.

But *West Wind* was not to be saved by incantations. It was Mato, a trained sailor, who late one afternoon saw in the distance a flock of birds flying with determination on a set course westward. 'There's land ahead. They're heading for it,' he cried. Tupuna and Teroro agreed, and when, a few hours later, the stars rose, it was reassuring to see that the Seven Little Eyes confirmed that they were near the end of their journey.

'A few more days,' Teroro announced hopefully.

And two days later, aching with hunger, Mato again spotted a bird, and this one was of special significance, for it was a gannet, poised seventy feet in the air; suddenly it raised its wings, dropped its head towards the waves, and plunged like a thrown rock deep into the ocean. It looked as if it must have split its skull on impact, but by some mysterious trick it had not, and in a moment it flew aloft with a fish in its beak. Deftly it flipped the food into its gulled, then plunged again with head-splitting force.

'We are surely approaching land!' Mato cried. But many on the platform thought of the gannet not as a harbinger of land, but rather as a lucky bird that knew how to fish.

In the early morning of the twenty-ninth day a group of eleven long black birds with handsome cleft tails flew by on a foraging trip from their home island, which lay somewhere beyond the horizon, and Teroro noted with keen pleasure that their heading, reversed, was his, and while he watched he saw these intent birds come upon a group of diving gannets, and when those skilled fishers rose into the air with their catch, the fork-tailed birds swept down upon them, attacked them, and forced them to drop the fish, whereupon the foragers caught the morsels in mid-air and flew away. From their presence it could be deduced that land was not more than sixty miles distant, a fact which was confirmed when Teura and Tupuna, working together, detected in the waves of the sea a peculiar pattern which indicated that in the near distance the profound westerly set of the ocean was impounding upon a reef, which shot back echo waves that cut across the normal motion of the sea; but unfortunately a heavy bank of cloud obscured the western horizon, reaching even to the sea, and none could detect exactly where the island lay.

'Don't worry!' Teura reassured everyone. 'When the clouds do lift, watch their undersides carefully. At sunset you'll see them turn green over the island. Reflections from the lagoon.' And so convinced was Teura that they were approaching some small island like Bora Bora with a lagoon that she chose the spot from which the wave echoes seemed to be generating and stared fixedly at it.

As she had hoped, towards dusk the clouds began to dissipate, and it was Teura who first saw the new island looming ahead. Gasping, she cried, 'On, great Tane! What is it?'

'Look! Look!' cried Teroro.

And there before them, rearing from the sea like an undreamed-of monster, rose a tremendous mountain more massive than they had ever imagined, crowned in strange white and soaring majestically into the evening sunset.

'What a land we have found!' Teroro whispered.

'It is the land of Tane!' King Tamatoa announced in a hushed whisper. 'It reaches to heaven itself.'

And all in the canoe seeing this clean and wonderful mountain, fell silent and did it reverence, until Pa cried, 'Look! It is smoking!' And as night fell, the last sight the men of Bora Bora had was of a gigantic mountain, hung in the heavens, sending fumes from its peak.

*

In the early light of morning it became apparent that the smoking mountain and its supporting island lay much farther away than had at first been supposed, and a final day of hunger and work faced the paddlers; but the visible presence of their goal spurred the famished men so that by nightfall it was certain that next morning the long voyage would end. Through the last soft tropical night, with the luminous mountain ahead, the crew of the *West Wind* followed their rhythmic, steady beat.

As they approached the end of a trek nearly five thousand miles long, it is appropriate to compare what they had accomplished with what voyagers in other parts of the world were doing. In the Mediterranean, descendants of once-proud Phoenicians, who even in their moments of glory had rarely ventured out of sight of land, now coasted along established shores and occasionally, with what was counted bravery, actually cut across the trivial sea in voyages covering perhaps two hundred miles. In Portugal men were beginning to accumulate substantial bodies of information about the ocean, but to probe it they were not yet ready, and it would be six hundred more years before even near-at-hand islands like Madeira and the Azores would be found. Ships had coasted the shores of Africa, but it was known that crossing the Equator and thus losing sight of the North Star meant boiling death or falling off the edge of the world, or both.

On the other side of the earth, Chinese junks had coasted Asia and in the southern oceans had moved from one visible island to the next, terming the act heroism. From Arabia and India, merchants had undertaken considerable voyages, but never very far from established coasts, while in the undiscovered continents to the west of Europe no men left the land.

Only in the north of Europe did the Vikings display enterprise even remotely comparable to that of the men of Bora Bora; but even they had not yet begun their long voyages, though they had at their disposal metals, large ships, woven sails, books and maps.

It was left to the men of the Pacific, men like cautious Tamatoa and energetic Teroro, to meet an ocean on its own terms and to conquer it. Lacking both metals and maps, sailing with only the stars and a few lengths of sennit, some dried taro and positive faith in their gods, these men accomplished miracles. It would be another seven centuries before an Italian navigator, sailing under the flag of Spain and fortified by all the appurtenances of an advanced community, would dare, in three large and commodious ships well nailed together, to set forth upon a voyage not quite so far and only half as dangerous.

from *Hawaii* by James A. Michener (1959)

A Treacherous Pilot

The Riddle of the Sands by Erskine Childers is more a spy thriller in the John
Buchan genre than a novel about the sea, since the action takes place
amongst the dangerous sandbanks and mudflats off the featureless, low-
lying shore inside the German Friesian Islands. The central character –
pseudonym 'Arthur Davies' – is a recent Oxford graduate who has spent
much of his spare time in his 30-foot gaff cutter *Dulcibella*, apparently
indifferent to all hazards of weather and shoal waters. At the turn of the
century, in the age of Cowper, Worth and Macmullen, a growing number
of yacht-owners looked for cruising grounds further afield than the West
Country, and explored in unwieldy boats unsuited to single-handed sailing
in extreme weather. Davies has become fascinated by the stretch of German
coastline within which lies the estuaries of the great rivers that sheltered
her growing imperial fleet, from the Ems to the Elbe. He scents strategic
possibilities for their waters' exploitation by the Emperor's Naval Staff, and
a possible unsuspected threat to England in wartime.

His suspicions are aroused during a passage from Nordeney to the Baltic.
By chance, he anchors close to *Medusa*, a magnificently converted Dutch
galliot of 60 tons, owned by a German called Dollmann, of whom he enquires
about prospects for duck-shooting. Dollmann insists that he would do better
in the Baltic and, since Davies is single-handed, persuades him to follow
Medusa through a short-cut to the Elbe. The description of how the weather
turns sour and *Dulcibella* is left to fend for herself on a lee shore with no
recognizable navigation marks could just as well apply to parts of Britain's
east coast which are guarded by unmarked sandbanks far out of sight of
land.

The little cutter survives against the odds which Dollmann has counted
upon to remove the inquisitive Englishman from a strategically sensitive
area. Davies then recruits a former Oxford acquaintance, Carruthers, to
join him at Flensburg in the Baltic, where he recounts his frightening
experience.

'It was his suggestion. He said he had to sail to Hamburg, and proposed that
I should go with him in the *Dulcibella* as far as the Elbe, and then, if I liked, I
could take the ship canal at Brunsbüttel through to Kiel and the Baltic. I had
no very fixed plans of my own, though I had meant to go on exploring eastwards
between the islands and the coast, and so reach the Elbe in a much slower way.
He dissuaded me from this, sticking to it that I should have no chance of ducks,

and urging other reasons. Anyway, we settled to sail in company direct to Cuxhaven, in the Elbe. With a fair wind and an early start it should be only one day's sail of about sixty miles.

'The plan only came to a head on the evening of the third day, the 12th of September.

'I told you, I think, that the weather had broken after a long spell of heat. That very day it had been blowing pretty hard from the west, and the glass was falling still. I said, of course, that I couldn't go with him if the weather was too bad, but he prophesied a good day, said it was an easy sail, and altogether put me on my mettle. You can guess how it was. Perhaps I had talked about single-handed cruising as though it were easier than it was, though I never meant it in a boasting way, for I hate that sort of thing, and besides there *is* no danger if you're careful—'

'Oh, go on,' I said.

'Anyway, we went next morning at six. It was a dirty-looking day, wind WNW, but his sails were going up and mine followed. I took two reefs in and we sailed out into the open and steered ENE along the coast for the Outer Elbe Lightship about fifty knots off. Here it all is, you see.' (He showed me the course on the chart.) 'The trip was nothing for his boat, of course, a safe, powerful old tub, forging through the sea as steady as a house. I kept up with her easily at first. My hands were pretty full, for there was a hard wind on my quarter and a troublesome sea; but as long as nothing worse came I knew I should be all right, though I also knew that I was a fool to have come.

'All went well till we were off Wangeroog, the last of the islands – *here* – and then it began to blow really hard. I had half a mind to chuck it and cut in to the Jade River, *down there*; but I hadn't the face to, so I hove to and took in my last reef.' (Simple words, simply uttered; but I had seen the operation in calm water and shuddered at the present picture.) 'We had been about level till then, but with my shortened canvas I fell behind. Not that that mattered in the least. I knew my course, had read up my tides, and, thick as the weather was, I had no doubt of being able to pick up the lightship. No change of plan was possible now. The Weser estuary was on my starboard hand, but the whole place was a lee-shore and a mass of unknown banks – just look at them. I ran on, the *Dulcibella* doing her level best, but we had some narrow shaves of being pooped. I was about *here*, say six miles south-west of the lightship, when I suddenly saw that the *Medusa* had hove to right ahead, as though waiting till I came up. She wore round again on the course as I drew level, and we were alongside for a bit. Dollmann lashed the wheel, leaned over her quarter, and shouted, very slowly and distinctly so that I could understand: "Follow me – sea too bad for you outside – short cut through sands – save six miles."

'It was taking me all my time to manage the tiller, but I knew what he meant at once, for I had been over the chart carefully the night before. You see the whole bay between Wangeroog and the Elbe is encumbered with sand. A great jagged chunk of it runs out from Cuxhaven in a north-westerly direction for fifteen miles or so, ending in a pointed spit called the *Scharhorn*. To reach the

Elbe from the west you have to go right outside this, round the lightship, which is off the Scharhorn, and double back. Of course, that's what all big vessels do. But, as you see, these sands are intersected here and there by channels, very shallow and winding, exactly like those behind the Friesian Islands. Now look at this one, which cuts right through the big chunk of sand and comes out near Cuxhaven. The *Telte* it's called. It's miles wide, you see, at the entrance, but later on it is split into two by the Hohenhörn bank; then it gets shallow and very complicated, and ends as a mere tidal driblet with another name. It's just the sort of channel I should like to worry into on a fine day or with an off-shore wind. Alone, in thick weather and a heavy sea, it would have been folly to attempt it, except as a desperate resource. But, as I said, I knew at once that Dollmann was proposing to run for it and guide me in.

'I didn't like the idea, because I like doing things for myself, and, silly as it sounds, I believe I resented being told the sea was too bad for me, which it certainly was. Yet the short cut did save several miles and a devil of a tumble off the Scharhorn, where two tides meet. I had complete faith in Dollmann, and I suppose I decided that I should be a fool not to take a good chance. I hesitated, I know; but in the end I nodded and held up my arm as she forged ahead again. Soon after she shifted her course and I followed. You asked me once if I ever took a pilot. That was the only time.'

*

'We soon came to what I knew must be the beginning of the Telte channel. All round you could hear the breakers on the sands, though it was too thick to see them yet. As the water shoaled, the sea of course got shorter and steeper. There was more wind – a whole gale I should say.

'I kept dead in the wake of the *Medusa*, but to my disgust I found she was gaining on me very fast. Of course I had taken for granted, when he said he would lead me in, that he would slow down and keep close to me. He could easily have done so by getting his men up to check his sheets or drop his peak. Instead of that he was busting on for all he was worth. Once, in a rain-squall, I lost sight of him altogether; got him faintly again, but had enough to do with my own tiller not to want to be peering through the scud after a runaway pilot. I was all right so far, but we were fast approaching the worst part of the whole passage, where the Hohenhörn bank blocks the road and the channel divides. I don't know what it looks like to you on the chart – perhaps fairly simple, because you can follow the twists of the channels, as on a ground-plan; but a stranger coming to a place like that (where there are no buoys, mind you) can tell nothing certain by the eye, unless perhaps at dead low water, when the banks are high and dry, and in very clear weather; he must trust to the lead and the compass and feel his way step by step. I knew perfectly well that what I should soon see would be a wall of surf stretching right across and on both sides. To *feel* one's way in that sort of weather is impossible. You must *know* your way, or else have a pilot. I had one, but he was playing his own game.

'With a second hand on board to steer while I conned I should have felt less of an ass. As it was, I knew I ought to be facing the music in the offing, and cursed myself for having broken my rule and gone blundering into this con-founded short cut. It was giving myself away, doing just the very thing that you can't do in single-handed sailing.

'By the time I realized the danger it was far too late to turn and hammer out to the open. I was deep in the bottleneck bight of the sands, jammed on a lee-shore, and a strong flood tide sweeping me on. That tide, by the way, gave just the ghost of a chance. I had the hours in my head, and knew it was about two-thirds flood with two hours more of rising water. That meant the banks would all be covering when I reached them, and harder than ever to locate; but it also meant that I *might* float right over the worst of them if I hit off a lucky place.' Davies thumped the table in disgust. 'Pah! It makes me sick to think of having to trust to an accident like that, like a lubberly Cockney out for a boozy Bank Holiday sail.

'Well, just as I foresaw, the wall of surf appeared clean across the horizon, and curling back to shut me in, booming like thunder. When I last saw the *Medusa* she seemed to be charging it like a horse at a fence, and I took a rough bearing of her position by a hurried glance at the compass. At that very moment I *thought* she seemed to luff and show some of her broadside; but a squall blotted her out and gave me hell with the tiller. After that she was lost in the white mist that hung over the line of breakers. I kept on my bearing as well as I could, but I was already out of the channel. I knew that by the look of the water, and as we neared the bank I saw it was all awash and without the vestige of an opening. I wasn't going to chuck her on to it without an effort; so, more by instinct than with any particular hope, I put the helm down, meaning to work her along the edge on the chance of spotting a way over. She was buried at once by the beam sea, and the jib flew to blazes; but the reefed stays'l stood, she recovered gamely, and I held on, though I knew it could only be for a few minutes as the centre-plate was up and she made frightful leeway towards the bank.

'I was half blinded by scud, but suddenly I noticed what looked like a gap, behind a spit which curled out right ahead. I luffed still more to clear this spit, but she couldn't weather it. Before you could say knife she was driving across it, bumped heavily, bucked forward again, bumped again, and – ripped on in deeper water! I can't describe the next few minutes. I was in some sort of channel, but a very narrow one, and the sea broke everywhere. I hadn't proper command either; for the rudder had crocked up somehow at the last bump. I was like a drunken man running for his life down a dark alley, barking himself at every corner. It couldn't last long, and finally we went crash on to something and stopped there, grinding and banging. So ended that little trip under a pilot.

'Well, it was like this – there was really no danger' – I opened my eyes at the characteristic phrase. 'I mean, that lucky stumble into a channel was my salvation. Since then I had struggled though a mile of sands, all of which lay behind me like a breakwater against the gale. They were covered, of course, and seething like soapsuds; but the force of the sea was deadened. The *Dulce* was bumping, but not too heavily. It was nearing high tide, and at half ebb she would be high and dry.

'In the ordinary way I should have run out a kedge with the dinghy, and at the next high water sailed farther in and anchored where I could lie afloat. The trouble was now that my hand was hurt and my dinghy stove in, not to mention the rudder business. It was the first bump on the outer edge that did the damage. There was a heavy swell there, and when we struck, the dinghy, which was towing astern, came home on her painter and down with a crash on the yacht's weather quarter. I stuck out one hand to ward off and got it nipped on the gunwale. She was badly stove in and useless, so I couldn't run out the kedge' – (this was Greek to me, but I let him go on) – 'and for the present my hand was too painful even to stow the boom and sails which were whipping and racketing about anyhow. There was the rudder too to be mended; and we were several miles from the nearest land. Of course, if the wind fell, it was all easy enough; but if it held or increased it was a poor look-out. There's a limit to strain of that sort – and other things might have happened.

'In fact, it was precious lucky that Bartels turned up. His galliot was at anchor a mile away, up a branch of the channel. In a clear between squalls he saw us and, like a brick, rowed his boat out – he and his boy, and a devil of a pull they must have had. I was glad enough to see them – no, that's not true; I was in such a fury of disgust and shame that I believe I should have been idiot enough to say I didn't want help, if he hadn't just nipped on board and started work. He's a terror to work, that little mouse of a chap. In half an hour we had stowed the sails, unshackled the big anchor, run out fifty fathoms of warp and hauled her off there and then into deep water. Then they towed her up the channel – it was dead to leeward and an easy job – and berthed her near their own vessel. It was dark by that time, so I gave them a drink, and said good night. It blew a howling gale that night, but the place was safe enough, with a good ground-tackle.'

from *The Riddle of the Sands* by Erskine Childers (1903)

Davies persuades Carruthers to forget about the pretext of duck-shooting on which he has been recruited and to join him in picking up the scent again in the Friesians. All ends happily – though not for Dollmann, who is unmasked as a traitor, an ex-regular officer in the Royal Navy playing a key role in developing secret German war plans for invading England using flat-bottomed lighters launched from the security of the island sandbanks. The scheme calls for brief naval supremacy in the North Sea – something which was accorded to neither Kaiser Wilhelm nor Adolf Hitler.

Things, however, did not end well for Erskine Childers. After fighting in the Boer and First World Wars, he threw in his lot with the Irish Republicans and was executed by sentence of court martial in Dublin in November 1922.

A Dangerous Rendezvous on the North Brittany Coast

Clare Francis's description of the hazards confronting navigators approaching the North Brittany coast in her bestselling novel *Night Sky* serves as a chilling warning, as urgent today as it has ever been. The wartime motor gun-boats based on West Country ports who made overnight trips to bring out agents, escaped prisoners-of-war and compromised members of the French Resistance took appalling risks, made all the greater by having to touch down on this most dangerous coast-line with all shore lights extinguished.

The coast is wild and rugged and utterly beautiful. From its border with Normandy to the point where the land turns to face the open Atlantic the North Brittany coast measures little more than a hundred miles as the crow flies. But this means nothing. It is so indented with bays and deep estuaries that its true length is at least twice that distance. Most of this length is impenetrable to anything but the smallest craft – and then only in good weather – for the land is defended by a great barrier of natural hazards.

A thousand storms have shaped the jagged cliffs and eaten into the soft rock, leaving a dense fabric of reefs, islands and islets to seaward. Some of the dangers stand proud and high in the water: great stacks of rock rising like dragon's teeth, or larger islands which lie cowed and barren before the wind. But most of the perils lie near the surface: sharp reefs marked only by breaking water, or islets so low that they are almost invisible. These dangers reach out four, five, sometimes twelve miles from the land.

Then there are the tidal streams. They run very strong along these shores, ripping across rocks and reefs, tearing through the deep channels, and swinging into bays and inlets, making accurate landfall difficult even for the most careful of navigators.

The strongest winds come in winter, blowing storm force from the Atlantic. They send before them armies of waves which curve in towards the shore, gathering speed until they break on the myriad of rocks and islets in a cauldron of white foaming surf, then advance, still snapping and roaring, on to the fragile mainland itself.

This coast is no friend to the sailor. Only those familiar with its dangers dare approach it with impunity; strangers must rely on good charts and blind faith. At night the dangers are marked by the powerful lights of all lighthouses; with the help of leading lights and channel buoys it is even possible for small fishing craft to navigate one or two of the estuaries in darkness. But for the most part this coast does not invite visitors; the great lighthouses serve to warn rather than welcome.

*

Motor Gunboat 309 had two outstanding characteristics: she was wet and she was as explosive as a bomb.

The south-westerly Force 6 was revealing the first of her attributes: her speed was reduced to thirteen knots and she was twisting and bucking like a wild horse. Every few seconds she dug her nose deep into a wave and chucked a wall of cold, very solid, water back along her 110-foot length, up and over the open bridge, drenching the four men who stood there peering into the impenetrable darkness.

There was a loud thud and a particularly large lump of sea flew up over the bows. Ashley ducked instinctively behind the reinforced glass screen. The water hit the bridge with a dull slap, showering spray in all directions. Ashley felt a rivulet of freezing water running down his back and reflected that things might be worse: an E-boat could at this minute be firing at them and igniting the perfect mixture of air and high-octane petrol in their fuel tanks. And what a lovely bang they would make, he thought. A nice big orange whoooomph! And the Jerries wouldn't have to worry about looking for survivors: there wouldn't be any. Instant cremation.

All things considered, he'd rather be wet.

As if reading his mind, Jones, the coxswain, shouted, 'When are we getting these new boats then, sir?'

'Ah, cox, when indeed? According to the Master Plan we already have them!'

'Yes, Sir.'

'But according to the grapevine, it'll be some time at the end of the year.'

Jones blew the saltwater off his lips and exclaimed, 'About bleedin' time too sir. This old girl's as wet as Glasgow on a Saturday night! If I'd wanted to be a submariner, I would have bleedin' well volunteered.'

Ashley smiled. 'On the other hand, Jones, a diesel-powered boat could be a real bore! A dry bridge, reliable engines, non-explosive fuel – there'd be no feeling of adventure. That first pint back in Dartmouth wouldn't taste the same at all!'

'Ha!' the coxswain retorted. 'After a ride on the Hamoaze ferry, lemonade tastes like bloody champagne to me, sir! But, you know, sir, I wouldn't mind about the weather, 'cept we've been having it all bleedin' winter. Not a break, 'ave we 'ad, not a single one.'

'No, cox,' Ashley admitted. 'We can't have been saying our prayers right.'

In fact, there had been breaks in the weather, but they had come during the full moon, or when *309*'s engines were out of action, or when there was no operation planned. Whenever an operation *had* been set up it had blown Force 5 or more. Nothing unusual for winter in the English Channel, but uncomfortable, wet and – for this kind of job – dangerously slow. A delay on the outward journey meant a late arrival, a nervous wait at the pick-up point, and a mad dash to get back across no-man's-land to British coastal waters before dawn.

Ashley peered at the luminous hands of his watch: it was already 2330 and, he guessed, another two to two-and-a-half-hours to the pinpoint. An 0200 arrival would give them only forty-five minutes – or an hour at the most – to make the pick-up. It would be horribly tight. In this wind it would take the beach party at least twenty minutes to reach the shore. Five minutes to sort out the passengers and get them loaded. On the way back they would have the wind behind them but it would still take, say, fifteen minutes. Horribly tight.

Worse, he had the unpleasant feeling the wind was freshening.

They'd had miserable luck all winter, one way and another. First they'd had an inexperienced navigator and, on one occasion, had waited at the wrong beach for over three hours. Then, a week or so later, the engines had started to play up. As the Chief, an inevitable Scot by the name of McFee, was always saying, 'Seawater and petrol don't mix.' He did his best with the three supercharged Hall Scott engines but even he couldn't make the damn things work when they weren't in the mood. Bad weather made them especially temperamental; 'Like a woman caught in the rain', the Chief said contemptuously. A week before, they'd packed up two miles off the Brittany coast, just as they were being opened up for the journey home. The Chief had managed to coax a couple of knots out of the starboard engine, just enough to get them out of sight of land before dawn. Eventually, water was found in the fuel system, was cleared, and they managed to get under way again, but not before getting a nasty fright from a patrolling E-boat.

Ever since, the engines had been giving trouble of some kind or another and they needed constant nursing to keep them going.

But at least they had got rid of the dodgy navigator: that was something. All then needed now was a break in the weather.

At this point the Captain realizes that his First Lieutenant is laid low with food-poisoning and will not be able to play any part in the recovery phase.

The Canadian was his best man; very keen and very able. He must be really ill to have agreed to lie down; if he was capable of getting to his feet, he would. Ashley gritted his teeth. He'd have to find a replacement – Macleod was leader of the beach party. Macleod was the only one who spoke decent French.

Apart from himself there was only one other officer on the boat: the navigator, a man called Tusker. He was RN (Retired) and had bamboozled his way back into active service by nagging the Admiralty to death. Unlike the first navigator, Tusker was brilliant at his job. He'd got *309* through rocks and narrow channels into countless pick-up points, in filthy weather and without a decent navigation aid in sight.

There was only one problem: he was forty-five and had a gammy leg.

Ashley made his way forward again, gripping tightly on to the available handholds. The boat pitched sharply forwards and then, trembling and shivering, heaved herself up once more, ready for the next wave.

Ashley climbed into the small space optimistically called the chart room. It was a wooden structure built on to the deck just in front of the bridge. Tusker was crouching over the collapsible chart table – a simple device which, when the boat pounded heavily, often lived up to its name. As usual, Tusker was making careful calculations. He never stopped, from the moment they left until the moment they got back, reworking the tides, the course, the speed, and the ETA.

'How we doing, Tusker?'

'Ah, should reach Les Vaches at 0135, and drop anchor at 0200.' He always used Les Vaches, a large pair of odd-shaped rocks three miles off the beach, as a navigation point. He aimed the MGB straight for them and then, as he liked to point out, when they almost hit them they knew exactly where they were. He'd never failed to find them yet, despite a shortage of navigation aids. All there was to confirm the dead reckoning position was an echo sounder ticking away in the corner of the chart room.

Tusker wiped some drips off the transparent plastic chart cover and pointed at the chart. 'We crossed the Hurd Deep forty-five minutes ago. I hope to pick up the edge of the Plateau de Triagoz in just over an hour. That'll give us a good lead in. Unless of course we have to reduce speed still further . . . ?'

'No, we must bash on, whatever the weather. Otherwise we'll be too late. We're cutting it a bit fine as it is.'

The two men braced themselves as *309*'s bows rose into the air and began to descend rapidly towards an approaching wave. There was a loud crash and the boat shuddered. Cascades of water thundered over the chart room, pouring down the windows and penetrating the cracks in the wood. Tusker methodically wiped the drips away and gazed down at the chart again. 'Whatever the revs say, I'd be surprised if we were doing thirteen knots in this sea.'

Ashley then has to make the hard decision to take the surf-boat into the beach for pick-up himself, leaving the navigator in charge of the MGB. Before landing he firmly orders the navigator to sail on the dot of the pre-arranged time, even if it means leaving him on the beach.

Tusker took some bearings and they pressed on towards the land. Because the wind was offshore and would carry the sound of their engines away from the ears of German sentries, Richard decided to risk a fast approach. Time was ticking away. It was 0150.

At two miles they reduced speed to five knots, searching for the familiar landmarks, feeling their way in towards the anchorage. Finally they were on station, one mile offshore in the open arms of a wide, rocky bay, lying to their grass-rope anchor. It was 0215. Only one hour at the most.

The beach lay in a cove in the western arc of the bay, its sides guarded by a myriad of small rocks. The surfboat was already in the water, the two crew waiting at their oars which were muffled with heaving sacking.

Ashley jumped down and sat in the stern, a compass in his hand and the wireless on the seat beside him. At his feet was their new gadget, a hydrophone, which, when its sensor was dropped in the water, would pick up the sound of *309*'s echo sounder and guide them back to her. They would need it tonight.

The surfboat buffeted her way through the waves, the water hissing and slapping at her sides. Already the MGB was a shadow in the deeper darkness behind them.

Ashley looked at his watch. It was 0222.

He couldn't help thinking that for once they really were cutting it a bit fine.

from *Night Sky* by Clare Francis (1983)

In the event, a traitor has alerted the Germans, who easily trap the surfboat's crew on the beach while the MGB makes good her escape without picking up any of those waiting for their chance of getting to England. Among them is the heroine of the story, Julie Lescaux, and her little son. They are finally reunited after the war when Ashley is released from POW camp.

SWEETHEARTS AND WIVES

A Pirate in Drag

F. Tennyson Jesse, the great-neice of Alfred, Lord Tennyson, was a prolific writer of plays, novels and film-scripts from 1912 for over forty years. She was also a brilliant criminologist, who edited six volumes of the *Notable British Trials* series. In later years she joined the ranks of great writers about the Second World War at sea with her classic of the torpedoed tanker *San Demetrio*, which was reboarded by her gallant crew and brought safely to port. Although she never wavered from the jingoist rhetoric of earlier adventure-story writers such as Stevenson, Henty, Kipling and Haggard, convinced that any Brit with a drawn sword could take on any two born east of Calais (or four if they chanced to be dark-skinned), her work does contain an underlying message that sets her apart from these authors.

The belief for which she quietly crusaded emerges in a dramatic denouement at the end of her novel about the pirate ship *Moonraker* and her unusual afterguard. Jacky Jacka is a Cornish lad who has run away from school and sailed for the West Indies in a brig – *Piskie* – which he picked up in Plymouth Sound after a witch had predicted that some fantastic adventures lay in store for him at sea. *Piskie* is 400 miles south of Bermuda when she falls in with a pirate ship of superior speed and armament and is summarily despatched.

> Jacky was taken along to the cabin of the pirate captain, and a fine cabin it was, taking up the whole of the stern, with square windows and rich panelling of polished wood. It was the hour of sunset, and the light lay on the water, turning it red, and the reflection of it struck like flame on the ceiling and filled the cabin with a ruddy glow.
>
> The Captain was a handsome young man, with a long lean brown face and a high nose, and deep wrinkles around his eyes, which were bright blue and innocent as a babe's. He looked as little like a bloody murderer as any one you could think of. And the queer thing was, that Jacky had a feeling that he had seen this face before, but he couldn't remember where, and the more he puzzled over it the less he could catch his memory, which was beating round in the back of his mind like a moth in a lantern. The pirate wore great gold ear-rings, and his name was Captain Lovel, which is a West Country name, and his mouth speech sounded homely to Jacky. He told Jacky he was to be his cabin boy, and that he would be treated well as long as he behaved himself, and that he would get a rope's ending if he didn't, just the same as in any decent vessel afloat.
>
> The brig was christened the *Moonraker*, and Captain Lovel had taken her

297

from the Yanks after a great fight, when she had been on her way back from the River Plate with specie and hides. She had been built at Salem for the north-west fur trade, and so she was heavily armed in case of Indian attacks, and made a fit craft for a pirate. She was copper-bottomed, and she carried single topsails, t'gallant-sails, and royals, and set stunsails on both masts. She also set every kind of Johnnie Green that she could crowd on; she looked a real lady when she was all dressed up in her best, clad in snowy muslin from head to heel. Her bowsprit, with the jibboom and flying-jibboom, was the hell of a length, and it was steeved right up so that the tip of the flying-jibboom looked to be above her foreyard. She was painted black, with a white band and square black gunports, and she flew the Jolly Roger from her spanker-gaff when in action, just like the pirates in the story-books. Her lines were as sweet and her heart as sound as any vessel's afloat. Poor Billy Constant couldn't have loved the *Piskie* better than Captain Lovel loved his ill-gotten *Moonraker*. You might have thought it would have made him understand another man's love of his ship, and be sorry for what he had done, but that was not Lovel's way. He saw well to her armaments, and kept her fit to commit her murders. She carried swivel guns on her bulwarks, and twenty-four cannon kept well shotted with grape or canister or langrage. Her quarter-decks were loopholed for musket fire, and pistols, muskets, boarding-pikes, and boarding-nettings were always ready to hand.

She was a sweet ship to steer, and Jacky, who had been born with his hands on the spokes of a wheel, could not but love her when the Captain tried him, to see whether he could stand his trick, which Jacky could, as well as an older man. He did not want to forget the *Piskie* and poor Billy Constant, and he grieved for them both. He felt he would never forgive Lovel for that killing, and the sight of the *Piskie*'s sails, lying flat over on the water, darkening as the swell took them more and more, like the wings of a wounded gull, stayed in his mind. Piracy was all very well to read of, and pirates were doubtless very good fun to fight when you beat them, but he had never imagined them winning. It made it all ugly and cruel instead of a great adventure. And now he was in a pirate vessel he might be forced to take part in these evil doings, and if they won, he would have to see honest sailormen killed and taken prisoner, and if they lost, he would be taken prisoner himself, and then perhaps he might be hanged from a yardarm as a pirate. It was all strange and confusing, and he tried to hate Captain Lovel; he knew he couldn't hate the *Moonraker*.

But it wasn't so easy to hate even the Captain. He was short and sharp, as was only natural in a skipper to a cabin boy, and there was something frightening about him apart from that; yet you couldn't hate him. He kept even his mates at a distance, instead of being free and easy and jolly, as you would have expected in a pirate ship. The only man he ever spoke with alone in a friendly way was old Red Lear, the bo'sun, a great hairy man, who had known the Captain ever since he was a nipper, so the other men said. They'd been picked up all over the Atlantic, some by shanghaiing, some by capture, and some because they were natural born robbers and murderers, and had wanted to ship in just such a vessel.

Lovel kept his word, and treated Jacky no worse than he said, and even a trifle better; for once, when the mate was going to flog Jacky for spilling the molasses all over him when he was waiting at the cabin table in half a gale, the Captain took the yoke-rope from him and flogged Jacky himself, and it must have been to let him off lighter, for the blows hardly stung him, though the Captain had been known to half take a man's back off. The discipline on that craft was sterner than on any law-abiding merchantman. You might have been in a ship of the line or an East Indiaman.

The *Moonraker* dodged about those waters for a while after sinking the *Piskie*, trying to waylay one of the many American ships that were trading constantly back and forth, bringing rich cargoes of nankeens and pepper, coffee and wine and tobacco, and taking iron and hemp and sailcloth and flax, all good things for another ship to get hold of by fair means or foul. She gave chase to one for a day, but the other vessel showed her a clean pair of heels, piling on her shining towers of cotton canvas. There was no going near Captain Lovel after that. He hated being out-sailed.

Jacky could understand that. He was praying with all his heart that the other craft would get away safe, and yet he hated not catching her. Besides, she was a Yank, and the *Moonraker* was British-owned now, even if by a pirate, so of course she ought to have won.

Soon afterwards *Moonraker* falls in with a laden French merchantman. After bitter hand-to-hand fighting the pirates prevail. One of the Frenchmen, a young nobleman named Raoul, fights bravely to the end and the Captain saves his life, just as the bosun Red Lear is going to despatch him with a belaying-pin. They carry him back to *Moonraker* as a prisoner, along with the merchantman's cargo of silks and wine. Raoul then persuades Captain Lovel to allow him to land on San Domingo under parole to go to the assistance of the black General Toussaint, who is bent on using his position as Commander-in-Chief to establish a republic of freed slaves, against the interests of the absentee plantation-owners in Paris. A punitive force of Napoleon's soldiers is closing the island to reassert their authority.

After many adventures in the hinterland of San Domingo, usually accompanied by voodoo drums throbbing in the distance, *Moonraker* sails away with a few passengers. Raoul brings with him the beautiful Miss Laura, whom he had first met in Boston during his time as a refugee from the French Revolution. In their different ways everyone fancies Miss Laura, although for Jacky she is firmly off-limits as the Captain's prize. The crew is bewildered that he does not immediately bed her down, as any other pirate captain would have done. But he explodes with rage when he finds Raoul in intimate conversation with her on the quarterdeck.

The brilliant blue sky and sea was overcast by a thin grey haze, as though one looked through smoked glass, the very foam seemed tinged with a livid yellowish cast. The *Moonraker* fled on, a high thin wailing in her shrouds. The Captain came on deck and saw the couple talking low and earnestly under the lee of the rail. A red colour ran up into his lean cheeks; he called to the young Frenchman to come and speak with him. Raoul said, over his shoulder, 'I am speaking with this lady,' and did not move. Jacky, at the head of the companion, the evening rum glasses in his hands, held his breath. Red Lear stared ahead, his cheek bulged by his quid.

Captain Lovel walked over to Mounseer Raoul and spoke again, in a thin hard voice.

'I command on my own quarter-deck, mister. By God, I'll have you put in irons if you disobey me.'

'You employ the wrong weapons to take a man captive,' said Raoul. 'They are all you have at your command, I presume.'

There was a moment of silence so profound that even the noises of the vessel's way seemed to have ceased. Then the Captain turned on his heel and came towards the break of the poop. Jacky saw he was walking like a man stricken by blindness, his blue eyes wide and staring, but seeing nothing. Jacky drew aside, and the Captain passed him by and went into the chart-house.

Jacky thought there was going to be trouble, and he was therefore surprised when the Captain, an hour later, told him to bid the guests to a dinner with him that evening in the stern cabin, and bade him make special preparations. The Captain spoke from the cabin he slept in since the arrival of the ladies, over his shoulder to Jacky; his voice sounded much as usual, and he was busy, Jacky saw, turning out a chest. Piles of rich silks, and a Cashmere shawl, were half poured out of the chest. Jacky stepped forward and asked if he could help, but the Captain told him sharply to get out, and Jacky went.

Evidently it was to be a festival for the crew as well as for the after guard; a cask of rum was sent for'ard and a whole side of pork. Jacky was bidden to set the table with the fine old silver stolen several years before from a Spanish vessel. There was much loot in the *Moonraker* that Jacky had never yet seen, things such as those silken garments in the chest, that the Captain had stored away by him for some reason, instead of selling them, or taking them home to his womenkind. But then, as far as any one knew, the Captain had no folks, no spot whither he could repair in safety and take his ease on shore. Other men might desert, or when they had made their pile, go home to spend it in the odour of respectability, but never either Captain Lovel or Red Lear. They were men above taking their ease, and they took their pleasure in the exercise of their chosen profession. Only when chasing and fighting did the Captain's eye light up, and the strong colour leap on his high cheek-bone.

Jacky, setting his silver, thought idly over these things, as often before, and thought what a strange being the Captain was, how hidden in his thoughts and swift in his actions, how violent and yet how quiet, with the quietness of an animal that waits and waits. Jacky always knew more or less what other people would do; Toussaint, black as he was, had acted like a man, and a finer man than many you would meet, thought Jacky. Once you knew him you knew what he would do, more or less. Mounseer Raoul now, he was a Frenchy, and yet you knew what he would do. It might be something rather highfalutin', because that was his nature, but at least you could make a guess at what it would be. Red Lear would growl and curse at every one but the Captain. As for Miss Laura, she might be haughty, though never with Jacky, only with Mounseer Raoul, because he was sweet on her, and that was a thing females always took advantage of, but otherwise she was just as sweet as new milk. Only the Captain had always been queer from the beginning.

At first Jacky hadn't noticed it; it was so strange to be on board a pirate vessel that it seemed natural every one on board should be strange too. Then the men had begun to seem just like any other men to him, which had been very upsetting to his notions of good and evil. Still, he had got used to that, but the Captain had never seemed to get like other men, and although he had changed from the man he had been, no one could say quite what he had been before or what he was now. Through everything he stayed unknown; all you could say was that now you knew still less what he was after or how he would turn. This dinner now, what did he mean by it?

Raoul was the first to enter the stern cabin. He was dressed with his usual care, in fresh linen and a fine broadcloth coat. He was pale and very grave. Next the two ladies came in, Mrs Pounsell still wan, but recovered from her sea-sickness, in her grey silk, looking a very proper gentlewoman. Miss Laura, for the first time, seemed the girl Jacky had seen that day in the little white house at Ennery. She wore the peach-coloured gown, very scanty and limp, as ladies' dresses were in those days, and girdled beneath her little breasts. Her hair was dressed high, and shone like a burnished helmet. Her cheek was pure and fresh, her eye bright and serene. She met Raoul's look as he hastened forward to meet her with one such as she had not given him for long past. Her little jealousies, her coldness, all were gone since Raoul had spoken to her and to the Captain on the poop.

The Captain's voice was heard shouting for Jacky, and he hurried to the cabin door. A moment later he returned with the message that the Captain was unavoidably delayed, and begged them to begin without him, and to drink of the old Canary that he had had specially broken out for them. After a polite demur they settled themselves at the table, and Jacky poured the wine and handed round the dish of prepared alligator pears. The hanging lanterns shone brightly, and the world beyond the ports looked blue and dense against the panes. No one spoke much; it was as though the very air held a sense of waiting for something.

In the silence, that was not broken but only marked more clearly by the slap and swish of the racing sea past the ship's side, and the creaking of her framework, the latch of the door suddenly made a sharp noise. Jacky sprang to open it and swung it wide. And there, the dark alleyway behind her, and the lights of the cabin shining full upon her wide silk skirts, stood a woman. Like a ship in full sail, rather than like any of the scantily clad women Jacky had seen in his life, she stood there, her breast rising sharply, and a creaking sound coming from the region of her waist.

Raoul had risen, checking the exclamation on his lips. The ladies sat, speechless and staring. Jacky, staring also, felt some memory that had always nagged at him slip into place in his mind. He saw again the reddened face and throat, the white shoulders, the hard proud glance that he had seen in the troubled water at old Tamsin True's. The Captain brushed past him, and came into the full light, head held high. The stiff old-fashioned silk, a yellowy white, made a noise like the rustling of waves past the ship's side.

from *Moonraker* by F. Tennyson Jesse (1927)

It takes time to persuade the guests that it is not a masquerade. Finally the woman tears open her bodice and the secret is out – and with it the author's stand as a feminist promoting the cause of equal opportunities for women. Had she lived long enough she might have written a novel around an SAS thug who is all woman beneath her jungle camouflage.

The mysterious bosun Red Lear turns out to be the Captain's father, who had shipped little Sophy off to sea as a boy in the belief that she was bewitched. All ends with an almighty bang. The crew mutinies unsuccessfully against the Captain, who has passed up too many chances of adding to their prizes. So Captain Sophy turns her passengers adrift in the longboat and then touches off a keg of gunpowder which blows the pirates and their unlikely Captain to kingdom come.

The Fiery Donna Clotilde

C. J. Cutliffe Hyne started writing short stories for *Pearson's* magazine nearly 100 years ago. During Edwardian days his central character, the legendary red-bearded Geordie tramp-steamer skipper Captain Kettle, had a larger popular following than the laid-back, opium-smoking occupant of 221B Baker Street, Sherlock Holmes. The Northcliffe weekly *Answers* built its huge circulation and the fortune of the Harmsworths with the help of regular instalments of the saga of the diminutive, hard-hitting Captain. Illustrated by Stanley Wood, most of the pictures show our hero repelling unwanted visitors to his ship or stamping his authority over the ill-disciplined dropouts his agent foisted on him as crew. As a rule he does so bare-knuckled, but he is ready to draw his loaded Service revolver from his oilskin pocket whenever the situation demands.

Two characters often form the background to these action-packed yarns: Kettle's genteel wife at home in South Shields, and the tight-fisted Newcastle shipowner Mr Gedge (see also pp.217-21), whose terms and conditions of employment drive him to accept command of ships long overdue for the breakers' yard, often in distant waters sailing under dubious orders. So the little Captain crops up in many seedy waterfronts, always with his peaked cap worn at a jaunty angle over his right eye, although I doubt whether Admiral Beatty caught the habit from reading *Answers*. He became as well known in South American tavernas as he was in Hallett's, the shipmasters' club on Tyneside.

Possibly out of deference to the proprietors of the magazine, Captain Kettle is untypically abstemious in taking advantage of the ladies of easy virtue who cross his path on the Pacific seaboard. However, it seems that he is wildly attractive to at least one woman, the fabulously rich and voluptuous Chilean heiress Donna Clotilde La Touche. At their first meeting her plans for him centre on forming her own navy with which to overthrow the warlord currently running the country. At £12 per month salary, with a £100 note for expenses, Kettle is launched as Commander-in-Chief (designate) of Donna Clotilde's navy. Thus it is agreed at their first meeting under the stars on the rooftop of a fashionable restaurant.

A bent agent in Callao palms off an over-aged barque as Kettle's flagship; with the glamorous name of *El Almirante Cochrane*, it is named after another Englishman who headed several South American navies in his time. She proves totally unsuited to the task; furthermore, her many years at the bottom end of the nitrate trade have left her with an all-pervading smell of guano. Nothing daunted (the phrase is inevitable in trying to precis any of Captain Kettle's tales), our hero hatches a scheme to start by capturing *Cancelario*, the modern 3,000-ton armoured flagship of the navy. His plan involves sailing the old barque straight into the warship as she lies at anchor in Tampique Bay.

The outline of Tampique Bay stood out clearly in bright moonshine, and the sea down the path of the moon's rays showed a canal of silver, cut through rolling fields of purple. The green-painted barque was heading into the bay on the port tack; and at moorings, before the town, in the curve of the shore, the grotesque spars of a modern warship showed in black silhouette against the moonbeams. A slate-coloured naphtha-launch was sliding out over the swells towards the barque.

Captain Kettle came up from below, and watched the naphtha-launch with throbbing interest. He had hatched a scheme for capturing the *Cancelario*, and had made his preparations; and here was an interruption coming which might very well upset anything most ruinously. Nor was he alone in his regard. The barque's topgallant rail was lined with faces; all her complement were wondering who these folk might be who were so confidently coming out to meet them.

A Jacob's ladder was thrown over the side; the slate-coloured launch swept up, and emitted a woman. Captain Kettle started, and went down into the waist to meet her. A minute later he was wondering whether he dreamed, or whether he was really walking his quarterdeck in company with Donna Clotilde La Touche. But meanwhile the barque held steadily along her course.

The talk between them was not for long.

'I must beseech you, Miss, to go back from where you came,' said Kettle. 'You must trust me to carry out this business without your supervision'.

'Is your method very dangerous?' she asked.

'I couldn't recommend it to an Insurance Company,' said Kettle thoughtfully.

'Tell me your scheme'.

Kettle did so in some forty words. He was pithy, and Donna Clotilde was cool. She heard him without change of colour.

'Ah,' she said, 'I think you will do it'.

'You will know one way or another within an hour from now, Miss. But I must ask you to take your launch to a distance. As I tell you, I have made all my own boats so that they won't swim; but, if your little craft was handy, my crew would jump overboard and risk the sharks, and try to reach her in spite of all I could do to stop them. They won't be anxious to fight that *Cancelario* when the time comes, if there's any way of wriggling out of it.'

'You are quite right, Captain; the launch must go; only I do not. I must be your guest here till you can put me on the *Cancelario*.'

Captain Kettle frowned. 'What's coming is no job for a woman to be in at, Miss'.

'You must leave me to my own opinion about that. You see, we differ upon what a woman should do, Captain. You say a woman should not be president of a republic; you think a woman should not be sharer in a fight: I am going to show you how a woman can be both.' She leant her shoulders over the rail, and hailed the naphtha-launch with a sharp command. A man in the bows cast off the line with which it towed; the man aft put over his tiller, and set the engines a-going; and, like a slim, grey ghost, the launch slid quietly away into the gloom. 'You see', she said, 'I'm bound to stay with you now'. And she looked upon him with a burning glance.

But Kettle replied coldly, 'You are my owner, Miss,' he said, 'and can do as you wish. It is not for me now to say that you are foolish. Do I understand you still wish me to carry out my original plan?'.

'Yes', she said curtly.

'Very well, Miss, then we shall be aboard of that war-steamer in less than fifteen minutes.' He bade his second mate call aft the crew; but instead of remaining to meet them, he took a keen glance at the barque's canvas, another at her wake, another at the moored cruiser ahead, and then, after peering thoughtfully at the clouds which sailed in the sky, he went to the companion-way and dived below. The crew trooped aft and stood at the break of the quarterdeck, waiting for him. And in the meanwhile they feasted their eyes with many different thoughts on Donna Clotilde La Touche.

Presently Captain Kettle returned to deck, aggressive and cheerful, and faced the men with hands in his jacket pockets. Each pocket bulged with something heavy, and the men, who by this time had come to understand Captain Kettle's ways, began to grow quiet and nervous. He came to the point without any showy oratory.

'Now, my lads', said he, 'I told you when you shipped aboard this lavender-box in Callao, that she was merely a ferry to carry you to a fine war-steamer which was lying elsewhere. Well, there's the steamer, just off the starboard bow yonder. Her name's the *Cancelario*, and at present she seems to belong to President Quijarra's Government. But Miss La Touche here (who is employing both me and you, just for the present) intends to set up a Government of her own; and, as a preliminary, she wants that ship. We've to grab it for her.'

Captain Kettle broke off, and for a full minute there was silence. Then some one amongst the men laughed, and a dozen others joined in.

'That's right,' said Kettle. 'Cackle away, you scum. You'd be singing a different tune if you knew what was beneath you.'

A voice from the gloom – an educated voice – answered him: 'Don't be foolish, skipper. We're not going to ram our heads against a brick wall like that. We set some value on our lives.'

'Do you?' said Kettle. 'Then pray that this breeze doesn't drop (as it seems likely to do), or you'll lose them. Shall I tell you what I was up to below just now? You remember those kegs of blasting powder? Well, they're in the lazaret, where some of you stowed them: but they're all of them unheaded, and one of them carries the end of a fuse. That fuse is cut to burn just twenty minutes, and the end's lighted.

'Wait a bit. It's no use going to try and douse it. There's a pistol fixed to the lazaret hatch, and if you try to lift it that pistol will shoot into the powder, and we'll all go up together without further palaver. Steady, now, there, and hear me out. You can't lower away boats, and get clear that way. The boats' bottoms will tumble away so soon as you try to joist them off the skids. I saw to that last night. And you can't require any telling to know there are far too many sharks about to make a swim healthy exercise.'

The men began to rustle and talk.

'Now, don't spoil your only chance,' said Kettle, 'by singing out. If on the cruiser yonder, they think there's anything wrong, they'll run out a gun or two, and blow us out of the water before we can come near them. I've got no arms to give you; but you have your knives, and I guess you shouldn't want more. Get in the shadow of the rail there, and keep hid till you hear her bump. Then jump on board, knock everybody you see over the side, and keep the rest below,'

'They'll see us coming,' whimpered a voice. 'They'll never let us board.'

'They'll hear us,' the Captain retorted, 'if you gallows-ornaments bellow like that, and then all we'll have to do will be to sit tight where we are till that powder blows us like a thin kind of spray up against the stars. Now, get to cover with you, all hands, and not another sound. It's your only chance.'

The men crept away, shaking, and Captain Kettle himself took the wheel, and appeared to drowse over it. He gave her half a spoke at a time, and by invisible degrees the barque fell off till she headed dead on for the cruiser. Save for the faint creaking of her gear, no sound came from her, and she slunk on through the night like some patched and tattered phantom. Far down in her lazaret the glowing end of the fuse crept nearer to the powder barrels, and in imagination every mind on board was following its race.

Nearer and nearer she drew to the *Cancelario*, and ever nearer. The waiting men felt as though the hearts of them would leap from their breasts. Two of them fainted. Then came a hail from the cruiser: 'Barque, ahoy, are you all asleep there?'

Captain Kettle drowsed on over the wheel. Donna Clotilde, from the shadow of the house, could see him nodding like a man in deep sleep.

'*Carrajo!* you barque, there! Put down your helm. You'll be aboard of us in a minute.'

Kettle made no reply : his hands sawed automatically at the spokes, and the glow from the pinnacle fell upon close, shut eyes. It was a fine bit of acting.

The Chileans shouted, but they could not prevent the collision, and when it came, there broke out a yell as though the gates of the Pit had been suddenly unlocked.

The barque's crew of human refuse, mad with terror, rose up in a flock from behind the bulwarks. As one man they clambered over the cruiser's side and spread about her decks.

Ill provided with weapons though they might be, the Chilians were scarcely better armed. A sentry squibbed off his rifle, but that was the only shot fired. Knives did the greater part of the work, knives and belaying-pins, and whatever else came to hand. Those of the watch on deck who did not run below were cleared into the sea; the berth deck was stormed; and the waking men surrendered to the pistol nose.

A couple of desperate fellows went below, and cowed the firemen and engineer on watch. The mooring was slipped, steam was given to the engines, and whilst her former crew were being drafted down into an empty hold, the *Cancelario* was standing out at a sixteen-knot speed towards the open sea under full command of the raiders. Then from behind them came the roar of an explosion and a spurt of dazzling light, and the men shuddered to think of what they had so narrowly missed. And as it was some smelling fragments of the old guano barque lit upon the after deck, as they fell headlong from the dark sky above.

Donna Clotilde went on to the upper bridge, and took Captain Kettle by the hand.

'My friend,' she said, 'I shall never forget this.' And she looked at him with eyes that spoke of more than admiration for his success.

'I am earning my pay,' said Kettle.

'Pah!' she said, 'don't let money come between us. I cannot bear to think of you in connection with sordid things like that. I put you on a higher plane. Captain,' she said, and turned her head away, 'I shall choose a man like you for my husband.'

'Heaven mend your taste, Miss,' said Kettle; 'but – there may be others like me.'

'There are not.'

'Then you must be content with the nearest you can get.'

Donna Clotilde stamped her food upon the planking of the bridge.

'You are dull,' she cried.

'No,' he said, 'I have got clear sight, Miss. Won't you go below now and get a spell of sleep? Or will you give me your orders first?'

'No,' she answered, 'I will not. We must settle this matter first. You have a wife in England, I know, but that is nothing. Divorce is simple here. I have influence with the Church; you could be set free in a day. Am I not the woman you would choose?'

But the Captain is not to be tempted and so, after the heiress has retired below, he takes the only way out. He casts himself adrift in the gig and watches the flagship disappear at 16 knots, taking the fiery temptress out of his life for good – or so he thinks. Much later, he awakes from an overdose of spiked Scotch to find that he has been shanghaied by a chance acquaintance in the Captains' Room at Hallett's and now is in a state room in a luxury steam-yacht heading westwards through the Pentland Firth.

By some subtle transference of thought, the woman in her berth below became conscious of his regard, grew restless, woke, got more restless, dressed, came on deck, and saw this man with whom she was so fiercely enamoured, staring gloomily over the bulwarks. With her light, silent walk she stepped across the dewy decks under the moonlight, and, without his hearing her, leant on the rail at his side and flung an arm across his shoulders.

Captain Kettle woke from his musing with a start, stepped coldly aside, and saluted formally. He had an eye for a good-looking woman, and this one was deliciously handsome. He was always chivalrous towards the other sex, whatever might be their characters; but the fact of his own kidnapping at the moment of Mrs Kettle's pressing need, made him almost as hard as though a man stood before him as his enemy.

'Miss La Touche,' he said, 'do you wish me to remember you with hatred?'

'I do not wish you to have need to remember me at all. As you know, I wish you to stay with me always.'

'That, as I have told you before, Miss, is impossible, for more reasons than one. You have done me infinite mischief already. I might have found employment by this time had I stayed in South Shields, and meanwhile my wife and children are hungry. Be content with that, and set me ashore.'

'I repeat the offer I made you in South America. Come with me, get a divorce, and your wife shall have an income such as she never dreamed of, and such as you never could have got her in all your life otherwise. You know I am not boasting. As you must know by this, I am one of the richest women in the world.'

'Thank you; but I do not accept the terms. Money is not everything.'

'And meanwhile remember, I keep you on board here, whether you like it or not; and, until you give way to what I want, your wife may starve. So if she and your children are in painful straits, you must recollect that it is entirely your fault.'

'Quite so,' said Kettle. 'She will be content to starve when she knows the reason.'

Donna Clotilde's eyes began to glitter.

'There are not many men who would refuse if I offered them myself.'

'Then, Miss, I must remain curious.'

She stamped her food. 'I have hungered for you all this time, and I will not give you up for mere words. You will come to love me in time as I love you. I tell you you will, you must, you shall. I have got you now, and I will not let you go again.'

'Then, Miss,' said Kettle grimly, 'I shall have to show you that I am too hot to hold.'

She faced him with heaving breast. 'We will see who wins,' she cried.

'Probably,' said Captain Kettle, and took off his cap. 'Good-night, Miss, for the present. We know how we stand: the game appears to begin between us from now.' He turned deliberately away from her, walked forward, and went below; and, after a little waiting, Donna Clotilde shivered, and went back to her own luxurious state-room.

But if she was content to spend the rest of the night in mere empty longing, Captain Kettle was putting his time to more practical use. He was essentially a man of action.

First he tries to get away in one of the yacht's boats, but is intercepted when its falls jam. In the ensuing commotion, it emerges that the yacht is half full of water, let in by Captain Kettle's opening all the bath-taps. After he has then set the yacht on fire, Donna Clotilde offers him parole to be on good behaviour for the rest of the voyage. When he declines, he is put in irons.

A second time Captain Kettle managed to get the yacht in a blaze, at the imminent peril of immolating himself, and then, from lack of further opportunity to make himself obnoxious, lay quiet in his lair till such time as the yacht would of necessity go into harbour to coal. The exasperated crew would cheerfully have murdered him if they had been given the chance, but Donna Clotilde would not permit him to be harmed. She was a young woman, who, up to this, had always contrived to have her own way, and she firmly believed that she would tame Kettle in time.

When the yacht passed the Straits she had only four days' more coal on board, and the executive (and Kettle) expected that she would go into Gibraltar and lay alongside a hulk to rebunker. But Donna Clotilde had other notions. She had the yacht run down the Morocco coast, and brought to an anchor. So long as she had Captain Kettle in her company upon the waters, she did not vastly care whether she was moving or at a standstill.

'You cannot escape me here,' she said to him when the cable had roared from the hawse pipe, and the dandy steamer had swung to a rest. 'The yacht is victualled for a year, and I can stay here as long as you choose. You had far better be philosophical and give in. Marry me now, and liking will come afterwards.'

Kettle looked at the tigerish love and resentment which blazed from her black eyes, and answered with cold politeness that time would show what happened; though, to tell the truth, indomitable though he was as a general thing, he was at that time feeling that escape was almost impossible. And so for the while he more or less resigned himself to captivity.

Under the baking blue of a Mediterranean sky this one-sided courtship progressed, Donna Clotilda alternating her ecstasies of fierce endearment by paroxysms of invective, and Kettle enduring both with equal coldness and immobility. The crew of the yacht looked on, stolidly non-interferent, and were kept by their officers at cleaning and painting, as necessary occupiers to the mind. But one or other of them, of their own free will, always kept an eye on their guest, whether he was on deck or below. He had given them a wholesome taste of his quality, and they had an abject dread of what he might be up to next if he was left alone. They quite understood that he would destroy the yacht and all hands if, by doing so, he could regain his personal liberty.

But others, it seems, besides those already mentioned in this narrative, were taking a lively interest in the smart yacht and her people. She was at anchor in the bay of the Riff coast, and the gentry who inhabited the beach villages, and the villages in the hills behind the beach, had always looked upon anybody and anything they could grab as their just and lawful prey. The Sultan of Morocco, the war ships of France, Spain, and elsewhere, and the emissaries of other powers had time after time endeavoured to school them in the science of civilisation without effect, and so they still remain to-day, the only regularly practising pirates in the Western World.

The yacht was sighted first from the hills; was reported to the beach villages; and was reconnoitred under cover of night by a tiny fishing-boat. The report was pleasing, and word went round. Bearded brown men collected at an appointed spot, each with the arms to which he was best accustomed; and when darkness fell, four large boats were run down to the feather edge of the surf. There was no indecent hurry. They did their work with method and carefulness, like men who are used to it; and they arrived alongside the yacht at 3 a.m., confidently expecting to take her by surprise.

But the crew of the yacht, thanks to Captain Kettle's vagaries, were not in the habit of sleeping over soundly; they never knew what piece of dangerous mischief their little captive might turn his willing hand to next; and, as a consequence, when the anchor watch sang out his first alarm, not many seconds elapsed before every hand aboard was on deck. The yacht was well supplied with revolvers and cutlasses, and half a minute sufficed to get these up from below and distributed, so that when the Riffians attempted to board, the defenders were quite ready to give them battle.

Be this how it may, however, there is no doubt as to which side got the first advantage. The yacht's low freeboard made but a small obstacle to a climber from the large boats alongside, and neither the deck hands nor the stokehold crew were any of them trained fighting men. In their 'prentice hands the kicking revolvers threw high, and were only useful as knuckledusters, and till they had thrown them down, and got their cutlasses into play, they did hardly any execution to speak about. The Riff men, on the other hand, had been bred and born in an atmosphere of skirmish, and made ground steadily.

At an early point of the scuffle, Captain Kettle came on deck with a cigar in his mouth, and hands in his pockets, and looked on upon matters with a critical interest, but did not offer to interfere one way or the other. It was quite a new sensation to him, to watch an active fight, without being called upon to assist or arbitrate.

And then up came from below Donna Clotilde La Touche, dressed and weaponed, and without a bit of hesitation, flung herself into the turmoil. She saw Kettle standing on one side, but neither besought nor commanded him. She would have died sooner than ask for his help then, and be met with a refusal.

Into the *mêlée* she went, knife and pistol, and there is no doubt that her example, and the fury of her rush, animated the yacht's crew, and made them stronger to drive the wall of their assailants back. To give Donna Clotilde her due, she was as brave as the bravest man, and, moreover, she was a certain shot at moderate range. But, after her revolver was empty and the press closed round her, it was not long before an expert hand twisted the knife from her grasp, and then the end came quickly. An evil-smelling man noted her glorious beauty, and marked her out as his special loot. He clapped a couple of sinewy arms around her, and bore her away towards the bulwarks, and his boat.

Some one had switched on the electric deck lights, and the fight was in a glow of radiance. Everything was to be clearly seen. Donna Clotilde was being dragged resisting along the decks, and Kettle looked on placidly smoking his cigar. She was heaved up on the bulwarks; in another moment she would be gone from his path for ever.

Still her lips made no sound, though her great black eyes were full of wild entreaty. But the eyes were more than Kettle could stand. He stooped and picked up a weapon from amongst the litter on deck, and rushed forward and gave a blow, and the Riffian dropped limply, and Donna Clotilde stood by the yacht's bulwark and gasping.

'Now you get away below,' he ordered curtly. 'I'll soon clear this rabble over the side.'

He does so with explosive ruthlessness. After the last surviving Riff has swum out of pistol range, the crew fall back in awe at this one-man army and are not inclined to deny him the authority he now assumes.

Captain Kettle was on the top of the deck-house which served as a navigating bridge, ostentatiously closing up the breach of the revolver after reloading it. He wished for a hearing, and after what they had seen of his deadly marksman-ship, they gave it to him without demur. His needs were simple. He wanted steam as soon as the engineers could give it him, and he intended to take the yacht into Gibraltar right away. Had anybody an objection to raise?

The red-haired man made himself spokesman. 'We should have to go to Gib anyway,' said he. 'Some of us want a doctor badly, and three of us want a parson to read the funeral service. Whether you can get ashore once we do run into Gib, Captain, is your own concern.'

'You can leave that to me safely,' said Captain Kettle. 'It will be something big that stops me from having my own way now.'

The men dispersed about their duties, the decks were hosed down, and the deck lights switched off. After awhile Donna Clotilde came gliding up out of the darkness, and stepped up the ladder to the top of the deck-house. Kettle regarded her uneasily.

To his surprise she knelt down, took his hand, and smothered it with burning kisses. Then she went back to the head of the ladder. 'My dear,' she said, 'I will never see you again. I made you hate me, and yet you saved my life. I wish I thought I could ever forget you.'

'Miss La Touche,' said Kettle, 'you will find a man in your own station one of these days to make you a proper husband, and then you will look back at this cruise and think how lucky it was you so soon sickened, and kicked me away from you.'

She shook her head and smiled through her tears. 'You are generous,' she said. 'Good-bye. Good-bye, my darling. Good-bye.' Then she went down the ladder, and Kettle never saw her again.

from *The Adventures of Captain Kettle* by C. J. Cutliffe Hyne (1898)

The Most Beautiful Navigator Afloat

In Robert Wales's *The Navigator*, Jim McBain is only twenty-one when he is given command of the crack sailing packet *Nantasket* on the Boston–Liverpool run in 1832. Before assuming command he meets and hastily marries the beautiful Amelia (Amy) Hall, in spite of her being jealously guarded by her sinister Aunt Dorothea. Amy joins him on *Nantasket*, where she is hostess to the passengers, but quickly she shows deeper interest in the ship's whole operation. The Mate, who is not qualified as a navigator, takes over the watch on deck as they clear Boston harbour.

'Take over, Mr Ludham,' James instructed him at last, thinking Amy might be getting too cold, and Ludham bellowed by name for a helmsman to come aft. James ordered the speed to be measured every hour around the clock, but if the mate had enough wit to realize that his new captain must have been very nervous about his navigation to want to know what distance he had covered with such frequency, he gave no sign of it.

'Come below now,' James said to his wife, taking her arm to lead her to the hatch.

'Can I wait to see what they do?' Amy asked, and James, only too pleased she was so interested, guided her to the starboard bulwark.

Amy watched the three men, two of them holding a pole with a loose spool, around which was neatly coiled line with knots at intervals, its outer end tied to a large piece of wood. At the same time as the wood was thrown over the side to hit the water and drift astern, pulling the line from the freely turning spool, the third man, who held a large sandglass, turned it over to start the timing. When the sandglass ran out the seamen immediately stopped the line from running and started to haul it back in, counting the knots.

'You see,' James explained, 'every knot represents a small portion of a sea mile, the sandglass the same portion of an hour, so by knowing what speed I'm doing I can tell what distance I'm covering over the water.'

'How clever!' Amy enthused, grasping it at once. 'How very clever, I'd never have thought of it.'

'Neither would I,' James admitted, 'and if I didn't have that and a compass and knew something about the currents I might be so far up the Charles River that only Indians would find me.'

Woodsmoke fled from the galley stovepipe that rose above the deck as they began to make their way down the companionway ladder.

'I remember now, James!' Amy said, suddenly stopping halfway down, 'I remember.'

'Remember what?'

'Apart from the fact that I love you,' she smiled, 'one nautical mile equals one minute of arc at the equator or along a meridian.'

'Where the devil did you learn that?' asked James, taken aback.

'Mr Hayne told us,' Amy replied, without having to confess that at the time she did not know exactly what a minute of arc was.

It was not the last surprise James was to get on his first day at sea as master. When they finally escaped from the passengers, all of whom wanted their attention, another awaited him after they had reached the privacy of their cabin.

'There's something I haven't had time to unpack yet, James,' said Amy.

James watched in mild curiosity as she opened the battered old sea chest she told him had been given her by Aunt Dorothea and took out two polished wooden cases and a much smaller one. He could hardly believe his eyes. Even before she opened the first he was familiar enough with its appearance to know what was inside. All the same, he found himself speechless as it was revealed in all its new and shining brass glory and at first he could only stare at it. He had known nothing of Amy hurrying up narrow, cobbled Broad Street and round the corner to Mr E.Hawkes, instrument-makers and suppliers, while he had been busy directing the hold stowage of his freight.

'How much is a sextant, chronometer and deck watch?' she enquired on reaching the counter and Mr Hawkes had just gaped at her. Never in all his years of business had a pretty girl come to ask for such things, and Amy quickly realised his confusion. 'I'm Mrs McBain,' she hastened to tell him, 'wife of Captain James McBain of the *Nantasket*'.

'Ah, Mrs McBain, of course,' Mr Hawkes said, enlightened, and with an appreciative eye thought what a lucky man the captain was. He produced the goods and gave her his prices. Amy looked at them, did a quick sum in her head, said, 'I'll be back, sir, or I hope I will,' and dashed out again in a whirl of skirts, leaving Mr Hawkes gasping for a second time.

'How much, sir?' she said in the jeweller's shop, producing her necklace, and the man to whom business always came before pleasure seemed to take forever to examine it, and in some disdain at that. It was a mistake to tell him, in her eagerness and apprehension, how much she needed. He reluctantly offered just a little more than that while, unknown to Amy, he had valued it to be worth four times as much. But Amy could not have been happier or more satisfied as she hurried back to Hawkes.

'I take it the captain has the Almanacs to go with it,' Hawkes said as his assistant wrapped up her purchases.

'Almanacs?'

'The sextant will be of no use without them, ma'am.'

And those, and the old second-hand sea chest she bought, used up every penny she had left.

*

. . . Later in the day, as the sun appeared, James fetched her on deck with the sextant.

'Lesson number one, Mrs McBain,' he told her, and patiently explained what had to be done. Amy was immediately intrigued but after a frustrating hour refused to give it up until she got the hang of it. Braced against the rail, eye glued to the small, telescopic eyepiece, she chased the wobbling sun through the world of filters, double images and mirrors, and lost it and found it and lost it again with the rolling and pitching of the ship.

'That will be enough for today, Amy,' James said, trying to get her to give it up.

'No, it won't, James,' she replied and tried again. James had never been so patient. Seven bells of the afternoon watch rang out on the foremast and the sun was already lowering towards the west, and still Amy would not give up.

'I've got it, I've got it!' she suddenly squealed in excitement, and all on her own brought the round, filtered ball down to set steadily on the horizon. Then she lowered it to read off the degrees and minutes on the arc as she had been previously shown.

'There, I have shot the sun,' she said with satisfaction, already having picked up the proper seamanlike term for it, 'and now we know where we are.'

James was astonished, not just by her having managed it so quickly but by having done so at all. In the navigation schools that existed in towns along the Eastern Seaboard it took men a long time to learn how to take a sun sight, and standing on dry land. He hardly had the heart to tell her that her achievement was only the beginning, but he knew she would not forgive him if he did not appear to be taking her seriously.

'Well, not quite,' he said. 'You have to have the exact time to the second as you do it, then there's quite a lot of work to be done with those Almanacs.'

'Then we'll do it all properly tomorrow, James,' she said, not at all dismayed, 'and once I know the rest there will be no need for you to bother with it.'

James could not have been more amused by such sweet innocence but thought he had better not laugh and managed to keep a straight face.

'Right,' he agreed, and she looked so adorable to him. He felt he had done an excellent job of taking her mind off the incident that morning. It was how he expected women to be, their interest jumping from one thing to another. There was no question in his own mind that once he showed her all the long, laborious calculations that could take hours in working out a position for the ship she would give up and turn her attention to crochet or stitching like most of the ladies usually did if they were not overtaken by seasickness.

But as wave after wave of the North Atlantic came rolling up from astern to raise the *Nantasket* and surge under her hull to push on ahead it was not the young bride who was being naive but the captain. For him, the real surprise was still to come.

They were only five days out of Boston when James came below to find Amy in their cabin, worriedly poring over the chart, surrounded by the Almanacs and the scribblings of many figures. She was holding the dividers in her hand.

'You'll have to help me, James,' she pleaded. 'I've made a mistake somewhere and for the life of me can't find out where I've gone wrong. My position is more than seventy miles from yours and I just can't get it right.'

It was as much to humour her that James had allowed her to continue as she wished and she had been on deck every time the sun appeared. And at night, the moon, too.

'Seventy miles is not at all bad, Amy,' James said, discreetly omitting to mention that near a coast in bad weather in poor visibility it could mean the difference between being safe at sea or wrecked on rocks with the loss of life for all those aboard. And for three whole hours, because he loved her, he patiently helped her to go over and over all her calculations and his own. Then the truth of it struck him.

'God damn my eyes,' he said in disbelief when nothing more could be done, 'it's not you who made the goddamned mistake, it was me. Your position's right and it's mine that's wrong.'

'Are you sure?'

'Of course I'm sure,' he replied, angry with himself.

Amy felt suddenly embarrassed for him. 'Anyone can make a mistake, James,' she offered in an attempt at giving comfort. 'Anyway, I'm tired of it and don't want to do it any more.'

But James was beginning not to be taken in by the look of innocence in her large brown eyes. Before him was positive evidence that his wife had a very unusual, natural talent for what he had always had to struggle with. It had taken him years to reach his level of proficiency and already Amy had shown him up. It was quite incredible. But he was no fool. He had been presented with a heaven-sent opportunity and he was not going to pass it up. It was only a matter of saving a little bit of face as he grasped it.

'Now, isn't that the greatest pity,' he said. 'And just as I was thinking about officially making you a member of my crew.'

'Me?' Amy questioned, her eyes even wider with surprise. 'A woman? A member of your crew?'

'Highly irregular, I know,' James said and shrugged. 'Ah, well, never mind, they would probably have laughed at me for it anyway.'

'Now, you wait a moment, James,' Amy demanded as he turned for the door, 'I'm perfectly willing to accept your offer if it's what you want.'

James stopped and turned back to her. 'But I thought you just said you didn't want to do it any more,' he reminded her.

'I have changed my mind,' Amy said. James held her apprehensive eye for a moment then smiled.

'Very well, Mrs McBain,' he said. 'From now on we share this particular duty and I'll inform Mr Ludham to that effect.' And a moment later the navigator was kissing the captain with gratitude and delight.

In truth, although Amy had wanted to be useful to James at sea, that was not why she had bought the sextant in the first place. She had done so simply because she knew James wanted it. It was not until she had raised it to her eye and become aware of the vast expanse of ocean surrounding her that the very idea of being able to tell exactly where the ship was on it drew her like a magnet. It was an almost mystical feeling, as though it was the answer to one of the questions on the mystery of the universe, a link with the sun, the moon and the stars that had some meaning. And it was far from all young Amy McBain wanted to know. How wide was the Gulf Stream? What currents were in it and where? What might the wind be doing elsewhere? How did you know you were steering your exact course when the movement of the ship was constantly swinging the compass all over the place? What was Leeway and how did you calculate it? Why was the Gulf Stream's eastward route the best? And many other mysteries. James was able to answer only a few of her questions, the knowledge handed down by tradition, and, as he told her, only God knew the rest. What she had as yet given no mind to because of her total confidence in her husband was that danger and even death stalked ships at sea.

*

It was to be over three weeks after setting out from Boston that, in good visibility, and with Amy's careful positioning, James was able to identify the small island of Inishtrahull off the north coast of Ireland, beyond which was Malin Head. For the *Nantasket* it was a respectable time and the passengers were pleased. But Amy was much more than just pleased. Not in all her young life had she felt so much satisfaction, so great a sense of achievement as having navigated to that landmark then seeing it there with her own eyes.

'It's like magic, James,' she said excitedly, but James knew full well it was she who was the magic. Not only did he have a perfect helpmate but a totally confident and competent navigator into the bargain, and he felt that no man on earth could ever have been so fortunate in his life.

Later, as they left Rathlin Island to starboard and headed down the North Channel, reaching on a fresh, westerly breeze, the flat was hoisted on the signal halyard to indicate to pilots they were Liverpool-bound. But it was not until after they had passed the Isle of Man that a Liverpool pilot cutter appeared. A rope ladder was thrown down the side and eventually the pilot was making a skilful leap for it to clamber aboard. In no time, the short, nuggety, whiskered man was to find himself bemused by the captain's pretty young wife questioning him on his knowledge of the Irish Sea and of the tides and currents on that part of the English coast. Not even his own wife had ever asked him such things, but it would have been superfluous to have pointed out to the ship's master what an unusual, engaging and fascinating woman he had in Mrs McBain. The pride in his young spouse was writ large all over the young American captain's face.

When Amy gets pregnant, the embittered Aunt Dorothea poisons her drinking water to such effect that her infant son Jamie is born sickly and retarded. Consequently it is some years before Amy is able to resume navigating at her husband's side. After a fast passage to London, she soon reveals to Mr Rivers, the Mate on James's new command *Amelia*, that she has intuitive skills as a metereologist as well, which are put to good use on the homeward passage.

. . . It was to be an even happier fast ship that set out on its westward voyage. All the way down the English Channel the wind was from the north, putting them on a fast reach, and it stayed like that until they were out into the Atlantic when it began to veer, then back, in a regular rhythm.

'I think we should go further north,' Amy advised James.

'What, and risk losing this great advantage we have? Only once in my life before have I had it this good.'

'It could be better north,' Amy persisted, 'with stronger winds.'

'What makes you think that?' James wanted to know.

'I just feel it,' Amy said.

But it was only because he so much wanted to please her and give her every opportunity that he ordered a change of course.

'I don't believe it,' he said in amazement when the wind gradually veered and strengthened until twenty-four hours later they were running with full sail before an easterly gale. Considering the prevailing winds at that latitude were almost always westerly it was incredible. Day after day it went on.

'Do you believe in the will of God, Mr Rivers?' James asked his first mate in restrained excitement as they stood on deck, the ship thundering, surging and streaking over the sea.

'Yes, sir, I do,' Rivers replied, 'and in your navigator, too.'

And both turned to look at Amy, hair blowing in the wind, who stood braced at the port rail, sextant raised. waiting for the moment the sun appeared between clouds again, the bosun by her side ready with deck watch and notebook.

The easterly took them more than halfway across the ocean on Amy's course before it eased off and after a day of calm started filling in from the south-west. James, not exactly a man to display his emotions by jumping up and down for joy, was almost ecstatic when the Floating Light off Sandy Hook came up dead ahead.

'By God, we've done it, Amy,' he kept saying, hardly able to stand still for a moment, and Amy had never felt so delighted for him, at the same time sensing that she had won round two against the London lady.

'The London packet *Amphitrite* owned by Messrs Merriman and Rudd and mastered by Captain James McBain, yesterday smashed the westward record from London by no less than *five days!*' ran the *New York Herald* the next morning and went on to give a full account of it to the public. Merriman and Rudd hurriedly arranged a celebration and, surrounded by admirers, James soaked up the attention like a sponge and got a little drunk. 'My navigator did it,' he said to all.

from *The Navigator* by Robert Wales (1989)

A Wife in Every Port

Traditionally the love-life of a sailor has always been enriched, although sometimes complicated, by fleeting opportunities for dalliance in foreign ports. especially if they are not likely to be visited again. It is not only Jack who has a wife in every port; even Captains are not immune to such waterfront temptations. But there are special problems lurking in the wings if a ship is on a regular run between the same two ports. In recent years Alec Guinness, in *The Captain's Paradise*, nearly got away with enjoying his pipe-and-slippers domesticity with Celia Johnson at the Gibraltar end of the Tangier ferry's run, in between frenzied bouts of the contrasting life-style offered by the sex-pot Yvonne de Carlo, who aroused the snake-hips-masher in him on cramped dance-floors under an exotic moon over Morocco.

His problems were trifling compared to those faced by Captain Fred Flower of the schooner *Foam*, plying between the London River and the east coast at the turn of the century. He manages to get himself entangled simultaneously with three young ladies, all of whom confidently expect to end up alongside him at the altar. Two of them are egged on by aggressively ambitious mothers, especially when word gets round that Flower will inherit his uncle, Captain Barber's estate, which includes *Foam* and thirteen cottages.

The story has all the ingredients which made W. W. Jacobs the leading writer of his day of humorous short stories about seafarers. The son of a dock-labourer in Wapping, he first went to work as a clerk in the Civil Service Savings Bank, but gave that up after a run of successes with short stories in *Strand* magazine. The short story was his forte, and a collection was published in 1896 as *Many Cargoes*. His full-length novels were less successful, but featured all the unexpected twists which were the hallmark of his stories.

Flower's uncle master-minds the preparations for the Captain's wedding at Seabridge, the East Anglian end of his regular voyages. When they reach the dressmaking stage, our sea-going Lothario realizes the time has come for drastic avoiding action. As soon as *Foam* slips and heads for Gravesend, he takes the Mate into his confidence.

'I'm in a desperate fix, Jack, that you'll admit', he said, by way of preparation.
The mate cordially agreed with him.
'There's Poppy down at Poplar, Matilda at Chelsea, and Elizabeth at Seabridge,' continued Flower, indicating various points on the table with his finger

as he spoke. 'Some men would give up in despair, but I've thought of a way out of it. I've never got into a corner I couldn't get out of yet.'

'You want a little help though sometimes,' said Fraser.

'All part of my plans,' rejoined Flower, airily. 'If it hadn't been for my uncle's interference I should have been all right. A man's no business to be so officious. As it is, I've got to do something decided.'

'If I were you,' interrupted Fraser, 'I should go to Captain Barber and tell him straight and plain how the thing stands. You needn't mention anything about Miss Tipping. Tell him about the other, and that you intend to marry her. It'll be best in the long run, and fairer to Miss Tyrell, too.'

'You don't know my uncle as well as I do,' retorted the skipper. 'He's as obstinate an old fool as ever breathed. If I did as you say I should lose everything. Now, I'll tell you what I'm going to do: – Tonight, during your watch, I shall come up on deck and stand on the side of the ship to look at something in the water, when I shall suddenly hear a shout.'

The mate, who had a piece of dumpling on his fork, half-way to his mouth, put it down again and regarded him open-mouthed.

'My foot,' continued the skipper, in surprisingly even tones, considering his subject, 'will then give way and I shall fall overboard.'

The mate was about to speak, but the skipper, gazing in a rapt manner before him, waived him into silence.

'You will alarm the crew and pitch a life-belt overboard,' he continued, 'you will then back sails and lower the boat.'

'You'd better take the life-belt with you, hadn't you?' enquired the mate, anxiously.

'I shall be picked up by a Norwegian barque, bound for China,' continued the skipper, ignoring the interruption; 'I shall be away at least six months, perhaps more, according as things turn out.'

The mate pushed his scarcely tasted dinner from him, and got up from the table. It was quite evident to him that the skipper's love affairs had turned his brain.

'By the time I get back, Matilda'll have ceased from troubling, anyway,' said the skipper, 'and I have strong hopes that Elizabeth'll take Gibson. I shall stay away long enough to give her a fair chance, anyway.'

'But s'pose you get drowned before anything can pick you up!' suggested the mate, feebly.

'*Drowned?*' repeated the skipper. 'Why, you didn't think I was really going overboard, did you? I shall be locked up in my state-room.'

The mate's brow cleared and then darkened again, suddenly. 'I see, some more lies for me to tell, I suppose,' he said, angrily.

'After you've raised the alarm and failed to recover the body,' said the skipper, with relish, 'you'll lock my door and put the key in your pocket. That would be the proper thing to do if I really did go overboard, you know, and when we get to London I'll just slip quietly ashore.'

The mate came back to his dinner and finished it in silence, while the skipper kept up a rambling fire of instructions for his future guidance.

'And what about Miss Tyrell?' said the mate, at length. 'Is she to know?'

'Certainly not,' said Flower, sharply. 'I wouldn't have her know for anything. You're the only person to know, Jack. You'll have to break the news to 'em all, and mind you do it gently, so as not to cause more grief than you can help.'

'I won't do it at all,' said the mate.

'Yes, you will,' said Flower, 'and if Matilda or her mother come down again, show it to 'em in the paper. Then they'll know it'll be no good worrying Cap'n Flower again. If they see it in the paper they'll know it's true; it's sure to be in the local papers, and in the London ones, too, very likely. I should think it would; the master of a vessel!'

Fraser being in no mood to regard this vanity complacently, went up on deck and declined to have anything to do with the matter. He maintained this attitude of immovable virtue until tea-time, by which time Flower's entreaties had so won upon him that he was reluctantly compelled to admit that it seemed to be the only thing possible in the circumstances, and more reluctantly still to promise his aid to the most unscrupulous extent possible.

'I'll write to you when I'm fixed up,' said the skipper, 'giving you my new name and address. You're the only person I shall be able to keep in touch with. I shall have to rely upon you for everything. If it wasn't for you I should be dead to the world.'

'I know what you'll do as well as possible,' said Fraser; 'you've got nothing to do for six months, and you'll be getting into some more engagements.'

'I don't think you have any call to say that, Jack' remarked Flower, with some dignity.

'Well, I wish it was well over,' said the mate, despondently. 'What are you going to do for money?'

'I drew out £40 to get married with – furniture and things,' said Flower; 'that'll go overboard with me, of course. I'm doing all this for Poppy's sake more than my own, and I want you to go up and see her every trip, and let me know how she is. She mightn't care what happened to her if she thinks I'm gone, and she might marry someone else in desperation.'

'I don't care about facing her,' said Fraser, bitterly; 'it's a shady business altogether.'

'It's for her sake,' repeated Flower, calmly, 'Take on old Ben as mate, and ship another hand forward.'

The mate ended the subject by going to his bunk and turning in; the skipper, who realized that he himself would have plenty of time for sleep, went on deck and sat silently smoking. Old Ben was at the wheel, and the skipper felt a glow of self-rightousness as he thought of the rise in life he was about to give the poor fellow.

At eight o'clock the mate relieved Ben, and the skipper with a view of keeping up appearances announced his intention of turning in for a bit.

The sun went down behind clouds of smoky red, but the light of the summer evening lasted for some time after. Then darkness came down over the sea, and it was desolate except for the side-lights of distant craft. The mate drew out his watch and by the light of the binnacle-lamp, saw that it was ten minutes to ten. At the same moment he heard somebody moving about forward.

'Who's that for'ard?' he cried, smartly.

'Me, sir,' answered Joe's voice. 'I'm a bit wakeful, and it's stiflin' 'ot down below.'

The mate hesitated, and then, glancing at the open skylight, saw the skipper, who was standing on the table.

'Send him below,' said the latter, in a sharp whisper.

'You'd better get below, Joe,' said the mate.

'W'y, I ain't doin' no 'arm, sir' said Joe, in surprise.

'Get below,' said the mate sharply. 'Do you hear? – get below. You'll be sleeping in your watch if you don't sleep now.'

The sounds of a carefully modulated grumble came faintly aft, then the mate, leaning away from the wheel to avoid the galley which obstructed his view, saw that his order had been obeyed.

'Now,' said the skipper, quietly, 'you must give a perfect scream of horror, mind, and put this on the deck. It fell off as I went over, d'ye see?'

He handed over the slipper he had been wearing, and the mate took it surlily.

'There ought to be a splash,' he murmured. 'Joe's awake.'

The skipper vanished, to reappear a minute or two later with a sack into which he had hastily thrust a few lumps of coal and other rubbish. The mate took it from him, and, placing the slipper on the deck, stood with one hand holding the wheel and the other the ridiculous sack.

'Now,' said the skipper.

The sack went overboard, and, at the same moment, the mate left the wheel with an ear-splitting yell and rushed to the galley for the life-belt which hung there. He crashed heavily into Joe, who had rushed on deck, but, without pausing, ran to the side and flung it overboard.

'Skipper's overboard,' he yelled, running back and putting the helm down.

Joe put his head down the fore-scuttle and yelled like a maniac; the others came up in their night-gear, and in a marvellously short space of time the schooner was hove to and the cook and Joe had tumbled into the boat and were pulling back lustily in search of the skipper.

Half an hour elapsed, during which those on the schooner hung over the stern listening intently. They could hear the oars in the rowlocks and the shouts of the rowers. Tim lit a lantern and dangled it over the water.

'Have you got 'im?' cried Ben, as the boat came over the darkness and the light of the lantern shone on the upturned faces of the men.

'No,' said Joe, huskily.

Ben threw him a line, and he clambered silently aboard, followed by the cook.

'Better put about,' he said to the mate, 'and cruise about until daylight. We ain't found the belt either, and it's just possible he's got it.'

322

The mate shook his head. 'It's no good,' he said, confidently; 'he's gone.'

*

At five o'clock, by which time they had chased three masses of weed and a barnacle-covered plank, they abandoned the search and resumed the voyage. A gloom settled on the forecastle, and the cook took advantage of the occasion to read Tim a homily upon the shortness of life and the suddenness of death. Tim was much affected, but not nearly so much as he was when he discovered that the men were going to pay a last tribute to the late captain's memory by abstaining from breakfast. He ventured to remark that the excitement and the night air had made him feel very hungry, and was promptly called an unfeeling little brute by the men for his pains. The mate, who, in deference to public opinion, had to keep up appearances the same way, was almost as much annoyed as Tim, and, as for the drowned man himself, his state of mind was the worst of all. He was so ungrateful that the mate at length lost his temper and when dinner was served allowed a latent sense of humour to have full play.

It consisted of boiled beef, with duff, carrots, and potatoes, and its grateful incense filled the cabin.

Unhappily, the Mate cannot let Captain Flower share in the meal, for he has mislaid the key with which he had locked him into the after cabin.

He found the key by tea-time, and, his triumph having made him generous, passed the skipper in a large hunk of the cold beef with his tea. The skipper took it and eyed him wanly, having found an empty stomach very conducive to accurate thinking.

'The next thing is to slip ashore at Wapping, Jack,' he said, after he had finished his meal; 'the wharf'll be closed by the time we get there.'

'The watchman's nearly sure to be asleep,' said Fraser, 'and you can easily climb the gate. If he's not, I must try and get him out of the way somehow.'

The skipper's forebodings proved to be correct. It was past twelve by the time they reached Wapping, but the watchman was wide awake and, with much bustle, helped them to berth their craft. He received the news of the skipper's untimely end with well-bred sorrow, and at once excited the wrath of the sensitive Joe by saying that he was not surprised.

'I 'ad a warning,' he said solemnly, in reply to the indignant seaman. 'Larst night exactly as Big Ben struck ten o'clock the gate-bell was pulled three times.'

'I've pulled it fifty times myself before now,' said Joe, scathingly, 'and then had to climb over the gate and wake you up.'

'I went to the gate at once,' continued George, addressing himself to the cook; 'sometimes when I'm shifting a barge, or doing any little job o' that sort, I do 'ave to keep a man waiting, and, if he's drunk, two minutes seems like ages to 'im.'

'You ought to know wot it seems like,' muttered Joe.

'When I got to the gate an' opened it there was nobody there,' continued the watchman, impressively, 'and while I was standing there I saw the bell-pull go up an' down without 'ands and the bell rung agin three times.'

323

The cook shivered. 'Wasn't you frightened, George?' he asked sympathetically.

'I knew it was a warning,' continued the veracious George. 'W'y 'e should come to me I don't know. One thing is I think 'e always 'ad a bit of a fancy for me.'

'He 'ad' said Joe; 'everybody wot sees you loves you, George. They can't help theirselves.'

'And I 'ave 'ad them two ladies down agin asking for Mr Robinson, and also for poor Cap'n Flower,' said the watchman; 'they asked me some questions about 'im, and I told 'em the lies wot you told me to tell 'em, Joe; p'r'aps that's w'y I 'ad the warning.'

from *A Master of Craft* by W. W. Jacobs (1900)

Mr Fraser then lures the nightwatchman to the galley long enough for Captain Flower to slip ashore and hole up in digs in South London under an assumed name. He re-emerges in the final chapter in time to see Captain Fraser walking down the aisle with his favourite girl.

POSTSCRIPT

Postscript

The meal is over. I hope it is one to be remembered with pleasure for the variety of its ingredients, the subtle blending of wines and food appropriate to the company at the table.

In putting it together I soon detected a common thread running through the stories of fiction-writers about the sea. In developing their characters and story-lines, they are shackled by the pervasive influence of the sea in all its changing moods, overriding other considerations. For the majority of novelists writing about events ashore, neither the quality of their work nor the characters they create are fashioned wholly by their chosen location.

Furthermore, except for the detritus of non-biodegradable pollution in coastal waters, mostly plastics and fossil fuels, the sea today is exactly as it was in St Paul's day. Superstitious sailors still stand in awe of the same inexplicable phenomena, and navigators still have to pick their way through inadequately charted hazards.

Even for modern writers, the greatest fascination is to be found in the age of iron men in wooden ships. Combat was normally resolved at point-blank range after broadsides of roundshot had softened up the target; grappling-irons, boarding parties and cold steel clinched the issue. All along those men knew that any tactical advantage might be lost if the sea and weather took a hand. Throughout the ages since the prose novel developed during the eighteenth century writers at all levels of literary competence have respected this self-evident truth. While their characters may vary enormously, they all must give a credible account of themselves in the same environment. Tug-boat Annie, Horatio Hornblower, Para Handy, Tom Cringle, Roderick Random and Richard Bolitho outsmart their rivals or overcome their difficulties because they are better able to ride the sea's punches. Current writers whose imaginations are fired by twentieth-century ships and weapons – Tom Clancy, Alistair MacLean, Hammond Innes, Lothar-Günther Buchheim – still have to pit their heroes against the same awesome, unpredictable sea.

Many authors whose finest work lay in writing about the sea were less successful when they turned their imaginations loose ashore. In my view, Nicholas Monsarrat was a case in point. His novels set in Africa, and the sordid tale of Esther Costello, will be forgotten long before *The Cruel Sea*. Some of the greatest writers were less comfortable, notably Robert Louis Stevenson, whose characters were always more at home on dry land, even with a wooden leg, an eye-patch and a parrot on their shoulder. Others, like Ernest Hemingway, Jack London, James Michener and Rudyard Kipling, left us only tantalizing glimpses of what they might have achieved had they looked seawards more often. And there are some wonderful surprises since I started to compile this anthology: I never expected to find a place in it for Evelyn Waugh, but the first chapter of *Vile Bodies* makes me wish he had sent his dotty lotus-eaters to sea more often. A writer about the sea in the genre of the tough modern detective thriller was sooner or later bound to emerge: Sam Lewellyn is a real find, the Dick Francis of the sea. His indestructible Charlie Agutter goes into action on thoroughbred hi-tech offshore racing yachts, with unscrupulous rich owners out to nobble the opposition in what used to be a Corinthian sport dominated by the likes of Tommy Lipton.

At the end of the meal some may be disappointed by its omissions: they might have looked for wines of more fashionable vintages, whereas I have hopefully decanted some of equal merit from lesser chateaux. None the less, I hope the piquancy of the sauces will provoke discussion among those fortunate enough to have known a love-hate relationship with the sea.

Now the wind rises, the windows rattle, the moon and stars are obscured by low scudding storm-clouds and the candles flicker.

The dogs grow restless . . .

J O C
30 November 1990

Acknowledgements

We are indebted to the copyright holders for permission to reprint extracts from the following:

FRANS BENGSTOON: from *The Long Ships* (Collins, 1954), by permission of David Higham Associates; TOM CLANCY: from *Red Storm Rising*, copyright © 1986 by Jack Ryan Enterprises and Larry Bond, by permission of The Putnam Publishing Group and HarperCollins; CLARE FRANCIS: from *Night Sky* (William Heinemann Ltd, 1983), copyright © 1983 by Clare Francis by permission of John Johnson Ltd and of William Heinemann Ltd; C. S. FORESTER: from *A Ship of the Line* (Michael Joseph, 1938), extracts from the *Captain Hornblower R.N.* Trilogy (Penguin, 1987), by permission of The Peters Fraser and Dunlop Group Ltd; PAUL GALLICO: from *The Poseidon Adventure* (William Heinemann Ltd, 1969), copyright © Mathemata Anstalt 1969, by permission of Aitken & Stone Ltd; WILLIAM GOLDING: excerpts from *Fire Down Below*, copyright © William Golding, 1989, and from *Rites of Passage*, copyright © William Golding, 1980, by permission of Faber and Faber Ltd and Farrar, Straus and Giroux Inc.; LOTHAR GÜNTHER-BUCHHEIM: from *U-Boat* (Collins, 1974), translated by G. Lawaetz, copyright © 1977 by Alfred A. Knopf Inc., reprinted by permission of HarperCollins and Alfred A. Knopf, Inc.; R. HAMMOND INNES: from *Atlantic Fury* and from *The Strode Venturer* by permission of R. Hammond Innes Esq., CBE; JAN DE HARTOG: from *The Captain* (Hamish Hamilton, 1968) copyright © 1966 by Jan de Hartog, by permission of Robert Hale Ltd and of Atheneum Publishers, an imprint of Macmillan Publishing Company; JOHN HEARNE: from *The Sure Salvation* (Faber and Faber, 1981), by permission of David Higham Associates Ltd; ERNEST HEMINGWAY: from *The Old Man and the Sea*, by permission of Charles Scribner's Sons, an imprint of Macmillan Publishing Company, copyright 1952 by Ernest Hemingway, renewed 1980 by Mary Hemingway; and from 'On the Blue Water: A Gulf Stream Letter', originally published in *Esquire* Magazine, April 1936, reprinted by permission of Charles Scribner's Sons, an imprint of Macmillan Publishing Company, copyright © 1936 by Ernest Hemingway, renewed 1964 by Mary Hemingway; C. J. CUTLIFFE HYNE: from *The Paradise Coal-boat*, and from *The Adventures of Captain Kettle – The War Steamer of Donna Clotilde and The Raiding of Donna Clotilde* (C. Arthur Pearson, 1898), by permission of IPC Magazines Ltd; W. W. JACOBS: from *A Master of Craft* (Methuen, 1900), by permission of The Society of Authors as the literary representative of the Estate of W. W. Jacobs; ALEXANDER KENT: from *The Flag Captain* (Century Hutchinson, 1973), copyright © 1971 by Alexander Kent, by permission of Random Century Group and Putnam Publishing Group; SAM LLEWELLYN: from *Dead Reckoning* copyright © 1987 by Sam Llewellyn, by permission of Michael Joseph Ltd, and of Summit Books, a division of Simon & Schuster Inc.; BILL LUCAS and ANDREW SPEDDING: from *Sod's Law of the Sea* (Stanford Maritime 1977) by permission of A. & C. Black Publishers Ltd; ALISTAIR MACLEAN: from

HMS Ulysses, copyright © Alistair MacLean 1955, by permission of HarperCollins, and of Doubleday, a division of Bantam Doubleday Dell Publishing Group Inc.; JOHN MASEFIELD: from *A Mainsail Haul* (Heinemann, 1905), by permission of Grafton Books, a division of HarperCollins Publishers Ltd, and The Society of Authors as the literary representative of the Estate of John Masefield; JAMES A. MICHENER: from *Hawaii* (Martin Secker & Warburg, 1960), by permission of The Peters Fraser and Dunlop Group Ltd; NICHOLAS MONSARRAT: from *HMS Marlborough Will Enter Harbour* (Pan Books), copyright © the Estate of Nicholas Monsarrat, 1947, by permission of Mrs Ann Monsarrat; CHARLES NORDHOFF and JAMES NORMAN HALL: from *Mutiny on the Bounty* (Little, Brown & Company, 1932) copyright © 1932 by Little, Brown & Company, copyright © renewed 1960 by Laura Nordoff, Marguerite Nordoff Chadwick, Sarah M. Hall, Nancy Hall Rutgers, and Conrad Hall, by permission of Little, Brown & Company; C. J. NORTHCOTE PARKINSON: from *The Life and Times of Horatio Hornblower* (Michael Joseph, 1970), copyright © C. J. Northcote Parkinson, 1970, by permission of Michael Joseph Ltd and Dr C. J. Northcote Parkinson; DUDLEY POPE: from *Ramage at Trafalgar* (Martin Secker & Warburg, 1986), copyright © 1986 by Dudley Pope, by permission of Martin Secker & Warburg Ltd and Dudley Pope; F. TENNYSON JESSE: from *Moonraker* (William Heinemann Ltd, 1927, extracts from Virago Paperbacks, 1981) and from *Tom Fool* (Evans Brothers Ltd, 1952), by permission of the Public Trustee Harwood Will Trust; H. M. TOMLINSON: from *Old Junk*, by permission of Jonathan Cape Ltd; ROBERT WALES: from *The Navigator* (Headline Book Publishing, 1989), by permission of Headline Book Publishing plc and of The Peters Fraser & Dunlop Group Ltd; EVELYN WAUGH: from *Vile Bodies* (Chapman & Hall, 1930), copyright © 1930 by Evelyn Waugh, copyright © renewed 1958 by Evelyn Waugh, by permission of The Peters Fraser & Dunlop Group Ltd, and of Little, Brown & Company; JOHN WINTON: from *We Joined the Navy* (Michael Joseph, 1959), by permission of the author.

W. W. Norton & Company apologizes for any errors or omissions in the above list and would be grateful to be notified of any corrections that should be incorporated in the next edition of this volume.

Index